Mary Hocking's many novels include *March House*, *He Who Plays the King*, *Look Stranger!* and *The Mind has Mountains*. She lives in Lewes in Sussex. *Good Daughters* forms the first part of a trilogy, of which the second and third parts, *Indifferent Heroes* and *Welcome Strangers*, will also be published by Abacus.

Mary Hocking

GOOD DAUGHTERS

First published in Great Britain by
Chatto and Windus 1984
Published in Abacus by
Sphere Books Ltd 1985
30-32 Gray's Inn Road, London WC1X 8JL
Copyright © 1984 by Mary Hocking

Printed and bound in Great Britain by
Cox & Wyman Ltd, Reading

TO BARBARA

I

In later years, Alice heard people talk as if those who grew up during the period between the two wars had lived their youth beneath the shadow of the swastika. But it had not seemed like that at the time.

Although in her childhood older people talked of the war that was just finished, and then, some ten years later, began to talk of the war which was to come, no shadow seemed to touch her until she was sixteen.

At the beginning of 1933 Alice was twelve and had lived in Shepherd's Bush for four years. The Fairley children had been born in Sussex which was the home of their father; their mother was a Cornishwoman. Most of their friends were first generation Londoners whose families' links with the shires had still not been broken. They grew up aware of an older, more stable way of life, though they were not to be its inheritors.

In the area around Pratts Farm Road where the Fairleys lived the present was eating determinedly into the past; but fragments of the life of other centuries were still to be found imposed as uneasily upon the twentieth century as one snap upon another when Alice forgot to wind forward the reel in her Box Brownie.

The houses in Pratts Farm Road had been built towards the end of the Victorian era. In nearby St Bartholomew's Churchyard, where the Fairleys' black cat, Smut, played with the field mice, there were tombstones dating back to the thirteenth century, and some people believed that beneath the present graveyard there was a Saxon burial ground. Alice, who equated history with romance, imagined Roundheads chasing Cavaliers along Shanks Alley, and Baron de Rothschild plotting with Disraeli in the temple by the lake at Gunnersbury Park. She peopled the Old Tuck Shop and the green at Gypsy Corner with characters derived from Dickens and Robert Louis Stevenson.

The newspaper boy who turned into Pratts Farm Road as the first tram clanged its way towards Shepherd's Bush saw nothing romantic in his surroundings. He moved in and out of gates with dispatch until he came to the two tall, semi-detached houses which stood a little apart from their terraced neighbours. Here, outside the gate of Number 29, he paused to examine the newspaper in his hand before going up the steps to the front door. Mr Fairley had made a fuss the previous day because he had found the *Daily Herald* lying on his doormat, an affront which he was ill able to tolerate at any time of the day, let alone first thing in the morning. This time, the *News Chronicle* was pushed through the letterbox with more than usual care. It landed title upward, proclaiming that this was the fourth of January, 1933, that the weather was likely to be bright and cold, and that Japan had laid waste a Chinese city.

The affairs of the wider world much exercised Mr Fairley. At the very moment that the newspaper landed on his doormat he was praying for the people of China. As he prayed he thought of his own experience of war – three years in the trenches during which he had sustained a cut finger – and of his happy marriage and his three beloved daughters still asleep in bed. He was torn between gratitude for God's goodness and a faint but persistent dissatisfaction that he had not been called upon to suffer more. It was possible, for he tended to make insufficient distinction between domestic and cosmic disorder, that he would have found cause for suffering adequate to his daily needs in the sight of his second daughter, now stumbling down the lane which divided the back gardens of Pratts Farm Road from those of Church Street.

The sunken path which divided the gardens was generally referred to as 'the back lane' although older people spoke of it as Shanks Alley. Along this path, a little over a century ago, drovers had passed to and from the farming settlements, and along it at this moment came Alice, in great discomfort of mind and body.

For some time Alice had been absorbed with secret passages. One such passage was reputed to have linked a manor house, recently demolished, with a priory which had come to grief in the time of Thomas Cromwell. Alice had spent fruitless hours digging in Shanks Alley. There were a lot of nettles here and she had been told that this usually meant that old walls were concealed beneath the earth. Her friend Daphne occasionally joined her in this enterprise. Second only to Alice's absorbtion with secret passages was her passion for midnight feasts. Daphne had challenged her to come to her house for a feast, after which they would search for a passage.

It had all started splendidly. Alice had successfully bribed her younger sister, Claire, to be silent; her escape from the home had been effected without waking Badger, the dog; she had been suitably terrified as she made her way along the dark alley: and the climbing of the tree by which she gained access to Daphne's garden had been just difficult enough to test her agility without diminishing her resolution. Most important of all, Daphne had not overslept this time and was waiting for her at the kitchen door. As Daphne's brother occasionally came home as late as two in the morning, the feast had had to be postponed until well beyond the witching hour. Alice found it a trifle disappointing: while Daphne had not failed in the supply of sugar mice, whipped cream walnuts, and other essentials, these proved not to be the fare which Alice's stomach craved so early in the morning. But to make up for this there was all the excitement of being in a strange place, a strangeness which Daphne shared to some extent since the kitchen was usually the servants' domain. It was this very lack of familiarity with their surroundings which eventually led them to investigate the trapdoor in the wall by the kitchen stove which must conceal a chamber of some kind. They pulled, it yielded, and out came something which fell soft as black snow upon the red-tiled kitchen floor.

Alice's reaction had been laughter; it was left to Daphne to assess the situation. 'You'd better keep clear. I can make some excuse for "discovering" this and explain away the soot on my clothes.' She had pushed her giggling friend out of the door and, aching with laughter, Alice had lurched down the garden path. Somewhere in Shanks Alley laughter had turned to tears. Now, as she made her way home, she asked why it was that for her adventures could not be adventure? Why must they resolve themselves into a matter of sooty fingernails and a churning stomach? Why should magic casements yield only soot? Where was all the glamour, the excitement?

She knew the answer, of course: the bitter truth was that she was twelve and should by now have outgrown secret passages and midnight feasts. They had passed her by and she must find sterner adventures more suited to her years. She reached the gate at the back of the garden which she had left open. As she came into the garden her conscience, that puritan destroyer of adventure, was waiting for her; she could feel it getting a grip on her as she tiptoed across the lawn. The light was on in the kitchen and she could hear her mother singing. Alice gritted her teeth and took hold of the lowest branch of the oak tree; both her strength and her spirits were low and she found it difficult to swing herself up. As she climbed towards the landing window she could distinguish the houses on the far side of Shanks

Alley with the spire of St Bartholomew's Church rising above them. To the right, where light sparked from the trams, there was the Uxbridge Road: in one of the big houses fronting the road Daphne must by now be announcing her 'discovery'. Alice rested in the fork between two branches. Tears of frustration trickled down her grimy face and as she looked into the darkness she murmured, 'Oh Kashmir, Kashmir!' It was not quite so wild a flight of fancy as might have seemed. Within the square formed by Lime Avenue, Croft Road, St Bartholomew's Lane and Saddler's Road there was a house surrounded by a high brick wall. From the topmost branches of the tree it was possible to see beyond the wall and Alice had often climbed up there to command this precious view. All around her lay the grimy town with its haphazard grey streets; then, secure behind the wall, set in green lawns and walled gardens, there was this inaccessible house, which had the secret look of a place out of its proper time. There were other old houses in the neighbourhood, but they had been incoporated into newer developments. The house, called Kashmir by an earlier seeker after adventure, had been built in Tudor times and re-faced in the Regency period. It was unlike anything in Alice's experience, except Hampton Court; but you could pay to go into Hampton Court and you could walk in the gardens and admire the formal flowerbeds. There was nothing in this to compare with Kashmir. The existence of places like Kashmir, where you had no right to be, was the essence of adventure. Cinemas ranked high in this category; films with titles such as *Forbidden* aroused an intense, almost desperate longing in Alice, who lived within scrupulously prescribed boundaries. In the case of Kashmir, there was the additional fascination that, being concealed, *it* seemed as though it had no right to be either.

This morning it was still too dark to see even the high wall which surrounded the house and Kashmir was more inaccessible than ever. By this time, Alice's puritan conscience was well in command and, as she climbed through the landing window, she would have been relieved to find her father waiting for her so that she could make him a present of her burden of guilt. But he was not there and she went upstairs to join Claire.

Claire had spent several hours wrestling with the temptation to sneak. As soon as Alice appeared, she said, 'Oh, Alice, I feel so *awful*, I've got the most *awful* tummy ache.' She rocked to and fro on the bed, holding her stomach and screwing her face into the contortion which she had perfected in her infancy when she discovered that the gnomes had more interesting things to do than the fairies in the preparatory school frolics.

Alice said, 'That's only because it's the first day of term.'

'Your face is *black*, Alice; what will Mummy say?'

'She won't know, *will* she?' Alice went to the washstand and spat on her flannel, then rubbed it round her face. She repeated this treatment until she was confident her face would pass her mother's cursory examination. Claire could be relied upon to attract the most attention with her pleas that she was too unwell to go to school. The pleas were usually unavailing but had become a pattern of behaviour that was as much a part of the first day of term as the tram conductors' jokes and the headmistress's less jovial welcome.

'Alice, what *happened*?'

'I'll tell you later.' Alice was undressing.

Claire watched, biting her lip, thinking that this time she really might manage to make herself sick. But then, while she was at home being cosseted, she would almost certainly tell; and this, Alice had made it clear, would be one tale-bearing which would not be forgiven. 'My tummy really is bad,' she said forlornly.

Alice got into bed. 'If you don't go today, you'll have to go tomorrow and that will be worse because everyone else will have got over it.'

Claire lay back against the pillows. All kinds of unpleasant things were happening. Faintly, she could hear her mother raking out the grate in the dining-room and, beyond the window, the distant clip-clop of the milkman's horse accompanied by the familiar rattle of bottles. Inexorably, the day was beginning. In the other bed, Alice was humped with her face to the wall, keeping to herself the secrets which couldn't possibly be shared with an unreliable, tale-bearing nine-year-old. Only recently, the new year had begun and Claire had made good resolutions not to show off or tell tales. Now, only a few days later, goodwill had dwindled. The school holidays were at an end and Alice would want to spend her time with Daphne and her other friends. Claire was aware that, in spite of being the clever one, there was no way in which she could prevent Alice from casting her off if that was what Alice decided to do. She stared up at the ceiling, contemplating the bleakness of her future. The milky pallor of her face contrasted with the brilliant red hair which was a legacy of her Cornish grandmother. Grandmother Tippet would as soon that Alice or Louise had inherited her glory, since she saw little else of herself in this nervous child, forever on the fidget, burning up energy to no good purpose. On the rare occasions when she was still, however, Claire's small face had a deceptively angelic quality – what Louise (who thought she was as tough as old boots) referred to as her 'not-long-for-this-world look'. Now, if only there had been someone to observe her, she did indeed look pathetic.

The milkman was getting nearer and another disturbing sound came to Claire's ears. 'Louise is playing music again,' she said to Alice.

Their elder sister had discovered delights which did not depend on the opening of trapdoors or the scaling of the walls of Kashmir. As she sat in her bedroom braiding her hair she was listening to a Schubert serenade played on the old phonograph which her grandmother had given to her. The sound was not good and the volume was turned down because her father would be annoyed if he heard it. Had Louise been more articulate in her musical appreciation, had she shown even a rudimentary appreciation of form and content, he would have been delighted; but a love of music in which the intellect played so small a part was something of which he disapproved in principle.

The milkman arrived just as Louise replaced Schubert with Mozart. Badger, the old Scottie, who was deaf and had not heard the paper-boy, made up for this omission by a long, bad-tempered display. Judith Fairley took in the milk and, having satisfied herself that the right paper had been delivered, looked to see if her husband's letter had been printed. 'Oh dear, there'll be two of you in a bad temper now!' she said to Badger as they returned to the kitchen. This was a good-sized room where the family ate their breakfast in winter to save lighting the dining-room fire. Judith opened the back door and pushed the dog out. 'You're not to bark and wake the neighbours.' She said this without much concern, having scant sympathy for anyone who was still abed at this hour.

The flames were roaring in the pipe of the Ideal boiler. Bacon was cooking and the kettle was boiling. The hands of the clock pointed to twenty-five to seven. Louise was already up; she had fetched her hot water and Judith could hear her moving about in her room doing whatever mysterious things kept her so occupied each morning. Probably the young ones were awake by now, Claire complaining of tummy trouble and Alice dealing with her practically. Judith thought of Alice with gratitude and of Claire with affection.

As she prepared breakfast she sang 'Bonny Mary of Argyll' in a manner more robust than the words would support. She was not a quiet worker, her activities would be unwelcome in a sickroom; there was a suggestion, too, that her store of patience would be limited. Her thick brown hair was drawn into a knot at the nape of her neck, a style well suited to one who had little inclination and less time for the fashionable. The face, strong-boned and a little heavy about the jaw, was remarkable for brown eyes informed by an intelligence which only the demands of three children and a strong-willed husband had prevented from becoming formidable: a woman whom some would find attractive and others a shade too forthright for their taste.

She finished her rendering of the song in operatic style, put the bacon in the oven, placed the porridge pan on a low gas, and poured hot water into a big aluminium jug; all the while giving the impression of having more than one pair of hands. Then she went upstairs to rouse Claire and Alice, pausing outside Louise's room to say, 'Turn that thing off, Louise, and get dressed.'

'I am dressed.'

'Well, turn it off anyway. It will disburb old Mr Ainsworth.' Mr Ainsworth, their neighbour, was deaf, but this fact was overlooked when Judith or Stanley wanted the children to be quiet.

When Judith entered the children's room only the top of Alice's head was visible, but Claire, surprisingly, was wide awake. 'It's cold,' she complained. 'And I've got tummy-ache.'

Judith put the hot-water jug down on the marble washstand. 'Nonsense! You won't notice it if you dress quickly.' Since Claire was the delicate one, she added, 'And don't forget to put on your camisole as well as your coms. School won't be well heated this morning.'

Claire sat up shivering, an art she had mastered so that she shook from head to foot. 'Rosalind has a radiator on the landing in her house.'

'Never mind about Rosalind or any of the others. I want you downstairs in ten minutes.' She went over to Alice's bed and made one of those remarks which made her family suspect that she had inherited second sight from her Celtic forebears. 'It's no use pretending, Alice. Up you get!'

'She *knows*,' Claire said in a sepulchral voice when their mother had gone out of the room.

Even if she didn't know, God did, Alice thought gloomily as she got out of bed. For the first time she understood something of the compulsion which led Claire to tell tales. As she washed she reminded Conscience that this was Daphne's secret as much as her own, and that loyalty to friends was important.

7

When Alice had finished washing Claire eased herself out of bed, shuddering as her feet touched the cold linoleum. 'You've made the water *black*,' she protested. 'What will Mummy think?'

'I'll empty it away.'

Claire dabbed at her face with a flannel. 'Rosalind and Marguerite have got a washbasin with running water in their bedroom.'

Alice made no reply and concentrated on brushing her hair which was straight and so long she could sit on it. As it was her one asset – her face being long and, by the standards of the film stars whom she revered, plain, and her figure regrettably plump – Alice paid a lot of attention to it, brushing it until lights glinted like gold-dust in sand and then weaving it into two plaits. The weight of the plaits on her shoulders gave her a feeling of reassurance, even of respectability, in the company of more elegantly endowed companions.

Claire said, 'You *are* going to play, aren't you, Alice?' There was a note of threat in her voice. 'You promised you would if I didn't tell.'

When their father was looking for a better teaching post their parents had prayed that he would get a headship where he was most needed. Alice and Claire had prayed he would be needed in Bognor where they would be able to swim every day. When God called him to a boys' elementary school in Acton, they comforted themselves by inventing the Maitland family who lived in a beautiful old Sussex farmhouse. An extra member was added to the family whenever they came across a name they could not resist, such as Marguerite or Imogen. But that was four years ago. Alice felt that the time had come to part company with the Maitlands.

'You promised,' Claire said ominously.

Alice said, 'Yes, all right; but we can't play now, can we?' She went out of the room carrying the basin. There was no one in the bathroom and she emptied away the water but had difficulty getting rid of the black rim around the side of the basin. She left the basin in the bathroom because she did not want to give Claire another opportunity to talk about the Maitlands. As she went downstairs she could hear her mother and Louise arguing in the kitchen. Her father was still in his study. She picked up the newspaper and with practised judgement opened it at the page that listed the films showing in the West End. Eagerly she scanned the column. *Movie Crazy* with Harold Lloyd, *Tess of the Storm Country* with Janet Gaynor, *The Midshipmaid* with Jessie Matthews, aroused little interest; these were films to which her parents might be persuaded to take her, provided their arrival on the local circuit was well spaced out. But there was no hope for *Trouble in Paradise* and *Rome Express*: if their titles did not condemn them, the stars would – Miriam Hopkins and Kay Francis were 'fast', while Conrad Veidt was 'sinister'. Alice put the paper down hurriedly as she heard the door of her father's study open.

In the kitchen, Louise was saying, 'Where does it say in the Bible that Jesus said all girls must have plaits?'

'You look quite grown up now that you've got your plaits up; you'll have to content yourself with that. It's no use arguing, because Daddy won't agree to you having your hair cut. Let Badger in, will you, Alice?'

Louise did not pursue the argument. She did not, however, appear to give in so much as to leave the matter lying there to be taken up again when times were more propitious. At the age of four Louise had realized, with the coming of Alice, that grown-ups were not to be trusted; and while she had made no objection to the sharing of what she had hitherto been led to understand was all hers, she had accepted her parents' inconstancy as a sign that she, too, could go her own way and had done so ever since without their being in the least aware of it. As she was not by nature unkind or aggressive, and as she was very fond of her parents, she made it her pleasure to be accommodating whenever possible and had so far done little to confound her father's picture of her as a 'dutiful' daughter.

To Alice, however, the sixteen-year-old Louise seemed to inhabit a different world from the other people in the house. From time to time she would come out with an observation which was out of keeping with the cherished principles according to which the Fairley family ordered their lives. She would drop these remarks as though herself unaware of their strangeness, unselfconscious as a tone-deaf singer. Her behaviour was equally unpredictable. Alice could tell that her mother thought the battle of the plaits had been won. Alice, however, remembered the first morning when Louise had come downstairs with her hair plaited on top of her head. A different person had walked into the room, but Louise had not displayed this new person with bravado, as Alice would have done, or with any of Claire's nervous silliness; she had walked into the room as unconcernedly as though she had worn her hair up for so long that it could not be a matter for discussion. The drawing away of the hair had uncovered a personality. In the moulding of this face no time had been wasted on subtlety, the lines of jaw and cheekbone were executed boldly and positively; there was nothing tentative about the wide mouth and the gaze of the eyes was direct. To Alice, the transformation had resembled that moment in a film when the person, head bent over a railway ticket, suddenly faces the camera full-on and you realize with a thrill of excitement that this is the star! Here, in the kitchen, the effect had been as startling but, perhaps because of the inappropriateness of the setting, not so pleasant. Alice, looking round, had seen that her mother and father were equally disturbed, though in a way she had not expected, for they seemed to be not so much angry as dismayed. Judith Fairley soon recovered and treated Louise with the confidence of one who is certain that, whatever may befall, she has the measure of her antagonist. Stanley Fairley became more authoritative than ever.

'I think your hair looks lovely like that, Lou,' Alice said, thinking of Daphne's soot-filled kitchen and anxious to avoid any more disasters.

'I've got an audition for the play today.' Louise spoke to her mother, ignoring Alice's attempt at peacemaking. 'We'll be late home.'

'Well, don't undertake anything that will intefere with your studies.'

Claire came in followed by Stanley Fairley.

It was apparent that the head of the house was now present. Although he lacked the stature for natural authority, being a little short of medium height, he nevertheless, on entering a room, contrived the impression of a substantial force; an effect achieved mainly by a certain fierceness of expression and the thrusting of his stocky body against the air as though he was forever pushing an unseen opponent before him. Forcefulness alone would probably not have been sufficient to sustain dominance over a long period of time, but he was fortunate in having his wife's support. She had suffered in her own childhood from the lack of a man at the head of the table and was not minded to go through her marriage as her mother had hers. She therefore reinforced her husband's position while not always accepting his judgement.

Mr Fairley, having made his entrance, put the newspaper down on the table and stood waiting while Claire took her place and Badger settled in front of the stove. He then pronounced grace in a deep, grave voice, sat down, shook out his napkin, and said, 'They can't take criticism, these fellows. They hand it out readily enough, but when it comes to themselves, they can't take it.' He drew bushy eyebrows into a frown as he sprinkled salt on his porridge. His brown hair, crowning his head like the bristles of a brush, gave an added abrasiveness to his appearance.

'Haven't they published your letter, Daddy?' Alice asked.

'No, my dear, they have not.' He uttered each word as though he had an individual quarrel with it. 'They are prepared to pay good money to a man like Robert Lynd to write a lot of nonsense about what he would do if he was the New Year Dictator, but when it comes to a sensible, balanced, well-reasoned . . .' He looked across at his wife and saw that she was smiling. His face went red and his eyes were like marbles; but even as the rage seemed about to burst from him, some unreliable element within turned traitor and his lips twitched. He said mildly to Alice, 'Your mother doesn't think much of my literary abilities, I'm afraid.'

'I don't know that "balanced" is a word I would use to describe them, Stanley, that's all.'

'And do you call it balanced,' he summoned his anger again, thumping his spoon in his porridge bowl so that Badger jumped and whined, 'to ask people to play the dictator? Do you see anything balanced about this word "dictator" that our Press is so enamoured of nowadays? It will all end in disaster. What do they tell you at school about Mussolini?'

'They've had four weeks' holiday and I expect they've forgotten everything they ever learnt.'

'My boys don't forget what I tell them!'

Louise, eyes on her mother, said, 'I don't want a fried egg.'

'You don't have a hot meal in the middle of the day, so you must have a good breakfast.' Judith Fairley put a plate of bacon, egg and fried bread in front of Louise.

'I shall be sick on the tram.'

Judith said, 'We really must get something done about the paint-work around the windows this summer, Stanley. I was wondering whether we might get Will Perry to do it. He's been out of work for so long.'

Stanley Fairley helped himself to mustard. 'What your mother means is that she doesn't want me to do it.'

' "Daddy does a thousand-and-one things between each brush stroke",' Claire quoted her mother.

For a moment it seemed her father was going to be angry; then he smiled at Claire and she gave the little-girl laugh which her sisters found so irritating.

11

Louise looked at Alice. When she was very young Claire had had diphtheria and had been incarcerated in the isolation hospital. Alice and Louise had run through childish ailments at an alarming rate and by the time they were ten there seemed little else for them to catch; but as none of these ailments had required a stay in the isolation hospital they never received the devoted attention which was paid to Claire's indispositions.

Louise wiggled her eyebrows at Alice and said, 'Snap, dumpling!'

'I had been thinking that Alice had lost a little weight.' Their mother came so automatically to the aid of whichever member of the family was under attack that it was not really a defence at all.

When they had eaten, Mr Fairley took the Bible down from the dresser and opened it at the place where the monthly Bible notes acted as a marker for the reading for the day.

' "By glory and dishonour, by evil report and good report, as deceivers and yet true; as unknown and yet well-known . . ." '

Louise listened with pleasure for her father read well, his strong voice rising and falling, faithful to the rhythm if not always to St Paul's intentions. Alice's stomach shifted uneasily at the mention of 'deceivers'. Judith, watching her, thought she was very puffy about the eyes and wondered if she was sickening for something. Claire, who needed the security of absolute truth and liked instructions to be unambiguous, wondered what she was supposed to do about "Be not unequally yoked with unbelievers: for what fellowship have right-eousness and iniquity, or what communion hath light and dark-ness?" She recalled that their headmistress had told them 'You should be tolerant about other countries which have governments different from our own, and should not make quick judgements about affairs in Italy.' Her father would surely think this was having communion with darkness.

The Bible was closed and they bowed their heads while Mr Fairley addressed God somewhat brusquely. Each morning a glance at the headlines convinced him that God had been about his business elsewhere in the cosmos and needed to be reminded of events on the planet Earth. This done, Mr Fairley asked God's blessing on the members of the Fairley household throughout the day. They said the Lord's Prayer together, after which there was a scramble to collect packed lunches and to find Alice's netball.

Then they left their home and took a tram to Shepherd's Bush Green, and from there they had a twenty-minute walk. Somewhere on this journey they ceased to be the Fairley family and became the pupils of the Winifred Clough Day School for Girls. By the time they entered the gates, Louise, Alice and Claire had separated and would barely acknowledge one another until the end of the day.

2

The school was founded in 1890 by Winifred Clough, suffragette, and heiress to a drapery business. It was sited at the back of Ladbroke Grove on Notting Hill. In spite of the comparative wealth of many of the people living in the area, the school was not, in Winifred's words, 'intended for the carriage trade', but for the daughters of parents of moderate means with scholarships for those of less than moderate means.

The building was a long red-brick structure, north facing; commonsense, rather than architectural conceit, had inspired its design. It knew itself to be worthy of respect but entertained no Gothic fantasies. Sober, modest, durable, it had the qualities which its Founder had looked for in its pupils. Subsequent headmistresses had looked for rather more. Each in her own way, they had sought to instil into the pupils an appreciation of beauty, a love of art, music and literature; to strengthen their qualities of loyalty, courage and fortitude; to give them a strong Christian faith and a desire to serve their country. Critics said that the school sent its pupils out into the world full of expectations which life would never fulfil.

Miss Blaize, the present headmistress, was well aware that many people questioned the aims of the school. She was not one to trim her sails to the wind. The fact that such concepts as beauty, faith, endurance, service to others, should occasion derision only showed the importance of ensuring that here, in this place, the laughable should be honoured. 'Cynicism,' she would say, 'is soon learnt, and scepticism demands less risk than belief.'

From the moment they passed through the school gates the pupils knew exactly what Miss Blaize expected of them in the way of response, behaviour, appearance, speech, deportment. When they left the school, they would, as one of the more rebellious spirits had put it, 'apportion our time between the soup kitchen, St Mary Abbot's, and the National Gallery; at all times being careful to observe the notices telling us it is forbidden to walk on the grass.'

Louise, who did not experience living in terms of aims and values, was largely untouched by the school's philosophy. Claire embraced it wholly. Alice had problems. She respected the school and was proud of it; but, like the uniform, it did not fit her very well.

Most of the staff were middle-aged, kind and caring; it was not an easy school for a young woman to teach in. Miss Lindsay, Alice's form mistress, had been at the school for two years. She was in her late twenties and had ideas which she regarded as advanced and others considered to be decadent. She was an expert at exploiting weakness.

'I wonder why my form is always late?' she greeted Alice on the latter's arrival in the classroom.

Alice halted at Miss Lindsay's desk, not sure what was expected of her. Daphne was seated at one of the desks by the window. She had been looking cool and composed, but as soon as she saw Alice she rolled her eyes heavenwards. Alice thought that perhaps her parents had found out about the midnight feast and sent a note complaining that Daphne had contracted an unsuitable friendship. Parents had been known to do this, but never in the case of one of the Fairley girls.

Miss Lindsay said, 'And how did you spend your holiday, Alice?'

Alice mumbled that she had had a good holiday, thank you.

'Have you ever *not* had a good holiday, Alice?'

Alice, bereft of speech, shook her head.

'You think it is written in the book of life that holidays are to be enjoyed? Pleasure is not mandatory, Alice. Do you know what that means?'

Alice said huskily, 'It means "by order".'

'It was the meaning of pleasure to which I was referring. An unfamiliar word in this establishment, but one with which you will one day have to become acquainted, even if only to deprecate it.'

At this point the handbell was rung and Miss Lindsay had to call the roll rapidly. Daphne whispered as Alice, seated herself in the adjacent desk, 'Just when she was going to tell you about illicit pleasure!'

'Daphne, what *happened*?'

'It's all right.' Daphne watched Alice's face relax in relief. As they lined up to leave the classroom, she said casually, 'We had to tell the police, of course.'

'The police!'

Miss Lindsay said, 'Whatever it is that Daphne wishes to communicate to Alice, I am sure it can wait until break.'

The door of the classroom was opened and the girls heard the sound of a march being thumped out on the grand piano on the platform in the assembly hall. The school, with the exception of the kindergarten, marched into the assembly hall, the various forms lining stairs and corridors, the girls waiting in good order their turn to enter two abreast. When they were all present, the head girl went to fetch the headmistress.

Miss Blaize mounted the platform to a hush which was a tribute to the respect in which she was held, if not to her popularity. Popularity was something which Miss Blaize would not have considered appropriate to a headmistress. She was a majestic woman with the proportions of a Wagnerian soprano who emphasized her regality by wearing ankle-length dresses of a purple hue. The girls were so used to this attire that the thought of being able to see Miss Blaize's legs was almost obscene (there was something obscene about the thought that Miss Blaize *had* legs). Her face, dark-skinned and blunt-featured, was heavily lined; underneath her black eyes were purple shadows tinged with orange at the outer edge; down one cheek ran a scar like a seam in the surface of a rock. Her hair was dark and worn in an uncompromising Eton crop; it refused however to lie flat, and hung across her forehead giving her a grotesque resemblance to that dreadful schoolboy, William Brown. Her very appearance at the end of a corridor was enough to strike terror into the heart of an oncoming pupil.

This morning she advanced to the rostrum and there paused to regard with apparent sorrow the faces gazing up at her. Alice thought: the police have been to see her. What shall we do?

They sang 'Hills of the North, rejoice!' Then a sixth-former read a passage from Isaiah. Prayers followed, the girls kneeling on the floor. When assembly should have been over, and they were waiting for the first chords of the march to be struck, Miss Blaize leant forward on the rostrum and said, 'Will you all sit down, please.' They sat cross-legged and waited, in doom-filled expectancy. Alice's face was scarlet; beside her, Daphne's composure was threatened only by a slight twitching of the lips. Seated on one of the built-in side benches, the gym mistresses cast expert eyes over the pupils to see that backs were straight, heads held erect.

Miss Blaize smiled; it was a mirthless smile, a stretching of the lips across the gums which produced a reptilian effect. The children preferred Miss Blaize not to smile. She spoke quietly in a voice which had a surprising and deceptive sweetness. They had, she told them, now returned from the school holidays; she hoped they had had a good Christmas and not eaten too much. The little ones, to whom this remark was addressed, tittered obligingly. She hoped that amid all the rejoicing they had remembered what it was that had happened at Christmas, that Our Lord had been born in a poor country into a poor home. She hoped they had remembered those less fortunate than themselves. Perhaps they did not think of themselves as fortunate? She herself had spent Christmas in Palestine and she told them about the conditions in which people lived there. Then she reminded them that in their own country there were nearly three million unemployed; and having thus suitably chastened them, she stopped. Miss Blaize never took long to make her points.

Alice began to breath more easily. Instantly, as though the relief had been communicated to her, Miss Blaize said, 'There is one other matter about which I must speak to you. Something very unpleasant happened this morning.' She paused, and in that small space of time Alice saw herself walking along Pratts Farm Road, wondering how she was to tell her parents that they were to take her away from school. Girls were never expelled from the Winifred Clough Day School for Girls; their parents always took them away. Miss Blaize was speaking again. She was saying that a girl had been seen riding her bicycle on the pavement, thus causing a pensioner to step into the road in front of the milkman's horse. She would like the girl concerned to come and see her in her study.

As they marched out of the hall, Daphne whispered to Alice, 'I wonder what happened when the sodding old pensioner and Dobbin collided!'

Alice did not care. All that mattered was that she had been granted a reprieve. 'Why did the police come, Daphne?'

Daphne laughed. 'It's all right. I didn't give you away.'

'But what happened?'

'I'll tell you at break when you've got your doughnut to build up your strength.'

Miss Lindsay, watching as they came into the classroom together, thought how unlike these two friends were. Alice Fairley was a good, solid child who would grow into a good, solid woman and contribute notably to the dullness of the Anglo-Saxon race. Daphne Drummond was a different matter altogether. At first glance, she seemed a real *Girls' Own Paper* type of girl: compact, alert, with crisp chestnut hair and – dear God, yes – mischievous hazel eyes. She had a trim figure and her blouse once tucked into her skirt stayed in place without need for the endless adjustment which so plagued her companion. She was good at games and would have been good at work had she put her mind to it. Of her kind are idols usually made and it puzzled her teacher that she did not run true to form, collecting no gang around her and attempting no domination either in the classroom or on the games field.

'With your gifts you could go a long way,' Miss Lindsay had once told her.

'But in what direction?' Daphne had replied with a bored lift of the eyebrows.

Miss Lindsay, who enjoyed ambiguity, had been taken aback. Her pupils were made ill at ease by her sarcastic manner and it was rare for her to encounter even the mildest cheekiness. The matter of Daphne's gifts had not been pursued. It was, however, her intention to choose Daphne as one of the form captains and observe what she made of responsibility. Each form had two captains, one chosen by the pupils and one by the form mistress. As soon as they had settled in their desks, Miss Lindsay asked the girls for their nominations.

Daphne said, 'I nominate Alice Fairley.'

Miss Lindsay said, 'Any other nominations?'

There were no other nominations; it was not a job which was hotly contested and Alice was popular. Miss Lindsay bent her head and made a note to occupy the time. It would not be a good thing to have two girls who were so friendly as form captains. She said, 'I nominate Joan Ashbury.'

'I hope you didn't mind being form captain,' Daphne said later when they were queuing for doughnuts during break. 'I didn't want to be Our Stella's choice; I could tell she was brewing up something for me in her nasty mind. Besides, I thought it would be good for you to atone for your sins.'

'Daphne, WHAT HAPPENED?'

'Wait a sec. I must find one with a nice crust. I always think doughnuts are like roast potatoes, don't you? They should be crisp on the outside and soft inside.'

Alice waited while Daphne singled out a doughnut to her liking. She knew her friend well enough to realize that the more she protested the longer Daphne would delay the telling. When they had paid for the doughnuts they walked towards the netball courts where several of the senior girls were practising.

'My father is away; so my dear brother is in charge,' Daphne said.

'Mother had hysterics. Angus can't bear to see her upset, though you'd think he'd be used to it by now. So he called the police to reassure her.'

'What did the police do?'

'Oh, poked around and asked questions.' She watched the senior girls throwing the netball from one to another. 'We ought to take them on, Alice. I reckon we're better than any of them.'

'But how did the police think the burglar got in?'

'Through the broken window, silly!'

Alice stared at her friend. 'You didn't . . .' Daphne was looking very merry and unconcerned, just as she did when she was the only member of her team not out and intended to hit several rounders. It was obvious Daphne had. The situation was becoming worse by the minute, layer upon layer of present guilt and guilt-to-be unfolding. 'Daphne, suppose they arrest someone? An old tramp, or the milk-man?' Milkmen, Alice knew from her parents' conversation, were particularly liable to suspicion. 'What will we do?'

'That's simple, isn't it? We either keep quiet or we own up. I know what I shall do.' Daphne finished her doughnut, rubbed sticky hands briskly together, then darted forward and snatched the netball. She set off running with it, passing it to Alice when her pursuers threatened her. It was some time before the angry seniors regained possession of the ball. When the bell rang, the two girls returned to the building with glowing faces. In the cloakroom, Daphne said, 'They found fingerprints, of course. It didn't matter about mine because that can be explained. I don't think you need worry. They're not likely to fingerprint everyone in Shepherd's Bush, are they?' She grinned at Alice as she said this.

'I don't believe you.'

'You wiped your fingerprints off everything before you left, did you? The ginger-beer glass and everything?'

'I don't believe they took fingerprints.'

Daphne looked astounded. 'Of course they took fingerprints! Whatever do you think the police do when people have been burgled – pray? Honestly, Alice, sometimes I wonder about you.' She went out of the cloakroom.

The double period between break and lunch was taken up with art. The art room was on the top floor of an extension recently added to the west wing; a spacious, lofty room, with big windows in the sloping roof to give north light. A greater degree of freedom was allowed here than elsewhere.

When the pupils entered the room they seemed at first to drift about languidly, some setting up easels, others looking at the work from the previous term displayed on the walls or studying potato-cuts in one of the side rooms. They were not called to order, but gradually they relaxed in this apparently casual atmosphere and without an effort being made to claim their attention, they settled to sketch one of the objects arranged around the room. The two mistresses moved about watching, occasionally making a suggestion.

The art mistresses were allowed, in their own domain, a degree of licence not permitted elsewhere, and wore brightly coloured smocks which made the girls think of them as 'Bohemian'. Miss Bellamy, who was in her early thirties and young by the standards of the school, laid further claims to this description by a vivacity of manner in no way diminished by her pallor and the pouches beneath her eyes. Among themselves the girls referred to her as Philippa and several of them had crushes on her which she did little to discourage. The older teacher, Miss Rosen, engaged in conversation with the girls on subjects not normally discussed at school; free love had even been known to be touched upon. Miss Blaize, more aware of the need for young creatures to have space in which to breathe and flower than her pupils would have credited, did not interfere with what went on in the art room.

Alice noticed that the one way in which art differed little from any other subject was that the better you were at it, the more acceptable you were to the teachers. Daphne was good at art and enjoyed long conversations with Miss Bellamy in which Alice had no part. The activities which Daphne related to Miss Bellamy were no more interesting than Alice's out-of-school activities, but she made them seem so. It was not so much that she embroidered, but rather that, as with sketching, she knew when to stop, whereas Alice did not.

When Alice came into the art room, Daphne was already talking to Miss Bellamy about the dancing of Anton Dolin. Alice drew up an easel next to Katia Vaseyelin. Katia was a sholarship girl who had only been at the school just over a year. She was also Alice's next-door neighbour. The two girls were friends, though at school they usually went their separate ways.

'My family knew all the great Russian dancers,' Katia said, looking contemptuously at Daphne. Katia did not tease, she just told lies. Alice accepted this with equanimity. If there was one factor governing Alice's choice of friends it was their ability to surprise and delight her; the 'nice' and the 'good' had little appeal to her. 'I bet your family didn't know Anton Dolin,' she said.

'He is a great friend of my mother.' The statement carried no conviction. In a sense, nothing about Katia carried conviction because she lacked a context in which to be convincing. She was so foreign. There seemed, for one thing, to be much more of her than was considered fitting for a thirteen-year-old. Yet she was not the tallest in her form. Perhaps it was her untidiness which called attention to her salient features: the constant parting company of blouse and skirt emphasizing well-developed bust and hips; while the straggling hair-ribbon drew the gaze to the mass of dark golden hair which looked so artificial. The English girls found it hard to believe that hair could be that colour and imagined it wanted only a good wash to become wholesome Anglo-Saxon honey. In manner Katia was foreign, too, seemingly unaware of words with such universal application as 'excuse me', and unable to master the art of looking without actually seeming to stare. Her eyes, which were large and slightly protruding, were particularly well suited to the practice of staring – one of her specialities was to see how many people she could compel to look at her in the tram on the way to school. Daphne did not like Katia. 'She comes to school with egg on her mouth.'

Over the recent holiday Katia had been staying with her grandparents in Germany and this was the first time that Alice had talked to her since her return. The grandparents and their impressive home were authenticated by the camera in whose veracity Alice was a profound believer. Bavaria was known to her by the same medium. She thought it very romantic with its snow-clad forests and buildings with cone-shaped turrets, like those in the Knights Castile advertisements. 'Did you go skating and was there lots of snow?' she asked.

Katia had started to paint a vase. She was clumsy and always managed to get as much paint on herself as on the paper. Now she was working with a desperate concentration not best suited to capturing the delicate lines of the Japanese design, and seemed reluctant to talk about her holiday. Usually she was only too willing to show off about the wealth and importance of her grandparents.

'It wasn't much fun this time,' she said, when Alice persisted. 'There was fighting in the town and they came and threw stones through the windows of our house.'

'Why did they do that?'

'Because my grandparents are Jewish.'

'But you're Russian.'

Katia, who was not as a rule afraid of being overheard, lowered her voice. 'My mother's family are Jewish.' For a moment, a shadow lay unmoving across the easels and Alice was aware that Miss Rosen had stopped and was listening. Katia said, 'My grandfather put the shutters up against all the windows and the house was dark. I hated it; it gave me the creeps.'

Miss Rosen said, 'What made you choose to paint the vase, Katia?'

'I liked the colours.'

Miss Rosen stared at Katia's painting for so long that Alice thought it must be good, but all Miss Rosen said was, 'You might have found it easier to start with something less ambitious.' She looked at Alice's sketch and passed on without comment.

Katia said, 'I'm going to Lyons on the way home. Why don't you come?'

She repeated this suggestion during the lunch hour when they were standing at the table reserved for pupils who brought packed lunches. The staff entered and took up their places at the high table. While the deputy headmistress said the grace Alice reflected on the temptation now presented to her by Katia. When Alice had told her mother that Katia would be coming to the school, her mother had said, 'You've got your own friends; you mustn't neglect them for Katia.' Daphne's instant dislike of Katia had proved the wisdom of this remark. But going to Lyons on one's way home could hardly be counted as neglect of one's friends.

'They have lovely doughnuts,' Katia said.

'But I don't need a doughnut then,' Alice said unhappily.

Alice's parents found it hard enough to meet the school fees without incurring any unnecessary additional expenses. Economics, however, were never represented to the children in terms of money, and as far as Alice was concerned she had a packed lunch because she had a good meal in the evening. There was no reasonable excuse for going to Lyons.

Reason, however, so important to the adult world, had little dominion over Alice. What Alice badly needed now was a refuge and it was Katia who seemed most likely to offer this.

To Alice it seemed that in their always dusky house which smelt of candle wax the Vaseyelins engaged in a mysterious masquerade which had something about it of the grotesque. In that alien sphere even the consequences of fingerprints in soot might not be terrible, the arrest of the milkman present no dilemma. From the way Katia talked, and from her own limited observation of their household, Alice was convinced that moral dilemmas, small or great, played little part in the preoccupations of the Vaseyelins. Loyalty to Daphne forbade the telling of the misadventure to Katia. But the thought that, even if presented with it, Katia would have made little sense of the knowledge, was in some way comforting, as though Katia's incomprehension of rights and wrongs which were so essential an ingredient of the Fairley daily diet, afforded a shelter which Alice needed. Just being with Katia would make it all less important.

Alice was tempted to accompany Katia to Lyons. But what of Claire? She looked down the table to where Claire was giggling with her companions. Claire's one concern would be to get home in time to listen to 'Children's Hour'. But was there any need to involve Claire in this? Louise would take Claire home, all that was required was an excuse for not accompanying them. As soon as this thought came to her she remembered the conversation at breakfast.

'I can't come today,' she said regretfully. 'We've got to wait for Louise. She's auditioning for the upper school play.'

'They don't do a play this term. Louise is having you on.'

Alice said, 'Louise wouldn't do that.'

Katia looked at Alice in a way which suggested that she knew a great deal more about life than did Alice.

When at the end of the afternoon the middle and upper schools assembled in the hall, Alice looked up to the balcony hoping to receive a reassuring signal from Louise, but she could not see her sister. The light was fading beyond the windows and it was cold in the big hall. The brief service always filled Alice with a sense of awe and mystery and, undisturbed by thoughts of mortality, she enjoyed the rather melancholy poetry of the prayers without feeling a need to explore their meaning. Today, however, she experienced some slight misgivings as she listened to Miss Blaize saying: ' "O God, from whom all holy desires, all good counsels and all just works do proceed; Give unto thy servants that peace which the world cannot give . . ." ' (Alice thought this particularly beautiful; it made her think of the pussy-willows on the towpath reflected in the river.) ' ". . . that both our hearts may be set to obey Thy commandments, and also that by Thee we being defended from the fear of our enemies may pass our time in rest and quietness; through the merits of Jesus Christ our Saviour." '

As she came out of the lighted entrance hall into the cold, windy street, Alice saw that Claire was waiting for her, jumping from one foot to the other.

'I walked to the end of the road with Marjorie Fowler. Shall we go in and wait for Louise?'

Alice was saved from replying by one of the seniors who approached them, saying, 'Louise will meet you at the tram terminus at Shepherd's Bush Green at five o'clock. You are to come with me. I'm going to the library and afterwards I'll walk to the Green with you.'

Alice said, 'We'll be all right on our own, thank you. We'll go to Lyons.'

The senior hesitated; there were a lot of girls walking down the hill towards Holland Park Avenue and she supposed these two would be all right. She did not want to be lumbered with Louise's sisters for the next hour.

'We're going to be awfully late home,' Claire said as they walked slowly down the hill. 'We shall miss "Children's Hour".'

There were lights on in the big houses and in one room they could see firelight dancing on a wall. As they watched, a maid came and drew the curtains across the window.

'Marjorie's parents have a maid and a cook,' Claire said.

They passed a postman, his sack over his back, standing in a gateway talking to a man delivering groceries. The man with the groceries was saying, 'I thought to myself, "I'll pickle your walnuts, my lady!" But what can you say? A word out of turn and I'd be on the dole.' Further down the street a woman was getting out of a cab followed by a man carrying big mauve and silver striped hatboxes. Grandmother Fairley had an enchanting collection of hatboxes. One of Alice's most precious treats was being allowed to open the boxes and take out the hats.

Claire said, 'You'll never guess what Letty Arnold's parents gave her for Christmas.'

'What?'

'A pleated skirt.'

'Gosh!'

They thought about this without envy, surprised at a glimpse of a life so different from their own.

'What colour was it?'

'It was tartan with a big pin.'

Letty would wear a neat blouse tucked into it and would look attractive because she had a small waist and a flat tummy. At the thought of this, some envy did creep into Alice's soul.

'Let's cross over and walk to John Galsworthy's house,' she said, brightening as they came to Holland Park Avenue.

'That's out of our way,' Claire said. 'I don't care about John Galsworthy. I want to get to the Green.'

Alice approached the Green reluctantly. In Holland Park she was aware of a life that ran along parallel lines to her own and never merged with it. When she was older, she intended to live in one of the elegant houses in Holland Park.

Outside the cinema facing the Green there was a big poster of a blonde woman, a silver lamé strap slipping low on one arm and a man standing behind her, nibbling the exposed shoulder. The woman had large, sad eyes, and appeared not to notice what was going on. Alice was about to look at the stills in the frame when a well-dressed man came up and offered to take them in with him.

'We don't want to go in, thank you,' Alice lied primly.

'What about the little one?' He smiled at Claire. The children could not imagine that anyone would be stupid enough to go with him; he had irregularly spaced teeth and sprayed saliva as he spoke.

The commissionaire strolled slowly towards them, staring at the man who hurried away. Alice and Claire walked in the direction of the shops, Claire imitating the man and trying to spray Alice's face. When they came to the teashop she stopped spitting to protest, 'We can't, Alice! What would Mummy say?'

'We're just spending our pocket money, that's all.'

'I don't want to spend my pocket money in Lyons.'

'We'll spend mine. I've been saving it.' Alice pushed open the door. 'And don't behave as though you've never been in a teashop on your own before.'

'Well, I haven't. And neither have you.'

The shop was crowded and most of the tables were occupied. The two children stood awkwardly just inside the door, wondering what to do. The Nippies in their black dresses and crisp white aprons looked very unapproachable. A woman at a nearby table which had two vacant chairs put her handbag on one of the chairs and glared at Alice. Adult disapproval had its usual loosening effect on Alice's stomach muscles and she was afraid she and Claire would have to make their exit, giggling ignominiously. Then she caught sight of Katia sitting at a table almost hidden by a pillar.

'I thought you might come,' Katia said. 'I bagged a place for you.'
There was no chair for Claire. Katia was unconcerned about this; her arrangement had been with Alice, and if Alice liked to lumber herself with her younger sister, that was her look out. The woman at the cash desk, who had big horn-rimmed spectacles, came to Alice's rescue, smiling like a friendly owl and pointing, 'You can take that spare chair.'

Katia was drinking tea. Alice picked up the menu and tried to study it composedly.

Claire moaned, 'I want to wee.'

'Don't be so childish!' Alice looked at her sister. Claire was sitting awkwardly, one foot hooked around the leg of the chair, giving the impression that at any moment she might overbalance; the frizzy red hair had pushed her school hat to one side and her features were contorted by inane laughter. What an awful little toad Claire was, and what an encumbrance to her own burgeoning maturity. 'Burgeoning' was a word which Alice had lately acquired. She liked to think of herself as burgeoning; it gave an acceptable quality to her plumpness. She said to Claire, 'I shan't ever come out with you again.'

'I don't want you to come out with me, so there.'

Katia poured more tea into her cup and said, 'You can't take her anywhere, can you?'

The Nippy came and Alice ordered two glasses of orange squash and two long iced buns. The Nippy said, 'I'm only supposed to be serving teas.' This convulsed Claire. Alice, who did not think she had enough money for two teas, looked at Katia, but Katia had become uncharacteristically abstracted and was staring dreamily towards the window. The cashier came to the rescue again. 'Don't be so mean, Doris.' The Nippy departed with an angry wiggle of her shoulders. In the interval before she returned Alice surreptitiously counted her money and made sure she had enough. As soon as the buns were put before them, Claire took one and proceeded to squash as much as possible of it into her mouth, a game she and her friends had recently devised to enliven the break period.

'Don't worry,' Katia said to Alice. 'My brothers play at which can break wind the loudest.'

Alice cut a small piece off the end of one bun and held it poised in her fingers. 'Did you go to the pictures in Germany?'

'I saw Marlene Dietrich in *The Blue Angel*.'

'Was it good?'

Claire, not used to being ignored, said, mouth full, 'I know a poem.'

'It was made years ago and she was plump, not like she is now. They don't groom them, you know. In French films you can see they've got underarm hair. And they *go* further, of course. It's not just kissing. They get very worked up and all that.'

Claire swallowed the last of the bun and inhaled until her whole body swelled up; she had lately been practising saying each verse in one breath.

'The breaking waves dash'd high on a stern and rock-bound coast;
And the woods against a stormy sky, their giant branches toss'd;
And the heavy night hung dark, the hills and water o'er,
When a band of exiles moor'd their bark on the wild New England
    shore.'

'You get shots of them in bed, too, and they haven't got anything on. I mean, you don't *see* everything, but enough, so that you can tell.'

Alice sipped her orangeade, trying to visualize how far was enough. As far as the waist?

'Not as the conqueror came they, the true-hearted came;
Not with the roll of the stirring drum, and the trumpet that sings of
    fame;
Not as the flying come, in silence, and in fear;
They shook the depths of the desert gloom with their hymns of lofty
    cheer.'

'How can you understand what's happening?' Alice asked.

'In England you get sub-titles. But I don't bother with them, they only tell you what they're saying and that stuff. You don't need sub-titles; it's all there in a Continental film without sub-titles.'

'Amidst the storm they sang; this the stars heard, and the sea,
And the sounding aisles of the dim woods rang to the anthem of the
    free . . .'

'We don't want to hear all of it,' Alice said.

People had been coming and going while they were talking. Now the door opened and a tall, shabby man in an old raincoat came in carrying a violin. He had a big head made bigger by a shock of curly white hair, against which his face looked sickly; his eyes were deepset and shadowed. Alice recognized him immediately as the man who played the violin outside the Shepherd's Bush Empire. He never thanked people when they gave him money – just went on playing as though he had not noticed. As he walked across the room, Katia stared at him so intensely that Alice was not surprised when he turned his head and smiled at her.

Katia pushed back her chair. 'Well, so long,' she said to Alice. 'I'll get my tea paid for now, I expect.'

'Katia, you can't!' Alice was aghast, and even Claire paused, open-mouthed, as Katia walked towards the man.

'We'll go,' Alice said. She went to the desk, followed by Claire declaiming:

'There were two men with hoary hair amidst that pilgrim band;
Why had they come to wither here, away from their childhood's
    land?'

The cashier said to Alice, 'Isn't it lovely? What is it?'
Claire said, 'It's *The Pilgrim Fathers* by Felicia Hemans.'
'What a clever little girl you are! Your Mummy and Daddy must be very proud of you.'
Claire looked odiously shy.

Katia and the man weren't having much to say to each other; he seemed more interested in the menu than in her. Alice thought she looked unhappy and that it served her right. As she and Claire made their way back to the Green, she wondered whether she should tell the Vaseyelins that Katia had been picked up by a strange man in Lyons. She didn't think she could do it, particularly as this would put a stop to any future visits to Lyons; but how would she feel if Katia were to disappear?

'There was woman's fearless eye, lit by her deep love's truth;
There was manhood's brow serenely high, and the fiery heart of
    youth . . .'

'Oh, shut up!' Alice shouted. 'I wish you'd died of diphtheria.'
'Josie Williams's sister is dying, did you know? Josie said it won't be long now.'
A few people were standing in the queue for the sixpenny seats

outside the cinema and a Jehovah's Witness was telling them the days of their wickedness were numbered. In a doorway two grubby urchins stood over an arrangement of shells and old buttons; as they passed, one said, 'Penny for the grotter,' and Alice, feeling reckless, gave him two pennies.

Louise was waiting at the tram terminus. 'Wherever have you been?' she demanded. 'We've missed a bus and a tram.'

'We went to Lyons,' Claire said. 'It was lovely.'

She finished the poem on the top of the tram to the amusement of the conductor. Alice looked out of the window. In a sidestreet she could see the lamplighter with his long pole poking at a lamp which had gone out. It was cold, and there was a smell of fog in the air. She felt churned up by her own and others' guilt. When they got off the tram and were walking towards their home, Louise said, 'I've auditioned for a part with the St Bartholomew's Dramatic Society. There's no need to say anything to Mummy and Daddy about it until I know if I've got the part.' It was all too much, and Alice had one of her tummy upsets that night.

3

On the other side of the party wall to the Fairleys lived an elderly gentleman known to the Fairley girls as 'the relic'. Mr Ainsworth, who was in his nineties, regarded the Fairleys as people with whom he could have little social contact. He acknowledged their existence by raising his hat to Mrs Fairley and the girls whenever he met them in the street, and by occasionally commenting to Stanley Fairley on events in the world of politics. Mr Ainsworth could recall seeing Mr Disraeli drive up to Gunnersbury Park to be greeted by Baron de Rothschild, and therefore regarded himself as an incontrovertible authority on all matters political. As Mr Fairley entertained the same conceit, without benefit of ever having seen Mr Disraeli, communication between the two men was necessarily brief – though invariably courteous. Mr Ainsworth, a widower, was looked after by a housekeeper. Mrs Peachey, a woman of great refinement, was even more aware of the decline of the neighbourhood than her employer, and it was many months before she could bring herself to walk on the same side of the street as the Fairleys. Mr Fairley said that Mr Ainsworth was a relic of the past, and as such instructive and to be studied with respect – a dictum he did not extend to include Mrs Peachey.

Mr Ainsworth was, however, part of a tradition out of which the Fairleys had grown. But the family who lived on the detached side of the Fairley property were of quite another kind. The Vaseyelins (or the Vaseline family as they were known locally) had come to Shepherd's Bush in 1926. Whether at that time there was a Mr Vaseyelin, the Fairleys did not know. Some people in the road said there had been a man in the house for a few years, but it was thought he was a lodger and he had now left. What was certain was that there were four children – one girl and three boys – now ranging from nine to eighteen. Jacov, the eldest, played the man's role in the household, and the role normally played by the woman in English households fell to Anita, who was possibly an old nurse, a governess, a dependent relative – or an amalgam of all three. Mrs Vaseyelin was a mysterious figure, seldom seen except in the evening, when she would appear wearing a long coat hemmed with fur and a hat with a veil which covered her face, and was knotted at the back of her head. No doubt in the past she had been accustomed to step from the house into her carriage; but if there was one thing which was known about the Vaseyelins, it was that they had no money. Several of the tradespeople were prepared to vouch for that. So, Mrs Vaseyelin, instead of stepping into her carriage, walked to The Askew Arms and took a Number 12 bus. What happened thereafter none of her neighbours knew.

When Mrs Vaseyelin and her family first arrived in Pratts Farm Road she had left her card at Numbers 25 and 29, but as the recipients had no idea how they were supposed to respond, this had not advanced intercourse between the households. By the time the Fairleys arrived in the autumn of 1929, the Vaseyelins were conditioned to isolation. The advent of three children next door, however, was of considerable interest to the Vaseyelin children. The first day that Stanley Fairley worked in the garden, Jacov Vaseyelin – having concluded from conversations with schoolfellows that cards were no longer exchanged, introduced himself in what he took to be a suitably informal manner.

'I am Jacov Alexei Anton Vaseyelin, sir, your neighbour. If I can be of service to you at any time, please to say.'

Stanley Fairley looked up in astonishment at the head with its mop of curly black hair affixed, in the manner of a surrealist sculpture, to the brick wall. Mr Fairley was deeply suspicious of surrealism, which he considered decadent. The face did nothing to allay his fears. It was apparently guileless, but it had that anarchic quality which can sometimes go with a certain kind of gentleness: the face of one of those unholy innocents who – seeming not to see the world as others see it – make havoc of the carefully constructed patterns of society. Mr Fairley, while being prepared to fight for intellectual freedom, was not prepared to brook any interference with the rules governing the day-to-day exchanges of his life. He was not a sociable man, and the last thing he wanted when he was working in his garden was to be made aware of neighbours, well-meaning or otherwise. He thanked Jacov Alexei Anton Vaseyelin brusquely, and went about the business of digging up a recalcitrant holly bush. When he swung round to throw down pieces of the uprooted holly, he saw that the head had been removed. Had he been dealing with a man, he would not have reproached himself; as far as he was concerned, the sooner you let the other fellow know the way you like to live your life, the better. But this was a boy, and he had been churlish to him. He stuck the spade in the flowerbed, and approached the wall to make amends. The rest of the unholy innocent was now in view: a thin youth, hunched crescent-shaped on a dilapidated garden seat, disconsolately poking at a hole in the sole of one shoe.

'You wouldn't have a pair of shears?' Mr Fairley asked grudgingly. 'I've sent mine to be sharpened.'

'Surely we must have!' The youth unwound himself with alacrity. He moved lightly and easily, but took a somewhat wayward course towards what was his obvious destination – the garden shed; it was as though it was not natural to him to approach anything directly. Eventually however, by way of a conservatory (where he pressed his face against the window and grimaced at someone within) and what was probably an outside lavatory, he came to the garden shed and, after some desultory rummaging, found a pair of shears on a shelf.

'Hmmm.' Mr Fairley examined the shears. 'These don't get used very often, do they?'

'I am sorry. No use?'

'I expect they might be with a bit of oiling.'

Later, he told his wife, 'I've spent the afternoon getting their shears into good repair. We really can't have too much of this kind of thing. We shall have to be careful to keep our distance.' He looked at her reproachfully, as though it were she who had borrowed the shears.

'I doubt if they will trouble you now that they've introduced themselves.' Judith guessed that it was her daughters in whom the young Vaseyelins were interested, and in this she proved correct. The back garden of Number 27 began to receive much-needed attention; the front garden, which offered no prospect of communication with the Fairley children, continued to be neglected, the hedge grown so high that it obscured the downstairs windows. In the spring there were frequent exchanges over the garden wall, and by the summer it was impossible not to include the Vaseyelins in Alice's birthday party. 'We can't have a party in the garden and leave them out,' Judith Fairley said reluctantly. The Vaseyelins were alien, and she did not want the bother of trying to understand them. She was busy enough without that.

The Vaseyelins arrived at the party stiff and too formally dressed. Nicholas and Boris, who were twins, took up their usual position on the fringe of events, heads close together, sharing secret observations. Katia, on the other hand, was soon shouting and screaming with the other children. Jacov seemed uncertain whether he belonged with the adults or with the children, and he made a nuisance of himself in the kitchen, offering to carry things and generally getting in Judith's way. In spite of his willingness, he was unable to complete the simplest task assigned to him effectively, because he allowed himself to become sidetracked into some other well-meaning activity.

'You can't do two things at once, Jacov,' Judith told him.

'But you do several things at the same time,' he pointed out.

'I know which things can be combined.' She was irritated at the way in which he spoke to her: not insolently, but as though he noted things about her. Her daughters' friends were not yet old enough to do this, and she was not accustomed to it.

After the party, the Vaseyelins kept their place on the far side of the garden wall. Judith was pleased about this. She had been afraid that they might have expected to come and go more freely.

Then at Christmas the party invitation was returned. This was obviously an event of some importance, and Jacov felt it necessary to approach Mr Fairley.

Mr Fairley found himself in a dilemma. He was careful about the houses which his daughters visited. He had refused to allow them to go to one house, because the parents played tennis on a Sunday: 'If they do that on the Lord's Day, goodness alone knows what goes on on other days of the week!' The membership of a social club, whether visited on a Sunday or a weekday, was an automatic disqualification for entertaining the Fairley children. The Vaseyelin household, however, kept its secrets, and all that Mr Fairley could with certainty pin on them was that they were foreigners and Russian Orthodox. Russian Orthodox was not as bad as Roman Catholic, but it was bad enough. 'Foreigner' was a different matter. Mr Fairley was a passionate believer in liberal values and, as a Methodist lay preacher, laid frequent stress on the rights of minorities and the needs of the underprivileged. He was aware that many people who would not have minded subjecting their daughters to the perils of an agnostic – or even atheistic – household, would not have wanted them to mix with the Vaseyelins because they 'did not belong'. But on a matter of such importance, would he be right to redress the balance in favour of the Vaseyelins? Should he not be concerned primarily with his children's well-being?

Jacov said, 'I hope you will do us the honour to say yes.'

At this point something happened for which Mr Fairley was unprepared. Mr Fairley could have taught in a grammar school; he had a good London degree; but the Lord had called him to teach the underprivileged and the less able. He did not do this in a spirit of patronage. Mr Fairley cared about his boys. Now, he was surprised to see in Jacov's eyes the same look he had sometimes caught in the eyes of a boy who is desperately afraid that – owing to lack of means – he will be left out of some longed-for treat, a sea cadet camp, or a day's excursion to the coast. On such occasions, Mr Fairley would dig into his own pocket to help. It was not money that was needed now. This party represented something to Jacov – perhaps it was honour that was at stake, or the need for once to be a giver. Mr Fairley had no understanding of the workings of Jacov's mind, but he did understand that the issue was an important one.

Jacov said, 'I will myself be responsible for your daughters.'

Mr Fairley, squaring up to him solemnly, replied, 'On that understanding alone, then . . .'

Mrs Fairley had sighed when her husband told her of his decision. 'I think the boy is to be trusted,' he said.

Judith Fairley did not believe that any human being, let alone a young male, was ever entirely to be trusted, but she saw no point in saying this.

So it was that at four o'clock in the afternoon of 21 December 1930 Alice stood at the dining-room window. It was cold, and the window was frosted so that she could not see clearly into the street; and in any case, the Vaseyelins' hedge was so high that it was not always possible to see people coming to the house. So far she had counted three people and the postman. She breathed on the window pane, moaning with impatience. Louise took a long time dressing and Claire started late, so Alice always had to wait for them. Her mother told her she was in too much of a hurry for her pleasures, but Alice was convinced that some moment of enchantment would be lost if she was late.

Louise came in and said, 'Anyone would think you had never been to a party before.'

Alice noticed that, in spite of being so casual, Louise was wearing the apple-green crêpe dress which Grandma had made for her, and which she kept for special occasions. It was a lovely dress, and Alice looked forward to the time when Louise would have outgrown it.

Outside in the hall Claire, who had been hurried, was saying, 'I don't want to go any more.'

Mummy said reprovingly, 'Think how disappointed you would be if people stayed away from your party.'

'I shan't know anyone.'

'You'll be with Alice and Louise.'

'*They* won't stay with me.'

'Yes, I will!' Alice rushed into the hall and put an arm round Claire. 'I'll stay with you all the time.'

Their father came with them to the door of Number 27. He knocked. There was no response. Claire tugged herself free of Alice's restraining arm and was about to protest, when they heard footsteps crossing the hall. The front door opened. In the dim light of the gas lamp they saw Jacov, shabby in a frayed brown suit with a bow tie. Behind him, a flight of uncarpeted stairs disappeared into the gloom of the first-floor landing. There was a smell of gas and damp.

Mr Fairley said he would come at six o'clock to collect the children. Jacov bowed and waited at the door while Mr Fairley walked down the path. The children peered about them uneasily, and Louise was moved to place a protective arm around the shoulders of each of her charges. On the left side of the hall there were heavy brown curtains in a material which resembled sacking; the sound of voices and laughter could be heard beyond the curtains. Had it not been for this, the house might have been unoccupied, so little evidence was there of its being lived in. Jacov closed the front door and took Alice's wrap from her. 'How nice. Is it sable or ermine, the collar?' He said this with no hint of mockery, as though sable and ermine were commonplace in Shepherd's Bush.

'I don't know what it is,' Alice answered. 'It came off a hat of Aunt May's and it moults.'

Claire and Louise gave Jacov their shawls, and he put them on top of a pile of clothes hung over the banister post. Then he parted the curtains grandly, as though they were velvet. Alice saw that only a few people had arrived. They were playing a guessing game. Claire, who always got on well at parties once she had broken the ice, immediately joined in. Louise was greeted by the twins, who stood one on each side of her, Nicholas saying she looked pretty while Boris giggled and stroked her hair. Alice started to talk to Katia, but she said 'Hush', because she was doing well at the game; so Alice sat on a stool by the fire and looked round the room, which was large with a high ceiling. It looked as though at one time there had been double doors leading to the hall, but these had gone, and in their place were the brown curtains. The absence of the doors made the room cold and draughty. The furniture had been pushed against the walls, revealing the holes which the castors of the couch had made in the brown linoleum. Patches of damp discoloured the yellow wall-paper. In a corner by the window there was a shrivelled tree left over from a previous Christmas, with a candle burning on the top. There were no other decorations; nor were there any photographs – not even one of Jacov's older sister, Sonya, who had died before the family left Russia. 'My mother does not speak of her,' Jacov had once said. Alice thought it was sad that there was no photograph of Sonya.

The wood fire was bright and made a pleasant smell, but it did not give out much heat. Alice was dismayed. In her own house she was surrounded by objects which had a history: the heavy Serpentine ornaments from Cornwall, one in the shape of a lighthouse, the other a buoy, which Daddy said must have belonged to Mummy's wrecker ancestors; the armchair which could be extended into a day-bed and had been left to them by Great Aunt Mathilda, who had spent a great deal of her life lying on it; the wheezy grandfather clock which was always wrong, in spite of Daddy constantly 'adjusting' the swing of the pendulum by attaching weights to it; these things were as much a part of the household as the people themselves. This room looked just like the sitting-room of Number 29 had looked on the day of their arrival, before any of their treasures had been unpacked. There were no tatting chairbacks, no embroidered cloths for vases to stand on so that they did not mark the table; there was not even a rug by the hearth. Alice glanced guiltily at the green enamel clock on the mantelshelf. Ten minutes past four. In two hours she could go home. She straightened out the skirt of her voile party frock, and wondered what she would do if she wanted to go to the lavatory.

There was a knock at the front door. Jacov introduced new arrivals. Several were foreigners who did not seem interested in the Fairley children, but there were three English boys who were plainly glad to encounter compatriots in this strange house. The most noticeable of the English was a boy of about Jacov's age. He had brown hair, thick and strong, falling in a tuft over his left eye and curling crisply at the back of his head and behind his ears. His ears were big and laid against his head as though they had been pinned there, just as they should. Everything about him was as it should be. He had blue eyes, a wide, smiling mouth, a straight nose with just enough freckles to be attractive, and no spots. He was the most handsome boy Alice had ever seen. His name was Guy Immingham.

The room was crowded now. The children jostled, screamed, laughed and improvised treasure hunts, which they enjoyed passionately and then dropped in favour of another activity, such as imitating film stars. It was not like an ordinary party where everything is carefully organized so that all are included, and a watch is kept to ensure that no one is getting over-excited. It seemed very odd at first. Claire scampered about, pushing, tickling, doing somersaults. A big, clownish boy told Louise what a rotter Guy Immingham was and she pretended to be shocked, head hung down so that the long brown hair curtained her face, while Guy squatted on the ground to see if she was laughing. Someone fell over him and upset orangeade. Everyone laughed, and Jacov poured some more orangeade, and no one fussed with a mop. The younger children screamed louder and louder, and Claire did cartwheels.

Alice sat on the stool, blowing up a balloon. The fire was warm now. She tossed the balloon up in front of her and, as she looked after it, she saw a tall woman standing between the curtains. It was Mrs Vaseyelin. Her dress was black and her hair was black and there was no colour in her face; yet she looked rich, and behind her the curtains really seemed velvet now. Dark hair parted in the centre and drawn back from the perfect oval face was, Alice knew, a recipe for beauty, and she had seen it demonstrated in photographs of Sylvia Sidney. But Sylvia Sidney was young. It was a surprise to see that a face could still be beautiful when it had tiny dry lines scoring the forehead, and shadows which looked as though they had been burnt beneath the eyes.

Alice felt as she did in the assembly hall, waiting for the school play to begin, when curtains were drawn across the platform to give the illusion of theatre. But whereas what happened on the stage was never as strange as she had anticipated, here was strangeness where she had not looked for it!

The room was quiet now. Everyone was staring at Mrs Vaseyelin. She walked across the room, not looking directly at anyone, but seeming to gaze at something beyond them. She sat in a chair by the window, a little in shadow. The voices leapt up again. Alice patted the balloon. It soared up and then came gently down towards her, orange and mauve in the firelight.

A man came through the curtains and joined Mrs Vaseyelin. He was tall, stooping and shabby. Alice thought there was something familiar about him, but as he was standing in the shadows she did not have a clear picture of his face.

The children shouted, tumbled, laughed and screamed. Claire was having a coughing fit. Louise imitated Al Jolson singing 'Sonny Boy'. Guy Immingham said, 'Gosh, you ought to be an actress!' and she said she was going to be, as though there was no question about it. The man and the woman watched without concern or interest. Every now and again fat, good-natured Anita lumbered in from the kitchen and shouted, 'The sweets, Jacov; don't forget to hand round the sweets!' or 'You must offer more ginger beer, Jacov.' No one was concerned when a chair fell over and a side-table was overturned. You would have thought they were used to their possessions tumbling around them.

Then, at a signal from Anita, the twins began to carry in trays of food. A table was moved into the centre of the room. The food did not look very exciting. Jacov brought candles and placed them on the table, then he turned down the gas lamps. He struck a match and bent forward. As Alice watched him leaning towards the candle, she felt that, in the shadows beyond the flame, the room had become much larger.

She looked around her. First, she saw that Mrs Vaseyelin had a shawl across the back of her chair; it was worn thin and the colours were faded, but the material was soft and it glimmered in the candlelight. Then, she saw the wooden figures on the mantelpiece which she had failed to notice before. They stood on a round base, a ballerina in a pretty flowing dress and a baggy-trousered clown; he was kneeling before her, she turning away, hand outstretched for something just beyond her reach. They looked so strange there, standing next to the green enamel clock.

Jacov handed Alice a blackcurrant drink. As she looked down into the glass, it glowed deep crimson. The cakes were from a shop in Shepherd's Bush High Street – not a very nice shop; they had a strange, spicy flavour. Alice said this to Claire, but Claire said she could not taste anything special, and anyway they were dry. Claire said she wished there had been some sherbet.

The candles flickered and shadows leapt on the wall, absurdly short, like a hunchback, and very long, like a beanstalk. Alice looked at Mrs Vaseyelin, who smiled pleasantly, but not as though she really saw her, and asked whether she would like another cake. Alice felt, as she watched the woman's eyes, that someone had come into the room and was standing beside her in the shadows.

While everyone ate and chattered, Alice went up to the mantel-piece. She stood on a chair and took down the carving. She knew this was a bad thing to do, much worse than spilling orangeade or knocking over a chair, but she could not help herself. Even if she was never asked again, she must touch these figures. She sat on the stool and stroked the folds of the gown, and the sad clown's face. The figures were mounted on a round base which had a key underneath; guiltily, Alice turned the key several times. Nothing happened. A voice said, 'She used to dance once. But no more.' Alice saw that Mrs Vaseyelin was looking down at her.

Alice said, 'I would love to have seen her dance.' She closed her eyes, and suddenly she was in a much bigger room; and in the centre of the room a girl was dancing and laughing as she danced. The curtains over the window were parted, and Alice was sure there was a glimpse of snow-laden trees. Then, as her fingers stroked the figure of the dancer, she heard the music of the dance – a long way off, but clear, like a music-box playing in another room. When she opened her eyes, Mrs Vaseyelin was still there, and Alice knew by something that flashed in her eyes that she, too, had heard the music.

Jacov came across the room. 'You are quiet,' he said to Alice. He took away the wooden figures and gave her a jam puff. 'Are you all right?'

'I'm having a lovely time, thank you.'

When Mr Fairley came to fetch his children, Alice did not want to leave. Mrs Vaseyelin and the strange man came out to the hall to see their guests off. Alice heard her say to the man, '. . . like our dear Sonya sitting there by the fire.' She stood on the top step and watched them go. It was cold, but there was no snow. In the yellow gaslight Alice saw that she was much older than she had imagined, and not in any way beautiful.

In the years since that party the Fairley children often saw the young Vaseyelins, but they seldom saw Mrs Vaseyelin, and they did not see the man again; although Alice thought she glimpsed him once walking down Acton High Street in the dusk, carrying a long case. Soon after the party, she had asked Katia, 'Was that man your uncle?' and Katia had shaken her head and changed the subject.

When the children described the party to their parents, they made much of Guy Immingham. It was then that they discovered that their father was acquainted with Guy Immingham's father, and that the Imminghams attended the Methodist Chapel in Holland Park.

'Why don't we go to chapel in Holland Park?' Louise asked her mother. 'It's no further than the Acton chapel.'

'We go to the Acton chapel because your father teaches in Acton, and he does a lot with the Acton sea cadets. There is no good reason why we should go traipsing off to Holland Park.'

Louise did not argue, and in this she was wise, because Guy Immingham began to visit the Vaseyelins quite often and it was no longer necessary to think of changing chapels in order to see him. Mr and Mrs Fairley thought him a likable enough boy, and a year later when the children had their own party no objection was raised to his inclusion.

It was as a result of her friendship with Guy Immingham that Louise was introduced to the St Bartholomew's Dramatic Society. Jacov produced plays for the society, and it was he who recruited Guy. Guy was by then studying for his accountancy examinations, and it was hoped that he would go into his father's firm; but like Louise he had leanings towards the stage, having played several leading parts in school plays with moderate success.

A few weeks after the audition, by which time Louise had been offered a part, Guy accompanied the Fairley family to chapel on a cold February evening. Mr Fairley was preaching and Guy had said that he would like to hear him. In spite of his quest for intellectual truth, which sometimes made him cavalier in his treatment of the pretensions of others, Mr Fairley liked praise. His wife – busy, practical and at times imperceptive – seldom met his needs in this respect, and was inclined to spoil his pleasure when others were more obliging.

'I don't think it is your words of wisdom that he's interested in,' she had said on this occasion, irritated that he should court Guy's good opinion.

'I see no reason to doubt his sincerity.'

Judith, walking with Claire while Louise and Guy followed some distance behind, reflected on man's infinite capacity for self-deception.

'Your father couldn't possibly mind your taking part,' Guy was saying. 'My father doesn't object, and he's a Methodist. There'll be a fuss when I tell him I'm going on the stage, of course; but that's different.'

'My father wouldn't think it was different,' Louise replied. 'I know exactly what he would say to that: "Play-acting is either right or it is wrong; whether it is professional or not is immaterial." ' She gave a passable imitation of her father.

They were walking past a terrace of small, two-storeyed houses, the occupants of which – judging by the smell – had all had boiled cabbage for their Sunday dinner. Although these people were at some pains to keep the houses decent, Guy was shocked to see how badly the paintwork had been allowed to deteriorate. He also noticed that in most cases the curtains were little better than threadbare scraps. In the rooms where the curtains had not yet been drawn there was no cheerful glow of firelight. Most of the houses fronted onto the pavement, but further on they came to two old cottages of an earlier period which had a few square feet of turned earth staked out by dilapidated railings. There were two women talking in the doorway of one of the cottages, and somewhere out of sight a child was howling dismally. Here, bad drains added to the all-pervasive smell of cabbage. The area reminded Guy of old photographs yellowing in albums. There was nothing dramatic about it, no sense of danger or depravity lurking in the shadows; it was simply that it failed to convince as a place in which real people lived and loved and had their being.

Beyond the cottages a group of boys were sitting in the gutter shouting encouragement to another boy who was climbing a lamppost. Judith Fairley stopped to admonish the climber; his companions eyed Alice and Claire stonily. Guy and Louise walked on.

'But your father doesn't object to school plays . . .'

'Oh, but he does! He went to see Miss Blaize about them.'

'What happened?'

'She convinced him that our "moral welfare" could be left in her hands and that, "although she is an Anglican, she has no leanings towards Rome." She also satisfied him on the subject of make-up. "We could hardly forbid the use of any kind of make-up in school and then permit theatrical make-up." ' Louise pronounced the word 'theatrical' in a deep voice. 'I'd love to have heard them talking.'

Guy was taken aback. If his father had made an exhibition of himself at his school, he would have been mortified beyond bearing. Louise, however, seemed not only to accept it but to feel a real affection for her father because of it. Guy, unable to respect any man whose opinions he did not share, was puzzled. He looked down at

Louise. He really knew very little about her, but this did not seem important because she was a girl. His own mother was a mystery to him. She was pretty in the manner of the ladies who advertised the MacDonald's permanent wave, and she talked about the superiority of MacDonald's over Eugene in a tone which made Guy imagine that it would be barely possible to mix with people who favoured Eugene. Her clothes were well-made and tasteful, but she wore them without pleasure, as though she was under an obligation to uphold the standards of her neighbourhood. Apart from her hairstyle and her clothes, he would have found it quite difficult to recognize his mother. He would have had no such problem with Louise. Although he might have found it hard to isolate any one feature which compelled his attention – the eyes, amused as though the whole of life was a huge joke; the tilted nose (which his mother thought a little vulgar); the mouth which could be twisted to express the impudence of Harlow or the hauteur of Garbo – she would be immediately recognizable by her liveliness. Now, walking along this dreary street, by her very presence beside him she made every step of the way exciting. He had always lived in anticipation until now – 'When you get into the main school, when you have matriculated, when you are articled . . .' Never before had he known what it was to enjoy the given moment.

'Doesn't it make you angry when your father behaves like that?' he asked.

'Daddy cares so much; I wouldn't have him any different.'

'If he cares about the wrong things, though . . .'

'I don't know about that.' She was indifferent to 'wrong things'.

'What will you do, then? About our play, I mean.'

'I'll wait to see how things go.'

The moment would come, she would feel it within her, just as she felt the sap rising in spring, and then she would tell her father. It did not occur to her to wonder whether the moment would be equally acceptable to him. She did not, in fact, distinguish very clearly between her own feelings and those of others.

They had come to the end of the road and Louise turned right under a railway bridge into another street, where the houses were interspersed with small shops and laundries. 'You're in soapsuds island now,' she said. 'George Bernard Shaw has his laundry done here, did you know? Mrs Haines, who collects, says he is a real gent and won't allow her to carry the basket down the steps.'

On the far side of the street Guy saw the Methodist chapel, a grim-looking building in dingy red brick, fronted by spiked iron railings. He experienced, George Bernard Shaw notwithstanding, a moment of dismay akin to fear. An atmosphere of mute hopelessness seemed to cling about him as though all the unemployed had breathed their sourness into this dismal area. He pulled himself together and said to Louise, 'Would it be helpful if Jacov and I talked to your father?'

'Perhaps. But he'll say no at first. If he does come round, it will take a day or so.'

'What will you do if he says no finally?'

'I haven't thought about that yet.'

A time would come when she would go her own way, but she sensed that it was not yet. Judith Fairley, Claire and Alice joined them, and they crossed the road to the chapel.

At the door, a rosy-cheeked man with a walrus moustache was talking to a chirpy little woman who waved to the Fairleys in a manner too skittish for a person of her age. 'That is Dot,' Louise told Guy. 'She's a bit simple.' A spotty-faced young man handed out hymn books, saying unctuously to Guy, 'Glad to have you worship with us, friend.'

The chapel was not like the Holland Park Chapel, which had stained-glass windows and an organ, and the appearance of being distantly related to the Church of England. It was small and bare of adornment. The platform was a space on which three objects had been deposited; an upright piano to the left, a pulpit to the right with a large Bible on a ledge and, back centre, a table covered with a green baize cloth on which stood a vase of yellow chrysanthemums. The room was lit by gas lamps which hissed and popped. After they had bowed their heads in prayer, Guy whispered to Louise, 'We have electric light in our chapel.'

The rosy-cheeked man at the far door broke away from Dot and moved along the row in front of the Fairleys to talk to a middle-aged woman, who looked plump not so much as a result of cheerful good living, but of wearing layers of clothes in order to keep out the cold.

'Did you hear the Minister forgot to ask Mrs Ravilious to open the bazaar?' the man asked, chuckling.

The woman replied loudly, 'I don't think it's funny, Mr Crockett. In this world, money matters, say what you will, and the way he goes on there soon won't be a Lord's House for us to worship in.'

Her companion, a bird-like woman with hairs bristling from a pointed chin, hissed, 'Forgetful he may be, but he's one of the saints of God, Miss Thomas.'

'Then the Lord has more patience than I have, Miss Dyer.'

This conversation was interrupted by a woman trailing a scowling small boy who squeezed past Miss Thomas and Miss Dyer, a process involving much fumbling with handbags, groping for gloves and the dropping of hymn books. As soon as they were seated, the small boy whispered to his mother, who said sharply, 'Not now.' A gloomy, cadaverous man came through the door at the back of the platform carrying a board with hymn numbers on it, which he hung on a nail at the side of the pulpit. The conversation in the hall died down, and there was silence save for the turning of the leaves of hymn books and the hissing of the gas. Claire and Alice looked at the woman with the small boy. They had heard older people say that Dolly Bligh was still attractive 'in spite of everything', but they could not understand this, because she was over thirty and sallow. Last week in chapel, while they had been waiting for their father they had heard Miss Thomas talking to the Minister. Mr Bligh, they knew, was in prison; what they had hitherto not known was that when he came out Mrs Bligh would have to choose between him and their daughters, because he was known to interfere with them. From the way in which Miss Thomas had spoken, they had been aware that the word 'interfere' was being used in a sense to which they were unaccustomed, and although no particulars had been given they had sensed, if not the exact nature, then the general area of the trouble. Alice wondered what the girls would do if Mrs Bligh chose her husband; Claire assumed she would stay with her children.

Mrs Bligh said to her son, 'You should have gone before you left home.' While he was debating this, the door at the back of the platform opened and the Minister came out. He was a tall, ungainly man who gave the impression of someone moving about on stilts. As he reached the pulpit, several sheets of paper fell onto the floor; he swooped to retrieve them and banged his head on the book ledge as he straightened. Miss Thomas sighed. The Minister glanced at the notes now topmost in the bundle and announced in a gentle voice, 'Let us begin our worship of God by standing and singing together hymn number one hundred and twenty-two, "Brightest and best of the sons of the morning".'

The pianist found herself confronted with a decision she was ill-equipped to make. While she hesitated, Miss Thomas began to sing in a resolute soprano, '"The day is past and over, all thanks, O Lord, to Thee".' The congregation supported her gratefully.

There followed prayers during which the small boy made repeated attempts to attract his mother's attention, an old man in the front pew murmured 'Amen!' fervently at frequent intervals and Dot shouted 'Hallelujah!' Miss Thomas then rose to read the notices. 'On Monday at three p.m. there will be the usual meeting of the Women's Bright Hour . . .' The small boy triumphantly announced that he had wet himself and, as the congregation rose to sing the next hymn, his mother led him out. Miss Dyer whispered to Miss Thomas, 'She shouldn't bring him out in the evening. He ought to be in bed.'

'She says its warmer here than at home.'

'Where's the girls, then?'

'They've been taken away, didn't you know?'

Alice looked at Claire; she was standing with her head bent over her hymn book, and it was questionable whether she had heard. They sang 'Fight the good fight', and then settled themselves for the sermon. While Mr Fairley rose from the front row and ascended the platform, the two sidesmen turned down the gas lamps in the body of the hall.

The room was slowly darkened and, by contrast, the little glow of light around the pulpit seemed to have an added intensity. The silence in the hall was broken only by the popping of one of the gas lamps and the distant sound of a train rumbling over the railway bridge. Mr Fairley frowned down upon the congregation. 'Our brethren in the Church of England will by this evening have repeated the Apostles' Creed and probably the Nicene Creed as well. We do not do this, and it is well that we do not do it. Tonight, however, I should like to examine the Apostles' Creed.

'"I believe in God, the Father Almighty, maker of Heaven and Earth, and in one Lord Jesus Christ, His only Son . . ." We would all say "amen" to that.' Miss Thomas exchanged a look with Miss Dyer, which made it clear that not everyone was prepared to make this concession to the Church of England. 'But *should* we say it so easily? "I believe": a tremendous statement to trip so readily off the tongue. Consider the world today. What evidence do we see of the hand of God in our affairs? Within the last weeks we have heard of the fall of the Daladier government in France and of the Hindenburg government in Germany; Adolf Hitler has become Chancellor of Germany; in Italy there is a dictatorship; in Russia a communist regime enslaves the people; Japan is at war with China; while in our own country we have two million, nine hundred thousand unemployed.' He enunciated each word with sombre clarity, so that the dead weight of numbers seemed to bear down on the unemployed among his audience, and they felt more diminished and hopeless than ever. 'It is not an encouraging picture, is it?' he demanded. 'God, we are told, created us out of chaos: it sometimes seems He is intent on returning us to chaos.'

At this point boys ran in from the street, banged on the doors and shouted messages which were only partly comprehensible, but unmistakably rude. The sidesmen, with expressions of grave reverence on their faces, got up and moved with unhurried dignity towards the doors; from outside there was the sound of an irreverent but not ill-humoured exchange, then they returned looking as grave as ever.

'Let us go on with this stupendous statement of belief: "conceived by the Holy Ghost" – well, I have reservations about *that*, but let it pass – "born of the Virgin Mary . . ." What sort of a world was He born into? A world not noticeably more full of hope than our own. Years before his birth, Sophocles wrote:

"Never to have lived is best, ancient writers say,
Never to have drawn the breath of life, never to have looked into
   the eye of day;
The second best's a gay goodnight, and quickly turn away." '

Miss Dyer nodded her head vigorously, which was her way of paying homage to poetry, whether by Ella Wheeler Wilcox or John Milton.

'By the time Jesus was born in Bethlehem, the brutal Roman civilization had succeeded the Greek and straddled the world, exhausting itself in the process. It was already divided, and dying – in my view – of lack of hope for the future and belief in itself.

'So, into this despairing world He was born, and the next thing that we are asked to note about Him is that He "suffered under Pontius Pilate . . ."' Mr Fairley gazed at them, eyes popping from beneath bushy eyebrows: his capacity for astonishment was infinite. 'Nothing between that birth and that suffering, no mention that He grew up working at His father's carpentry bench, made friends and walked with them through cornfields in Galilee, turned water into wine at a marriage at Cana; only birth, suffering and death. Yet for nearly two thousand years men have followed Him and tried to make His way their way. Why? We should ask ourselves these questions from time to time.' He allowed a pause for them to put the question to themselves. Mr Fairley's family obligingly registered concern; the old man who had said 'amen' during the prayers slept peacefully, each outward breath producing a noise like the blowing of a contented horse; the Minister had the look of a man troubled in spirit; the rest of the congregation waited in varying attitudes of stoicism. 'Why?' Mr Fairley repeated. 'What did He offer them? "If any man would come after me, let him deny himself and take up his cross and follow me . . ." "I came not to send peace, but a sword . . ." "Nation will rise against nation, kingdom against kingdom, and there will be famines and earthquakes in various places . . ." Hard words, if you think about them, which we seldom do.' The dark, cadaverous man nodded in dismal approbation and cracked his knuckles.

'But He did make certain promises: "I am the resurrection and the life; he who believes in me, though he die, yet shall he live . . ." "I will not leave you desolate; I will come to you . . ." Not, I suggest, as the Man of Sorrows will He come, but as the man who drew all manner of folk to Him who were enriched and invigorated and made eternally joyful by His company.'

While Mr Fairley was saying this, the boys ran in from the street and banged the doors. The sidesmen withdrew, this time accompanied by Dot, who could be heard shouting that the devil was in one Harry Rowbotham. The old man woke up and stared unblinkingly at Mr Fairley to show how alert he was.

'Why do we listen to these promises? Others have said splendid things; but their voices die. This voice speaks to us directly, as though no centuries separated us; it is a voice which challenges us at the deepest level of our being, and we need no one to interpret for us in order that we can understand what it is that is required of us.' He felt the challenge himself, every moment of every day. Early in his life he had acquired a taste for his own way, and this made for confrontation rather than contemplation. His protruding eyes brimmed over with emotion as he said, 'If we decide to answer His call, we may stray from the path, but we do so knowingly; for there is that within us, and within all men, that knows it is answerable to Him. He is our

47

master and we prove it every day, in every decision that we make, in every encounter with another human being.' Miss Thomas scratched at a mark on her coat, and then carried out a morbid inspection of her fingernail.

'And the Creed says, "And after three days He rose again from the dead and ascended into Heaven and sitteth on the right hand of God, from whence He shall come to judge both the quick and the dead . . ." And I say NO!' Mr Fairley banged the pulpit and Mr Crockett, who had been counting the congregation, lost his place and began a recount. 'I cannot accept this as the bare bones of my belief. For I believe He broke through not only the bonds of death, but of time. The agonies that came upon Him in the Garden of Gethsemane were indeed the sins of the world, of my sins and your sins, then, at that moment, bearing down upon Him.'

Alice thought of Jesus hanging on the cross, knowing that police in Shepherd's Bush were investigating a burglary that had never taken place. The hissing gas lamps had a hypnotic effect. She bent her little finger back, which was something she had been told was a cure if you felt faint; it was certainly painful enough to occupy her mind until the urge to stand up and confess her sin had passed.

Mr Fairley was glaring angrily, a flush of colour on his cheeks; his voice became louder, vibrating with the force of his emotion. Judith thought: he'll have a stroke when he's older; it's in the family. 'And He is crucified now and the Resurrection and the promise are now. My Christ is not sitting at the right hand of God watching the miseries of the world and waiting to come in judgement. He is here among us. But do we look for him, my friends? Do we go where He will be?' Mr Fairley paused. It was plain he would not be pleased to be answered in the affirmative.

'How many people in London turned out to support the hunger marchers? Or offered them accommodation for the night? Most people were too busy for that. But on the days when these men were marching, cinema attendances were good. People weren't too busy for that! And of one thing we can be certain: we shall not find Him in the cinema.'

Alice felt the hand of God laid on her as her father continued: 'It is all glitter and glamour and tinsel morality; a world in which, above all else, it is essential to be attractive; where the problems of personality can be solved by a change of lipstick or a new hairstyle. We say it is only entertainment; but there are young people who go to the cinema two, three times a week and, without their knowing it, the values of the silver screen become an integral part of their way of looking at life.'

A further thumping on the chapel doors jerked Mr Fairley back to his pursuit of God. 'Our situation today demonstrates that without Him "things fall apart, the centre cannot hold".' Miss Dyer nodded, quick to recognize the poetic tone. 'There is an essential person somewhere within each of us who eludes us. We long for all the fragments of personality to be gathered together so that we are whole. We can't do this for ourselves. Isn't this because we are created by God and only He sustains us? Without Him, we cannot sustain our lives; we, too, fall apart and gradually cease to be. The proof of this is all around us.'

Alice clenched her hands and prayed that he would stop and he did. He had not got very far with the Creed, and would have to deal with such matters as the communion of saints and the forgiveness of sins, to say nothing of the Holy Ghost, on another occasion. He concluded, 'My friends, we must take Christ out of history, or our religion becomes a long, backward glance. He is here and now always. We have our being in His presence. It is that or nothing. As we walk home tonight, along Acton High Street, past the Globe Cinema and The King's Head and the Napier Arms Factory, the road leads – as it always has led and will always lead – to Emmäus.' Dot, the tears streaming down her face, shouted 'Hallelujah!' Mr Fairley concluded sombrely, 'And now, in the name of the Father and of the Son . . .'

They bowed their heads and groped for hymn books. The Minister announced the hymn, and they rose to sing:

> 'Oh Beulah land, sweet Beulah land
> As on thy highest mount I stand
> I look away across the sea
> Where mountains are prepared for me
> And view the shining glory shore
> My Heaven, my home for evermore.'

They sang loudly and the bare, uncomfortable room was suddenly full of people who had come alive and were briefly happy; the old man's paper-thin face glowed as though the rosy light of the promised land already fell upon him. This, their voices said to Mr Fairley, is the kind of thing which is needed in these dark days!

When the service was over, the old man came along the row to Miss Thomas and said, 'We should have opened the church hall to the hunger marchers; I shall raise it at the next vestry meeting.'

'They were communists, Mr Plumley. It said so in the *Morning Post*.'

Miss Dyer said, 'I was surprised to hear mention of the Virgin Mary. We'll be having candles on the communion table next.'

It took several minutes to get out of the chapel, because the Minister and the sidesmen were shaking hands with people at the door. By the time his family had reached the door, Mr Fairley had joined them. The Minister gripped his hand and said, 'Splendid! We must have a talk some time about your interpretation of the Ascension . . .'

'I didn't think that last hymn was very appropriate,' Mr Fairley said bluntly.

'No, perhaps not, but Mr Plumley particularly asked for it.'

'The reward of the good; I don't begrudge that, dear old chap,' Mr Fairley said philosophically as they left the chapel and turned towards the railway arch. 'I just wish he could have had his reward at morning service.'

A few flakes of snow were beginning to fall. There was a tram coming when they reached the High Street, and in the hurry to catch it all else was forgotten. They did not speak about the service until they sat down to supper. After he had said grace, Mr Fairley turned to his wife. 'Startled them, talking about the Creed, I'm afraid. Does them good to be startled every now and again.'

'It's not the Creed that startled them; it's the films you see!'

'I haven't *seen* them,' he said irritably.

'That's what you tell us!' She smiled at Guy. 'Do you go to the pictures much?' She was aware of her husband's displeasure, but Louise was coming to an age when she would bring young men home, and they must learn to talk about these things. She was relieved, however, when Guy said with obvious sincerity, 'I agree with Mr Fairley; the cinema's full of rubbish.'

Mr Fairley looked approvingly at Guy from under bushy eyebrows; he was about to lead the conversation round to his sermon, when Guy went on, 'It's the theatre which interests me.'

Mr Fairley said, 'Really?'

'In fact, I belong to a rather good dramatic society.'

'You mean you actually . . . perform?'

Alice was sitting opposite Guy, and the consternation reflected in her face warned him. He said, 'I have done a bit, yes; at school . . . Shakespeare and that kind of thing . . .'

'*Which* of Shakespeare's plays?' Mr Fairley was not the man to be silenced by the magic of a great name.

'The historical plays – *Henry the Fifth* and . . . er . . . *Julius Caesar*.'

Mr Fairley nodded. The danger had passed. Claire, who did not like to be left out of a conversation, said, 'And *The House with the Twisty Windows*.'

'The WHAT?'

'*The House with the* . . .' Claire, aware of the angry looks of her sisters, went scarlet; her eyes filled with tears.

'What is all this about?' Mr Fairley looked at his wife as though she were involved in a conspiracy against him.

'I've no idea. What are you being so silly about, Claire? Is this house-with-whatever-it-was something you've heard on the wireless?'

Claire began to cry.

Louise said, 'It's a one-act play. The St Bartholomew's Dramatic Society are putting it on with two other one-acts.'

Mr Fairley said, 'St Bartholomew's?'

'It's not a church dramatic society, Daddy; it broke away from the Church of England five years ago because the vicar kept interfering with the plays they put on.'

'Why didn't the vicar like the plays they put on?' Judith Fairley asked, watching her daughter closely.

'It was all right as long as they did things like *Quality Street* and *Cranford*, but if they did anything in modern dress he found it wicked.'

'I am not at all clear,' Mr Fairley said, 'why we are talking about this.'

Judith caught her daughter's eye and shook her head, but Louise had recognized her moment. 'They want me to play a part in *The House with the Twisty Windows*.'

'You!'

'There's nothing surprising about it, Daddy.' Louise remained calm in the face of something rather stronger than surprise. 'Several people we know belong. Jacov produces for them.'

Judith said sharply, 'Louise, be quiet. What Jacov does or does not do is of no interest to your father.' She turned to Claire. 'If you're not going to eat any more, you had better go upstairs. It's past your bedtime, anyway.'

Claire got up; on her way to the door she paused behind Louise's chair. 'Lou . . .'

'Oh, go and eat sour apples!'

Claire went out of the room crying.

Mr Fairley said to Louise, 'We will say no more about this, you understand? We will say no more about it.'

Alice clenched her hands on the sides of her chair and prayed. 'Oh God, please don't let Louise argue with him, please don't let her argue.'

Louise looked at her father. This was an occasion which demanded lowered eyes and trembling lips, and to Alice it seemed there was something alarming about the very steadiness of Louise's gaze.

'I see now that no one was listening to me this evening,' Mr Fairley said. This hurt him and deflected his anger. 'While I was castigating the congregation about superficiality, and making that good old man, Plumley, feel guilty about the hunger marchers, my own family was racked with concern about a one-act play called *The House with the Twisty Windows*!'

'I thought your sermon was splendid, sir,' Guy said.

For a young man who hoped to make a career on the stage he had a poor sense of timing.

When Guy left, Alice feared hostilities would break out, but neither protagonist appeared to relish a confrontation. Mr Fairley retired to his study and Louise followed Alice and her mother into the kitchen.

'Mummy, why shouldn't I?'

'I've no sympathy with you. I warned you and you took no notice. You always think you know best, my lady, and it will lead you into trouble.'

'But Daddy doesn't even know the play. If that isn't an example of knowing best, I don't know what is.'

'Don't be pert, Louise. He knows you deceived us.'

'It wasn't deception, it was you who assumed it was the school play I was talking about.'

'And you encouraged Claire and Alice to deceive us.'

'As soon as Claire got involved, I told Daddy about it.'

'Only because Claire had given the game away. You see everything from your own point of view, Louise; if you want a thing, it is right, and people who don't agree with you are wrong.' She went into the dining room to clear the table.

'I know someone else who suffers from that complaint.' Louise waited until her mother had passed out of earshot before she said this.

'Who do you mean, Lou?' Alice asked, feeling, as she so often did when an oblique remark was made, that she must be the person at fault.

'Why, Daddy, of course.'

Louise was showing more of herself than she usually revealed to Alice. This made Alice feel elevated. 'What do you mean about Daddy, Lou?' She managed to say this in a sensible, interested tone, just as she would have talked in class about the character of Darcy or Mr Collins.

'If he wants a thing, he talks about it as though it had happened – like me going to university; so it becomes an accepted fact. We can argue about *which* university and *what* course, but the fact of my going is incontrovertible.'

'I thought you *were* going.'

'You see how well it works!'

'*Aren't* you?'

'No; I'm going to be an actress.'

'Lou!'

Alice looked at her sister in awe. This was not the Louise of childhood, but a new person. And such a marvellous person, so brave and resolute, yet so cheerful with it. Alice had the same feeling of fear and exultation she experienced when her father and his friends talked about going over the top; but Louise's non-combatant bravery seemed more splendid than the vision of men charging with bayonets. It was also more real, something she might come to herself one day.

'But that's some way off.' Louise became active at the sink, pouring hot water into the bowl and grabbing a handful of soda. She had shaken herself and felt some compunction about the effect she must have had on Alice. 'I'm just as fond of Daddy as you are. Don't take what I say to heart.' She looked at her sister quizzically, then she put a finger on the tip of Alice's nose and pressed. Mrs Fairley came in with a loaded tray and the two girls laughed conspiratorially.

Claire was in an agitated state when her father came in to say goodnight to her.

'You mustn't blame yourself for what happened,' he told her.

It seemed, however, that it was something she had overheard in chapel which was now upsetting her. 'Mummy wouldn't ever send us away, would she?'

He tracked this down to Miss Thomas's comments about the Bligh family, and comforted Claire by pointing out the unfortunate fact that not every family was as loving and united as her own. He then read her a 'William' story (a great concession, as this was Sunday), after which he returned to his study and his own distress.

When Alice came into the bedroom there was a ridge of snow several inches deep on the windowsill. She put the stone hot water jar in her bed, and began to undress. Claire said, 'Is Louise still cross with me?'

'I expect so.'

'I didn't mean it; it just came out.'

Alice went to the washstand.

The windows were blotchy with snow. 'The pipes will freeze,' Claire said mournfully. She hunched down in the bed, contemplating the misery which would befall them when the boiler had to be put out, and the cold established its iron grip on the whole house. The paraffin lamp would be placed on the landing but would be found to smoke, or there would be a strong draught from the landing window which would make it dangerous to keep it alight. Louise would make an awful fuss about the state of the lavatory. Daddy would go up in the attic with a blow-lamp and Mummy would say, 'Now we shall have a burst.'

There was a place just above the lavatory window where a waterpipe curved outwards, inviting the attention of the east wind. It was only a small length of pipe, but the plumber informed the Fairleys on each of his more than occasional winter visits that they could save themselves the bother of lagging the pipes because the water would always freeze at this point. Although it was such a small length of pipe, there were reasons – which he could not bring himself to divulge – why to bring it into the house would involve a major alteration of the whole water system.

The burst, when it came, was always a source of excitement to the children. First, it must be located, and the house would echo to cries of 'Not in here!' until eventually damp patches were discovered (not infrequently in the linen cupboard); then there would be much rushing about with buckets and cries of 'Ahoy down below!' from Mr Fairley in the attic. But enjoyable though all this undoubtedly was, it did not compensate for the misery which had gone before; and the long, cold spells gave rise to constant grumbling on the part of the children, by no means muted by their parents' recollection of greater hardships endured in their youth.

Claire's discomfort differed from that of her sisters. It was not just that she could not stand the cold and inconvenience; there was something sinister in the failed apparatus itself. She went in dread of the first sight of a damp patch, and at night the thought of the burst pipe dripping somewhere unknown in the house filled her with terror. While diphtheria had not permanently undermined Claire's health, banishment to the isolation hospital had left her subject to unspecified fears which she could not fight, because they never confronted her in the open, but engaged in a kind of shadow-boxing just beyond the range of sight and sound.

Claire sniffled, thinking that this time she would have to bear Louise's anger as well as the malignity of leaking pipes and smoking oil stoves. 'Badger's the only one who understands,' she mourned.

Alice, who had finished washing, went to the window to draw the curtains. 'It's all white, Claire. I expect Kashmir looks lovely.'

Mr Fairley sat alone in the sitting-room, his book unopened. Judith was putting washing in to soak in case the water had frozen by the morning. Mr Fairley poked the fire and sighed. The very idea that his daughter had deceived him was scarcely credible, conflicting as it did with his cherished impression of his family as a united one in which each person could speak freely to the other. Mr Fairley made a number of assumptions about his life which usually worked out very well. On the occasions when an assumption was proved false, he had a long journey to make back to the reality of his situation. He took such setbacks badly; they disrupted him, and he often had a bad turn. He was feeling sick now.

He gazed into the fire. If the freezing of water was one of the miseries of the winter, firelight was surely its greatest joy, offering such homely pleasures as roasting chestnuts and toasting crumpets. Best of all was watching the faces in the fire. At first barely discernible, so that there was much discussion as to how it would emerge (Mr Fairley tended to see men like Jack Hulbert with long chins, while Alice favoured a sailor, like Nelson, in a cockaded hat), the face, as the flames worked on it, became clearer so that all could see that it was, in fact, the hawk-nosed gypsy which Louise had predicted. How often they had stared at the face in the fire until either some movement of the coals broke it apart or the flames, burning steadily, ate it away! But by then another face would be forming, only to be consumed in its turn, and so it would go on until, as evening turned to night, the flames hollowed the last face to glowing embers. Tonight, the wind howling in the chimney had accelerated the process. Soon the embers would dwindle to ash. Mr Fairley, who had no taste for the end of things, went out of the room and began his nightly round of winding the clocks.

4

The blizzard was the worst for fifty years, but the snow cleared as rapidly as it had come, and brought floods to many parts of the country. Days followed which were bright and clear. On one such day in March Joseph Tippet, sitting at the window of his house high in the old part of Falmouth, had a fine view across the harbour and the Carrick Roads. He looked steadily, eyes narrowed – not against the sun, for he was looking north-east – but in order to focus on the particular period on which he was gazing, which was certainly not the present. But then, what was the present? Joseph's present had never been other people's present. He had lived most of his life at sea, and his brief excursions ashore had been like the intermittent waking of a Rip Van Winkle. Now, as he looked out of the window he was seeing in his mind's eye the last of the clippers. It did not seem possible that a thing of such grace and beauty could vanish so quickly from the earth once its commercial value was gone. Although he had spent a lifetime in steamships – and traders at that – he had little time for commerce. He gave a deep sigh. 'There wasn't anything to touch them!'

His wife turned the pages of the letter she was reading. 'Three pages about this Reichstag fire and one about the family!' There was very little she missed at close range, but she had no understanding of foreign affairs beyond the Tamar. Not that her horizons were limited; they were just different from those of other people.

'What's the news of the family, then?' Joseph asked without shifting his gaze from the harbour.

'He says Judith thinks it would do Alice good to come down on her own this summer. Claire is very much the baby still, and Alice is growing up.'

'And Louise?'

'He doesn't mention Louise. There's something wrong there.'

'Now, don't you go seeing things, Ellen!'

Ellen Tippet's red hair had long lost its fire, but the light blue eyes, which sometimes seemed strangers to the face, were as disquieting as ever. It was well known that she had 'the gift'. In her case, however, second sight did not go hand-in-hand with any notable powers of interpretation. Just as a hunting dog may sniff out a man without knowing what manner of crime he has committed – or even that he is a criminal – so Ellen might 'see' trouble in a person's face, without having any idea of the particular form it would take. She herself was unaware of any discrepancy between her powers of foresight and diagnosis. Some said she caused more harm than she ever did good. But the gift was genuine, and laughter at her pronouncements was always tinged with uneasiness.

'Well, there it is,' she said with the wry briskness with which she would acknowledge bad fish, or any other catastrophe for which there was no remedy. 'Louise will be happy because she means to be, and that won't suit Stanley. Stanley thinks happiness is measured out according to our deserts.'

'Don't go upsetting Stanley, Ellen.'

Joseph got slowly to his feet, looking around with his habitual expression of one who has wakened to find himself in a strange place.

'Don't shift yourself; I'll get it for you.' She was always ready to busy herself on other people's behalf, whether they needed her ministrations or not.

'This is one thing you can't do for me, Ellen,' he said mildly. 'I wonder you didn't know that, with your powers.' A few seconds later she heard the kitchen door open as he went down the garden path to the lavatory.

'Now, what's Stanley got to say?' he said when he returned.

'It's mostly politics.' She handed him the letter.

'He's a clever man, is Stanley.' Joseph liked his son-in-law because he listened to his stories about the sea.

'Clever he may be . . .' She left the unfinished sentence trembling on the brink of disaster. There was no one whom she made more uncomfortable than Stanley Fairley, who had a dark inner world, and didn't want Ellen paddling in those pitchy waters. 'If you'd had your mother's eyes, I wouldn't have married you,' he had said more than once to Judith.

Joseph unfolded the letter, and carefully eased out the creases on his knees. 'When Alice came down in 1927, the *Herzogin Cecilie* was out there.' He enjoyed his grandchildren, who were still of an age when he could relate to them, whereas his own children had passed beyond his understanding while his back had been turned.

'First man that offered and she married him! "There's something in you he'll never satisfy," I told her. But she wouldn't listen.'

She remembered Judith telling her that she was going to marry Stanley, whom she had met while on a visit to Dover to stay with a cousin.

'You don't know anything about him. It's the uniform's turned your head.'

'I met him at chapel, and we all had lunch at the Minister's house.'

'I've seen many a bad match made in chapel! You are only nineteen; you're much too young.'

'It's the first time you've ever told me I was *young*.' Being the oldest child of a family of seven which was to all intents and purposes fatherless had been a responsible position. 'Harry can be the responsible one now. I want a life of my own.'

'A life of her own!' Ellen said to Joseph, who was reading Stanley's letter. 'Who has a life of their own? Not even a man. Your life belonged to the shipping line. That's the way it is. But Louise will be the same. She'll want a life of her own, too.'

He put the letter down. He had difficulty in coming to terms with distances on shore, but sporadically something close at hand would claim his attention. On this occasion it was his wife. 'Would you have liked a life of your own?' he asked.

'With children? I said to Judith, "In a few years you'll have children of your own instead of a life of your own, whatever that's supposed to mean."'

'No point in being angry about it now, Ellen.'

'I'm not angry. Why would I be angry after all these years?'

He was amused to catch her on the defensive. When he was alert like this, one could see the humour in the eyes and a certain firmness of character in the line of the mouth; once, when he had had decisions to make, he had been effective and resourceful.

Ellen said, 'Maybe she did care about Stanley; there weren't many young fellows around here a girl would look at twice. I don't blame her for wanting to go.'

'Not blame her? For leaving Falmouth!'

'You did, didn't you?'

'But I came back. I always came back to Falmouth.'

And saw it as it had been when he was a young man, just as he saw her as the vivacious girl he had married; whereas the boy she had fallen in love with was now incongruously cloaked in the withered flesh of an old man. 'I've had more of that old flesh than I ever had of the young,' she thought.

She looked at the clock; it was half-past eleven. There was plenty of time to walk down to the High Street and tell Charlie and Prue that Alice would be coming in the summer.

'Will you come?' she asked when she had put on her coat and hat.

'No, I'll walk down to the harbour later.'

On an impulse, she came and kissed the top of his head. 'Put on your overcoat, then; the wind's keen.'

That same afternoon, Alice was with Grandmother Fairley in her house in Holland Park.

'I'm going down to Cornwall in the summer all on my own,' she said.

'To stay with your Granny who was a slave?'

Granny Tippet was a Hocken from Looe. When he had been studying the old records on one of his visits to Cornwall, Stanley Fairley had come across the case of Edward Hocken for whom nineteen shillings and two pence had been collected in church in 1677, he being a slave in Turkey. Claire had told Grandmother Fairley, 'My other Granny was a slave.' This had been a family joke ever since, and Grandmother Fairley had never failed to refer to it whenever Granny Tippet was mentioned. Louise said she had to have funny things to repeat, because she had no sense of humour. Louise disliked her grandmother, who was always reminding her that she paid her school fees.

Agnes Fairley was a tall, thin woman who still had some claim to beauty – if bone structure and elegance of feature are accepted as the criteria of good looks. Her face, however, expressed little save the tight-lipped resignation of the sufferer from neuralgia, a suffering which was emphasized by the way in which her sparse white hair was clawed up on top of her head so that the network of veins seemed taut as wires. When her husband had been alive, she had been an active woman, and had enjoyed her life in Sussex. But on his death she had insisted on returning to Holland Park, where she had failed to make friends. She and Judith Fairley did not get on well. 'I married beneath me,' she would say to her sister Charlotte, 'and now my son has married beneath him. It seems to be a family failing.' Her marriage had, in fact, been a good one; but now, left alone in old age, she had reverted to the attitudes of her socially ambitious parents. The beginning and the end of life had become the realities for her; the middle seemed only a dream.

Alice had established a rapport with this rather wintry old woman, because she liked to hear her talk of her childhood in London. There was, however, another reason why these visits were precious. Neither Claire nor Louise enjoyed visiting their grandmother, so Alice often went on her own. On these excursions she began to realize that she was not the Alice Fairley whom her family and schoolfriends knew. Solitude was rare, and for most of her life she had seen herself in the eyes of others; her mother's acknowledgement that 'Alice has the nicest nature of the three, if only she wasn't so obstinate'; her father's less qualified approval, 'Alice has to be allowed to work things out her own way – she is going to be the thinker'; the verdict of the school report, 'Alice has been a responsible member of the form and she has worked hard'; the judgement of her peers – Podge Fairley, a cheerful companion and good at games. Aware of the images presented to her, she tried dutifully to mould this composite picture into one person. She failed. Then came the surprising discovery that when she got off the bus and headed towards the road where her grandmother lived, all the images remained behind on the far side of the Uxbridge Road. She felt unencumbered, and often experienced a sudden fear that she had left something behind on the bus. She was not nearly as sure of things she knew she should be sure of, and she did not care about things she spent the rest of the week caring about.

Today, when she arrived at her grandmother's, and the crumpets had been toasted, she deliberately selected the one towards the bottom of the plate – which would be more buttery – and settled herself on the window-seat, something which would not have been countenanced at home, where meals must be eaten seated at table.

Grandmother Fairley put the hot water jug in the hearth and poked the fire, the rustling of her long black skirt accompanying her movements. 'You were late today, dear. I expect you caught a later bus.' She lowered herself slowly into her chair, and panted for a few moments before continuing mournfully, 'But then, it's very good of you to come and see an old woman when you would much rather be out playing.'

Alice had caught the earlier bus, but as the day was sunny she had walked in Holland Park. She did not want to tell her grandmother this, so she said, 'I enjoy coming to see you.'

'That's nice of you, dear.' It seemed, however, to make Grandmother Fairley even more mournful and she sighed, dabbing with her handkerchief at the butter which ran down her chin. 'It's more than your mother would say. And my own son, when do I ever see him?'

'Daddy came on Sunday.'

'He didn't stay long. But he's busy, I know that.' She wiped her fingers on her napkin, and repeated, 'I know, I know . . .'

'May I have another crumpet, please?'

'Yes, dear. Have as many as you like, they're all for you. I don't eat much myself now. My teeth don't fit so well. Your mother didn't say anything about my dental appointment?'

'I don't think so.'

'They're all too busy to see me. It's weeks since I saw anyone.'

'Aunt May comes in every day, doesn't she, Grandma?'

The old woman sniffed. It was her adored son whose company she longed for; her daughters did not interest her. She bent down and took another crumpet from the plate in the hearth. 'Take all the jam, dear. I can't manage with the pips.'

They sat in silence for a little while, and Alice looked down into the road. It was mysteriously different from the road where she lived, the houses being tall and plain with no balconies, gables or turrets, and the windows long, coming close to floor level. From where she was sitting, she could see into the ground floor room of the house opposite; there was a grand piano with photographs on it, and a lot of paintings on the walls.

'You're going on your own, all the way to Cornwall, then?' Grandmother Fairley said. 'I hope they know what they're doing.'

'Daddy is going to put me on the train at Paddington and Grandfather will meet me at Truro.'

'You won't talk to anyone on the train, will you, dear? And don't take any sweets if they're offered.'

'No, I won't.'

'Ah well, I suppose they know what they're doing.'

'It must have been so peaceful when you were young.' All that Alice could see to disturb the peace of the tree-lined road was a newspaper boy on a bicycle, and a postman with his sack over his back. The remark, however, served its purpose, and Grandmother Fairley turned willingly towards the past.

'It wasn't all that peaceful. The farm carts made a terrible noise going up to Covent Garden in the morning.'

Alice asked, 'Did you see Oscar Wilde and Holman Hunt and Dante Gabriel Rossetti?'

She had asked this often in the hope that Grandmother Fairley would ransack her store of memories and come up with an overlooked trifle concerning one of these great men. Granny Tippet knew all about the important people in Falmouth, none of whom was of interest to Alice. It seemed inconceivable that Grandmother Fairley, who was so well connected, should have lived surrounded by the great without ever having noticed them.

'No, I can't say that I did, dear.' In spite of her social pretensions, Grandmother Fairley was strictly truthful in her reminiscences. 'I did see that woman who writes those books, Beatrix Potter. She was a girl then, of course.' She smiled mistily down at her fingers and then, remembering how arthritic she was, flexed them, noting the pain with morose satisfaction. 'And when I was very small, I was taken to Acton to see the mummers. I remember there was one of them called King George who used to fight a Turk and kill him, and then the Turk would be given a big pill which would bring him back to life. I always wondered why they wanted to bring him back to life if King George had seen fit to kill him.'

The postman pushed something through the letterbox and they heard his familiar rat-a-ta-tat.

'You were allowed to see theatricals, then, Grandma?'

'It wasn't quite the same, dear. We didn't go into a theatre to see them; the mummers came to us, and it was all in the open air.'

There was a young woman walking along the pavement. She had dark auburn hair curling beneath a hat pertly tilted over one eye. As she walked she turned her head slowly from side to side, looking at the trees and the houses, and giving enchanting views of her face from many different angles – just like the heroine of a film. She wore an emerald green velvet coat with the prettiest little cape trimmed with fur, which tickled her chin. Her appearance made Alice wonder what opportunities she herself might be allowing to slip by. Were there famous people in Shepherd's Bush, whom she passed daily in the street without being aware of their identity? It did not seem very likely. In fact, she could not think of a single person whom she knew who might become famous – except, perhaps, Jacov. I must start to keep a diary, she thought, just in case . . . At this moment, the girl was greatly surprised to recognize a man who had been approaching her from the opposite direction. They met in the shade of a tree where Alice could not see them. Her grandmother was offering her a cream horn, and when she had taken it the man and the woman were going into a house where the front door stood open.

'Do they always leave their front door open?' she asked.

'The house is divided into flats.' Grandmother Fairley sounded disapproving.

'Like your house?' Alice said naughtily.

'This house is mine, dear. I have two lodgers, and they are both from the chapel.'

A thought struck Alice. 'Grandma, you must know Mr and Mrs Immingham. They go to your chapel.'

'I don't recall, dear; my memory for names is so bad.'

'They have a son, Guy; he is friendly with Louise.'

'Oh, courting, is she?' Grandmother Fairley's interest sharpened, and Alice wished she had not mentioned the Imminghams. 'No wonder she doesn't have time to come and see me any more.'

Alice said nothing, hoping her grandmother's grievance would overcome her curiosity. She looked at the house which was divided into flats. I shall start a diary tonight, she thought, and I shall make a note about the auburn-haired woman. She wondered whether she should give her a name, such as Zelda, but decided that she must confine herself to what she actually knew and saw.

An hour later, when she was leaving, her grandmother picked up the letter which the postman had delivered, 'This is for Number 31.' She was overcome by sadness at the mistake. 'I should have know it wouldn't be for me. There's no one left to write to me; they've all passed on.' She did not believe in speeding her departing guests on their way with brisk good cheer. Alice, who always tried to get away before she said, 'I'll see you next week, dear, if I'm not in glory by then', took the letter and said, 'I'll drop it in on my way.'

Grandmother Fairley said, 'Immingham, did you say?'

'I'd better hurry, Grandma; I'm meeting Mummy at half-past five at Pontings.'

'If she's at Pontings, I wonder she couldn't come here to fetch you. But you'd better run along; you mustn't keep her waiting since she's so busy.'

Alice kissed the old woman's cheek, which was cold and smelt of Lifebuoy soap. 'Thank you for giving me such a lovely tea. I'll come again next week.'

'If I'm not in glory by then.'

Alice hurried down the path. When she reached the gate she looked back, but her grandmother was not standing at the window as she often did; perhaps she had gone to the lavatory, in which case she could be occupied for the next ten minutes, as her bowels took a long time to move. Alice darted across the road and went in at the gate of Number 33. It was surely near enough to Number 31 for her to say she had made a mistake if anyone spoke to her. 'I'll just stand in the doorway,' she thought. 'That's all I mean to do.' But when she reached the doorway she thought it would be all right to walk into the hall; after all, the building was divided into flats, so it wasn't like intruding in someone else's home. On the right of the hall was a door with Number 33a on it. Beyond, a passage led to a glass-panelled door through which Alice had a glimpse of a garden with a grubby stone cherub, who looked as if he wanted to fly away, but had one foot secured in concrete. Now she could hear the faint sound of music, and she recognized the voice of Jessie Matthews singing 'I want to be happy'. Alice was drawn towards the music. Slowly, heart thumping, she walked down the passage towards the door leading to the garden, urging herself on by the thought of what a promising start this would be to her diary. From now on, she would put off childish things, like midnight feasts and secret passages, and find adventure in the here and now of life. All that was needed was a little intrepidity. Beyond the glass-panelled door the branches of a tree swayed gently to and fro in the spring breeze, casting moving shadows on the wall. Alice opened the door and went into the garden. To her right there was a long window with a drawn curtain; the window was open at the top. She decided she would just walk to the window. When she came to it she saw that the curtains did not meet properly in the centre. The music was close now. Alice imagined a man and a woman dancing, bodies close and hardly moving, like the people she had glimpsed in trailers of films she was not allowed to see. She placed one foot in the flowerbed and, leaning forward, pressed her nose against the window.

What Alice saw was a man half-turned from her and bending forward to take up an article of attire from a chair. Although it was the first time Alice had seen a naked man, one of her Cornish cousins had once described the organs on which her gaze now rested. Dizzy with shock, Alice clutched the window-sill and waited, whether for the wrath of God or further confirmation of Lucy's descriptive powers, she would have been hard pressed to say. The man spoke. 'My dear girl, let's try to be reasonable, shall we?' The voice was master of that adult trick of saying one thing while meaning another. 'There's nothing I'd *like* more, dear heart, but you know how damned difficult things are for me.' While he was stepping into his pants, the auburn-haired woman came between him and the window, drawing a negligée about her with shameless leisureliness. She had a pretty face with upturned nose and slanting eyes, like a friendly, compliant cat; one could imagine her curled up on a couch, purring and flexing her claws ecstatically. The negligée had a satin sash at the waist, and as she tied it to one side her wandering gaze was arrested by the gap in the curtains. Her eyes met Alice's; one hand went to her breasts, a raw, involuntary movement as though Alice had thrown a stone.

The man was saying, 'My wife could scarcely be described as demanding; however, even she . . .'

Alice extricated herself from the flowerbed. Unfortunately, her legs, which had borne her here so eagerly, were now unable to perform the function of retreat with equal dispatch. By the time she reached the glass-panelled door, the woman was waiting for her.

'Who put you up to this?' A change had come over her. The pretty face wasn't held together properly; the cheeks were quivering, and she was having trouble with her mouth. She looked quite old; thirty at least.

Alice, her own mouth painfully dry, managed to say, 'I brought a letter, it . . .'

'Well, what about it?' The woman snatched the envelope and looked at it without seeming to make much sense of it, the paper shaking in her hands. The spring breeze ruffled the frothy negligée, which looked rather absurd; the material so buoyant, the woman's body now so heavy.

Alice croaked, 'It's for Number 31, I don't know where that is . . .'

She looked round, indicating her lostness. The garden was shadowy, and the sky which had been so bright earlier on was pale and cold. The cherub stared past her with sightless eyes. An air of disapproval seemed to enfold her.

'You little liar!' The woman looked at her with such loathing as Alice could not believe directed at her. 'Why did you do it? Why?' She said this so forcefully that it did indeed seem it was Alice and not she who had something to answer for. She was behaving as if she did not know she had been dishonoured.

Alice burst into tears. 'It was the music,' she sobbed. 'The music made me do it . . .'

The woman's hands grasped her shoulders; the pressure of the fingers was cruel, but the bewildered eyes insisted that it was Alice who had done the hurting. 'God, I could kill you!' She smelt of one of those perfurmes which Alice's mother described as cheap, although

66

they came in expensive containers. How could she wear that kind of perfume and still be hurt?

'I didn't mean anything,' Alice wailed. 'I didn't mean . . .'

The woman swung her round. 'Go on, sod off before I do something I'm sorry for.' Her knee came up and jolted Alice in the behind.

This attack on her posterior was particularly shocking for Alice, whose person had hitherto always been treated with respect. She stumbled across the hall and out of the front door. The sky was more remote than ever now; even the trees and houses seemed to have distanced themselves as though they wanted nothing to do with her. So much for another adventure! She had been expecting something so different – a misty, floating loveliness – when she looked through the window. But now, the nastiness in the room seemed to have reached out to her.

She was too frightened and ashamed to think of telling anyone what had happened. By the time she met her mother at Pontings, she was sufficiently in possession of herself to explain her pallor by saying she had eaten too many cream horns. When they reached home, they were greeted with the news that Claire had spots and a high temperature. The doctor was called, and diagnosed chicken-pox. Alice, on this occasion, was not sorry to be up-staged by Claire.

What was to be made of all this? The trouble was, it was neither one thing nor the other. It wasn't farce, with the woman caught out not having really done anything and looking delicious in satin cammiknickers; and it wasn't drama, because the words couldn't be made to fit the attitudes of the players – *Dishonoured*; *Tarnished*; *Her Shame*; *Bad Company*; *Betrayed* . . . Only *Betrayed* fitted, because that was how the woman had looked at Alice. But it wasn't Alice who had betrayed her. It didn't make any sense at all. Oh, if she didn't get to see any more than the trailers, how was she ever going to sort life out?

One evening, when she had finished her homework, and her mother and father were in the front of the house with Claire, she climbed the tree and looked towards Kashmir. Perhaps in that forbidden world lay the answer to the questions she scarcely knew how to formulate.

A few evenings later, her mother discovered her up the tree. She was not annoyed as Alice had expected, having been a tomboy herself when she was Alice's age; all she said was, 'As long as you never climb it while we're out.' She began to unpeg clothes from the line.

Alice looked down through the branches of the tree and said, in a rush of gratitude, 'I can see Kashmir. They're playing croquet.' She wondered if she might tell her mother what she had seen through the gap in the curtain.

The mention of playing games had reminded her mother of something. 'You'd better come in now. I want you to fetch Louise. She has been in the Vaseyelins' for the last hour; it's time she came in. I don't want her spending too much time hanging around in there.'

Alice went reluctantly, knowing her mission would not make her popular. It was a windy evening, and the sky was a lurid orange, across which rags of sooty cloud scurried as though there was a fire somewhere – but a long way off, as no fire bells were ringing.

She knocked on the Vaseyelins' door, but there was no answer. The window frames rattled, and there was a constant spatter of loosened concrete as though the wind was gradually dismantling the house. Somewhere upstairs Katia was practising the violin, a desolate sound unredeemed by evidence of talent. Alice was about to knock at the door again, when it opened to reveal Mrs Vaseyelin swathed in an indeterminate black garment and wearing a violet turban. Alice was not sure whether she was on her way out or to bed. Mrs Vaseyelin started guiltily.

'It's me, Alice, Mrs Vaseyelin, from next door. I've come for Louise.'

Mrs Vaseyelin, perceptibly relieved by this identification, said, 'Yes, please,' and made a gesture indicating that Alice might take Louise and whatever else seemed appropriate. It was obvious she did not expect to be involved in the transaction.

As it was not possible to enter without pushing Mrs Vaseyelin to one side, Alice waited. 'It's a windy night,' she said, feeling it might be necessary to remind Mrs Vaseyelin – who was now looking about her furtively – of her presence.

Mrs Vaseyelin said, 'Excuse me,' and turned her back on Alice. After some fumbling Alice heard the clink of coins; Mrs Vaseyelin was counting money. When she turned she said, quite brightly, but without seeming to see Alice, 'I don't suppose you would have sixpence?'

Alice shook her head. 'But I expect Mummy has.'

'Oh dear no, no, no!' Mrs Vaseyelin was vehement. 'It is of no consequence.' As she walked past Alice she must have been telling herself an amusing story, for her lips moved and emitted a tinkle of disdainful laughter. The wind worried at the black cloak, and she held it tightly about her.

Alice stepped into the hall and shut the door; she had to lean against it, the wind was so strong. She went to the bottom of the stairs and called Katia; but either the door of Katia's room was closed, or the agony of the violin drowned all other sound, and there was no reply. Although she had been in the house quite often, Alice had never been taken upstairs. She did not see this as an indication that upstairs was forbidden territory; rather as an oversight on the part of the Vaseyelins who, not being interested in their home, could not imagine that it would be of interest to anyone else. She went to the half-landing; here, the stairs turned to the left.

The landing was dark, but in a recess a candle burned beneath a small painting on wood of the Virgin and Child, elongated and quite unlifelike. In spite of the flame which flickered wildly in a strong draught of air, there was a aura of stillness around the recess, not in any way related to the rare moments of quiet prayer in the chapel. Here, there was neither question nor answer, neither a reaching out nor a drawing in. As Alice gazed, she felt the fear, not that something awful was going to happen, but that nothing would happen, now or ever. At first, she was conscious of her own breathing; then there seemed only to be breath and no Alice. No home with parents waiting, no clock to record the period of absence. Nothing. Her eyes were wide and unblinking. Then some thing that was hard and breakable crashed outside the house – a tile, perhaps. Alice turned and ran down the stairs, taking two at a time.

She must have made a noise. The kitchen door opened and there was Anita, holding a basin in which she was pounding something which had a musty smell. The twins were watching her.

'I'm looking for Louise,' Alice said.

'They are down there.' Anita jerked her head in the direction of the cellar. The twins put their heads together and whispered.

The cellar was used by the young Vaseyelins to entertain their friends. It had rush matting on the floor, two dilapidated cane chairs, a Victorian day-bed with the stuffing coming out of it, and a couple of tea-chests on one of which stood two ornate but badly tarnished candlesticks. As elsewhere in the house, Alice always felt uneasy in the room, but with a different kind of uneasiness. Here, she sensed a certain anticipation, as though the room waited, indifferent, for things to happen.

She opened the cellar door and heard laughter abruptly broken off. 'It's me, Alice,' she called as she went down the stairs. 'Mummy asked me to come.' She had expected to see members of the St Bartholomew's Dramatic Society; but there was only Jacov and Louise and a dark, lowering girl whom she did not know. The latter was the only one to welcome Alice's arrival.

'Is this your kid sister come to take you home?' she said spitefully to Alice.

Louise said to Jacov, 'Let's have one more record.' She was sitting on a cushion with her back against the wall. She looked pale in the candlelight and there were shadows beneath her eyes. Alice thought she was probably having period pains.

Jacov looked from Louise to Alice, his brow furrowed. He read emotions as other people read thoughts, and he found conflicting emotions troublesome. They were all aware of his hesitation. Louise braced her back against the wall. The dark girl stretched herself out on the day-bed, making a shadow-play with her hands in the candlelight; she wore a black woollen dress and the seams had split under the arms. Alice thought crossly, 'Can't he see it's up to him?' In your home people had to do things your way, just as at your party you chose the games. Didn't he know what he wanted? Alice knew: she wanted Louise to come quickly because she felt uncomfortable, and because there were roes on toast for supper. The girl on the day-bed knew; although she seemingly wasn't paying attention, there came very strongly from her the wish that Louise would go away. But Jacov might have been watching a film in which he was not taking part, and so could not influence the action. Background music he was prepared to provide. He put a record on the gramophone. While he was winding, Alice whispered to Louise, 'I'm sorry, Lou.'

Louise turned her head and looked at Alice. All her movements were slow, as though a weight was pressing down on her.

Alice said, 'Is your tummy bad, Lou?'

'It's not what you think; not what you think at all.'

'What is it, then?'

Louise turned her head away. 'I don't want to spend my life being sensible.' She spat out the word sensible.

Mystified, Alice listened to the music, which sounded Eastern, but wasn't 'In a Chinese Temple Garden' – which was the one piece of Eastern music with which she was familiar. Looking down, she saw that she had scratched her knee. She dabbed at it with her handkerchief.

'I was up the tree when Mummy called,' she said, defending herself against Louise's unspoken hostility. 'I didn't want to come.'

The dark girl sneered, 'Me, Tarzan – You, Jane?'

'I was looking at Kashmir,' Alice said loftily.

The dark girl said, 'Pardon me!'

'Alice aims to be an explorer.' Louise said this in a way which made Alice seem silly. She was not behaving at all like her usual self.

'Why is it necessary to climb the tree if you want to get into Kashmir?' Jacov was perplexed by so much effort. 'Why do you not climb the wall?'

'I couldn't do that!' Alice was aghast. 'What would I do when I got to the other side?'

Jacov acknowledged the difficulty, but Louise said, You'd have to worry about that when you got there. If it was something you really wanted, more than anything else, wouldn't it be worth it?'

Alice, at a loss, pretended to study the label on the record while Jacov wound the gramophone again.

'It's *Hassan*,' Louise said, unrelenting. 'Have you read *Hassan*, Alice? You're always reading.'

'I'm reading *The Mill on the Floss* now.'

'That morbid thing! Death by drowning as a punishment for sin!'

'Louise prefers the "Golden Road to Samarkand".' Jacov was lazily amused.

'I don't care about the *pilgrims*. It's the *lovers*. They are offered one night of love at the price of eternal torment.'

'How awful,' Alice said warily. Torment, to her, was having a tooth drilled on the nerve, and it was much more real than anything she had so far been able to discover about the delights of lovers.

Jacov said mockingly, 'And they choose love, of course.'

'Yes, of course,' Louise was scornful. 'But it's the wrong way round; it's *The Mill on the Floss* thing all over again. Why can't people understand? You have the offer, and if you *don't* accept it, the price is eternal torment. That's the truth of it, Alice, and don't ever let them tell you different.'

The girl on the day-bed said, still making dancing shadows with her hands, 'I don't think Guy is coming, do you? He's never as late as this.'

Jacov looked at Louise, his head on one side. Alice thought that at last he was going to tell Louise she should go. But he put his hand on the top of her head, and then ran a finger right down her face to the place between her breasts, which Alice thought was a bit much. He said, 'Not tonight, Louise.'

Alice, pink with embarrassment, said, 'Well, I'm going. I want my supper.'

Louise followed her out. The dark girl stayed behind. 'What's she doing there?' Alice asked as they let themselves out of the front door.

'I'm sure I wasn't such a baby when I was your age!' Alice was surprised to see that Louise was close to tears.

From outside, the Vaseyelins' house had a dark, untenanted look. Then gaslight came on in an upstairs room. For a moment the Fairley girls could see Katia standing beneath the lamp; her arms upstretched, she seemed to reach out of the shadows into the circle of light in a gesture that had something appealing about it, almost a supplication.

Their mother called to them from their own front door. There was nothing vague or indecisive about her; she was very positively angry, and Alice had never valued her more. 'It was Louise,' she said. 'She wouldn't come.' She left Louise to make her own explanations, and went into the sitting-room to talk to Claire.

Claire lay on Great Aunt Mathilda's chair, which was extended to form a day-bed in times of sickness. Seeing her there, Alice felt a great gush of happiness. In after years, this kind of chair aroused in her a wave of yearning for a vanished security of which firelight and the smell of a peeled orange were the other ingredients. There would be people pushing to and fro in the world beyond the window-pane, heads bent against driving rain while she lay cocooned in love and comfort. Sometimes she would drift away, floating in mindless contentment, and wake to see her mother drawing the blinds and know without regret that the day had passed while she slept. Her father would bend over her, repeating the family joke (he had once been accused by Louise of 'not asking how I am') 'Well, how am you?'

Claire, who still looked like a spotted dick, said, 'Will you read me a William story?'

Alice complied, knowing that she read well. Claire listened, completely absorbed, the usually animated features still, the eyes deep pools in the spotted face. The boys Claire met were bits and pieces of a boy; William Brown was the complete boy, in comparison with whom they were imperfect imitations – good enough in their way, but not getting this business of being a boy quite right. This was what books did, Claire thought: they gave you the real thing, and you measured up to it as best you could. 'I'm going to be a librarian when I'm grown up,' she said to Alice. 'What will you be?'

'It's no use asking that,' Alice answered with unwonted scepticism, 'because whatever I say it will happen differently.'

5

There was always one moment when Alice noticed that the trees had grown tender leaves, and that instead of having a long view from the kitchen window, the garden had closed in on them, and Number 29 was a world on its own. She wrote in her diary that she would always remember these times: Daddy in the garden resting on his spade, calling out, 'The labourer is worthy of his hire!' and Mummy saying, 'Alice, come and take your father's tea out to him.'

Yet the very fact of appreciating the small, intimate joys of family life, of luxuriating in the slow passage of the lengthening days, seemed to cut Alice off from Claire. Claire, whether lying in the hammock reading, or playing with Badger on the lawn, lived completely in the golden hours as though evening would never come; and Alice was aware of something she had lost. She was also aware of Louise moving away from them all.

Alice and Louise had spent a weekend together with their uncle and aunt in Sussex. One afternoon they went for a walk on the edge of a wood. Alice had taken an exercise book so that she could record the wild flowers which she saw for later entry in her diary. Louise walked ahead. At every step in the wood you trod flowers. The hedgerows were rampant with Queen Anne's Lace, stitchwort, celandine, self-heal and more flowers than Louise could have named had she cared about naming; the hawthorns bent beneath their burden of blossom. This, she thought, was more than abundance, it was a madness of praise and affirmation. How it must embarrass the prudish, how they must wonder at God for allowing this unseemly sensual riot! She closed her eyes, quite dizzy with joy as she smelt the hawthorn blossom. Alice, coming up behind her, said, 'Do you think I should call it May or hawthorn?' Louise took the book out of her hands and threw it in the hedge. It was the last time they went for a country walk together for some time.

Alice was also subject to moods at this time. She loved her family passionately, but was finding it much harder to get on with the individual members. She was discovering how complex love is, how it seems to incorporate all other emotions, even hate. She wondered whether she might be able to explain this to her mother, but she doubted whether her mother could be made to understand. It was so very long ago that her mother had been young. When Alice looked at the old pictures in the family album, she saw no break in the continuity until her own time; her mother, wearing dresses down to her ankles, seemed to belong more to the world of her grandparents and great-grandparents than to Alice's own world.

So Alice did not tell her mother how impossibly difficult life was just now. She became argumentative, and was increasingly jealous of her small pleasures. She grumbled because she was not allowed to have her friends to play in the evenings. 'I can't always be with Claire. Why can't I have Daphne to tea?' It mattered so much, every moment of every golden evening mattered, but her mother could not be made to see this.

'Daphne doesn't have you to tea. I expect she has plenty to do with her own family.'

'She and Cecily don't get on, and Angus is at Cambridge. It's ever so dull for her.'

'Alice, I'm not interested in Daphne's problems. I can't think what has come over you lately. You used to be such a contented child.'

At half-term, Alice and Claire were invited to tea at the Drummonds.

'I don't suppose you want to come, do you?' Alice said to Claire. The Drummond children seldom invited their friends to their home and, apart from the disastrous midnight feast, this would be Alice's first visit. She did not want to have to contend with Claire's silliness as well as her own nervousness.

'Yes, I do,' Claire retorted. 'I sit next to Cecily in class.'

Claire was adamant. So later in the day Alice announced to her parents that she and Claire were to have tea with the Drummonds the following Monday. Usually, she would have asked permission, and her mother, looking at her, noticed the obstinate set of her mouth, and wondered why Alice was so difficult lately. Stanley Fairley said, 'What do we know about the Drummonds?' He had thought of taking the children to Kew Gardens for the day, but as he preferred to work in his own garden he was prepared to regard the Drummonds in a favourable light if no evidence to the contrary was produced.

Alice said, 'You know them by sight; we pass them on our way to chapel. They go to St Bartholomew's.'

Judith said, 'They are faithful after their fashion, so don't be so critical, Stanley.'

Their faith, though a poor thing, was sufficient to justify them in Stanley Fairley's eyes, and he raised no objection to the acceptance of the invitation.

'It won't be what you're used to,' Alice told Claire as they walked along the Uxbridge Road towards the Drummonds' large, double-fronted house. 'They have a maid and a cook.'

'It's not what you're used to, either,' Claire retorted.

'So long as you don't giggle when the maid answers the doorbell.'

It was Daphne who opened the door. She looked cool in a sleeveless tennis frock. She and Alice greeted each other with restraint, not yet having experience of each other's social behaviour. 'Shall I take your blazers?' she said politely. She hung the blazers on the coat-stand, a procedure to which they were unused, as they always took friends up to their bedroom when they arrived. She looked at their feet. 'You've worn plimsolls. Good. My father gets mad if we cut up the lawn.' She led them into a big room at the back of the house which had french windows leading into a garden large enough to accommodate a tennis court, flowerbeds and another, smaller lawn. Mrs Drummond was sitting on a sofa with a book on her lap, which she was not reading. Daphne did not introduce her to Alice and Claire, but walked straight through the room into the garden without glancing at her mother.

Cecily was standing on the grass surrounded by tennis rackets and balls, and a man was sitting beside her in a deckchair. He said, without turning his head, 'Don't make a racket if you're going to play.' Claire giggled at the pun, but no one else behaved as though there were any occasion for amusement.

Daphne said, 'Suppose we take on Alice and Cecily, Claire?'

The younger children missed the ball more often than they hit it, and soon Alice and Daphne began to hit the balls to each other. After a few games, Claire and Cecily departed sulkily to play on the far lawn, and Daphne and Alice began to enjoy themselves. They were well matched. Daphne's reactions were quick and her footwork was good, but Alice hit the ball harder and volleyed better. Neither gave any quarter. By the time the maid came out to say that tea was ready, Alice had won the first set 6-4 and Daphne, who never gave up, led 4-2 in the second.

Daphne's brother, Angus, joined them for tea. Although Daphne often talked about him, it was the first time Alice had met him. He was tall and dark, and had the same compact look of being turned out all in a piece that Daphne had. Alice was sorry that no one thought to introduce her to him. She supposed he was on holiday from university, but did not like to ask him.

The maid placed plates of sandwiches and cakes on a sidetable and departed, leaving the business of pouring out the tea to Mrs Drummond – a task which seemed to present her with such a bewildering number of options that Daphne eventually took over from her. As she handed her father his cup they exchanged an amused glance. Cecily, an ungainly, owlish child, unlike any of the others, began to talk to Claire about the Robert Mayer concert she had recently attended. The remainder of the family made desultory conversation, taking little notice of their guests. Alice ate in silence, unable to think of anything to say. There were no family jokes, and the Drummonds seemed to behave as though they did not know one another very well. Daphne had become a different person, older and less spontaneous. Mrs Drummond asked Alice if she would have liked toast. As there was no toast, Alice said politely that she preferred cucumber sandwiches. This did not reassure Mrs Drummond. She was a tiny, fluttery woman with gossamer hair and pale, worried eyes. She never seemed at rest, and as soon as the people about her had settled she looked uneasily round the room, trying to find a reason to get them moving again. Was Alice in a draught? Would Claire be more comfortable in a lower chair, Angus in a deeper one? Had Daphne got the sun in her eyes? When this attempt at all-change failed, she plucked the pleats of her silk dress. Mr Drummond, a handsome man with a neat moustache, talked with off-hand assurance on any topic which was raised. Although his manner conveyed the impression that the people in the room were barely worthy of his notice, there was that about him which suggested he was aware of the crumb at the corner of your mouth. Mrs Drummond made occasional remarks which did not seem to be connected with anything her husband had said. They were the oddest married couple Alice had ever encountered – seeing them like this, one at each end of the room, it was as though two wrong bits of a film had been joined together.

Gradually, as she listened, Alice found herself paying more attention to Mr Drummond than to anyone else. Something about him was beginning to disturb her. He was, for one thing, quite different from her own father, and she suspected her parents might have regarded him as 'suave'. But it was not her parents' possible disapproval which concerned her most; it was an uncomfortable feeling in her stomach. As his eyes swivelled indifferently from one person to another, she had the sensation of taking part in a kindergarten game (which she had always found frightening) where someone sent a top spinning and, if you were the nearest person to it when it stopped, you had to pay a forfeit. It didn't matter whether you had done anything to deserve it; there was no escape if the top chose you. Now, as she nibbled her sandwich, she was afraid that, however inconspicuous she might make herself, Mr Drummond's attention would suddenly spin her way, and he would engage her in a conversation as meaningless and hostile as her namesake's conversation with the Red Queen.

'Well, where is it to be, then?' he was saying. 'We have to make our minds up soon, though I appreciate that mind-making doesn't come easily to us.' He looked at his wife in amusement, and then his gaze transferred itself to Daphne. He looked at Daphne as though there was an understanding between them which did not exist between his wife and himself. Daphne responded – not in her usual unconsidered, forthright way, but carefully.

'What shall it be, Mother?' she said. 'The South of France?'

'It's such a long journey.' The corners of Mrs Drummond's mouth turned down.

'Germany, then?' Mr Drummond said. 'Curt tells me he knows just the place in Bavaria.'

'I don't think we want to go to Germany, do we?' Mrs Drummond looked nervously round the room, as though seeking the support of unseen witnesses. 'They were throwing stones at people the other day.'

'Only at Jews.'

'Oh, Alan!' For the first time she looked directly at Alice, saying rather inappropriately, 'It's a good thing we all know you.'

'My dear girl, let's be reasonable about this, shall we?'

As he spoke these words, there came vividly to Alice's eyes a picture quite at variance with the debonair image now presented by Mr Drummond. She saw him reaching forward – not for a cucumber sandwich, but for an article of attire of which he stood in total need. From that moment onwards, it became quite impossible, despite the services of an expensive tailor, for Alice to see Mr Drummond clothed.

Mr Drummond, unperturbed, went on. 'They segregate themselves, they never integrate, never give anything to the country in which they live – although they *take* a hell of a lot. It invites persecution – always has, always will. I'm sorry about that, but they have no one to blame but themselves.' The voice went on, just as it had when Alice first heard it – saying one thing and meaning another – and all the time he was looking at his wife, his lips curled in amusement, making sure she was aware that he was needling her. Cecily had stopped talking to Claire, and was looking unhappily at her mother. Mr Drummond said, 'Extortioners and usurers.'

Angus said, 'Isn't that because historically they were debarred from taking up other professions?' He had something of his father's manner, for – although he spoke civilly enough – he was not really asking a question.

'Oh, nonsense, old chap, nonsense! You've got Jews at Cambridge, so has Daphne at school. They'll be competing with you in whatever profession you take up – provided there's money in it!'

Angus said, leaving space between the words, 'I said "historically".'

Mr Drummond went on as if his son had not spoken. 'Hitler is a bit strident, I'll allow that; but it's not *all* nonsense that he talks. There are too many Jews in controlling positions. Banks, for example . . . You'll allow me to know a little about banking, old chap.'

Mrs Drummond, who had been looking at her son's face, was moved to a flurry of activity. She crossed the room and rang for the maid. 'I think we'll have toast,' she said. 'I'm sure these girls want toast.'

When they went out to continue their game, Daphne said to Alice, 'I didn't know you were so bothered about meeting my father.' Alice's stomach lurched. Daphne went on, 'Don't look so stricken! He thought it was very funny. He has a marvellous sense of humour.'

'Funny?'

'He wouldn't have liked it if it had been the morning room, but he didn't mind about the kitchen. Mother doesn't know, of course. She still thinks it was burglars.'

Alice said slowly, 'You mean, you told your father about our feast?'

'Well, I had to,' Daphne said reasonably. 'Suppose the police had picked up some tramp or other? What would we have done? Luckily my father knows the police superintendent. He thought it was funny, too.' She tossed a ball to Alice and said, 'You can stop worrying about your fingerprints now.'

How unfair life was, Alice thought as she served into the net: when one worry is removed, a greater one takes its place! And added to this was the realization that even one's very best friend is not to be trusted.

Claire was unusually silent on their way home.

'Didn't you enjoy yourself?' Alice asked.

Claire shook her head.

'I told you you shouldn't have come.'

They walked in silence until they reached the end of their road, then Claire said, 'Mr Drummond has . . .' She looked down at the pavement, scarcely knowing how to say it. '. . . another woman.'

'How do you know?'

'Cecily told me.'

'But how does she know?'

'Daphne told her. He goes away at weekends. Mrs Drummond knows all about it. Cecily says Daphne says they are staying together for the children's sake.'

'How does she know?'

'I don't know.' Claire stamped her foot. 'You ask her; she's your friend.'

Alice thought; the more she thought, the worse it seemed. 'Claire,' she said eventually, 'you mustn't tell Mummy and Daddy about this. If they find out, we won't be allowed to play with the Drummonds.'

'I don't want to play with them.'

'You are *not* to tell!' Alice said angrily. 'You told about Louise and the play. You can't tell any more tales, or neither of us will have anything to do with you.'

They began to walk towards their home. 'I shall feel so awful not telling them,' Claire pleaded.

'It's kinder for them not to know,' Alice answered. 'It would upset them so much.'

But even for her it was not easy to keep quiet.

'Grandma will be disappointed if you don't go to see her,' Judith Fairley said the following week. 'She looks forward to your visits.'

'I'll take her to Pontings for tea.'

'Whatever for?'

'Why shouldn't I? Other girls do.' She had not, in fact, encountered anyone who took their grandmother to tea at Pontings or anywhere else, but she did not want to go to her grandmother's house for fear of meeting Mr Drummond and the auburn-haired woman.

'I thought you were saving your pocket money for a bicycle.'

'I'd rather spend it this way,' Alice said miserably.

6

Miss Blaize gazed out of the window of her study and was afflicted by melancholy. It was her fear that the old balance between man and his world had already been destroyed. Man thought of himself as master now; madness was abroad. What could one do about it? A generation was growing up which had no instinctive sense of the natural order. For this reason, she always laid great emphasis on the importance of the children understanding the cycle of the seasons, and their own part in it. At this moment the third-formers were working on the flower border. One child had just pushed another into a rose bush; while a third, having dug a small hole, appeared to be drowning a plant in it. Miss Blaize could not believe that their activities were doing much to increase the third-formers' awareness of themselves as part of the woof and warp of creation.

There were times when Miss Blaize looked at her pupils and wondered whether the school really had any effect on them at all. The rules and regulations which they found so irksome were not imposed for their own sake, but because Miss Blaize believed that life was not easy, and unless the habits of self-discipline and respect for the rights of others were inculcated at an early age, it would be hard indeed for either the individual or society to survive. But how much did they absorb? Children were as unpredictable as a whirlwind: once in motion, there was no knowing what course they would take.

Miss Blaize moved away from the window and sat at her desk. She looked at the notes which she had prepared for this morning's scripture lesson. When she thought of the young faces which would soon be staring up at her, she felt a profound sadness. She believed that hope was essential to the survival of the human spirit, but there were times when she herself almost ceased to hope.

There was a knock on the door. Colette Biggs, form captain of Lower Four Aleph, had arrived. She would now conduct Miss Blaize, like a guard of honour, to the classroom, while the other form captain maintained that atmosphere of meditation necessary to the occasion. The advent of Miss Blaize was usually awaited with some trepidation, and pupils were anxious to re-read notes, so that they would have a ready answer if called upon to summarize the contents of the previous scripture lesson. Something, however, seemed to have gone wrong on this occasion. As Miss Blaize and Colette walked along the passage above the assembly hall, it was apparent that whatever else was happening to Lower Four Aleph, it was not meditation.

The girls had settled quickly after the change bell had sounded. Monica Pilgrim, the other form captain, was away sick. Alice, as last term's form captain, was in charge. She wiped down the blackboard, and said to the other two girls who were arguing about tennis practice, 'Leave it until break; we can sort it out then.'

Valerie Pewsey, a precocious girl who spent the greater part of lessons curling her hair around her fingers and thinking about Ginger Rogers's latest film, said to her neighbour, Ena Pratt, 'Lend me your notes; I can't find mine.'

'You should listen,' Ena said virtuously, 'then you wouldn't need notes.' She made no move to produce her own.

Valerie poked Katia between the shoulder-blades. 'Lend us your notes. You don't need them anyway.'

The Jews and Roman Catholics were excused scripture lessons, and arrangements were made for them to be instructed by members of their own faith. As no such facility was available for members of the Russian Orthodox faith – and as her family seemed unconcerned – Katia attended scripture lessons. She had had the benefit of more concentrated religious instruction than most of the other girls and, although her contributions were not invariably congenial to Miss Blaize, she nevertheless scored some notable successes during discussion.

Ena, who longed to impress, but had never learnt that her brand of sanctimonious Protestantism was anathema to Miss Blaize, said, 'Why don't you let Val have your notes? You know it all.'

'And anyway, it doesn't matter to you: you're not a Christian,' Valerie said reasonably.

Katia was incensed. 'You're one to talk about being a Christian! I've seen you in the back row at the Roxy.'

'Never mind about the Roxy now,' Alice said. 'You can have my notes, Val.'

Valerie said sweetly, 'At least I don't go with old men.'

Alice said, 'Leave this until break, will you?'

'What's this about old men?' Daphne felt this was a situation which would not improve with keeping.

'I've seen her at the ABC in Hammersmith with the old man who plays the violin outside the tube station.'

Katia seemed to balloon out of her seat, and to grow larger and larger as she towered over Valerie. Her sallow face paled to ivory. She sucked in saliva and spat at Valerie. Consternation reigned. Those who had seen what happened expressed their views noisily, while those who had not stood up, determined not to miss any further action. Sympathy was almost entirely with Valerie. 'Mucky little sod,' Daphne said as Valerie scrubbed her face.

Katia surveyed them, and said with grand impartiality, 'I despise you all. You are insignificant creatures whose mothers think of nothing but housework.'

A stunned silence greeted this judgement, which was quite out of keeping with the usual classroom repartee, and was in fact attributable to Mrs Vaseyelin. Alice took advantage of the lull to say loudly, 'Have we all got our Bibles open? It s the Acts of the Apostles, Chapter Five.' She was pleased to see several people hastily flipping over pages; the insurrection was over. Miss Blaize's arrival coincided with what Alice regarded as her victory. The room was quiet, and the girls were studiously regarding their Bibles.

'Who is in charge here?' Miss Blaize stood in the doorway looking thunderous, but speaking softly; behind her, Colette peeped at her form-mates as though expecting to witness a Bacchanalian rite.

Alice said that she was in charge.

'Why are you not wearing your form captain's badge?'

'I'm not form captain this term, Miss Blaize – only for today because Monica Pilgrim is away.'

'So you feel that exonerates you from any attempt to exercise authority?'

Alice, who felt that she had right on her side, said, 'I *was* trying to exercise authority.'

'But, my dear, you weren't succeeding, were you? I could hear the noise from this room as I came up the stairs.'

'It took a bit of time,' Alice admitted. 'But they were quiet when you arrived, Miss Blaize.'

Miss Blaize, who regarded this as entirely due to her presence, was not impressed. She looked at Alice sternly. Katia got to her feet. 'It was my fault, Miss Blaize; it was all my fault.' She was sweating, and her voice shook with emotion. Miss Blaize looked at her without favour.

'I am not at this moment concerned with who was responsible for the commotion.' She turned her attention again to Alice; 'What concerns me, my dear, is that you were afraid to fetch a mistress to quiet the class because of what your friends would say about you.'

Alice's friends looked woodenly at their desks. Katia and Alice spoke in unison.

Alice said, 'I didn't fetch a mistress because I *was* quieting them; we were just looking up Chapter . . .'

Katia said, 'It wasn't Alice's fault, Miss Blaize, it was . . .'

Miss Blaize said, 'Will you both sit down. I will see you later in my study.'

She walked across the room, and Colette, thus released, scurried to her desk. Miss Blaize opened her Bible and looked at the class. If she was searching for weakness, she had no difficulty in finding it; the pupils maintained that in this respect she had a nose like a bloodhound. She said to Valerie, 'Will you remind us of what we know about St Paul?'

Valerie rose to her feet and intoned, 'He came from a little town where he would not have had much opportunity for learning . . .' The members of the class bowed their heads while Valerie proceeded to make a neat reversal of everything she had been told about St Paul.

When she had finished, Miss Blaize said, 'You *were* here last week, I suppose, my dear?'

'Yes, Miss Blaize.'

'Don't you keep notes, my dear? You obviously have a very bad memory. So it is particularly important that you should make notes.'

Valerie said that she had lost her notes.

'You mean you have lost your scripture notebook? That will include the whole of this year's work, won't it?'

Valerie, not wanting to pursue this any further, said that she had left her scripture notebook on the bus. Miss Blaize gazed at her, and Valerie hung her head and was silent – she had long ago learnt that this was the best way to weather storms. Miss Blaize, unprepared to be led in labyrinthine pursuit of Valerie's notebook, turned her attention to St Paul. Ignoring Ena, who had been eagerly waving her hand for some time, she said to Daphne, 'What can you tell us about St Paul, my dear?'

Daphne briskly reinstated St Paul, taking care to quote that he was a citizen of no mean city, so that Miss Blaize would not assume that she was merely taking up the options left to her by Valerie.

When the lesson was over, Miss Blaize left the room trailing Alice and Katia behind her.

'Now, my dears,' she addressed them when they were seated in her room. 'You have been faced today with a testing situation, and one which I myself have come up against in the past – and which, I admit, I found very difficult.' She paused, looking out of the window. The third-formers were no longer gambolling in the flower border. 'Most of us have our failures,' she said sadly. 'There is something inhuman about a person who has never had a failure. The important thing is to learn from failure.'

She paused. Katia was resentful. Miss Blaize was aware that reason would make no impression on her. Katia was ill at ease with life, and no wonder: the girl had had a bad beginning; even her Russian ancestry was not pure. These mixed origins produced an irrationality which was not conducive to sober consideration of the facts of a situation. Miss Blaize looked at Alice.

'I didn't think I *had* failed, Miss Blaize.' Alice spoke quietly, surprising both herself and Miss Blaize by her composure.

Miss Blaize talked about St Paul, about moral courage, about the need to stand firm even when all one's friends have forsaken one. 'Even Demas,' she added, striking a sombre note as though at the recollection of a personal betrayal.

Alice listened. Miss Blaize, as she looked at the girl's attentive, good-natured face, could almost have imagined that Alice Fairley was humouring her. She appealed to Alice, and beyond Alice to all those girls who, on leaving school, must uphold the tradition of dedicated service in an increasingly undisciplined world. 'You told yourself that it was wrong to speak. So you chose to neglect the responsibility placed upon you as form captain. Did it occur to you that this was not only a responsibility to your fellows who were in your charge, but also to the people who trusted you to fulfil your duties?'

Alice admitted that she had not looked at it in this way. She was surprised to find that it was possible to escape relatively unscathed from a difference of opinion with authority. She had no mind to push matters much further, but was not happy with the present conclusion. 'I didn't think about sneaking,' she said.

Miss Blaize studied her thoughtfully and then asked, 'Do you now think it would have been advisable to fetch a mistress to control the class?'

Alice, having no quarrel with 'advisable', conceded that it might have been. They observed a few moments' silence. Miss Blaize decided to rest her case.

'I should like you to reflect on this, Alice,' she said. 'Then come to see me on Wednesday.'

When the girls had gone, Miss Blaize took time for reflection. She had presented Alice Fairley with a suggestion which the girl could accept, and Alice in her turn had appreciated that Miss Blaize was defending discipline in the school, and that discipline must not be seen to lose ground. It seemed quite a mature understanding to have reached with a girl whom she had previously thought of as a nice currant bun of a creature.

She sent for Miss Lindsay.

'How is Alice Fairley getting on? I know the little one is rather too clever for her own good, and Louise uncommonly attractive. Alice must have some gifts, one imagines?'

Miss Lindsay drew thin brows together and tried to imagine Alice's gifts. 'She *is* good at English, but I doubt that she'll make much of it. She is the kind who doesn't expect to be better than anyone else at anything – except scoring goals at netball.'

'Some of this may be our fault?'

'She hasn't any spark.'

'Sparks can go out. I should like to see one or two of Alice's essays.'

When Alice and Katia returned to their formroom, notes of apology had been left on their desks, Daphne's embellished with spirited drawings representing them as Christian martyrs confronting a gigantic Nero. 'What happened?' Daphne asked Alice.

'I've got to see her on Wednesday morning when I have had time for reflection,' Alice answered.

Daphne said coolly to Katia, 'None of this would have happened if you hadn't been so ready with your spit.'

Katia turned away; it was apparent she was very upset.

That evening, Alice said to her mother, 'May I go next door? Katia was upset at school today, and I'd like to see that she's all right.'

'As long as you don't stay too late.'

It was a dry, windy evening, the rambler roses bobbing about and the spent lilac dropping its last blooms. The Vaseyelins' front garden was a tangle of long grass and briars. The windows on the ground floor were open and the thin curtains billowed out, catching on the ivy.

Jacov opened the door. He had no jacket on, and had his shirt sleeves rolled up. He said that Katia had gone to bed, feeling unwell. Alice followed him down the corridor into the kitchen. He said, 'Excuse, please,' and turned off the tap over the sink, which was full of pots and pans. There was a smell of spice and greasy washing-up water. 'My mother and Anita are out tonight,' he said, 'so I am in charge.'

Alice offered to help with the washing up, but he refused, so they sat at the kitchen table and talked. Honeysuckle grew heavy as thatch above the window and made the room dark. The wind rattled window-panes, and somewhere above a door banged insistently. Alice said, 'Katia was upset because one of the girls had seen her with the man who plays the violin outside the Empire . . . Actually, I've seen her with him, too.' She was unhappy at betraying Katia, but she had thought a lot about it on the way home from school, and decided that for Katia's own good she must tell. She could not imagine Jacov being angry, but the Vaseyelins were unpredictable. 'I don't want to get her into trouble. Only, I thought . . .'

Jacov said kindly, 'There is no trouble. He is our father.'

'Your father!' Alice stared, uncomprehending. Was it to meet him that Mrs Vaseyelin went out to catch the Number 12 bus at The Askew Arms in the evenings? It seemed a very odd way of going on. 'But why doesn't he live with you?'

'Because there are too many of us.' Jacov smiled as though this should have been self-evident.

'You mean there isn't room?'

Jacov shrugged his shoulders. 'In a way, yes. Before we came to England, we had a big house with servants, and he did not have to see us often. But in England we are too much for him. So he lives alone and my mother goes to see him. Sometimes he comes here, but only occasionally. It is hard for him.'

'Doesn't he love you?' Alice asked.

Jacov appeared nonplussed by the question, as though love – which for Alice seemed as essential to family life as yeast to bread – to him represented the unknown factor in a difficult equation. He sat with his elbows on the table, head bowed as he examined the past. His shirt was damp under the arms, and Alice could smell sweat.

'I think he loved Sonya.' He said this as though making an offering to Alice which he hoped she would find acceptable. As she still seemed troubled, he went on, 'She was the first child, so I suppose it was not so irksome for him, just having the one around. Then she died, which was satisfactory.'

'Satisfactory!'

He raised his head and looked at Alice. 'Satisfactory is not a good word to express what I mean. The dead are secure, nothing can change them, you understand? My father can love Sonya and she will never hurt him; he can imagine how she would have grown up, what she would have become, and none of it will be painful because she will not be there to disappoint him.'

'How dreadful!' The idea that it might be better to be dead than to disappoint one's parents was worrying.

The evening breeze stirred the tangled greenery around the open window, and the sharp-sweet smell of honeysuckle drifted in from the garden. 'How seriously you take everything, Alice.' Jacov's tone did not imply that she was wrong to be serious – he was merely recording an observation about a person whom he liked, but who was different from himself.

Alice, wanting him to be the same as herself, said, 'Aren't you angry with him for caring about Sonya and not being interested in the rest of you?'

'I may have been angry at one time.' He was not at ease talking about his feelings, but he seemed unable to bring the conversation to an end, perhaps for fear of hurting Alice. 'It is a mistake to be angry for long. It turns into bitterness, and bitterness only hurts the person who is bitter. One cannot afford to be bitter. You see, I am concerned with self-preservation.' He grimaced comically, inviting disapprobation.

Alice said, 'I think you are very good.'

'No, no, you mistake.' He became anxious. 'I am selfish. I forgive my father, if there is anything to forgive, and I try to understand him, because it will be better for me that way.' A moth fluttered through the open window and dropped on the table between them. Jacov looked at the clock; it was half-past eight. No doubt he was aware that Mr Fairley would not think it correct for him to be sitting alone with Alice in the evening. He ran his fingers through his curly hair and sighed. Alice thought he was unhappy. Had he scraped his chair back a few inches, she would have guessed that he wanted her to go.

He was released from the need to act by the arrival of Louise.

'The front door was open, so I came in. You've got a moth, did you know?' She bent forward and trapped it in cupped hands. 'Shall we put it out in the garden?'

Jacov, who had risen to his feet, said, 'You are not afraid?'

'I don't think so.' She smiled at him in the warm, direct way which Alice admired because it seemed so brave. Tonight, however, her gaze wavered. 'I can feel it fluttering. Ugh!'

Jacov opened the kitchen door; she went to it and released the moth, which flew back into the kitchen.

'Do we catch it again?' Jacov asked.

She remained in the doorway, the wind ruffling her thin dress. She put up a hand to her head, twisting a tendril of hair into place. 'We'd better go. Mummy sent me to fetch Alice.'

They walked round the side of the house to the back gate. The wind made a dry rustling in the leaves of the trees, and the brambles tore at their dresses; one caught in Louise's hair.

'Let me do it,' Jacov said as she raised a hand. 'Otherwise you will prick yourself.'

'But you will prick yourself.'

'It is my bramble, so I am responsible.'

They were so close that when he leant forward Louise's breasts brushed his shirt, and Alice felt a discomfort in her own breasts.

'This is bad,' he said. 'I shall have to take this fastening out. Will it all come down?'

'I don't know.' She looked at him as though he had surprised her. Alice could see that she was breathing more quickly. He began to take the hairpins out, one by one, not hurrying, releasing Louise's hair very gently, in a way which Alice found excruciatingly embarrassing. She turned away, and stared into the back garden. It had been hot in the kitchen, and now the wind cooled the sweat on her body and made her shiver.

Jacov said, 'There, you are free! I must make amends. Shall I cut you a rose?'

'You haven't got any, have you?' Mummy would have said that Louise was being very pert. 'I mean, you've only got brambles.'

There was a slight scuffling, and he said, 'You mustn't move, or you'll be caught by them again.'

Louise gave a little gasp, half laughter, half anger, and then a smothered sound about which Alice could not be specific. After what seemed a long time, Louise's voice rang out cheerfully, 'Come along, Alice! Don't stand there mooning.'

When they were out in the road, she said, 'Well, I never thought he had it in him! Come along, we'll walk as far as the pillar-box while I put my hair up again.'

That night, after their parents had said goodnight to Alice and Claire, Alice found it hard to sleep. She remembered what Jacov had said about Sonya not living to disappoint her father, and she felt very guilty about concealing the state of affairs in the Drummond household. She prayed that matters might be so arranged that her parents would be spared disappointment without the necessity of anyone dying young.

Miss Lindsay wondered what was behind Miss Blaize's interest in Alice Fairley. Was this her way of intimating that Miss Lindsay was paying too much attention to Ella Philpotts and Emmie Barker? Both girls had a crush on her and, since they were clever and amusing, she allowed them some licence – though she was always careful to appear disdainful. She asked a mystified Alice for her English notebooks, and drew Miss Blaize's attention to the best of Alice's work in the hope that this would prove that others besides Ella and Emmie benefited from her teaching.

When the time came for Alice to keep her appointment with Miss Blaize, she approached the headmistress's room with apprehension. It seemed, however, that the incident of the scripture lesson was not to be the subject of discussion. Instead, Miss Blaize talked generally about English literature, and told Alice about her travels in Greece and the Holy Land. Finally, as Alice was about to leave, she said, 'I have been reading some of your essays. You do realize that you have a gift for expressing the English language?'

Alice, anxious to be agreeable, said, 'Yes, Miss Blaize.'

She was relieved to have got off so lightly, and did not at the time think much about what Miss Blaize had said.

7

Summer seemed no sooner to have come than it was on the wane; the school had broken up and the Fairleys were preparing for their annual holidays, a procedure requiring no little delicacy and ingenuity. Mr Fairley was good about relatives in theory, but not when actually confronting them. His intentions were invariably praiseworthy, but the need to maintain an appearance of affability over a period of days – let alone weeks – in the company of people who did not share his ideas was beyond him. Consequently, evasive action had to be taken and the Fairley family usually spent their holiday at a place too far removed from either Cornwall or Sussex for there to be any question of visiting relatives. Neglect, however, was unthinkable and so ambassadors must be dispatched. This year, Alice was to go to Cornwall and Louise to Sussex. Claire and Mr Fairley were going to camp, Mr Fairley with the sea cadets and Claire with the Crusaders at Jordans. At the end of August the entire family would have two weeks at Sheringham.

'What is the weather report?' Judith asked at breakfast.

Claire said, 'Where will Lobby Lud be next week, Daddy?' She enjoyed going up to men in straw boaters and saying, 'You are Mr Lobby Lud. I claim the *News Chronicle* prize.' The prize was ten pounds – twenty if the previous town had failed to produce a successful challenger – and Claire had made a list of things she intended to buy with it, including a new sewing machine for her mother.

'Wherever it is, it won't be Jordans.' Her father put the paper down and Alice, on the pretext of looking for Lobby Lud's timetable, turned the pages and had a quick glance at the entertainment guide. The notorious *Story of Temple Drake* had come to the West End; she had read that George Raft had refused to play the title role. What could be so uniquely dreadful that even George Raft, who had played so many gangster roles, should condemn it? Claire asked, 'Where is he going to be?'

'I can't find it. You look for yourself.'

Later, when they were in their bedroom sorting out the few personal possessions they wanted to take with them, Claire said to Alice, 'You're going to miss Cru. camp.' Her face wrinkled in displeasure. She liked others to share her enthusiasms; if they failed to do so, she began to question their worth.

'I'm not all that keen on Crusaders.' Alice leant out of the bedroom window. It was a warm, sunny day and she could hear the sound of someone hitting a tennis ball against a wall. 'Daphne's out in her garden practising.'

Daphne and her family were going to Germany in spite of Mrs Drummond's protests. Katia was going to her grandparents. As her grandparents lived in Bavaria, and Mr Drummond had talked about a holiday in Bavaria, Alice wondered whether they would meet. It was obvious from what Katia said that her grandparents were important people who lived in a very superior style; so perhaps this would impress the Drummonds, and then Katia and Daphne would be friends, which would make life much simpler.

'You don't play our game any more; and now you don't like Crusaders.' Claire sounded forlorn. She enjoyed her sister's company more than that of anyone else, and was finding it hard to accept that companionship depends on the consent of both parties.

Alice sat on the bed beside her. 'I'll think about you camping. Every evening, I'll think of you sitting round the fire singing choruses.' She began to sing, 'Wide, wide as the ocean/High as the Heaven above,' and Claire joined in, 'Deep, deep as the deepest sea/Is my Saviour's love.'

Claire said, 'Rub noses,' and they rubbed their noses together, which was a family sign of reconciliation.

Louise would be in the sixth form in the autumn. She had only scraped through matriculation but it was hoped that, provided she worked hard, she would get her Higher School Certificate. If she was successful in this, a long period of strain and unhappiness would lie ahead of her at university. Louise realized that the only way to convince her father of her unsuitability for the academic life was to take her exams and fail convincingly. It seemed a waste of two years of her life. If this was not hard enough to bear, her parents had arranged that she should spend a month on her uncle's farm in Sussex, so that she could study in peace.

'I would prefer to go to Falmouth,' she had protested to her mother.

'You'd never manage to do any studying with my mother around you!'

It was not of study which Louse had been thinking. 'Guy and his parents are staying at St Mawes for the next three weeks,' she told Alice. 'I've given them the grandparents' address, so maybe you'll see something of them. It'll be a change from looking after the tribe.'

They had a large number of Cornish cousins, all younger than Alice. Alice, who liked them but did not want to spend all her time looking after them, said hopefully, 'I expect they've got friends of their own.'

'They'll bring their friends with them,' Louise said.

On arrival in Truro, Alice was confronted with an unexpected addition to her relatives. Her grandfather was waiting at the ticket barrier with a tall, bony young man who looked about him as though he wished he was somewhere else. On being introduced to Alice he studied her face thoughtfully, apparently not being one to commit himself to a 'Good day', let alone a smile without good reason.

'This is your Cousin Ben,' Joseph said while Ben was deciding what was due to Alice.

Alice, having little expectation of surviving prolonged scrutiny with credit, said, 'I haven't got a Cousin Ben.' This, her expression made plain, was a conviction she intended to uphold.

Ben responded with a gust of laughter as inexplicable as his previous surliness. 'There should be a law that no one has cousins thrust upon them without notice.' He picked up Alice's suitcase. 'When I become Attorney General it will be my first consideration.' He walked towards the exit swinging the heavy suitcase and menacing those around him. He seemed at one moment to be both self-conscious and unaware.

On the bus he spoke little until the woman in the seat behind him began to tell the conductor about a sheep she had seen on her way in to Truro: it had been lying on its back, and if it was still lying on its back this evening, she wondered whether she should get off the bus and find the farmer. Ben turned round. 'Why didn't you do that this morning?' His tone was so accusing that the woman embarked on a long defence involving an aunt in hospital in Truro and a dog with poor bowel control in Falmouth. Her days, it seemed, were passed travelling anxiously between the two. Ben gazed at her as if weighing her veracity in a matter of exceptional gravity.

The sheep was still on its back when they came to the field, and Ben said he would investigate.

'If it was like that this morning, it's dead by now,' the conductor said.

'You'll have to walk home, there isn't another bus,' Joseph warned.

But Ben got off, and as the bus drove away they saw him climbing the gate leading into the field, body arching forward, neck stretched out, as though straining ahead of an unseen challenger. Joseph was moved to make one of his rare observations on a fellow man. 'That's how it will be with Ben, always climbing gates before he's given them a push.'

'I haven't got a Cousin Ben, have I?' Alice appealed to Ellen as soon as they were alone together.

'He's Joseph's Cousin Cedric's grandson. Your third cousin that would make him – or maybe he's Joseph's third cousin?'

'Mummy never talks about him,' Alice disposed of any claim to kinship.

'She never got on with Lizzie, and she couldn't forgive her for marrying first. But you did meet Ben once when you were very small. They lived in Bodmin, he and Lizzie. She died last month. That's why he's staying with us.'

'Hasn't he got a father?'

'He has not,' Ellen replied with satisfaction. 'Lizzie married an American journalist, Walter Sherman. Everyone said at the wedding what a fine couple they made.' She paused, staring at the wall as though visualizing the wedding party grouped on it.

Alice, accustomed to such pauses, prompted, 'Did you see something, Granny?'

'I saw in his eyes he wasn't going to live long. They didn't go to America at once because he was travelling round Europe. Then in 1915 he went to New England to make arrangements for his family, though why he couldn't have taken them with him, I shall never know; Lizzie was tough as wire, and she could have put up with a bit of discomfort until they found a place to live. But he was the kind must do it all himself. And when everything was settled to his liking he set off to fetch them. On the *Lusitania*. You know about the *Lusitania*?' Alice nodded. 'Two thousand drowned and Walter Sherman among them.' Her eyes moved to the window, less piercing in their gaze as she regarded her old adversary. 'He wasn't even a sailor, but it took him just the same. Poor Lizzie.'

'How old was Ben?'

'He'd have been a year old. Lizzie was a hard woman and thought

94

a lot of herself, but she was a worker. She put her pride in her pocket and took in lodgers. Scrimped and saved to give Ben a good education. He's going to study for the law at London University, Alice. The first Tippet to go to university. Joseph didn't say much when Ben told him, but I could see how proud he was. He put on his best suit and went down to The Crossed Keys that evening.'

Alice tried to be sorry for Ben. The death of a parent was almost too dreadful to contemplate. But he did not grieve in any way recognizable to Alice, and although every morning she made a resolution to notice his suffering, other matters usually claimed her attention. At mealtimes she was aware, as he helped himself to more potatoes without being asked, that his bony wrists extended too far from the sleeves of his jacket. The jacket was also tight across the shoulders. His clothes had a hand-me-down look. He didn't have much in the way of manners, either. He ate faster than his companions, and drummed his fingers impatiently on the table while he waited for them to finish. He was not greedy, however, and could never be tempted to another helping once he had had sufficient.

'No wonder you're fat,' he said when Alice accepted more treacle pudding.

'Alice enjoys her food,' Ellen said fondly.

Ben hardly ever mentioned his mother, but he talked a lot about his father. To Alice's surprise, he had decided to help her to amuse the tribe. They played cricket on the sands, and Ben made up his own rules. Alice noted that the young did well under Ben's dispensation. He told them stories about General Sherman who, he claimed, was his great-great-uncle, and he taught them 'Marching through Georgia'. They marched up and down the beach, singing:

' "Sherman's dashing Yankee boys will never reach the coast",
So the saucy rebels said, – and 'twas a handsome boast,
Had they not forgot, alas! to reckon with the host,
As we were marching through Georgia.'

'Hurrah! Hurrah!' the tribe shouted. 'We bring the Jubilee!'
They had no idea what that was, but they waved their spades triumphantly in the air. They strutted beside the English Channel, shouting, none more exultant than Ben:

'So we sang the chorus from Atlanta to the sea,
As we were marching through Georgia.'

One evening in the second week of her stay, as they walked back from the beach together, Ben said severely to Alice, 'This is your holiday.'

'Yes, I know.' She wondered what she had done wrong.

'You're much too good-natured. You should ditch the kids and do whatever you want.' They walked in silence for a few moments, then he said rather awkwardly, 'I would like to give you a treat.'

'What's that, then?'

'*I* don't know,' he replied irritably. 'You have to decide. Surely there is something you'd like to do.'

'Oh, there is!' she responded immediately. 'I'd like to go to the pictures, please.'

'The pictures!' He had obviously envisaged something he would also enjoy. 'In this weather?'

'It's called *Spy 13*. It's got Gary Cooper in it.'

'Gary Cooper?' He studied her face and then, making an effort not to sound grudging, conceded, 'Well, I can see we have to go.'

They set out for the cinema the following afternoon. The sun glinted on the still water in the harbour; the pavement was hot beneath Alice's sandals, and the salt in the air stung her face. She waited for Ben to say he could not go to the pictures on such a glorious day, but he merely asked where she wanted to sit. She said in the shilling seats if he didn't mind – 'in case of fleas'.

By the time the censor's certificate came up with the words *Spy 13* written on it, Alice could barely nerve herself to look at the screen. When Gary Cooper first appeared, she screwed up her eyes and only gradually allowed herself to discover him. Miraculously, he was all she had dreamt he would be. The action took place during the Civil War. Alice did not like to see real blood, but the sight of Gary Cooper with a bloodstained bandage round his head made her feel as though something inside her head had melted and liquid warmth was spreading through her whole body.

'What about Gary Cooper, then?' Ben asked when they came out of the cinema.

'I liked him,' Alice replied sedately.

'But the film . . .' he began and then, seeing her face, contented himself with saying, 'I don't think civil war is like that.' He talked about General Sherman.

It was not of General Sherman that Alice was thinking. At last she had discovered the kind of hero for whom she was looking. He was tough and manly, but with an ingrained sensitivity; beneath that hard shell of bone there was a heart that beat in time with Nature, an understanding that could penetrate the mysteries of a woman's reserve. Whatever his past errors – be it jail break, cattle rustling, gambling – he would do the right thing at the right moment. Cousin Ben undoubtedly lacked Gary Cooper's gentle strength; and she suspected that not only would he fail to do the right thing at the right moment, but he had no awareness of what constituted the right moment. She held her dream to herself and said nothing.

That night as she lay in bed, Alice thought about the film and relived the more romantic moments. She thought of the men in their uniforms, and the women in their pretty dresses and the magnolias and the moonlight, and she wished desperately that she could go through an experience like that. It was so unlike her father's war memories: civil war was much more poignant.

Towards the end of the week the Imminghams called. Both Guy and his father wore white flannels and blue blazers. They looked alike in other ways, both tall and shy, though Guy had an eagerness about him which his father lacked. Mr Immingham gave the impression of a man who fears he may at any moment accidentally do something wrong. He stuttered slightly as he greeted Ellen.

Mrs Immingham was dressed in a cream linen costume, and she wore a cream panama hat which shaded her face and kept her skin from getting burnt. As she entered the sitting-room she darted little glances around her, noting objects, such as the ship in the bottle, as though their unfamiliarity threatened her. When Alice pointed out the view of the harbour, she replied, 'We always stay at *St Mawes*.' Her offended tone implied that Alice should have known it was impossible for the Imminghams to stay anywhere else.

She was a soft, pink woman who wore an expression of doing something to which she was unused; she even sat down as though this was an exercise involving no little risk to her person. Once settled, her plump hands soothed the folds of her skirt. While the others engaged in the usual introductory chatter, she gazed reproachfully at her husband and Guy. It was apparent she had not wanted to come, and could not imagine why her menfolk should have subjected her to this.

'And you know Alice, of course, Louise's sister,' Ellen said.

Mrs Immingham looked more reproachful than ever. Guy greeted Alice with warmth to make up for his parents' lack of response.

'And this is Ben. He is staying with us before he goes to London University,' Ellen said proudly.

Mrs Immingham responded to this as though it was a claim on her own private territory. 'London? That's just institutes, surely? Guy's headmaster said he would certainly have gained a place at *Oxford*.' The word Oxford invoked an upward lift in her otherwise flat voice.

Alice, who was sitting beside Ben, looked at him, half expecting he would say something awful. His face had a raw, startled look; he blinked rapidly as though his eyes were stinging. Alice thought perhaps he was remembering his mother, who had scrimped and saved to give him a good education. She hated Mrs Immingham.

Guy intervened awkwardly, 'Anyway, I'm not going to university.'

'But you *could* have gone to Oxford; the headmaster said so.' She turned to Ellen and announced, much as a biologist might have introduced a new strain in the human species, 'Guy is going to be an *accountant*.'

'I'm going to have six months in America before I get down to swotting,' Guy said, trying to change the subject. 'We have relatives in Tennessee.'

'Ben's great-great-uncle led the march through Georgia!' Alice said breathlessly before Mrs Immingham could tell them about Tennessee.

Ellen, who had no intention of taking an interest in Guy's plans now that Ben's achievement had been dismissed, said to Mrs Immingham, 'I'm going to prepare a good Cornish tea for you. Alice says you're staying at the Cotters' guest house and I know they don't feed you very well there. He's a dry old stick twice her age. Every so often they have a row and she goes off to her mother for a few days. Then he has to do the cooking as well as everything else, poor man.'

Mrs Immingham said, 'They have never had a row while *we* have been staying there.'

'She'll break out one of these days and then there'll be blood in that house.' Ellen spoke in the dry, matter-of-fact tone which she reserved for such pronouncements and then, being unwilling to draw the veil of the future further aside, departed for the kitchen accompanied by Alice, who was too disturbed to stay behind.

Mr Immingham took advantage of his wife's affronted silence to say to Joseph, 'You were with the Hain Steamship Company, I understand?'

'Nigh on fifty years.'

'Ship's engineer, I believe? A cousin of mine was first mate with the Ellerman Lines. I wonder if you ever came across him – Jasper Immingham?'

Mrs Immingham found voice to correct this. 'Your cousin was in the *Merchant Navy*.'

Mr Immingham said mildly, 'The Hain Steamship Company is Merchant Navy, my dear.'

Mrs Immingham shook her head. 'There's some difference, I do know that. They were *big* boats your cousin was on, and they went to the *Far East*.'

Ben, who had been looking at her with increasing contempt, gave a snort of laughter.

Guy said to Joseph, 'It must have been a wonderful life. I have always wanted to go to sea.'

'You've never said that before.' There was distress in Mrs Immingham's eyes. 'It's not the kind of life which would have suited you at all.'

'In the age of sail, I meant,' Guy amended.

'Oh, that's different.' She was mollified; even so, her eyes strayed momentarily to the window, where a few sailing boats could be seen bobbing about in the harbour.

Ben got up and strolled to the window.

Mr Immingham and Joseph began to talk about the way in which the sailor's life had changed since the coming of steam, and Guy listened to them, only occasionally contributing a remark. From time to time he glanced at Ben. He knew he had made a bad impression, and wanted a chance to redeem himself. Eventually, he got up and joined Ben at the window. 'We come to St Mawes every year,' he said. 'Have you found the good places to swim from?'

Ben, whose time had been occupied with the tribe and the cinema, had to admit he had not.

'We must have a day out together,' Guy said. 'I assume you are a swimmer.'

The challenge was unmistakable and was duly accepted. By the time Ellen and Alice came in carrying trays, it had been agreed that they would meet next day.

Mrs Immingham ate hardly anything, which necessitated her husband and son eating more than was good for them. Her conversation centred on the affairs of the family, which she appeared to regard as of unique interest. When she spoke of her husband as 'an *accountant* and he works in *Holborn*', one might have supposed this to be the only coming together of Holborn and accountancy; while the possession of a house in Maple Road, Shepherd's Bush, was something to which few could aspire. Ben sat silent and dour.

When they left, Mr Immingham courteously praised Ellen's saf-fron cake, and she insisted on packing a substantial wedge for him to take with him. Guy reminded Ben of their engagement for the next day and Ellen, who was annoyed with the Imminghams for being so superior, said, 'And you can take Alice with you. She is a splendid swimmer; I wouldn't be suprised if she wasn't better than the pair of you.'

The next day the three of them set out together. They walked to the far end of the beach where there were few people. The sun was shining in a cloudless sky, and the sand was hot beneath their feet. Alice felt less at ease than usual. She found it difficult to know what to say to Guy, who seemed to her to be very 'deep' because he did not talk a lot.

Once they had settled themselves, they did not go into the sea immediately but sunbathed. Divested of his smart flannels and blazer, Guy looked rather defenceless: his long, thin body was white, like a plant deprived of sunlight. Ben was more muscular, his body hard and hairy. After they had been sitting for half an hour, Guy had to put his towel around his shoulders. 'I burn easily,' he said apologetically. The two young men talked. Guy was at a loss as to how to strike the right note with Ben, while Ben was indifferent to the impression he made on Guy.

When eventually they decided to swim, Guy said loftily to Alice, 'You can sit and guard our clothes.'

'I'm not Badger,' she protested. 'I'm coming in, too.'

'You're not to swim out too far,' Guy told her, and looked to Ben for support. He had little idea how to behave with people younger than himself.

Ben said, 'If you get into trouble, we shall leave you to drown.'

'Granny says I'll be as good as either of you and I bet I am,' she retorted, and to prove it she ran into the water, not stopping until it was up to her waist. They followed slowly, seeming reluctant to commit themselves. She plunged in and came up gasping at the shock of the water on her burning shoulders. 'It's lovely!' Ben waded in until he was breast high in water, then lashed out in a fierce crawl which sent up showers of spray. Guy began a leisurely breaststroke. For a time, Alice kept at Guy's side, then she turned over and began to do backstroke. After a while she floated, staring up at the blue sky, feeling happier than she had ever felt in her life. Before, there had always been anxious people on the shore shouting at her not to go too far. She had, however, a strong sense of self-preservation and kept a weather eye on the coast; at the moment when she judged she had reached her limit, she raised herself, treading water, and shouted, 'I'm going back now.' It was Ben who was swimming close to her; Guy was a long way ahead.

Alice towelled and changed into her frock. How good life was! She felt the warm, salt goodness of it across her shoulderblades, tingling on her legs; the wonder and mystery of it whispered across the sand, and she felt it welling between her toes as she walked to the sea's edge to rinse the sand out of her bathing costume.

Soon, Ben came wading towards her, breathing with difficulty. 'Wasn't that lovely?' she said. 'I feel tingly all over.'

He walked past her without replying and, snatching up his towel, buried his face in it. Alice though he was not well, but when eventually he began to dry himself, still refusing to speak, she realized he was angry.

Guy returned a quarter of an hour later. 'Good old Alice!' he said, a shade too boisterously. 'You're a remarkably good swimmer for your age.'

Ben turned over, propping his face on his folded arms. Guy stretched out in the sun. He did not seem at all winded. Alice thought now nice he was, innocently enjoying his triumph but not really crowing.

They were all tired and lay for a time without speaking, listening to the waves hissing on the sand. It was very peaceful. A motor launch moved slowly across the bay, white patterns of spray forming in its wake, lethargic as marshmallow.

After another half-hour, Ben sat up and said cheerfully, 'Who's for ice cream? State your preferences.'

'Get a paper, too,' Guy called after him when he went away to fetch their orders. 'I want to see who has won the Davis Cup.'

Guy and Alice watched him walk away. 'He started off so well,' Alice said. 'Did you think he would win?'

'Not thrashing about and sending up all that spray.'

'I'm sorry he was such a bad sport; burying his face in the sand.'

'Literally biting the dust.' Guy sounded happy. But as he watched Ben returning, there was a certain wistfulness in his eyes. He would have been very distressed had he lost the contest, but he would never have shown it, and he was a little envious of Ben's ability to show his feelings, and more than a little envious of his ability to shake off his defeat so soon.

'It has to be the *News Chronicle*,' Ben said, handing the paper to Guy. 'Alice has to check up on Lobby Lud.'

' "Perry beats Merlin!" ' Guy read. 'We've won. Hurray!'

'Listen to this!' Ben exclaimed. In a side paragraph it was reported that the Nazis had established the first Institute of Racial Hygiene, which was to be consulted by engaged couples to see whether their choice of partner was favourable in the racial hygiene sense. Married couples would be advised before deciding to have children. Dr Karl Astel, in opening the Institute, said that responsibility towards race, and not love, should be the guiding motive for marriage. Ben read the paragraph aloud. 'How's that for romance, Alice?'

'Two of my friends are on holiday in Germany now.'

'I don't suppose the Institute of Racial Hygiene would worry about them; they're racially pure.'

'Katia's half-Jewish.'

'Poor Katia! No Gary Cooper for a husband!'

'I've been thinking about that film, and the lovers being divided by the war.'

'You have?'

'My ancestors were in the packet service, and perhaps your ancestors on the American side were privateers. We should have been on different sides then.'

'My maternal great-grandmother was in service,' Guy said cheerfully, and then looked uneasy, feeling he had let his mother down.

'That's great!' Ben said. 'She works up at the big house and the wicked squire takes advantage of her; and her hotblooded lover kills him and has to flee the country, so he signs aboard the Falmouth brig (smuggling her aboard) and somewhere off Newfoundland an American privateer attacks them . . . Are you getting this down, Alice? You're the one that's going to write it. Where does Gary Cooper come in?'

'Not as a privateer.'

'No? Well, we'll have to get them all shipwrecked. Then, outlined against the skyline, this lean, lanky figure appears on horseback . . .'

'The Virginian!' Alice exclaimed.

'And it all ends happily,' Ben said.

They stayed until the sun went down. Ben had recovered his good humour completely by this time. The green hills beyond the bay were darkening as they walked beside the sea singing,

' "Sherman's dashing Yankee boys will never reach the coast . . ." '

8

The summer came to an end. Katia and Daphne returned from Germany where their paths had not crossed. There seemed even less likelihood of their becoming friendly. Katia reported that the Germans were being asked to boycott Jewish-owned department stores; this was very bad for her grandparents, who owned a chain of shoe shops.

'The Germans are jealous of anyone who makes money,' she said. 'They are too stupid to make it themselves.'

Her grandparents' wealth meant a lot to Katia, who spent most of the year in straitened circumstances which must on no account be acknowledged. Jacov had found his way of dealing with this and the twins lived in a world of their own, but Katia was confused and angered by the contradictions in her life.

Daphne dismissed Katia's fears. 'My father says Hitler has a lot of sound ideas,' she told Alice as they walked home after a game of tennis in Acton Park. 'He heard him speak at an open air rally.' She stopped and pointed at a greengrocer's stall. 'Pomegranates! We must have one.'

When they had bought a pomegranate each, Daphne said, 'Why do you take so much notice of Katia?'

'It's not just Katia,' Alice said. 'My father thinks Hitler is bad.'

'Why?' Daphne bit into her pomegranate.

'He wants to get rid of people.'

'Only gypsies and useless people like that.'

Alice could not think what to say in the face of this lack of sensitivity. Then she noticed that Daphne was throwing away the seeds of the pomegranate. 'Daphne, what are you doing?'

'I don't like the pips.'

'But there's nothing else.'

'I can't help it; I don't like them.'

Alice, who didn't like anything about a pomegranate except its name and the fact that she never had one at home, munched in silence. She wished the people she loved could get on with one another better.

Claire was having the same problem in a more extreme form. She had made a bosom friend at Crusader camp. Alice was able to sustain several friendships at the same time; but Claire could not do this. Each friendship was exclusive and tended as a result to break down, since few could equal her capacity for singleminded devotion. Judith warned her about this tendency, but to little avail – it was as much a part of Claire's make-up as red hair and freckles. In answer to her complaints that her friends were unfaithful, Judith would say, 'You ask too much of your friends, Claire. You mustn't always expect them to behave and feel like you.'

'But I do expect that.'

It seemed she had found what she expected in Maisie Richards. Maisie, a scholarship girl, was a form higher than Claire, and they had not been friendly until they met at Crusader camp.

Maisie had told Claire about her working-class family, who had no time for religion. 'It's the same as voting Conservative to my Dad.' They had talked a lot about this, and prayed for the conversion of Maisie's family. Claire had told Maisie how upset she was because Alice no longer wanted her, and they had prayed about that, too.

When they returned to Shepherd's Bush, Claire visited Maisie and was distressed by what she saw. The house was small, and Claire felt frightened by the proximity of people and furniture in the tiny overcrowded rooms. The garden in her own home was treated as another room in the house, used and tended; but here it was a waste area in which wood and coke, the handlebars of a bicycle, a broken handcart and other mechanical failures, had been dumped. Mr Richards, who was unemployed, sat in his shirtsleeves staring at the empty kitchen grate, and did not raise his head when Maisie and Claire came into the room.

Maisie took Claire up to the room which she shared with her younger sister and which, to Claire, seemed little more than a cupboard. 'The beds weren't made,' she told Alice later. 'And the chamber-pot was full of number two. I thought I was going to be sick.'

The stairs were uncarpeted. There were no pictures on any of the walls, and there were no flowers about the house. Flowers were very important to the Fairleys. Every Friday Claire saw her father come home with a bunch of flowers, which he presented to her mother with a joke about its being his 'peace offering'. It was hard to imagine what peace offering would be acceptable to Mrs Richards, who raised her voice whenever she spoke, and always seemed to be angry.

Judith disapproved of the intensity of this new friendship. She hoped the attraction would pass, but as the autumn term wore on it seemed that Claire had found a friend whose devotion equalled her own.

There were arguments at Christmas. Claire painted a desolate picture of the way in which Maisie would have to pass Christmas Day. 'They won't go to chapel, and there won't be any decorations or turkey or . . .'

Judith was adamant. Alice and Louise could not have friends on Christmas Day and neither could Claire. Christmas Day was given over to the family – including Grandmother Fairley, Aunt May and Ben – and six of the old folk from the chapel.

Louise took Claire's part. 'If Maisie can't come, I don't see why we have to have Ben.'

Since he came to London, Ben had been a welcome visitor at the Fairleys' home. Stanley Fairley enjoyed having masculine company about the house, and Judith had suggested that Ben might like to live with them. He preferred, however, to remain in his digs in Camden.

'I'll be better off on my own,' he had told Judith. 'I've got to study.'

'Don't overdo it. All work and no play makes Jack a dull boy.'

'All the Jacks I know are going to be dull because they were content to stay where they were and play.' University acceptance was the second great achievement of Ben's life: getting his scholarship had been the first. He was moving well ahead of his contemporaries at home, and he wasn't fool enough to slacken his pace when he had a commanding lead.

'He means to make people take account of him,' Judith thought, and liked him for it. Louise disliked him for the same reason.

On Christmas morning Ben arrived while Mr Fairley and the girls were at chapel. He made himself useful to Judith in the kitchen. She could tell from the unfussy way he set about the small tasks she entrusted to him that he had been used to helping his mother. She wondered whether now was the time to have a talk with him about Lizzie; but it was difficult to know what to say, particularly as she hadn't liked her.

Ben, in fact, was thinking how much Judith reminded him of his mother as she had been before hard work and illness wore her down. He went into the hall to put a piece of holly over the mirror. The door of the sitting-room was ajar, and he could see that the fire was alight. He stood in the doorway, observing the flames reflected on the long wall; and the neat preparedness of the room with bowls of nuts and boxes of dates, sugared almonds and Turkish delight upon the side tables, the piano open with music on the rack. The feeling of love and family closeness oppressed and confused him. He thought of Judith with resentment, because life had been so much kinder to her than to his beloved mother. Yet he was half in love with her and jealous of Stanley. He hated Louise, who would come in at any moment and draw the dancing firelight to herself. She, more than any of the others, made him aware of his emotional inexperience.

He felt an urge to run out of the house and get some space around him. But it was too late even for flight into the garden, because he could hear Stanley and the girls coming up the path. He was drawn into the ceremony of present-giving: at least he had come well prepared for that.

At dinner even Grandmother Fairley, who sighed over Christmases past, ate heartily and had two helpings of Christmas pudding. Claire, however, maintained an air of tragedy. In the afternoon she shut herself in her room, because she and Maisie had agreed to put aside a time when they thought about each other. She was not, however, proof against the enchantment of charades. This was the one theatrical entertainment permitted in the Fairley household. The dressing-up trunk was brought out and its treasures re-examined; mother-of-pearl fans and painted parasols, lace shawls and little sequin bags, long black taffeta skirts (there was a preponderance of black, as many items had been donated by Grandmother Fairley), white kid gloves which reached above the elbow and had little pearl buttons to draw them tight at the wrist, straw hats decorated with cherries, and a feather boa which had to be handled carefully, because it was moulting so badly.

Whatever the word chosen, the scenes enacted reflected the spirit of Punch and Judy rather than Christmas, and Claire and Ben were particularly uninhibited in their performances.

On Boxing Day evening the Fairley children had a party to which the Vaseyelins were invited, together with Guy, and Daphne, Angus and Cecily Drummond.

'Why couldn't I have Maisie?' Clare complained to Alice.

'Because if Maisie came you wouldn't take any notice of Cecily.'

'At least Maisie's father hasn't got another woman.'

'It's the first time we've been allowed to have a party on Boxing

Day. You mustn't do anything to spoil it, or we'll never have another.'

The party went well. The Drummonds were a great success: Daphne had an instinctive social sense which enabled her to get everything right without making any effort, Cecily was polite and anxious to please, while Angus was adjudged by Louise to be 'rather sophisticated'. Alice was proud of them. Ben and Jacov engaged in lively conversation on a wide range of subjects, Ben showing off shamelessly and Jacov matching his mental gymnastics without apparent difficulty. Guy, who always experienced a compulsion to adjust his personality to the requirements of the company in which he found himself, watched them with a certain amount of envy. Louise, who had also been watching them, said to Guy, 'I wouldn't have expected those two to get on; they are so different.'

'I was thinking they were rather similar. Both a bit clever.'

'Ben talks out of the top of his head.' She shrugged Ben aside as not worthy of interest. 'Jacov makes me feel there are things he knows that I don't know.'

'What sort of things?'

'Dark things.'

As the party continued, Alice began to feel lonely. Claire had reconciled herself to Maisie's absence, and she and Cecily were sitting in a corner whispering secrets. Daphne was being mildly provocative to the Vaseyelin twins, and Ben was arguing with Jacov. Louise and Guy were sitting on the rug by the hearth, roasting chestnuts. As Alice watched, he leant forward and poked one chestnut free, then he peeled it and offered it to Louise. She opened her mouth like a soft, downy bird, and he broke off a piece and fed it to her. In the glow of the flames, they looked warm and very happy. Louise said to him, 'Can you see the gypsy in the fire?' Alice wondered why Louise always saw a gypsy in the fire. As she watched Louise pointing, and Guy pretending to see – although it was obvious he couldn't really – she felt an odd pain in her tummy. She looked round the room. There was no one here who was particular to her. She had never hitherto felt this as a loss, but now it began to matter. Katia would not speak to her, because Daphne had been asked to the party and she was now talking to Angus Drummond in a loud, showing-off voice. The sophisticated Angus looked a bit alarmed, which wasn't surprising since she had bushed her dark gold hair so that she looked heathen as a Hottentot, and her eyes fairly popped out of their sockets in their attempt to rivet his attention.

Across the room, Alice could see her mother looking at her. The last thing she wanted was for her parents to feel sorry for her because she had been left out. She got up and went out of the room, coughing as if she had a piece of one of the chestnuts she hadn't been given caught in her throat. She had a drink of water in the kitchen, and then studied herself in the hall mirror. She had parted her hair in the middle and secured it with pink bows, which stuck out like extensions to her ears; a pink velvet band across the top of her head connected the ears and compounded the silly, pantomime effect. Her dress, the pattern for which she herself had chosen, had tucks and pleats in all the wrong places. She returned to the sitting-room, where her absence appeared to have passed unnoticed.

They were about to play charades. In a surge of self-pity, she thought how all the other girls would enjoy letting themselves go and looking ugly, because they knew inside themselves that they were attractive – even Cecily seemed quite pleased with herself today. Jacov had produced a brown paper bag and was taking something from it; he spoke in his most foreign way, as if he was making a speech, 'Our contribution to the dressing-up trunk, which you have often so generously shared with us!' He took out of the bag a peacock-blue shawl studded with ruby and amethyst beads, unpatterned, as though jewelled dust had been blown across it at its making. The thing was quite dazzling in its beauty: whoever conceived it was a foreigner to sober English notions of unpretentious good taste, and it looked strange and exotic in the Fairley's homely sitting-room. It was obviously old because Alice, who was now sitting on the piano stool close to Jacov, could smell the stale perfume which hung about it – but this only added to its enchantment. It was old because it was the Arabian nights, the desert sky into which God had tossed the stars . . . it was . . . oh, she would think of other things when she wrote about it in her diary at night. Perhaps Louise might let her take it up to her bedroom if she promised not to crumple it. Alice looked at Louise, rosy in the firelight, eyes shining: beyond a doubt, the shawl must be hers.

Louise looked at the shimmering silk in admiration but, confident that life would bless her, she was neither acquisitive nor competitive, and did not stretch out a hand. Guy, however, looked at the shawl and then at Louise as though it already adorned her; and Alice felt the pang in her stomach again, but sharper this time. She said, 'It will go with Claire's hair, won't it?' It was one of her few moments of pure spite, and as Claire's face lit up she got no pleasure from what she had done, and would have spoilt things for Claire, too, had she seen her way to it.

Then Jacov had one of his unaccountable lapses. It had been noted before that he seemed on occasions to suffer from a defect of vision, which made him see things quite differently from normal people like the Fairleys and their friends. He had, moreover, the disturbing ability to fracture their clarity and impose on them his own distorted impressions. Now, easily and unselfconsciously, as though performing an act they were all awaiting, he took up the shawl and, turning so that he stood behind her, laid it around Alice's shoulders. 'Alice is to be its custodian.'

Alice sat dumbfounded with the glory of the shining thing about her. Although in fiction she relished the moment when the self-effacing heroine is honoured by the hero to the chagrin of those who judged themselves better qualified to receive his attentions, she now discovered in herself a strong aversion to being thus singled out. It was not something for which her life had prepared her, being a middle child at home and a middling performer at school. Not only was she unwilling to accept this undreamt-of gift, but she rather resented the threat to her middlingness, and felt a need both to question the motives of the giver, and her own worthiness to receive. Jacov must surely know that of all the girls present she was the least suitable, not being the youngest, or the most beautiful, and not having either the style or the confidence to wear such a gorgeous thing. He was making fun of her.

Yet it was not mockery which most troubled her. It was an unfamiliar, prickly sensation occasioned by the feel of his hands laid on her shoulders; light though the touch was, she was aware of each fingertip, and it seemed as though the gesture as well as the shawl was a gift to her. Alice felt an impulse to sink down beneath this gentle pressure, overwhelmed by so much individual attention.

Her mother said, breaking the surprised silence, 'Alice will take care of it. Alice always takes good care of things.'

They were all going to be kind about it, and she hadn't earned the kindness. Above all, she hadn't earned the shawl. If anything, it was a reward for spite and envy! She smoothed it over her wrist. The material was so fine that even the movement of her soft flesh against it produced a slight friction. It was altogether too exquisite for her. She did not know where to look.

Ben said, looking at Louise, 'Alice should have the prize; she is a nice, modest girl.'

Louise said, 'Alice has a beautiful nature. She's not one of those people who are always getting at other people.'

It was so unexpected, so unsuitable and so undeserved . . . Oh, the very un-ness of it! She wanted to run out of the room and hide herself.

Her mother said, 'It is most generous of you and your family, Jacov. Alice is so pleased she can't speak.'

When the party was over, Alice put the shawl away in a drawer and did not take it out again for many years.

9

The New Year did not begin auspiciously. Badger died on the morning of the first of January and the family stood round, weeping, while Stanley Fairley buried him in the plot at the end of the garden where Smut, the black cat, was now buried. 'He won't like that,' Louise said.

'All are reconciled in Heaven,' her father answered. But he felt melancholy without the dog. It was a grey, smoky day; fog had been forecast. The rag-and-bone man's raucous cry came to his ears as he returned to the house; and soon he saw him pushing his cart in the company of a man from the chapel who had recently lost his job, a decent fellow now looking sadly defeated. He sat down at his desk, and wondered what was coming to the world. They should bring back Lloyd George, he thought.

Alice pressed her nose against the pane of her bedroom window, and hoped the fog wouldn't get bad before she went out in the afternoon. Miss Bellamy was taking a small party of girls to the National Gallery, and afterwards they were invited to her flat for tea. Alice thought of Christmas as 'the dead of winter', and was always dismayed to realize with the coming of January that the worst of the winter lay ahead. This year, however, the sense of anticlimax was not quite so hard to bear. Christmas had offered rather too much. As she stood by the window, Alice was looking forward to the outing, not so much for any cultural benefits which might accrue from it, as for the pleasure of being with Katia. Katia could be relied upon to draw so much attention to herself that she provided a screen in whose shelter Alice could once more pursue her own activities in blessed anonymity.

By noon, the day looked no different from any other dull January day, and Alice was allowed to set out. The afternoon passed pleasantly enough. Alice and Katia giggled at the big women in the Rubens paintings; accustomed to Hollywood standards of beauty, it was difficult to understand what motivated painters in their choice of model. They tried to guess which Gainsborough lady did the bowing for Gainsborough films, and stared puzzled at a portrait by Goya until Alice exclaimed, 'She's like you!' Katia made a vulgar noise. Yet the portrait hinted not so much at a resemblance as a possibility. In contrast with the neatness of many of her schoolmates, Katia seemed rather coarse; but the potrait showed what she might become – a handsome woman, and passionate.

When they came out of the National Gallery the fog had become dense, and it was not possible to see across Trafalgar Square. Philippa decided they must all go home and come to her flat on another occasion.

'I don't want to go home,' Katia said as they walked disconsolately in the direction of Leicester Square. 'Let's have tea.'

Before they reached Lyons Corner House they passed a cinema. The film showing was *The Bowery* with Wallace Beery and George Raft. The combination of George Raft and the Bowery could surely mean only one thing; here was Alice's chance to see the America of the gangster era which must pass away now that Prohibition had been repealed. 'It will be almost historical in a few years' time,' she argued.

'I don't care about history.' Katia studied the stills, and Alice watched her anxiously. Katia was very particular. She wrote to film stars for photographs, and was usually rewarded. In the evenings, Alice had sometimes waited at the garden gate with Katia to see whether the postman was carrying any large envelopes.

'What do you *say*,' Alice had asked recently. 'To the men, I mean.'

'I told Clark Gable I was sorry for him having to play opposite Carole Lombard and I said I could have done the love scenes better. I sent him a picture of myself.'

'You sent *your* picture to Clark Gable? I bet he preferred Carole Lombard.'

'She hasn't got any breasts.'

'You don't *act* with your breasts!'

'I act with all of me. If I played opposite Clark Gable, I wouldn't stand there like a lamp-post when he touched me.' Katia's flesh had quivered so violently that Alice had visualized Clark Gable's hands laid upon places where the Hays Office would never have allowed them to be.

Katia, who was looking at the stills without enthusiasm, said, 'Is this the one there was all that fuss about because he ripped her dress?'

Alice said, 'Yes.' She had no idea whether this was true, but it looked the kind of film where anything might happen.

They had a disagreement, because Katia wanted to sit downstairs. Alice's mother always insisted on sitting in the circle, and Alice imagined that – quite apart from people eating oranges – something nasty would happen if she sat in the stalls.

'If I'm going to get the tickets, we're going downstairs,' Katia said, well aware that the woman in the box office would never admit Alice to an 'A' film unaccompanied.

Alice said, 'I'll pay the extra. I had money from Grandma for Christmas.'

This was a much grander cinema than the one in Falmouth; it had a big, winding staircase on which four or five people could have ascended side by side. Before they reached the top, they could hear the clatter of crockery and the sound of voices; people were having tea in the cinema restaurant which was sited in the lounge adjoining the entrance to the auditorium.

The lights were on inside, and the usherettes were leaning listlessly against the wall. Alice and Katia sat at the end of a row sufficiently far from the entrance not to be troubled by people coming and going. Soon after they sat down a man came and sat by Alice, which was odd as there were many unoccupied seats. When the lights went down, she felt his fingers on her knee; obviously in the West End the circle was no more free of vice than the stalls. She got up. Katia said, 'What *are* you doing?'

'We're going to move,' Alice hissed at her.

'I don't want to move. If I go any further forward, my eyes don't focus.'

'We've got to move.' Alice began to struggle past her; while they were wrestling, the man got up and walked away.

'You should have stuck a pin in him,' Katia said when Alice explained.

Katia concentrated on the screen. Alice closed her eyes and tried to prepare herself for the experience she was about to receive. Soon, she would enter that forbidden world she had glimpsed in trailers. A woman, wearing a backless evening dress with a fox fur slung across her shoulders, would walk through a crowded nightclub, a sad, disdainful expression on her face, and all eyes would turn to follow her, conveying a sense of expectation heightened by an almost unbearable awareness of imminent danger. There would be shots of a man and a woman gazing at each other, and the lowering of eyelids, the twist of a mouth, would speak volumes in a language Alice did not yet understand but desperately wished to learn. And surely in the

Bowery there would be tenement blocks with fire escapes where people slept at night because it was too hot indoors; and there would definitely be narrow streets from which a man, walking half in shadow, would emerge at a crossroads, glance nervously from side to side, rush forward – and then, from nowhere, the fast car . . . She had seen it all in trailers, but had never had the opportunity to witness the sequence of events which led to the lowering of the eyelids, the words spoken out of the corner of the mouth, the fleeing figures, the murderously-driven car. It wasn't the happy endings which made films so appealing to Alice; it was the possibility of things going unimaginably wrong. She felt sick with excitement when the change in the music heralded the arrival of the big picture.

She opened her eyes and immediately became aware that the cinema seemed to be full of dirty cotton wool; several people were coughing badly. The censor's certificate had come up, but the words *The Bowery* could barely be seen. A small figure appeared by a corner of the screen. It was the manager. He said that because the fog was so bad it would be impossible to show the film.

Alice was overcome with rage and disappointment. It was not until they had, at Katia's insistence, been reimbursed, and had moved out of the foyer, that it dawned on her that London was at this moment providing drama on a scale to rival the goings-on in the Bowery. The buildings on the other side of the street, the street itself, even the pavement on which they stood, had been obliterated, but nearby a great wall loomed out of the fog, and very faintly they could see two fuzzy lights. People screamed and pushed back into the cinema foyer as a two-decker London bus edged along the pavement and came to a halt only a foot from the cinema's sweets and cigarettes kiosk. 'You're on the pavement,' the trapped assistant shrieked at the driver. In a moment, he could be heard shouting, 'I'm not going any further!' and soon ghostly shapes detached themselves from the bus.

'How are we going to get home, my man?' A woman's voice. 'I have to get to Hampstead.'

'Not on this bus, lady.'

'Let's go upstairs and sit in the lounge,' Katia said.

'But they'll expect us to buy something to eat, and anyway, we've got to get home. Mummy and Daddy will be terribly worried.'

A car crawled along a few feet from them; a man in evening dress crouched on the running-board directing the driver.

Alice said to the man in evening dress, 'You're on the wrong side of the road.'

'Are we? Thanks most awfully.' He shouted to the driver, 'Whoah!'

Light flickered, and the figure of a man carrying a hurricane lamp slowly emerged from the fog, a bus crawling behind him.

'I'm afraid we seem to be in your way,' the man in evening dress told him pleasantly. Perhaps the conductor of the bus had been carrying the hurricane lamp for some distance, or perhaps he simply did not like people in evening dress; whatever the reason, his reply fell somewhat short of the courtesy which one benighted traveller might be expected to extend to another. Alice and Katia edged away. They stood in the doorway and discussed their situation.

After a few moments the man in the bookshop opened the door and said, 'Why don't you come in?' The notice outside the shop said CLOSED.

'We're all right, thank you,' Alice said warily.

'Fuck off, then!'

They moved away hurriedly. 'We're in Charing Cross Road,' Alice said. 'If we keep walking, we'll come to Tottenham Court Road tube station. The tube trains are bound to be running.'

'I don't want to go underground,' Katia said sharply.

Alice took her hand. 'Come on. Let's make an adventure of it.' She stepped boldly forward and tripped over a pile of papers which had been abandoned by a newsvendor.

Katia crouched beside her. 'Are you hurt?'

'I've got a hole in my stocking, and I think I've cut my knee.' People stumbled into them while Alice was binding a handkerchief round her knee.

'I don't like this, Alice!' Katia's voice was rising.

A man asked, 'Where do you want to go?' He sounded young and unperturbed.

'Tottenham Court Road tube station.'

'I'm going there. Hang on to my arm.'

Katia readily grabbed his arm, her good spirits restored. They moved forward slowly, unable to see one another; they could hear the sound of traffic quite close. The young man said, 'The first road we come to will be Shaftesbury Avenue at Cambridge Circus.' They shuffled along for what seemed to be an interminable time, their eyes smarting, their throats raw. Katia giggled and made constant ejaculations. As they came near to Cambridge Circus, light again penetrated the fog. A policeman on point duty was trying to direct the traffic with the aid of an acetylene flare. There were several abandoned cars in Shaftesbury Avenue, and they edged gingerly between them. This manoeuvring made them lose their way, and they found themselves on an island with no idea in which direction they should move. Katia, alternately excited by the presence of the young man and terrified by the feeling that a choking blanket had been thrown over her head, began to whimper. The young man said, 'If the bobby is in the middle of the road – and we'll hope he is – we want to go towards him and then veer to the left.'

'We'll be run over,' Katia protested.

'We may be run over if we stay here,' the young man said cheerfully. 'Onward and upward!'

They started forward again, Katia clinging to the young man's arm while he flourished an umbrella and Alice pawing the air with her free hand. They made contact with three cars, two pedestrians, a lamppost and a pillarbox, but as the traffic was now jammed because of the abandoned vehicles, they came to no harm. In this way, and with one or two changes of course, they came eventually to Tottenham Court Road tube station. Katia had stopped giggling; whenever she tried to take a deep breath, there was an odd whistling noise in her chest. Alice, who had wound her scarf round her mouth and nose, was not so badly afflicted, but her knee was throbbing.

'Which way do you go?' the young man asked.

'Shepherd's Bush.'

'I'm for Holborn. Will you be all right from here?'

'Yes, thank you,' Alice said politely.

They listened to his departing footsteps. 'It would have been nice to have seen him,' Katia said dejectedly.

'Take your chance.' The clerk in the booking office said sourly, 'Keep well away from the track.'

Katia hung back at the top of the escalator. 'Don't let's go down there, Alice.'

'Come on! We're nearly home!'

The platform was crowded. After five minutes a train came inching out of the tunnel; a guard shouted, 'Keep back! Keep back!' When the doors opened, Katia and Alice were swept up in an onward rush. Alice, clinging to Katia, felt herself lifted off her feet and hurled forward. She had not experienced such force since the time an Atlantic roller had plucked her up and flung her on the beach at Newquay. People had said how lucky she was to be tossed on the shore when the sea might just as well have sucked her into its great maw. She had not felt lucky, but terrified by the power that had had her in its grasp. She did not feel lucky now, the breath knocked out of her body, although there were people on the platform who had not managed to get onto the train.

When she had recovered herself, she said to Katia, 'We'll go down the centre of the carriage. There won't be so many people there.'

'We'll never get out!'

But Alice was more afraid of being spewed out at the next station, and she began easing her way towards the centre. 'Remember Miss Pym.' Miss Pym, their lacrosse mistress, always maintained that a good lacrosse player could get through any crowd. It was congested even in the centre. The train started, and proceeded in a series of jolts. The air was foul and the press of people alarming.

Katia said, 'I don't like this, Alice.'

Alice said, 'Look up, it's much better if you look up.'

Admittedly, visibility was a bit better, but the sight of the rounded roof above their heads reminded them that they were in a tunnel.

As the train rattled and shook, and people pushed and strained, Alice became aware of a sound which seemed to go on beneath all this activity – a deep roar, as of something monstrous awakened in the underground. She shook her head and rubbed her fingers in her ears. Katia was gripping her tightly. Alice looked at her, and saw that a change had come over her friend's face. It had become like a face in a dream, known and yet not known, the face of someone who was not quite a person. The eyes, of whose compelling power Katia so proudly boasted, seemed to get larger as Alice looked, but they were empty of intention, as though they had swallowed up all the people on whom Katia had ever played her game, and now the eyes had nothing to hope for. Alice said sharply, 'What's the matter, Katia?'

'I don't like this, Alice.'

'It's all right. We'll be at Oxford Circus soon.'

Alice recited the familiar names to herself: Oxford Circus, Bond Street, Marble Arch, Lancaster Gate . . . The train stopped at Oxford Circus. People fought to get to the door while others fought to get into the train. Alice could feel Katia trembling; there was a lot of Katia to tremble, and the vibration was unpleasant. Someone was screaming and a guard was shouting. Alice had never realized people could behave in this way, clawing one another like animals. She began to believe Katia was right, they would never get out, they would have to go to the end of the line; but that would only be Ealing Broadway, there was nothing dreadful about Ealing Broadway. She repeated 'Ealing Broadway' aloud. The familar words brought no reassurance. There was a blackness which seemed to surround the two of them, and she could not believe she would ever see Shepherd's Bush or Ealing Broadway. Panic threatened her. She tried to think of pleasant things. How lovely it had been walking by the sea's edge at Falmouth! But the goodness which had welled up between her toes now seemed a small thing against this blackness. She thought of her home, of the table laid with tea and toast and cup cakes, but instead of bringing comfort, the image of her family sitting down to tea filled her with desolation. If she were to cry out for help, no one would come, they would be too busy helping themselves to jam. The possibility of abandonment had never before entered her head; when she had a nightmare, she had only to cry out and there would be Claire, or her mother, at her side when she awoke. She prayed, 'Please, God, let me get home to Mummy and Daddy.' Bodies pressed in on her, tight-packed as a lost-property cupboard full of pieces of people, knuckles, shoulder-blades, elbows, chins.

The doors closed, jammed, opened, closed again. The train moved slowly. 'People will start getting out at Lancaster Gate,' she rallied Katia. 'And by the time we get to Holland Park it will be quite comfortable.'

It was less crowded, but it was not comfortable. They managed to ease their way towards the doors so that they would be in position when the train arrived at Shepherd's Bush. Here, there was a big crowd waiting, and as soon as the doors opened people surged forward. Katia and Alice were sucked into the foul mouth of the carriage. Alice, forgetting Miss Pym, used not only her shoulders, but elbows, knees and feet, to say nothing of every ounce of weight, to fight her way out. She reached the platform, triumphant and surprised by her own ferocity. The doors were closing. To her dismay, she saw that Katia had not managed to free herself. Katia's face stared at her, passive and ludicrously despairing. Yet what was there to despair about? There would be no crowds at Wood Lane. But such mischances always engender fear of a separation which will be longer than the journey back from the next station. Alice was intensely afraid. 'My friend!' she howled. 'My friend's in there!' She put a foot in the door; when the driver opened the doors, she caught hold of Katia's coat and tugged with all her might so that Katia fell out of the train and sprawled on the platform.

'Why didn't you push?' Alice shouted, panic making her angry.

'You've ripped my coat!' Katia snivelled. 'You've ripped out the sleeve.'

Alice squatted beside her. Now that it was over, her legs were shaking. Katia said, 'I'll be better in a minute. I don't mind about the coat. I don't mind about anything now I'm out of that train.'

'I still don't understand why you didn't push. You're pushy enough most of the time.'

Outside, the above-ground world had not yet reassembled itself, even the station-name was blotted out. Alice, never good at orientating herself, was unsure which way to turn. While they hesitated, a policeman loomed up and pointed them in the direction of The Askew Arms.

They got home safely after a long walk, and there *was* tea with toast and cup-cakes. Alice was allowed to sit by the fire and as she ate, warm in the glow of the flames, she felt ashamed of the horrible things which had come into her mind in the train. 'Whatever came over me?' she wondered, reaching for a cup-cake. Tomorrow, she would have forgotten about it.

10

In February, Grandmother Fairley had a stroke and went to stay with Aunt May in Notting Hill. Aunt May was quiet and gentle and loving, but all that Grandmother Fairley thought about was that Judith had not had her to stay. 'Oh, my son, my son, what have I done that he should treat me so?' she would ask, although he came to see her regularly.

Louise became angry about this. 'What's so special about a son? Why doesn't she care about her daughters?'

'Her mind is wandering,' Judith said.

'Her mind's as sharp as a tack. The moment you go out of the room she stops all that moaning and sighing; I've watched her in the mirror in the hall. She's a wicked old woman! You'd better not let me go to see her, because I shall tell her so.'

Louise was at odds with life. Many of her contemporaries were enjoying being in the sixth form, because they were treated by the staff as though they were adults. But Louise, not regarding the staff as adults, did not find that the more informal atmosphere compensated for having to work harder than she had ever worked before.

'You should be grateful for your opportunities,' her mother told her.

'I bet that's the kind of thing they used to say in the eighteenth century when they arranged a good marriage for their daughter! And things are no better now. In those days a woman had to get married; now she has to be educated. Either way, someone else decides what's good for her.'

'Is it Guy that is making you feel like this?'

'There you go again! There are just two possibilities: go to university and make a career for yourself; or get married.'

'If you don't want a career and you don't want to get married, what do you want?'

'I'm only seventeen. I don't have to have the whole of my life mapped out as though it had already happened, do I?'

'That's how life is, Louise. If we don't grasp our opportunities, they don't come again.'

'Is that why you married Daddy?'

'Don't be impertinent.' Judith was almost as edgy as her daughter.

'You asked me about Guy.'

Judith found the question difficult to answer. She had known that Stanley was the one who would change her life. Now, when she returned to Falmouth, she saw that the lively boys she had grown up with had allowed their small businesses to drain their resources; they were spent forces, and their wives had the look of women whose husbands were no longer interested in them. She was proud of Stanley's intellectual alertness, and prouder still of his undiminished sexual energy. 'I thought we would suit each other very well,' she said in answer to Louise.

'But were you in love with him?'

'Oh, how you do go on about being "in love"! That sort of feeling doesn't last.'

'Doesn't last, you say! At the rate I'm going, I'll never have had it. Do you realize I've never been allowed to go to a dance?'

'Is that what this is leading up to? A dance?'

'Not exactly.' There was a pause while Louise marshalled her forces. 'St Bartholomew's Dramatic Society is doing *Dear Brutus* in the autumn, and they want me to play Margaret, the dream child. Why shouldn't I? Daddy can't find much wrong with *Dear Brutus*, can he?'

'You'll have to slim down before the autumn if you're to play a dream child.'

'Does that mean you'll ask him?'

'We'll see. There's sometime between now and the autumn. In the meantime, perhaps we can persuade Daddy to take us to the theatre.'

After this conversation, Judith found herself re-examining her own adolescence, arousing old yearnings which gave rise to new discontents. It was in this uneasy mood that she tackled Stanley later that week when they were sitting together after the children had gone to bed. She was aware of a certain pleasure in the prospect of combating his objections; a desire, in fact, to pick a quarrel.

She watched him reading the *Methodist Recorder*, innocently savouring the attack which he would make on one of the articles. She sat quietly for a few minutes, allowing her resentment to simmer. He moved and re-settled himself in his chair, like a log shifting comfortably in the fire. She said, 'Do you think the children would enjoy this *Richard of Bordeaux* the critics are so enthusiastic about?'

'*Richard of Bordeaux*?' Stanley lowered his paper and stared at her. His time alone with Judith was precious. So was his peace. He imagined it was understood between them that they sat in silence while he read the paper and she pursued her womanly chores: the silence of a companionship too deep for words was how he liked to think of it.

'It's on in the West End,' she continued to promote this extraordinarily irrelevant conversation. 'John Gielgud is in it and . . .'

'Yes, I have read about it,' he said testily. 'A highly romantic piece of special pleading for a thoroughly bad king.' His disapproval of the man was growing by the minute.

'You did agree to Louise seeing *Richard II*.'

'That was Shakespeare, and it was in her school syllabus.'

'When she goes to university, she will see things which aren't in her syllabus.'

He could scarcely believe that she intended to squander these precious moments talking about the school syllabus. He said, 'There will be a certain freedom, undoubtedly, and one that I would want her to experience. What she makes of it will be up to her. She will not have had bad examples set in her own home.' In case his briskness had not sufficiently emphasized that the conversation was concluded, he returned to his study of the *Methodist Recorder*.

Judith said sharply, 'Example is one thing, a refusal to allow her to begin to find her own way is another.'

'Her own way?' He was outraged both by the sentiment and the continued interruption of his reading. 'What is all this talk about finding her own way?'

'You found your own way, didn't you?'

She was looking quite flushed and angry, some woman's disturbance, he supposed. He said mildly, without – he prided himself – a hint of rebuke, 'That's different.'

'In what way is it different?' Her manner was almost belligerent. 'Because you are a man? How do you think of me, then? As a parcel handed over by my father to you at the altar?'

Sighing, he folded the paper and prepared to listen, though with an air of exaggerated meekness. 'If I ever thought that, I've spent the remainder of my days learning otherwise.'

'Louise will have to find her own way and you will have to be tolerant about it.'

'Tolerant!' This was too much. 'I don't think you could find anyone more tolerant than I am. But if what we are talking about is not tolerance but indifference, that is another matter. I am not prepared to walk through the streets of South Acton and come away tolerant about unemployment.' He was resorting to his usual practice of changing the subject so that he should be seen to be standing on firm ground. 'Nor am I prepared to tolerate the endless delays of this bungling government in its slum clearance programme; the degradation of human beings is a matter on which I shall ever be intolerant . . .'

'Can't you forget what is happening to the nation and think about what is happening in your own home just this once?'

'How can you say such a thing, Judith? I am simply arguing that . . .'

'I am suggesting an outing to the theatre, and you have to respond by talking about slum clearance programmes! We take them to the cinema; is the theatre so different?'

He picked up the poker and inserted the point in a log, twisting it round and round as he pondered this. Beneath his irascible exterior he was a vulnerable, rather shy man and the mechanics of theatre-going bothered him. He was most at ease in his house, his school and his chapel.

'A good deal more licence is allowed in the theatre,' he said, giving a particularly vicious twist to the poker.

'It doesn't sound as if the morals in this play are any worse than in the Ralph Lynn/Tom Walls farces we take the children to see.'

'These are live people,' he protested.

'What has that got to do with it?'

He was embarrassed at the prospect of seeing live people on stage behaving in an emotional and undisciplined manner. It was not so much that he disapproved of emotion, as that his own emotions were too easily aroused. The log broke apart and he contemplated it unhappily.

Judith said, '*I* should like to see *Richard of Bordeaux*. It would make a change.'

He stared at her in astonishment. 'A change? But you do so much, my darling.'

'What? What do I do? Name me one thing, apart from house-work.'

Her daily life being rather a mystery to him, he could only say, 'Well, there's the Women's Bright Hour . . .'

'The Women's Bright Hour!' Her face was reddened by firelight and her eyes flashed with scorn. 'Thank you, Stanley. Is that really how you think of me? Those boring women!'

'Good women in their way.'

'Boring in every other way.'

Stanley laid the poker down carefully in the hearth. 'If the thing's so popular we probably won't be able to book tickets.'

'You don't have to book for the pit.'

'I am not going to be seen queuing outside a theatre, you can put that out of your mind!'

'Louise and I will queue while you take Alice and Claire for a walk.'

It had been a tactical mistake to allow himself to get into an argument about the method of obtaining tickets.

They went to see *Richard of Bordeaux* one Saturday afternoon. Once he had dealt with the business of handing over the tickets, buying programmes and refusing tea in the interval, Stanley Fairley set himself to examine his fellow theatregoers. They did not, in his opinion, amount to much. Certainly, there were no women present who bore comparison with his wife and daughters. He settled more comfortably in his seat and examined the programme for errors.

Claire found the presence of real people on stage threatening, and her father advised her not to look when they became angry or emotionally distressed (there was rather a lot of emotional distress). Louise was enchanted by the theatre itself, the people around her, the safety curtain, the slow fading of the lights, the way in which the actors made their exits and their entrances, their gestures and their manner of wearing their costumes. Beside her, Alice sat so still she seemed scarcely to breathe; by the time it was over she was in love with John Gielgud – a love which was to last long after the hold of the silver screen had been broken.

Judith was not interested in the play, but she was very moved by the occasion. She felt, as she sat in the first row of the pit, surrounded by her family, that she had accomplished rather more than a visit to the theatre. They had taken a step forward, and life would not be the same again.

When they came out of the theatre, there were a lot of policemen about. The Blackshirts had been on the march. Fortunately, they did not discover this until the next day, and so they could discuss the play over supper.

II
═══

By the summer the activity of the Blackshirts had led to riots, and Miss Blaize thought it necessary to address herself to the problem.

'I have told you many times,' she said to the girls at assembly, 'that you should be prepared for leadership. I have asked, without a noticeable response, that you should not always choose the same people for form captain, because it is important that as many as possible should have the opportunity to lead.' She has in mind some quite horrid enterprise during the school holidays, Daphne thought – working in Bethnal Green or some other dreary place; when she asks for volunteers to stand up, I'm going to be one of those with a gluey seat. 'But as you grow older, it is likely that more of you will be led than will lead. You must never be led like sheep; even those who follow have their responsibilities. They must examine the quality of leadership, they must ask where it is that they are being led.' She's seen someone out with a boy, Katia thought; it's time I had a boy. She experienced an unholy upsurge of joy. 'However brilliant and compelling a man may be, there can never be an excuse for involving himself in activities which lead to gross public disorder. Mob violence is a terrible thing.' Her pupils, most of whom had experienced nothing worse than minor disorders on bonfire night celebrations, gazed at her politely while they tried to identify among their acquaintances any who might be described as compelling, let alone brilliant.

Miss Blaize, studying their inexpressive faces, thought that if she were to announce the imminent end of the world they would continue to look like this. Although she had done her best to inculcate in them qualities of self-discipline and composure, she regretted the absence of volatility. She herself found Mosley very compelling; had her life taken a different turn, she might have become one of his followers. There were volcanic powers in Miss Blaize. She returned to her room saddened by the inability of life to match itself to the grandeur of her needs.

'It's time we had a boy friend,' Katia said to Alice when they returned to their formroom.

'I don't want boys.' Alice was scornful; it was men like Gary Cooper and her new idol, Ralph Bellamy, who appealed to her.

'Boys are all right.' Daphne often talked about her exploits with boys which usually consisted of fights which she won. 'I punched him and he cried,' she would say. Recently she had been out with the vicar's son, but they did not fight. 'We play tennis. He's not very good.'

Miss Blaize's comments about riots had passed over the heads of her pupils, but an incident occurred a few days later which had more effect on those who witnessed it.

Cynthia Applestock, one of the more eccentric members of Alice's form, maintained that the daily round of school life was only tolerable if she could drive the mathematics mistress to the verge of tears by the end of each lesson. This was not the result of particular animosity, but rather part of a grand design. Every Commemoration Day the school sang 'Let us now praise famous men'. Cynthia said that this was one of the most exquisitely funny moments of her life, and doubted whether subsequently there would be anything to equal it. Certainly, it had a relevance of a kind for, as some are born to praise, so Cynthia seemed constitutionally formed to destroy what others construct. She went about her mission quietly, but with the dedication of one whose concentration never fails or falters, and whether spoiling play on the games field by constant misfielding, or delaying a rural science outing by losing one shoe on the railway track, she let no opportunity slip by. In the curriculum, mathematics offered her the most scope. For one thing, it was a subject which many pupils found difficult enough without its principles being turned inside out just as they were getting some grasp of them. And then there was Miss Punnett. A large, humourless woman, unable to deal effectively with the most harmless misdemeanour, she was never angry, only disappointed, sad, reproachful, forever appealing to better natures which her pupils did not possess. When she rebuked them individually, she put her face close to theirs and moisture sprayed from her wet mouth. She smelt of sweat-soaked wool. Cynthia, not being given to unnecessary exertion, disrupted Miss Punnett's lessons by the simple expedient of feigning bewilderment whenever a new formula was introduced. Mathematics being prone to formulas, there was ample occasion for bewilderment. Not only Miss Punnett, but her form-mates had come to dread the languidly raised arm which signalled that Cynthia had found a flaw in an equation which mathematicians of no mean repute had not hitherto found wanting.

In spite of Miss Punnett's unpopularity, there was something about the way in which Cynthia teased the woman which made the other girls uncomfortable. On one occasion, when Miss Punnett had left the room very close to tears, Daphne had said to Cynthia, 'When you've made her cry perhaps you'll be satisfied?'

'Oh no!' Cynthia had looked as surprised as was possible for a girl with such indolent features and no eyebrows. 'Hadn't you realized? The whole point is never actually to make her cry. This kind of enterprise requires very careful judgement; otherwise Miss Blaize would put a stop to it!'

'Sod you!' Cynthia was the one person who could needle Daphne. 'I don't know why you make such a fuss about Hitler,' she had once said to Alice, 'when you've got a little flower of evil like Cynthia right on your doorstep!'

The form as a whole suffered from Cynthia's 'enterprise', enduring long moral strictures from Miss Punnett, and sometimes missing break periods while she harangued them. Cynthia was unperturbed by their protests. In fact, it seemed she courted hostility as assiduously as others court popularity, and it was difficult to tell which was more important to her – the exasperation of her fellows or the torment of Miss Punnett. It was certain that she reserved her worst behaviour for days when it might pose a threat to some activity dear to her companions.

On this particular bright summer afternoon, the mathematics lesson was followed by a games period. Miss Punnett, unaware of this stimulus to Cynthia's creativity, stood facing the blackboard. The lesson had been punctuated by interruptions of which fire drill had taken up the most time, and Cynthia had so far been denied her form of sport. Perhaps it was this which led her to resort to tactics of a cruder nature than those she usually employed, or perhaps there was an element of hysteria which made itself felt when she found herself thwarted. Certainly, her languor seemed exaggerated to a point where a more alert teacher might have wondered about her health.

Miss Punnett, traditionally garbed in a rust-coloured sack loosely roped by a girdle, raised a hand to the blackboard, and the girls could see the sweat-bleached patch around the armpit. Katia put her fingers to her nose, but no one laughed. It was a sunny day and only ten minutes left of the lesson. Miss Punnett drew an octagon on the board and said, 'You should have a figure like mine.' Katia whispered, 'I'd sooner die!' and this time was rewarded by the merest ripple of laughter. Had Miss Punnett ignored it, the laughter would have died away without causing any disturbance; but she lacked judgement, and must make it the occasion for a lecture on manners. 'You are old enough to have learnt to consider the feelings of others. It is possible to be very hurtful to other people; I am not speaking of myself, of course . . .' Her pink face, quivering like an unfirm blancmange, gave the lie to this. The girls watched her with distaste.

When she had finished rebuking them, Miss Punnett asked Cynthia to clean the blackboard, hoping by this means to have the girl harmlessly employed. While Miss Punnett was returning homework to members of the form, Cynthia, who believed in using what opportunities the gods give, wrote on the board, 'Miss Punnett is a silly old trout'. Her form-mates were surprised. 'Silly old bag' would have been acceptable but 'trout' had a dash of style about it which seemed to give an air of adult authority to the statement. Miss Punnett, reacting with unaccustomed alacrity to the gaze of her pupils, turned round before the words could be wiped off the blackboard.

Until this moment Alice, and many others, had imagined that for every act of insurrection there was an appropriate response which could not be withheld for one instant. Retribution was an important part of their upbringing. They waited. In five minutes one of the prefects would be ringing the changing bell. Miss Punnett, purple-faced, stared at Cynthia, a trickle of saliva at one corner of her mouth; in spite of much evidence to the contrary, she believed that a reproving glance has a greater effect than words. Cynthia took advantage of the silence to wipe the message off the blackboard; she then returned to her desk as though nothing had happened.

Miss Punnett said in a hoarse voice, 'Leave the room, Cynthia; I will speak to you later.'

Cynthia appeared to toy with the idea. A ray of sunlight falling aslant the inkstained desk created no sensation of warmth in the girl. She had an overbred appearance with her ash-blonde hair, white eyebrows and thin, colourless lips, and at this moment, narrow shoulders hunched, looked as though she lacked the energy to move. Miss Punnett's glasses misted over, and her upper lip trembled. The girls wriggled in acute discomfort. At this rate, not only would they lose their games period, but probably swimming after school as well.

At the back of the room, Katia snorted with laughter and pressed a hand to her mouth.

Miss Punnett said, 'That girl who laughed is as guilty as this wretched girl.'

Cynthia slewed sideways. Initially, she did this in order to get a view of Katia; then, it must have occurred to her that this was the moment literally to turn things upside down.

The changing bell was rung clamorously. The girls shuffled their books. Miss Punnett was now afraid that if she dismissed the class Cynthia would walk out unpunished. She said, 'No one will leave the room,' and then, realizing that this was unlikely to advance her cause, added, 'until you have done as you are told, Cynthia.'

Cynthia, hanging out from her desk at an angle which invited collapse, yet maintaining her balance with the inconsequential ease of a circus performer, allowed the top of her forehead to touch the floor.

Miss Punnett came and stood by Cynthia's desk, sternly regarding the upside-down face. 'I have spoken to you, Cynthia.'

Cynthia said, 'Yes, I know you have, Miss Punnett. I am now meditating on what you have said.' Having come thus far, she probably realized it would be difficult to find a way back; certainly it would be tedious: the Winifred Clough Day School for Girls was unlikely to permit itself to be viewed from this angle again. Perhaps these thoughts and the rush of blood to the head were responsible for something hectic in her manner. 'I can see right up your hairy nostrils into your brain, Miss Punnett. Your brain is full of common denominators and terribly vulgar fractions, did you know that?'

Daphne got up. 'We have a games period now. Did you know *that*?' She came up to Cynthia, grasped fistfuls of hair and yanked hard. It was almost possible, looking at the long, thin, colourless girl, to see her as a recalcitrant weed which Daphne, legs set sturdily apart, had committed her strength to uprooting. Cynthia's fingers, like thin tendrils, clung to the desk with all the tenacity of a parasite. Daphne bared her teeth in a fierce little grimace, and put a knee to the small of Cynthia's back.

Cynthia cried out, 'Why can't you control your class, Miss Punnett?'

Slowly, her face reddening with effort, Daphne applied herself to her task, as unyielding and grimly determined as when she hauled for her side in a tug-of-war. 'I warn you, you're going to look as if you've got ringworm.' Gradually, with tremendous concentration, adjusting balance and grip when required, she addressed herself to the razing of Cynthia. Alice thought she had never seen such dedication in Daphne, and wondered what it was in Cynthia which could rouse her friend. The girls at the back of the room were standing up to watch the struggle. What was at stake, whether their right to a games period or to scalp one another when it took their fancy, they could not have said.

Miss Punnett, seeing she now had no chance of restoring order, uttered the ultimate threat, 'I shall fetch Miss Blaize.'

Cynthia screamed, 'Hurry up then, you daft cow!' This was the end of her resistance. A moment later, she broke away from Daphne and ran into the corridor, announcing her intention of slashing her wrists to two astonished sixth-formers and closely pursued by Miss Punnett.

Katia, eager to keep the excitement going for a little longer, said, 'She does have a razor blade to sharpen her pencils.'

Daphne said, 'It's blood she doesn't have.'

One or two girls thumped Daphne on the back, but she shook off their congratulations.

Twenty minutes later, when Miss Blaize came to speak to the form, she found the girls bent industriously over their exercise books.

'Who was the girl who laughed?'

Katia stood up.

'Were there any other girls who thought that what was happening was funny?'

Miss Blaize waited. She looked more awesome than ever. Her cropped dark hair had been slicked back, and the late sun highlighted features of the utmost severity. From their deep sockets, her eyes seemed to confront some appalling knowledge from which she was too resolute to turn aside; her lips were pursed and her mouth sunk in grim pain. It was the face of one who has looked on degrees of depravity mercifully hidden from most of mankind. As though mesmerized, several girls stood up. Alice and Daphne remained seated; Alice thought she had sufficient sins on her conscience without confessing to ones she had not committed, and Daphne thought, 'I'm not going to be jerked up and down like a yo-yo by this woman.'

An extraordinary change came over Miss Blaize. Pain was mercifully lifted from her. She became genial, and as she smiled at them it was as though she had it within her compass to feel affection, a quality they had not previously recognized in her. She began to talk and they felt a power encircling them, drawing them together. This, they were to understand, was not their headmistress, but a fellow human into whose being had been sewn the same incompatible instincts and desires, who felt the same pull of good and evil, who was as incapable as they of resolving the contest one way or the other. 'It goes on all our lives,' she said, not in her dramatic vein but in a quiet, matter-of-fact tone, 'and the sooner we accept this, the better for all of us.' She spoke then of an incident in her own past, not looking at them but towards the window, as though it opened into another world, and her voice – always a superb instrument of her moods – conveyed such an impression of pleasure and regret, sweetness and sorrow, that she held them under her spell although the incident she related was trivial enough. It was the early summer, and in her Sussex home her father was dying; in the last days of his illness it was necessary to employ a nurse, a good enough woman who fulfilled her duties to the letter but who was quite lacking in sensibility. She would insist on closing windows and drawing blinds, when all that the old man wanted was to look out to the hills. 'There are some people who can never raise their eyes to the hills, whose capacity for life is limited, and sometimes we find ourselves tempted to hate instead of pity them. One day when the nurse was particularly churlish, I thought, "What am I going to do about this? If I'm not careful I'm going to be very angry with her, and that won't help anyone." And do you know what I did? I made tea and took it up to her. When we are angry it is often best to let our hands have their way . . .' (Had she not been told of the use to which Daphne had put her hands? It was inconceivable that she could approve it.) '. . . to busy ourselves doing something practical and positive. We shall all meet people who anger us; and, more difficult perhaps, people whom we despise. We must be positive in our dealings with such people; otherwise we may be driven into bullying and tormenting. It is easier than you may imagine to become the tormentors of the weak and stupid.'

It was by now apparent that Miss Blaize had little respect for Miss Punnett, and when she left the room having given no punishment to the form as a whole, Daphne said, 'I bet Miss Punnett won't be coming back next term. Miss Blaize would never have talked like that otherwise.'

One or two people said, 'Good riddance', but without zest.

That afternoon at evening prayers, Miss Punnett sat among the staff, her face puffy and her eyelids swollen. Cynthia Applestock had been sent home, and she never appeared at the school again.

'What an old fraud Miss Blaize is!' Daphne exclaimed in the cloakroom. 'Talking to us about not bullying and then taking it out on poor old Punnett.'

'She wasn't much use, was she?' Alice said.

'She never did anyone any harm.' Alice was surprised to see that Daphne was really angry. 'I'm going to apologize to her.'

'Well, I'm not.'

Miss Punnett's unequal contest with Cynthia had left Alice with a question in her mind. What would have happened if Cynthia had persisted in her refusal to leave the room? Once, when she was a small child, Alice had dreamed that the Leaning Tower of Pisa was about to fall on top of the house. The dream itself was not important. What had been important was that when her mother had comforted her, it had dawned on Alice that her mother could not have prevented the Leaning Tower of Pisa from falling had it so decided. Until that moment she had imagined her parents as a tower of strength. Belief in authority had survived, however, because she saw it upheld in home, in chapel, in school, in the ordered streets around her home. Now, it seemed that authority depended on people like Cynthia being prepared to accept it. The maintenance of authority was obviously a more precarious exercise than Alice had imagined.

Authority, at another level, was under threat at home. Louise had told her father that she wanted to act in the next production of the St Bartholomew's Dramatic Society. It had now been decided that it would not be possible to do the whole of *Dear Brutus*, and instead it was proposed to present the dream sequence and two one-act plays.

Judith and Stanley discussed the matter after the girls had gone to bed. Louise was playing her records and, as Stanley talked, in the dark garden Susanna sang of her love for the untrusting Figaro.

Judith, who had been listening to the music which was being played louder than usual, threaded more wool into her darning needle and said, 'Whether it's right or wrong, we have to agree.'

He stopped speaking, his cheeks flushed so that in contrast his rather colourless eyes seemed more flinty than usual; his head jerked back on its short, thick neck, and the movement thrust out chest and paunch. 'I can hardly believe I have heard you aright, Judith.' Even to his ears, deaf though they were to the music, this had a false ring about it.

'We can't be Louise's right and wrong forever.' Judith herself was surprised at the ease with which she laid down the burden of right and wrong.

Stanley's eyes expressed a wounded incredulity which must surely have shamed her had she paid attention to him. The contest between them was unequal. He, in spite of his vehemence, was vulnerable to attacks which she repelled without effort. She seemed impregnable, able to hold herself together as a person against whom his personality stormed in vain.

'I only ask that you should listen to me.' Although he meant to be reproving in a gentle, tolerant manner, he merely succeeded in sounding huffy.

Judith put aside her darning and stuck the needle in the arm of the chair. 'I have listened.'

He became angry. 'I don't think you could repeat half of what I said.'

'Well, what do you want me to say?'

'*Want* you to say! What a way to talk to me, Judith. As though I would ever dictate to you what you are to say! I want the truth, of course. If you don't agree with me, you must say so roundly; I shan't take it amiss. But you must give me your *reasons*. That is not an unreasonable demand, surely? Instead of which, you are behaving as though I was the sort of person with whom it is impossible to have a reasoned discussion.'

He spoke loudly, shutting out the voice from the garden which sang of things other than reason. It was important to him that it should be accepted that at all times he behaved reasonably. It was even more important that it should be understood he was tough-minded and disdainful of flattery. 'I would sooner people attacked me than flattered me.'

This was far from true. Stanley Fairley never attempted to ingratiate himself with others by offering false praise; indeed, when dealing with adults (he was generous to his boys), it might have been said of him that he was somewhat miserly of praise. But he was very anxious that others should praise him – although this must be done in a way that was utterly frank, and without the least hint of insincerity which he would unfailingly detect. To set about praising Stanley Fairley as he wished to be praised was a task to be attempted only by people of fortitude and integrity, whose intellectual credentials were impeccable.

'Am I so very difficult to talk to?' he asked, allowing his hurt to be apparent in the hope – no, the belief – that she must then respond with a reassurance so warm as to sweep away all doubt. But while he was talking of reason, Susanna was concerned with the erotic; and Judith had been thinking that Susanna had somewhat the better of it. She replied, 'It's just that we look at things in a different way.'

'You say that so calmly, almost as though it didn't much matter.'

'It doesn't most of the time.'

'Most of the time! Are you saying that "most of the time" we look at things differently?'

'Yes, I suppose I am.'

He was very agitated; a gulf yawned between them, and she seemed unconcerned about it.

'You talk as though we are strangers,' he said, and he thought that all these years they had lived together and yet must have been quite separate, seeing a different world taking shape around them every day.

Judith laughed. 'What nonsense! I know you better than I know myself. It's only your thinking I don't always follow.'

Only his thinking! He so longed to share with her his enthusiasms, his ideals, his perplexities. Every day he tried to wring from her the responses he required, and every day he was snubbed, defeated and puzzled, his disappointment as sharp as on the first day of their courtship: while long ago she had accepted him as he was, and made her way around his angularities without attempting to soften them.

'In what way do we look at things differently?' The agitation in his breast was so great, he was scarcely able to draw breath while he waited for her to reply.

'You see things as they ought to be, and I see them as they are.'

'But those are two aspects of one view, surely, my dear? I see further ahead than you, but you see what is before us more clearly. We complement each other as husband and wife should.'

The song had ended and, in the silence, Judith found herself considerably less sanguine about many things than she had been before.

She said impatiently, 'We can't prevent Louise going out of the house and finding her own amusements for much longer. At least on this occasion we know the people she will be with, and many of them are young people we have received here in our own home. We may not always be as fortunate as that.'

He sat with bowed head. Her words conjured up a picture which was distressingly different from his own view of their loving, united family. 'We can't prevent Louise going out of the house . . .' as though they were gaolers, when he had seen them as shepherds, gently, wisely guiding their children along the right path.

'If you are saying we should not try to influence our children,' he re-phrased, 'have you thought of the other forces which will certainly influence them?'

'If we don't allow them as much freedom as other children, it begins to look as though we're afraid our influence won't last.'

'Not allow them freedom!' This was an unfair blow. Stanley Fairley was not obsessively possessive, and provided he felt his family were pointed in the right direction, he did not attempt to intrude himself into the meandering patterns of daily life. If one of the children spent a whole afternoon shut away in her bedroom, he did not see it as his duty to stand at the bottom of the stairs shouting, 'What are you doing up there all this time?' and if he saw them lying idly in the garden, he did not immediately break into their daydreams with suggestions of things for them to do. Whatever else might be laid at his door, his was not the tyranny of the love which seeks to share each moment's pleasure with the beloved. 'Not allow them freedom! I fought in one world war for my unborn children's freedom, and I would fight in another for them.'

'Well, then, you must let them have their freedom, otherwise there won't have been much point in your fighting.' She was irritated that he could not discuss this without dramatizing himself and bringing his war service into it.

'We started by talking about Louise and now we are talking about you. We always end up talking about you, Stanley. But freedom for Louise means being able to do things *you* don't approve of.' She picked up her pile of darning, and began to put it in her basket, afraid of what else she might say. 'I'm going to make our cocoa now.'

He stayed up long after she had gone unrepentantly to bed. 'We always end up talking about you, Stanley.' How could she have said such a thing? He thought about his family all the time, more than they thought about him. Judith would have forgotten much of what he had said by the morning, whereas it would be a long time before the words she had said this night ceased to disturb him. How could she have accused him of being self-concerned? He was so proud of her. When they gathered round the piano to sing and he saw her, so lively, not holding back like some of the silly women his friends had married, he could have cried with gratitude that he was blessed with such a wife. Was *she* proud of him? Sometimes she spoke to him rather in the manner of a school prefect – 'your elder sister voice', he would tease. Did she really think he was selfish and a bad father? He, who was always so pleased and excited by the children's small successes – Claire's recitation of 'Meg Merrilies' at the chapel concert, Alice's poem in the school magazine, Louise's performance as Elizabeth Bennet in the school production of *Pride and Prejudice* . . . Louise! He had almost lost track of how this had begun. Now, in his concern about Judith's unjust attack on him, he no longer found this business of Louise's play-acting so important. It was probably a whim. By this time next year Louise would be interested in something else. That was the way of the young. The important thing was to keep a sense of proportion.

He said to Judith the next day, 'If we had been able to have a rational discussion, I would have been able to make my point without being accused of trying to be "Louise's right and wrong". Because we are discussing drama, there is no need for us to be dramatic!'

Judith, sensing that this speech was a prelude to surrender, held her peace.

'I merely wished to make the point that we should not overlook the effect this may have on Louise's studies and to suggest that we should speak to her teachers. It is Sports Day this week, and there is always an opportunity for informal talk.'

'What a very good idea.' Judith was not displeased at having the final decision passed on to more objective adjudicators.

Sports Day dawned grey with a thin drizzle of rain, but by two o'clock in the afternoon, the rain had cleared away and folding chairs and benches had been put out for staff and parents. When Judith and Stanley arrived, the Middle School Rounders Final and the Upper School Tennis Final were in play and contestants were being lined up for the first track event of the afternoon, the City Train Race; these consisted of very young children, each child having at its feet a man's hat, scarf, overcoat, umbrella, newspaper and briefcase. When the whistle was blown several children looked around to see what their neighbours were doing, and one parent shouted, 'Put Daddy's hat on, Marjorie!' Marjorie put on a bowler and her face disappeared; she then grovelled on the grass and fell over the briefcase belonging to her neighbour. Some discord ensued. Meanwhile, one sturdy creature, a trilby rammed around its ears, was already stumbling towards the finishing tape clasping paper, briefcase and umbrella and, despite becoming entangled in the trailing coat and rolling over, reassembled itself in time to win. Marjorie was by now in tears, and two other contestants had failed to start, but seemed in no way disheartened.

'Do you remember Claire winning this?' Judith said to Stanley.

'And not knowing she had won because she couldn't see.'

This was probably the only way Claire was likely to win on the sports field, since in this one area she was quite lacking in the competitive spirit. Later in the afternoon she lost the relay race for her form, fumbling the baton exchange and subsequently falling further and further behind.

'Never mind,' Alice said when she consented to speak to her parents. 'She's enjoying herself taking snaps of all the people she's cracked on.'

'Is she cracked on many people?' Judith asked.

'One or two prefects and several members of staff. Claire never does anything by halves.'

Claire had already taken snaps of the prefects and members of staff on whom she was cracked when Miss Blaize came into sight, strolling towards the pavilion with the Chairman of the Governors, Mrs Brinley Harris. Miss Blaize, looking more massive than ever in purple Donegal tweed and an inverted chamber-pot hat in pale pink, was nodding and smiling at pupils and parents, seeming to invite a familiarity which would not have been tolerated on other occasions. When developed, most of the snaps showed staff looking at the pupils with amused resignation; a look quizzical, as though uncertain whether their pupils really knew how to handle their apparatus, but kindly and quite lacking in selfconsciousness, a look which they probably wore most of their school life. Only Miss Blaize betrayed in front of the camera a lack of social assurance as she tried uneasily to temper majesty with benevolence.

Shortly after she had been snapped by Claire, Philippa Bellamy met Mr and Mrs Fairley. None of the Fairley children excelled at art, but Miss Bellamy liked Louise because she did not suffer from the malady which affected so many sixth formers. Sixth formers, in her view, did not study, they appropriated whole subjects to themselves, put up a palisade and signalled the less gifted to keep out. Within the magic circle, they spoke of great artists and writers with amused condescension as though they had established a personal relationship with them. Miss Bellamy not only found this boring, but offensive. However unconventional her appearance, there was a sense in which she remained at all times very much a mistress.

When Mr Fairley told her that Louise was hoping to take part 'in one of these little amateur theatrical events' she cried, 'Bravo! I must try to see it.' The sun was hot now. Miss Bellamy's bony face was greasy, and powder had clotted in the open pores in her large nose; but she radiated such exuberant goodwill that Mr Fairley, who liked women to be lively, thought her very handsome.

In answer to his enquiry as to whether Louise's studies might be adversely affected, she said vehemently, 'Absolutely not! Do her the world of good. Blow away a bit of this hothouse atmosphere.' Seeing his surprise at this description of sixth-form life, she went on, 'They get much too intense about it, you know; take themselves too seriously. I'm all for them having time off, quite a bit of time off, seeing other things.' She waved a hand vaguely. 'You don't want Louise to be an academic, do you?'

'I doubt if she is suited for that.'

'I should hope not!'

They chatted for a few minutes and then she strolled away. 'More a woman of the world than some of the others, wouldn't you say?' Mr Fairley asked Judith as he watched Miss Bellamy's orange bandana mingling with the more sober hats.

Judith was looking at Miss Lindsay, who was wearing a particularly sober hat and suit in mud-coloured linen. As Miss Lindsay took Louise in English and History, whereas Miss Bellamy – however worldly – only taught art, Judith decided to ask her opinion.

Miss Lindsay, who did not believe in saying what people wanted to hear, even if it happened to be the truth, meditated. Pain tautened her never very happy face. She had bad period pains and was disposed to be spiteful. As she was more intelligent than Miss Bellamy, she was immediately aware of all the nuances of the situation. 'They have said "yes" and now they wish they had said "no",' she thought. And of course, in their terms, it would have been wiser to have said 'no' – particularly if they wanted Louise to have the slightest hope of getting her Higher School Certificate. But the only interesting thing about Louise, who could hardly have been said to have a first-class brain, was that the morals and values dear to the Winifred Clough Day School for Girls had failed to have a deadening effect on her. In this respect, she was not unlike Daphne Drummond, but there, of course, the resemblance ended: Daphne was an altogether more fine-bred, subtle creature than Louise Fairley, who had a streak of the peasant quality one noticed in her mother. Daphne Drummond might well lead a life of great daring, whereas the most one could hope for from Louise would be a little irregularity here and there. Nevertheless, the girl was in her way an original, and it would be amusing to promote her extra-curricular activities.

She said, 'I really don't think a little play-acting will affect Louise's university prospects one way or the other.' She chose her words carefully, because she did not want to lie in giving an intellectual assessment: on the intellectual level, she refused to compromise even in the interests of making mischief.

'I don't know what we are to make of that,' Stanley Fairley said when Miss Lindsay had left them.

Claire came running up to them. 'You must come and watch the high jump. Maisie is in it and her parents aren't here, so you *must* come.'

The next day Stanley Fairley spoke to Jacov, who was producing the dream sequence and had responsibility for the production as a whole.

'I will consent to my daughter taking part on the understanding that you do this dream business first and she comes home immediately afterwards.'

'I'm sure we could usually manage that at rehearsals . . .'

'I'm not interested in "usually".'

'At rehearsals, then. But it would make a more balanced evening if, on the night, we did the two one-act plays first and ended up with the *Dear Brutus* scene. It is much the best, you see, and the evening will lead up to it . . .'

'You can have a balanced evening, or you can have my daughter playing Margaret. It is up to you to decide; I don't seek to dictate to you on artistic matters.'

'We will do the dream first.'

'And I shall want her home not later than nine o'clock each evening.'

'Yes, we will see to that, except at the dress rehearsal . . '

'*And* at the dress rehearsal.' Stanley Fairley had in his view made a considerable concession, and he was determined that he would not give an inch more.

Louise was delighted. But Judith, as she watched her daughter, was uneasy. In some ways mother and daughter were alike, high-spirited and strong-willed in pursuit of their objectives. There was, however, a big difference between them. In Falmouth in her youth Judith had perceived very clearly the pattern of life, and had determined within the limits set by the pattern to make the best of things for herself. Louise intended to break out of the pattern. Judith was a little hostile to her eldest daughter, unable to forgive her this nonchalant attitude to constraints which had shaped her own life; just as Judith's mother had never quite forgiven her for turning her back on Falmouth. Yet, Louise moved her more than the other two; and she could not bear the thought of all that energy and hope being drained away by Guy Immingham, who was conventional and pedestrian, and would grow up to be the kind of man from whom she had escaped when she left Falmouth.

'I hope you're going to be sensible about this, now that Daddy has given way,' she said.

Louise said, 'Yes, of course,' though what was her view of sense was anyone's guess.

Louise, in fact, had one more scheme in mind. For some time she had wanted her parents to meet the Imminghams, and this had now become a matter of some urgency; it would be unfortunate if they met for the first time on the night of the play, when her father might not be at his best. Her attempts to bring this about met with little response from her mother. 'Your father knows Mr Immingham, what more do you want?'

'Just because Daddy has preached at their chapel, it doesn't mean they know each other.'

It was, however, through the chapel that Judith and Mrs Immingham were to meet.

In the first week of August the Women's Bright Hour had its annual trip to the sea. This year, not without some disagreement, it had been decided that the sea cadets should be included in the party. They could travel in a separate compartment, accompanied by two of their officers, and there was, Mr Fairley insisted, no reason why they should in any way inconvenience the members of the Women's Bright Hour. 'The beaches are surely extensive enough to accommodate both parties.' Mr Fairley, unfortunately, would be unable to accompany the sea cadets because he had to attend a headmasters' conference; he would, however, meet the party at the station on its return and receive the good reports of his officers. Mr Fairley took his position as commander of the sea cadets very seriously.

An invitation had been sent to other chapels whose women's groups might wish to join the party. Guy represented this to his mother as a personal invitation from Mrs Fairley. His mother was not best pleased at the amount of time which he spent with Louise, and he was naïve enough to imagine that closer acquaintance with Louise's parents would remove her objections.

'I shall be going,' he told her.

'Don't be silly, Guy! You don't belong to the Women's Bright Hour.'

'I shall help with the sea cadets.'

Mrs Immingham, suspecting he would spend his time with Louise, consented to join the party.

It took Mrs Fairley and Mrs Immingham only a short time to realize that the only thing they had in common was the dislike of the friendship of their offspring. Mrs Immingham thought Mrs Fairley rather too swarthy of countenance; and the Cornish accent, which years in the civilizing atmosphere of London had failed to eradicate, sounded harshly in Mrs Immingham's sensitive ears. Judith thought Mrs Immingham a silly, affected woman. When they arrived on the beach, further differences became apparent. Judith liked to paddle and sunbathe. Mrs Immingham liked to sit in the shade as far from the sea as possible.

Deck chairs were hired and Mrs Immingham sat, still wearing her panama, a parasol in one hand while with the other she tried to secure her frilly voile dress from the breeze. The members of the Women's Bright Hour regarded her with tolerant amusement as though she were a harmless freak. Louise said to Guy, 'Didn't you tell your mother we'd be spending the day on the beach?'

He had noticed on previous holidays that his mother wore more formal clothes than other people, but had accepted this as a mark of her superiority. Now he began to be embarrassed for her. 'I'd better see what the lads are up to,' he said. 'I promised to lend a hand.'

Louise sat in the shelter of the deck chairs and began to change into her bathing costume. 'You need to find a bathing hut, my lady!' Mrs Immingham said, joky but unamused.

'The bathing huts are down the posh end. We never go down the posh end.' She gave a final wriggle and pulled her dress off over her head.

Mrs Immingham turned her attention to the other people on the beach. It worried her to see them enjoying themselves in circumstances which would not be acceptable to her. 'I can't see why people want to sit so near the sea, can you?' she said fretfully to Judith. 'There is a lot of spray coming off the sea, and the sand is so much finer here; wet sand is very unpleasant. I'm sure we are in much the best place.' She looked around her cautiously for a few minutes and then said, 'I can't understand why some people wear headscarves. They don't protect the eyes, and the sun must be very hot on the head. It is so much better to wear a panama.' She looked at Judith. 'You don't wear anything on your head.'

'I don't feel the heat.'

'Yes, well, you have got very thick hair, haven't you?'

She watched disapprovingly as Louise rubbed oil on her legs. There was something offensive about so much glistening flesh. 'I always use Cool Tan,' she said. 'Cool Tan is really much the best way to prevent burning. It's not so messy as oil, either, *and* it doesn't smell.'

'Oil makes you go browner.'

'Go brown, indeed! I'm sure your mother doesn't want you to go a horrid brown.' She looked at Judith, but Judith happened to be paying no attention.

'Could you do my back for me?'

'I'll do your back.' Judith turned from whatever had preoccupied her. 'Mrs Immingham doesn't want oil all over that nice dress.'

They watched Louise as she walked towards the sea, toeing the sand lightly, not hurrying, making the sea wait for her. Judith was aware of that lessening of noise which can come when a lot of different conversations are momentarily suspended. She felt proud, yet dismayed, because Louise made the most of her opportunities – and where might this power to attract lead her when she grew older?

'She doesn't wear a bathing cap, then,' Mrs Immingham observed. This reminded her to worry because Guy was not wearing a panama. While Mrs Immingham talked, Judith watched the people bathing. One young woman was accompanied to the water's edge by a ragged black-and-white mongrel. He was not apparently a sea-going dog; shepherding was more his line. He marked a stretch of beach to west and east of his mistress's position and ran up and down, occasionally stopping to take a fix on his errant charge, sitting alert and worried, but with no intention of getting his paws wet. When she finally emerged, he leapt about in hysterical relief that this madness was over – or perhaps he was telling her that, if things had really gone badly, he would have attempted a rescue.

'Dogs are great companions,' Judith said.

She had touched a chord in Mrs Immingham. 'They are, indeed! And so affectionate. As long as I was there our Sandy was happy; he didn't want anyone else. No one gives us love like that. I cried for a week when he died.' There were tears in her eyes now; tears were never far below the surface, springing from some reservoir of untapped grief within her. She dabbed her eyes. When she could see clearly, she was rewarded by a sight, the memory of which would give her cause for tears for the rest of her life. Guy had now left the sea cadets and was standing at the sea's edge, while Louise, breast-high in water, lured him with siren calls and outstretched arms. While Mrs Immingham watched, he suddenly let his trousers drop. He had bathing trunks on, but they were light-coloured and just for a moment . . . Mrs Immingham was sick with shock and disgust. Ever since the untoward disclosures of her wedding night, she had turned her head away while her husband undressed. She hauled herself unsteadily out of her deck chair, calling out, 'He mustn't . . . not when he's so hot . . .' She began to thread her way down the beach, which was like an obstacle race – full of castles and sunken canals, with the added menace of hard-flung quoits and misdirected toddlers. There was a strong smell of seaweed and oily bodies which made her faint with nausea, but she hurried on, impelled by a premonition that calamity threatened her son. She waved to him, moaning under her breath, 'Oh, my boy, my boy!' He did not turn his head and, long before she reached him, he had swum out to join Louise.

'It's very safe swimming here,' Judith said, idly aware that all was not entirely well with Mrs Immingham when she returned.

'Guy burns so easily. He shouldn't go in when he's hot.'

'Young people are never sensible, are they? I suppose we weren't ourselves.'

Mrs Immingham rummaged in her handbag for her cologne.

At half-past twelve lunches were unpacked. Mrs Immingham had not brought any food. She looked at Guy. 'I think perhaps we should look for an hotel, dear.'

Guy rubbed an irresolute hand across the back of his neck, which was fiercely red.

'You can have some of ours,' Louise intervened, and turning to the members of the Women's Bright Hour she called out cheerfully, 'Loaves and fishes, everyone!' It was plain to see she was a very managing young woman.

A miscellany of jam sandwiches, sausage rolls, bananas and treacle tart were good-naturedly provided.

Judith said to Louise, 'Perhaps Mrs Immingham and Guy would prefer to go to an hotel. You must leave them to decide.'

Louise looked at Guy. Decision did not become him. He said

awkwardly to his mother, 'Well, since these good people have so kindly offered . . .' He stretched out a hand for a banana.

When their lunch had had time to settle, several of the women expressed a wish to go out in one of the motorboats that did a trip round the bay. Judith would have liked to accompany them, but Mrs Immingham said that she was already feeling sick with the heat of the sun, and could not possibly go 'tossing about out there'. Her face had become moist and blotchy, and she looked so sorry for herself that Judith felt she should not leave her alone. 'I'll just see them off and take a few snaps.'

'I'd like to go in a speedboat, wouldn't you?' Louise said to Guy.

'Better not,' he said uncomfortably. 'My mother gets awfully upset if my father or I go out in a boat.'

'Don't you ever do anything she doesn't want you to do?'

'Yes, of course, when it really matters. Only there's no point in spoiling her day, is there?'

'What about spoiling my day?'

He looked down at her in concern. The way in which he responded to her most unconsidered remark was one of the things which endeared him to her. I could do anything with him, she thought, anything! She found this exciting, though of course she would never do anything which would really hurt him. 'Aren't you enjoying it?' he was asking. 'I am so much and I thought . . .'

'I was only teasing. Don't you tease one another in your family?'

He put his arm round her waist. As his fingers touched her ribs, her head came up sharply and they looked at each other, surprised by a sensation more exciting than the speed of a boat or spray whipping sunburnt flesh. 'I'm going in again,' she cried, 'Come on, come *on*!' She danced ahead and then turned, flicking water at him until he caught her by the shoulders and ducked her; after which they trod water, laughing as they clung to each other. He told her that if she lay still on her back he would show her how to lifesave, but she twisted away from him and he caught at her foot. Sure of their powers of survival, they drifted, she on her back and he holding her foot, unconcernedly beyond their depth. Louise was not such a good swimmer as Alice, but she was more reckless and had little respect for the destructive power of the sea. To Guy, the sea had always seemed friendly, the one element in which he felt free. He enjoyed seeing the figures on the beach growing smaller and smaller.

Mrs Immingham, meanwhile, had consented to walk down the beach with Judith to watch the party embark. As they walked, she drew Judith's attention to the fact that there was indeed a stronger breeze here, and the sand was undoubtedly wet, and the people who were sitting here would have been much better advised to sit further back.

The Women's Bright Hour had been haggling with the boatmen and had now decided in favour of the *Saucy Sally*, which was newly painted in bright blue. It was at this moment that the Women's Bright Hour and the sea cadets came together. The sea cadets were naturally interested in the launching; indeed, they would have liked to go out in the boat, but had insufficient money. Abandoning their game of cricket, they came and splashed around the boat while the man in charge was taking ticket money. They were mildly envious, but far from having bad intentions. The weather was fine, they had had a good lunch, enjoyed their games on the sand and felt at one with the world.

The sea was choppy and the boat rose and fell; the members of the Women's Bright Hour let out shrill cries of delight mixed with pleasurable anticipation. 'We shan't go out of sight of land, shall we? Now you promise us that.' Spray fell on burnt arms and they gasped. 'Not going to be sick, are you, Lill? She's green already, look at 'er!' The motion of the boat was of professional interest to the sea cadets, who had been told that a boat is pushed out on an incoming wave. Now, they decided, was the time for them to demonstrate their seamanship. The man in charge was taking the last of the tickets and the whole party was aboard. A particularly big wave was coming in and, obeying a common impulse, the sea cadets put their shoulders to the boat and heaved. The sea cadets had been trained in seamanship. The Women's Bright Hour had not. When the sea cadets pushed the boat out, several women – unevenly distributed fore and aft – stood up and screamed. The boat up-ended, and the women came out like so many shelled peas.

One moment Judith had been taking a snap of a group of brightly arrayed women, the next she was helping to pull ashore so much lank, streaming seaweed. Mrs Immingham, who was doing nothing to help and getting in everyone's way, was pushed aside by a fisherman, causing her to stumble. Not only did she sit in wet sand; she fell foul of a very tarry rope.

Judith's mind worked quickly as she assisted in the rescue. When a count had been made, and all the women found to be present, if not correct, she knew what was necessary. She asked the fishermen to direct the party to the nearest laundry – not for nothing had she spent years in chapel in 'soap suds island'. They set off along the promenade. Mrs Immingham looked round for Guy, but he was nowhere to be seen. She experienced all the terror of the abandoned. What was she to do? Her inclination was to stay on the beach. This, however, would make her the sole female representative of this ill-fated band of women, and she could see from the discussion which was taking place between the owner of the *Saucy Sally* and the harassed officer in charge of the sea cadets, that negotiations were not going to be conducted in a congenial atmosphere. Already several sea cadets were applying to her as witness. 'We never done nothing but push, did we, mum? It was them silly cows standing up what done it. You saw, didn't you, mum?' She had no alternative but to hasten in pursuit of the gaggle of half-drowned women. The wet sand in her shoes rubbed her tender feet, bringing up painful blisters, and she was uncomfortably aware of the tarred patch on the seat of her dress. As she staggered along, holding her parasol in one hand while she clutched alternately at her panama and the ruined dress, some dreadful schoolboy, egged on by giggling fellows, came up to her and said, 'You are Mr Lobby Lud; I claim the *News Chronicle* prize.' All in all, the progress along the promenade and through the streets of the town to the laundry was the most humiliating episode of her life.

The staff at the laundry were sympathetic and anxious to be helpful. Their business, however was with clothes which usually arrived separated from their owners, and they had no changing facilities. This difficulty, at Judith's suggestion, was ingeniously overcome. When Mrs Immingham arrived, she was greeted by the unnerving sight of long rows of up-ended laundry bales from each of which protruded, like the carving at the top of a Roman pillar, the head of a member of the Women's Bright Hour. The atmosphere in the room was warm and the dousing in the sea had made the women feel tingly and, now that their wet clothing had been removed, remarkably healthy. Their good humour was restored, and they were singing, 'Throw out the lifeline, someone is sinking today.' The only person who appeared to have suffered real injury was Mrs Immingham, who had been abandoned by her beloved son, and whose expensive dress had been ruined.

In half an hour, the Women's Bright Hour – washed, ironed and refreshed by tea – emerged, rosy-cheeked, and made their way singing to the beach, where the sea cadets were still explaining in aggrieved tones that their intentions had been entirely honourable.

The owner of the laundry was very impressed with Judith's resourcefulness and had refused payment.

Mr Fairley, waiting in full uniform on the arrival platform, could tell from the gloomy expression of his second-in-command that all had not gone well. The tale, when recounted, struck Stanley Fairley as inordinately funny, and he had the greatest difficulty in concealing his amusement.

There was no mirth in the Immingham household that evening. Guy had failed to support his mother in her distress, and had even muttered on the way home, 'Oh Mother, don't fuss so!' Nothing would reconcile her to the Fairley family and when, later in the week, Guy told her that he had been invited to spend a few days with them on holiday in Devon, it was made perfectly plain that on no account was he to accept.

Mr Immingham pleaded his son's cause. 'Mr Fairley is a good sort of fellow, my dear, and quite a figure in Methodism.'

'He teaches in an elementary school. And he has no control over his boys. You should have heard their language! What can they be taught in that school!'

'I think all boys use bad language among themselves, my dear,' her husband said gently. 'It's part of being a boy.'

'Part of being a boy!' She looked from one to the other of her menfolk. If this were true, then there was a part of her son which must be unknown and unknowable. She appealed to Guy. 'I hope *you* don't swear, Guy.'

'Nothing very terrible, Mother.'

'You've changed since you met Louise; I've noticed it for some time.'

'Then I must have changed for the better,' he said angrily and went out of the room.

This was the first rift between Mrs Immingham and her son, and she was alarmed. 'That girl means to have him,' she said to her husband. 'You should have seen the way she flaunted herself on the beach!'

Mr Immingham tried to comfort her. He believed in his wife's goodness, because disbelief would have undermined the foundations on which their marriage was built. He was, however, too kind and thoughtful a man not to feel certain qualms, and early in his married life he had withdrawn from serious discussion with his wife.

Guy had grown up in a house that was unnaturally quiet, as though it harboured an unseen invalid who must not be disturbed.

Breakages aroused in his mother an almost superstitious terror. 'You go,' she would say when they heard a clatter in the kitchen. 'I dare not look.' When she cleaned out the china cupboard, the fragility of its contents terrified her.

Once, when Guy and Louise had been going through articles for a jumble sale in aid of the dramatic society, Guy had dropped an imitation Chinese vase which had been given by Mrs Fairley. He had looked so horror-stricken that Louise had laughed, 'It's only a broken vase!'

'But it belonged to your mother. She'll wonder what happened to it.'

'She won't mind. It's not as if you did it on purpose.'

His dread of breaking china had been so great that he had never thought beyond the moment of breakage. And here was Louise, laughing as it were from the other side of disaster, holding out her hand to help him across.

Now, pacing up and down his room, he equated this rift with his mother with the incident of the broken vase. It would all turn out much better than at one time he could have expected.

Until now, there had never been any trouble between Guy and his parents. He loved his father, who was a gentle, moderate man, and he was grateful to his mother who looked after his creature comforts with such loving, if fussy, care. Perhaps there had been something missing, some indefinable thing which made itself felt in the exhilaration which he experienced when on the stage he expressed emotions and performed acts quite foreign to his mild temperament. His determination to go on the stage was not something which he had mentioned to his parents. His first consideration must be to win their acceptance of his friendship with Louise. Although he was confident, he could see that it would be wise to take a step at a time.

He was unduly optimistic. There would never be a time when his mother was ready to share her son's affections with another woman.

The Fairleys went on holiday to a farm in North Devon and they went without Guy. Louise, looking forward to rehearsals, was more philosophical about this than was Guy.

'It's only a fortnight.'

'It's the principle. My mother can't expect to dictate to me all my life.'

He expressed himself more strongly to Louise than to his mother, because he was afraid that Louise might think him weak. Louise, however, did not think of him as weak or strong, but as a young man who aroused in her delicious sensations she had not known before.

It was an uneventful holiday. There were no impressive adventures, no notable misfortunes, and only the most modest of pleasures to recount to friends on their return. The sun shone much of the time, but the farm was isolated and they were unable to get to the coast, so swimming costumes were never unpacked from the trunk. Yet, looking back, it seemed to the girls that this was the happiest holiday of their lives. There would never again be anything to compare with those meanderings along the Bagworthy Water, and the time when their father forded it carrying the lunch basket, and his family was prevented from joining him because the icy water, though not deep, ran swiftly over the stones; nothing so breathtaking as Exmoor lightly brushed with the first bloom of heather, stretching level to the horizon; no such contentment as on the slow return to the farm, walking along dusty cart tracks, smelling the meadowsweet, too hungry to be saddened by any thought of summer's end. Nor would plain food ever be more welcome, nor sleep as deep. None of the children had yet lost that excitement, half fear, half joy, which comes on waking in a strange room, sunlight on unfamiliar walls, momentarily unable to knit together the bits and pieces, curtains, chest of drawers, ottoman, and give an identity to the whole.

'Aunt Patty's,' Claire said drowsily when she woke on the first morning.

'We're in Devon, silly,' Alice said affectionately. She looked round the poky little room with its sloping walls and white-painted floorboards. 'Isn't it heaven?'

They all agreed there was nothing to compare with a small room tucked away beneath the rafters. Even the lattice window that could not be adjusted without the fear of bringing down the eaves had an enchantment, and as for the basin in which Alice washed dirty socks one morning so that there was no clean water for the rest of the day, in years to come they had only to see a similar ewer and basin to be overcome with nostalgia.

Once, they went out long after their parents were asleep.

'If we're caught, we can't all say we've been to the privy,' Claire protested. 'We ought to have stayed in and had a midnight feast.'

But Louise needed something more daring than a midnight feast to stir her imagination.

They walked down the farm track into a meadow where they stood close, listening to the distant hooting of a barn owl, a scurrying in the grass at their feet, their own breathing. Louise longed for Guy, and for the first time she became aware of an insistent ache in her belly, and she thought, 'I didn't know I could miss anyone so much.' Although the pain brought tears to her eyes, she was pleased by this proof of suffering. Now she knew that she was really in love.

For Alice and Claire it was all quite different. Although they were growing up, they had not yet achieved the complete separateness of human beings from the natural world. Here in this darkness in which there was only the mass of earth and the enormity of sky, they could experience a sense of mystery and vastness, and yet be aware of the miracle of tiny things close at hand, glow-worms like stars in the grass. Their breath came light and shallow: they felt themselves embraced in the mystery and were full of wonder and a primitive fear.

Alice's hearing was so sharp she felt she could discern the movement of each blade of grass. Beside her, Claire whispered, 'Doesn't everything smell? Even the earth smells.'

When they returned, Louise said, 'We won't tell Mummy and Daddy.' She and Alice looked at Claire. Claire made no objection.

Their parents thought how well they all behaved. Claire did not complain unduly when she was bitten, Alice did not grumble too often about not being able to swim, and Louise was a good-natured companion to her sisters, and chased the moths out of their bedroom. Stanley said to Judith how blessed they were in their daughters. Only Judith wondered whether this might be the last holiday they would have together as a family. The children had no thought of last things, confident that everything lay ahead of them. Yet, as though unconsciously reluctant to leave childhood behind, they lingered in the lanes, leisurely exploring hedgerows; and the older girls spent hours lying in the meadow, chewing grass and talking. 'What do they think about?' Judith thought as she watched Alice and Louise. 'Lying there for hours on end, just talking and doing nothing.' If there had ever been a time when she could do nothing for hours, she had forgotten it.

The holiday represented to the children, and particularly to Alice, a kind of simplicity, not a part of their own childhood but of some other idealized country childhood.

On their way home, they broke their journey to visit relatives in Sussex, and here Louise one afternoon wandered into a country church. There had been a festival that week, and the little building was full of cheerful, if not always harmonious, colour. The work of decoration had obviously been done by many hands, and Louise was pleased to think that her mother would have made a better job of the altar vases. One person, however, had an outstanding gift. Beneath a neatly written inscription, 'a Magdalen', there was a trite little verse, but there was nothing trite about the decoration of the window itself. The container was not visible and the flowers seemed not to thrust upwards, but to have a downward movement, giving the appearance of a robe in which one colour gradually shaded into another. A pale, waxy pink warmed to apricot and then the flamboyant beauty of poppies with their dark centres yielded to a damask rose, and the rose deepened to crimson folds which fell in drifts of amethyst and violet and came to rest in the fullness of deep purple. Louise was much moved. This was the way to speak; they could throw away all the texts and sermons! 'This says it all,' she said to herself ecstatically, although in fact she had very little notion of what it was that the flowers were saying. She thought perhaps that she could sketch it, and then she thought that being a rotten artist, she would only spoil it by attempting to translate it to paper. She would sit and look, making no attempt to capture it. And this she did, emptying her mind so that she experienced an intense reality in which all the complex, quivering strands of life came together and were contained in the one still image. She felt enriched when eventually she walked out of the church and stood in the sunlight, watching sheep grazing in the graveyard.

12

The cane-mender sat in the gutter mending one of the dining-room chairs, and Claire and Judith watched him. He came from near Wrexham, where there had been a bad colliery disaster in September.

'Closed up the pit and left all those men down there; sealed it up and left them to die,' he said.

'Wasn't gas coming up the shaft?' Judith asked.

He looked at her, his face beneath his blue cap hard and wrinkled as a walnut. 'Ay, so they said.'

'I don't think they would just leave men to die, would they?'

'If you'd seen the things I've seen, you wouldn't say that.'

Claire wondered what else he had seen. The man's mouth was tightly pleated, and he went on with his task as though she and her mother were not there.

Alice was sitting at the kitchen table looking at pictures of Princess Marina's trousseau. When Claire tried to talk about the colliery disaster she looked up, keeping a finger on a woollen coat with a draped collar of astrakhan, and said to her mother, 'When are we going to have another dog?'

Claire went upstairs to their bedroom. The conversation had upset her, not only because of the men who had been left to die, but because it reminded her of Maisie, whose uncle was a miner. What was Maisie doing now that she did not want Claire's friendship any more? Probably she was out with her new friends, the slum girls who shouted coarse words at Claire when she and Alice went to Lyons in Shepherd's Bush Green.

When Maisie suddenly turned against her, Claire had run home and, flinging open the kitchen door, she had cried bitterly. Her mother had offered practical comfort. 'Let's walk down to the pet shop and see if the tortoise is still there.' Claire, needing a major modification in human behaviour, had been angry at being offered a tortoise.

'You'll have to come to terms with small comforts, or you'll be very unhappy when you grow up,' her mother had said. But Claire would not accept this, and so had lost both Maisie and the tortoise.

How unfair life was! Alice, who had so many friends, had only been in her new form a few weeks before she had made another friend, Irene.

She heard Alice's footsteps on the stairs and squeezed out a few tears; but Alice walked straight past her to the chest of drawers. 'Cheer up,' she said, without turning her head to look at Claire. 'Mummy says we can have a dog, but we've got to take it out for walks and not always leave it to her.'

'I don't want a dog. I want Maisie.'

'Do you? I'd much sooner have a dog.'

Alice took a sanitary towel from the top drawer and went out of the room. She had had her first period the day after the family came back from the summer holiday. On her return to school she had joined those in her form who were excused swimming once a month. She was surprised that this sign of womanhood should come to her before Daphne.

She wrapped the soiled sanitary towel in newspaper and took it downstairs to burn in the kitchen stove. Her mother was turning out a brawn and she said, 'Here, take Princess Marina upstairs. I can't have all this clutter in the kitchen. Show the pictures to Claire, or play a game with her.' ·

'I'm sick of Claire.'

'And don't forget to dust your bedroom.'

Alice was beginning to feel obscurely different; but if this was the maturing process, then it seemed she was maturing into a rather nasty person. For one thing, she was increasingly resentful of all the moral duties which were imposed on her, and she had recently made one small, mean rebellion. Each year the school assembled to consider the disposal of the money which had been collected for charities. The staff, although present, Miss Blaize presiding, took no part in the allocation process. Speeches were made urging the merits of particular charities, and the girls then voted. As a result of this exercise in democracy, the Holloway Prisoners' Aid Society regularly topped the list because the girl who spoke for it, as well as being articulate and persuasive, had no little gift for drama. For several years, Alice had spoken for the Sunshine Homes for Blind Babies. This year, she had refused to speak. She admitted that no blind baby could be held in any way responsible for the moral pressures which so irked her, that to abandon blind babies was an act for which there could be no pardon: nevertheless, she had abandoned them, and it was no thanks to her that they improved their standing, a more eloquent speaker taking up their cause.

Now, as she went up to the bedroom, she felt bodily discomfort to add to her meanness of spirit. Her clothes no longer fitted her properly; her dress pulled beneath her breasts and was too tight under the arms. She had a headache, and her hair felt messy.

She went to the window without speaking to Claire. She liked the winter view when the trees had lost their leaves and she could see much further. It was nearly four o'clock. The sun had set, although the sky to the west was still tinged with a pale, frosty pink. The street lamps had not yet been lit, but there were lights in several rooms and chimneys were smoking. The chimney fires made her think of crumpets, and this made her think of Grandmother Fairley. Her grandmother was now very ill, and Alice had only been to visit her once. She should have gone with her father this afternoon, but had made out to her mother that her period pains were bad. She did not even feel sorry.

It was becoming dark and very cold in the room. Claire had her dressing gown on and the eiderdown wrapped around her. In spite of all this discomfort, Alice suddenly felt excited when she thought of the mysterious life that was going on in shaded rooms where the lights had not yet been lit. Her moods swung unpredictably lately. She opened the window and leant out into the sharp, smoky air. She wanted to reach out, to be drawn into, to take part . . . But in what?

'I've made up a story about Kashmir,' she said to Claire. 'Do you want to hear it?'

'As long as you shut the window.'

Alice put on her dressing gown and sat on her bed with the eiderdown draped across her stomach.

'There's this mysterious place which travellers have always sought. No one knows where it is, you see. Some people have searched for it down the Amazon, and others in the Himalayas, and in deserts, too. And all the time, it has been hidden away in an ordinary town like Shepherd's Bush.

'People see the brick wall from different angles, like we can see part of the wall of Kashmir from this window; but no one sees the whole wall so they don't realize there's a place hidden away there.

'Then this boy and girl decide to climb the wall because they have been told there is an old mulberry tree there and they haven't ever had mulberries. And when they get over the wall . . .'

'*How* do they get over the wall?' asked Claire, who felt all the interesting things were being left out.

'I haven't worked that out yet.'

'Do they go in the house?' Claire asked impatiently.

'No, they sit on the grass.'

'Sit on the grass!'

'You see, it's the garden that matters.'

'What's so special about the garden?' Claire was plainly disgusted.

'You can sit on the lawn and pick the flowers; there's nothing forbidden.'

Claire screwed up her face trying to think of rules she might like to break. 'Is that all?'

Alice had seen it in a dream, just two people, a girl and a boy, sitting on the grass making a garland of flowers. It was hard to understand what was so disturbing about that; and yet, in the dream, when the image came to her there came with it the sense of something dreadful awaiting these two beyond their border of flowers. She had been at once entranced and terrified. The one sensation did not follow the other: the enchantment and the menace were inextricably part of the image. But it was the terror which had been uppermost when she awakened. If only she could write the story, perhaps she could recapture the enchantment. 'It's not finished yet,' she said to Claire. 'I'll have to do a lot more work on it.'

Their mother called to them that tea was ready, and they went downstairs talking about the sort of dog they would have.

The next day was Sunday, and they went on a bus to hear their father preach in a chapel in Cricklewood. Alice's new friend, Irene, came with them, and she and Alice sat together. Claire looked out of the window. They were travelling through an area which seemed to consist entirely of railway arches and coalyards; the few houses, sooty and dour, were unnoticeable until the bus was on top of them and, once passed, faded quickly into the grime. It was hard to imagine Kashmir hidden away here, but not so hard to imagine the families of the men who had been left to die in the coal mine.

It was a solemn service, because this was the first Sunday Armistice Day since 1928. They had heard on the wireless before they left home that thousands of people had been to the Cenotaph, and there was a mountain of wreaths there. Mr Fairley preached a particularly long sermon as befitted the occasion.

As they went through the dingy streets on their way home, Alice commented on the lack of window-boxes. Even in the poorest areas of Acton there were window-boxes, and in most of the streets there were houses with laurels in the front gardens and an occasional tree. There was no green here, and the whole area looked and smelt as if it had been sprayed in coal dust.

'Do they have enough to eat?' Claire asked her father.

'I'm sure they don't,' he said grimly, looking at his watch and thinking they would be late for their own dinner.

They sat down to eat at half-past one. Irene, an only child, was three months younger than Alice, but seemed older. She had an air of grave assurance, and spoke as one used to being taken seriously. In answer to Mr Fairley's question, she said that her parents went to the Church of England, although her father had been a Quaker. 'I've been to one or two Quaker meetings, and I haven't made up my mind yet whether I want to be confirmed.' The Fairley girls were impressed that something so important was to be left to Irene to decide: this, presumably, was the way with the notoriously lax Church of England. Mr Fairley put in a few good words for the Quakers.

'I'm not very good at being silent.' For a moment a more mischievous person showed an inclination to take over, but was apparently banished when Mr Fairley expounded his views on the Quaker silence. Irene, used to attention herself, was also an admirable listener. There was, however, a not entirely appropriate merriment in her eyes as she regarded Mr Fairley which suggested she might be enjoying his performance as much as his ideas. At school, she had the reputation of being a good mimic.

She left before tea, saying her thank you as though it must be a matter of some importance to the Fairleys to know that she had enjoyed herself. Obviously she did not see her visit as an incidental part of their busy day. Irene had not yet found that undemanding position which lies between being of integral importance in the lives of others and of no importance at all.

Alice accompanied Irene to the bus stop. Mr Fairley, watching them from the window, said, 'A firm little character that!' He was by no means disapproving.

'And such pretty *bobbed* hair,' Louise said. Her own thick, springy hair would look splendid bobbed.

'You can't play this dream child with bobbed hair,' her mother said. 'Irene will be a good influence on Alice. Perhaps she won't see so much of Katia now.'

'It's Katia who won't have time for Alice,' Louise laughed. 'She's going to prompt our play.'

'I'm surprised at Jacov encouraging her.'

'So am I. She's an awful prompt; all she thinks about is the boys.'

'At her age!' Mr Fairley was shocked.

'She was fifteen in September,' Judith said. 'She's older than Alice.'

'But she's still a child,' he insisted, thinking of Alice.

Alice did not throw one friend over for another, and she continued to see Katia and enjoyed listening to accounts of rehearsals on their way home from school. While Claire raced ahead to the tram terminus to help the conductor turn the seats the other way, Katia told Alice about the boy who was stage managing. 'He says I'm always under his feet. He picked me up and sat me in a wastepaper basket the other day. Then on the way home he wanted to make it up with me. He pulled me into Shanks Alley.'

'What did you do?' Alice asked with interest, for who knew but that similar experiences might lie ahead of her.

'He tried to kiss me and I spat at him.'

This seemed to Alice a foreign solution, like kissing hands and clicking heels, and she could not imagine herself adopting it.

On the day of the Royal Wedding they went for a walk in Holland Park. Neither was much interested in the royal romance, but they were glad of the day's holiday. Katia told Alice, 'I've got a boyfriend in Germany. He tried to take my knickers down.'

Alice, as taken aback by the crudity of the statement as the act itself, said, 'How awful, Katia! Weren't you frightened?'

'I was at first; my legs went shaky. But it's surprising how hard you can fight when you have to. I felt fine and he got scared; so I let him kiss me and fondle me a bit.' Then, as Alice was silent, contemplating fondling, she added, 'Of course I wouldn't do that with Brian; he's got a spotty face and I don't really like him. I wouldn't go too far with Ernst, either.'

How far was too far? Alice wondered. She asked, 'What does Jacov think?'

'He doesn't notice me; he only thinks about your sister. They're all mad about your sister, Jacov and Ben and Guy.'

'I didn't think Ben liked Louise. He's always so nasty with her.'

'That's *because* he's mad about her, stupid! If I was Louise, I'd have him.'

'Don't you like Guy? I think he's ever so handsome.' And he would never push Louise into Shanks Alley or try to take her knickers down.

'You haven't got a pash on Guy, have you? He's soft!' Katia spat her contempt. 'Ugh! It must be like kissing butter.'

The way that Katia said this gave the impression of her having watched someone kissing Guy. Perhaps Louise had to kiss Guy during rehearsals, or perhaps she kissed him after rehearsals? When a suitable opportunity arose, Alice decided she must have a talk with Louise about kissing – and about fondling and this 'too far' business.

That evening, however, Alice had other business to attend to. The play was to be presented on the Friday and Saturday of the following week, and tonight there was a dress rehearsal with make-up. Louise had said to Alice, 'If I'm going to be back by nine o'clock there won't be any time to get my make-up off. I shall have to rush home and Daddy will be horrified if he sees my face. If you can let me in I can go up to the bathroom and get it off before he sees me.'

So Alice, eiderdown wrapped round her, was sitting by her bedroom window anxiously staring into the dimly-lit street. It was a wild night, and the wind blew the branches of the trees and howled in the chimney. In the sitting-room where Stanley Fairley was listening to the wireless, smoke gusted out of the fireplace and Judith said, 'This will bring the fence right down.'

He said testily, 'Yes, yes, I know it needs to be done.'

'By tomorrow morning it won't be there to be done.'

In the street, two figures passed beneath the light of the gas lamp and one waved a hand. This was Alice's signal. She tiptoed down the stairs, not daring to put on her dressing gown for fear of losing a second. As she undid the latch a huge gust of wind buffeted the door, sending it flying back. Alice's nightgown whipped straight over her head. She heard a startled ejaculation. Then the front door closed and someone rushed past her. She just had time to pull down the nightdress before her father came into the hall.

'What are you doing here?' he asked sternly, thinking of the fence which must indeed have come right down.

Alice, red in the face and very distressed, stammered, 'I came down because I heard Lou. I let her in.'

'My dear, why were you waiting for Louise? Were you afraid she was going to be late, was that it?' He could think of no other reason for his daughter's distress. 'Am I really so severe that you are frightened of me?' He kissed her. 'Off you go. Louise is only five minutes late. I shan't be angry with her.'

Later, Louise came up and said to Alice, 'Thanks, my pet. It was rather an unconventional way to greet us, but never mind.'

'Who was with you?' Alice asked anxiously.

'Ben. He walked home with me; the others are still rehearsing.'

When next she had her bath, Alice crept into her parents' room and, slipping off her dressing gown, studied her body in the long mirror in the wardrobe door. As she turned this way and that, she was dismayed to find herself reminded of the Rubens paintings she and Katia had laughed about. It wasn't an exact image, of course, only a kind of half-way creature, a cherub come to adolescence. She was deeply ashamed that there was so much of her for Ben to see, and resolved then and there to lose weight.

The incident spoilt her enjoyment of the entertainment provided by the St Bartholomew's Dramatic Society. It was only when Louise was on stage that Alice was aware of what was happening. Whereas the gestures and grimaces of which Guy's performance was made up most notably displayed his stagecraft, Louise acted without apparent effort. One forgot she was not suited to the part. When the moment came for the poignant cry, 'I don't want to be a might-have-been!' even her family, who knew her to be too resilient for such a fate, were persuaded of the possibility. Mr Fairley had tears in his eyes, and Judith felt chilled as she looked at her daughter.

Louise joined them during the interval. People were watching her and there were whispers of 'Who is that girl?'

They remained in their seats while tea was brought to them, inexpertly balanced on trays by such members of the society as could be spared by the backstage staff. Alice looked uneasily around her, hoping that if Ben appeared she would see him first and have time to make an excuse for leaving the hall. When her father asked where he was, Louise said, 'He's doing the lighting,' and pointed to the rafters.

'Good gracious! Is he safe?'

'I shouldn't think so.' Louise laughed. She was very happy.

For the rest of the evening Alice thought of Ben up there, seeing but unseen, and her flesh prickled.

She was glad that when it was all over her father refused to go backstage to see Guy and Jacov. Louise, who hoped to persuade him to let her stay to the party on the following night, held her forces in reserve. Alice pushed rudely as they made their way out of the hall; but her haste was of no avail because Ben was waiting outside and accompanied them home.

'What did you think of this girl who played Margaret?' he asked cheerfully, falling into step between Alice and Judith.

'I wouldn't mind her for a daughter,' Judith said. 'She's a much better listener than some people I know.'

'Oh, she's got the gift, no doubt of that.' He bent to look at Alice. 'Everything all right down there?'

Alice said, 'I thought it was very good' in a constrained voice.

He chuckled and tweaked her ear. When they were in the house he did not take much notice of her, and by the time he left she was at ease with him again.

Judith said to herself as she watched his departing figure from the front door, 'Oh, how I wish . . .'

But how could she make wishes for Louise? She often tended — because she was busy and it was convenient to generalize — to talk about her children as though she had the measure of them. But in her quiet moments, she began more and more to suspect that the family home of the future would not be as she had once imagined it, spilling over with loving children and grandchildren, herself the central figure which held all the pieces together. She went into the kitchen to fill the hot water jars, not wanting to join the others in the sitting-room. They would come home, she thought, looking at the steam misting the windowpane, but in their own way: her hopes and dreams would not be the controlling factor.

13

In late January Alice and Claire visited their grandmother who was still living with Aunt May. Rain and wind battered the window of Aunt May's living-room and Dickie, the bullfinch, swung on his perch cheeping bad-temperedly.

'It said in the paper the gales were particularly bad round Porthleven,' Claire said. 'Granny Tippet said Charlie Tremayne's son was washed away while he was watching the high seas.'

Grandmother Fairley rolled her eyes heavenwards. It offended her that another person's misfortunes should be discussed when she had been so ill. 'Porthleven, eh?' It took some effort to enunciate Porthleven, and her teeth slipped. She adjusted them with a shaking hand and said, 'Why didn't your mother come, then?'

Alice and Claire exchanged glances and Alice said sulkily, 'She's coming later. She had to go to a meeting at the YWCA. She's on the committee.'

Grandmother Fairley's interest was aroused. 'Always out at meetings now, ain't she? I wonder she finds the time with a house to run and all of you to look after.'

'We're growing up,' Claire said, the corners of her mouth turning down.

'Yes, dear, but you're all at home still.'

'I think it's nice for Mummy to go out,' Alice said grudgingly.

Claire thought that her grandmother smelt rather badly and hoped nothing had happened. She said, 'I'll go and see if I can help Aunt May.'

'Tell her it's no use putting out jam with pips in it for me, dear.'

Claire repeated the message to her aunt and added, 'But you needn't worry about Alice and me; we can eat raspberry jam.' She looked with interest at the food spread out on the kitchen table. Aunt May always provided a good tea.

'Grandma smells a bit,' she said.

'Does she, dear? I expect we need a window open, only the wind is so strong.'

'Do you think she wants to go to the lavatory?'

'She would say if she did. She's not incontinent, you know.' Aunt May smiled at Claire. 'Does it worry you, dear, seeing her like this?'

'I don't like her face being so twisted.'

'It's much better than it was. But if you don't like it, you can help me butter the bread.' She began to cut bread and Claire fetched the butter which had been warming near the stove. 'Your mother said she would be here about five, didn't she? Is it the NSPCC meeting?'

'No, this is the YWCA. Mummy goes to ever so many meetings now.'

'We've been appointing a new warden,' Judith said when she arrived. 'I'm not sure we've got the right person even now.' She kissed Grandmother Fairley's cold forehead.

'It sounds like a prison,' Grandmother Fairley said, looking at Alice and Claire to see if they had appreciated her joke.

'I sometimes think it looks like one, too. We really shall have to do something about the bedrooms.' She looked at her daughters who were both watching her unsmiling. Their resentment of the fact that she was no longer always there when they needed her had not escaped her. '*You* wouldn't like to have an uncomfortable bedroom, would you?'

'Our bedroom is cold,' Alice said.

'And my bedcover's frayed,' Claire said.

'Oh, the younger generation!' Grandmother Fairley looked benevolently on the ungraciousness of her granddaughters, pleased to take their side against their mother. 'But I do remember how important it was for me that my dear mother was always there when I came in.'

'Did you ever wonder what she was doing while you *weren't* at home?' Judith asked.

'She was resting, I expect. She had poor health.'

'Well, I haven't got poor health and I don't need to rest.'

Aunt May poured tea and talked, contriving to agree with everything that was said, however contradictory.

'What does Stanley think about all these meetings, then?' Grandmother Fairley asked.

'Daddy goes out a lot,' Claire said. 'He's always at sea cadets.'

'You are poor, neglected little things, aren't you!' Judith exclaimed, thinking how tiresome children could be, always letting one down when one least expected it.

'I think perhaps Alice needs some brimstone and treacle,' Aunt

May whispered to Judith as they took their leave. Grandmother Fairley insisted on giving money to Claire and Alice. 'That will help to cheer you up.' She could not forbear adding, 'And because I may not be here much longer.'

They walked to the bus stop in silence, neither enjoying the feel of the money in their hands. As they came into the main road, Claire linked an arm in her mother's and said impulsively, 'I shall put my money in the box for the Distressed Families.'

Alice said mutinously, 'I shall spend mine on silk stockings.'

Claire wanted to sit at the front of the bus where there was only one vacant seat, so Alice sat with her mother. Alice said, 'You tell us that you go out now because we are growing up.' Judith waited, aware from the tone of voice that Alice had a bargain to strike. 'Well, if I'm growing up, I ought to be able to please myself about some things.'

'I suppose that's fair enough,' Judith said unwisely. Louise had recently had her hair bobbed and she thought that Alice was probably going to make the same demand, which would be a pity because Alice would not benefit from a closer comparison with Louise.

'I don't want to go to Crusaders any more.' Alice spoke quietly, yet as though the words were the final summary of a long argument.

'Why ever not?' Judith thought of Claire, to whom Crusader meetings were so important and who would be unhappy going alone.

'I hate them.' Alice turned her head away and addressed her reflection in the bus window. 'I hate the things they say.'

Judith could have slapped her. But she knew that her anger was caused partly by the guilty awareness that she had unsettled her family by turning her attention outward; so she merely said, 'You can't give things up just because someone says something you don't like.'

Alice clenched her hands. As the bus passed the Drummonds' house the look of anger in her face turned to something nearer to despair.

Alice had had a disturbing experience. Crusader meetings were held in a classroom at a private school. One afternoon in early January, while Alice was putting the chorus books away in the stockroom after the meeting, she had overheard one of the older girls talking to the leader of the group, Eileen Palmer. Alice did not know the girl in question, and had been surprised when during prayers she had prayed for Daphne and her family. Now, the girl was telling Eileen that her aunt had at one time been employed as a companion to Mrs Drummond, but had had to leave because the atmosphere in the house was unhealthy. 'She said he paid too much attention to his elder daughter.'

Eileen replied primly, 'I think you should be careful about repeating anything like that.'

The following Saturday Alice and Irene had spent the afternoon at the Drummonds'. Mrs Drummond had been in bed with a migraine. On arrival they went into the garden. Daphne produced tennis rackets and a ball. 'We can't play on the grass because the ball won't bounce,' she said. 'I suggest I hit it against the wall and Alice hits it back before it bounces and then Irene hits it back.'

Irene looked at the racket as if unsure which was the business end. 'I can tell you how long we shall keep *that* up.'

Daphne regarded her thoughtfully and then decided to ignore the remark. 'I'll start.'

Daphne hit the ball hard against the wall and Alice returned it well. Irene was not good at games. For one thing, she was not in the least interested and, for another, she had no ball sense. This did not, however, appear to give her any feeling of inferiority. Bright-eyed, red-cheeked with the cold, diminutive as a woodland creature and wielding her racket much as she might have done a wand, she darted here and there, first sending the ball spinning so high that if Daphne had not caught it, it would have landed in the garden next door, then edging it into the shrubbery, and then into the front garden.

'It isn't possible for you to hit the wall once in a way?' Daphne asked after she had retrieved the ball from the Uxbridge Road.

By way of reply, Irene took a wild swing and, rather by luck than judgement, sent the ball crashing against the wall whence it rebounded into Alice's chest.

So she continued until dusk, impervious to their annoyance. When the ball finally went into the garden next door, Daphne said, 'We might as well stop now; it's teatime anyway.' She collected the rackets, and Alice and Irene waited while she carefully screwed them into the presses. It was nearly dark, and the trees at the end of the garden were no longer sharply defined. Irene, standing by the shrubbery, glowing with mischief, looked as though she might at any moment step back and merge into the undergrowth. Daphne showed them to the downstairs cloakroom and went to see about tea.

'I enjoyed that,' Irene said as she combed her hair.

'That's more than we did.'

'If you don't like the way I play, you should have done something else.'

'It was two of us to one of you.'

'I can't be bothered about that!' In the mirror Irene's eyes looked at Alice, saying, 'You didn't know I could be like this, did you?'

Alice in her turn did not hide her irritation. 'Anyone can tell you're an only child,' she said.

They felt they knew each other better after this exchange. Their sense of companionship was strengthened as they walked down the corridor. They were in a strange house which was dark and silent, and Daphne seemed further away than the distance between them and the drawing-room. When they came to the room, Mr Drummond and Daphne were standing by the fire, their backs to the door; he had one hand on the mantelshelf, the other teasingly ruffled her hair and then rested at the nape of her neck, shaking as one would shake a puppy by its scruff. His voice was teasing. 'I hope *you* never ape Betty Barton and Company.'

Daphne said, 'They are my friends.'

'And will grow into worthy women much given to good works, particularly the ponderous Alice. As for the other one, if she'd broken one of my windows, I'd have had her breeches down and given her something to squeal about.'

Alice and Irene withdrew and tiptoed back down the corridor. Upstairs, Mrs Drummond called fretfully for one of the maids. Alice banged the cloakroom door, and she and Irene talked loudly and nonsensically as they again approached the drawing-room. Their exertions in the garden, together with the heat of the fire, adequately accounted for their pink faces.

Daphne rang for tea and a maid soon wheeled in a trolley. Mr Drummond took a packet of De Reszke from the mantelpiece and remained astride the hearth, keeping the warmth of the fire to himself. Neither Alice nor Irene had any inclination to talk to him, so they engaged Daphne in chit-chat about school. Irene talked about the coming production of *A Midsummer Night's Dream*, in which she was to play one of the fairies.

When Alice had first visited the house she had been aware of a Daphne who was obscurely different from the Daphne she knew at school. She had thought this change a sign that Daphne was more grown-up than was she, more at ease with the different types of behaviour appropriate to different situations. In Irene's company, this explanation no longer seemed sufficient. In the garden, Irene had had a spritelike quality which amply explained why she had been chosen to play one of the fairies; but now, sitting beside Alice on the sofa, talking amusingly and articulately about why she disliked Shakespeare's fairy plays, she was crisp and sharp and very much the sort of person who would sparkle more brightly in a drawing-room than in a wood near Athens. Yet, in spite of this unpredictability, Alice still felt in touch with Irene, and quite able to accommodate the inconsistencies in her personality.

'If I played anyone, I'd like it to be Helena; but it looks as though I'm doomed to be a fairy all my life because of my height.'

When Alice turned from Irene to look at Daphne, she saw a person with whom she seemed to have little in common. Daphne was speaking about school as from a distance, as though it was much further away than a bus journey up the Uxbridge Road.

'Fairies!' Mr Drummond interrupted the conversation. 'Good God, is this what I spend all that money on fees for?'

Irene, who could not bring herself to look at him, let alone speak to him, occupied herself with a cup-cake.

A door banged at the back of the house, and after a few minutes footsteps sounded in the corridor. Cecily came into the room, dragging a satchel by its straps, spilling sheet music and leaving a welt on the carpet. Mr Drummond said, 'What do you think you are doing?' He seemed to welcome the intervention; his eyes were so bright he might have been laughing. 'Go out of the room and come in properly.'

Cecily went out of the room and they heard the thud as she threw the satchel down. She remained in the hall, whimpering. Mr Drummond strode briskly to the door.

'Come here! You heard me, didn't you?' He slapped Cecily lightly across the face with the back of his hand. 'Then do as you are told.'

Irene and Alice sat as though turned to stone while Cecily walked stiffly into the room. Mr Drummond pointed, and she bent to gather up the sheet music. Alice had a piece of cake half-swallowed and prayed she might not choke. Daphne lifted the lid of the teapot and inspected the contents, then poured in more hot water. Mr Drummond pointed to a chair. 'Sit down. I am going to the morning-room to read the paper in peace; and if I hear any more from you, my girl, I can promise you something to wail about.'

He went out of the room. As soon as the door closed, Cecily began to weep quietly. Daphne picked up the teapot and refilled cups.

'He's only talking like that because he wants to shock you,' she said to Irene and Alice. 'He never beats us.'

'He hit me,' Cecily blubbered.

'Oh, don't be such a baby. You can hardly have felt it.'

'He's always picking on me.'

'You play up to him, that's your trouble. When he twists my arm I make up my mind I won't cry out and he soon stops.'

'But he still does it.'

'It's just a game. He likes to test my spirit every now and again to make sure I won't grow up like Mother.'

'Don't you hate him?' It would have taken Alice a long time to get round to saying this, but Irene came out with it as though it was the most natural remark, which, in the circumstances, it perhaps was.

'No.' Daphne looked at Irene with dislike. 'He wants people to stand up for themselves, like he does. But Mother is always ill, and Cecily is always crying. It's awful for him.'

'I think we ought to report him to the NSPCC,' Irene said later as she and Alice walked along the Uxbridge Road. She said it because she needed to imagine Mr Drummond under threat, and this was the worst threat she could bring to mind. Neither girl had any intention of telling her parents. This, they knew instinctively, was the kind of situation to which parents would react by making matters worse. They would be forbidden to go to the Drummond house again, and something might even be said to teachers at school. They were not sure that they wanted to go to the Drummond house again, but preferred to be left with the option.

'This is the second nastiest thing that has ever happened to me,' Alice said.

'What was the nastiest?'

Alice told Irene about the journey on the tube train with Katia. Irene, still shocked by what she had seen and heard that afternoon, was not impressed. 'But we *know* Daphne and Cecily and their parents,' she said. 'You didn't know any of those people who were pushing and shoving; they probably lived in Goldhawk Road.' She herself lived a respectable half-mile away in Holland Park.

They waited for Irene's bus, not talking much. When Alice imagined Daphne's spirit being tested by her father, it produced an uncomfortable sensation in the lower part of her body. She wondered if Irene had the same feelings, but did not like to ask. She was ashamed, as though she herself had done something wrong. The unpleasant sensations persisted. When she went to bed, she lay thinking of Mr Drummond twisting Daphne's arm, and she remembered the girl at Crusaders saying that the atmosphere in the Drummonds' house was unhealthy. In fact, of course, it was wicked; wickedness, unlike sin, was something new in her life.

At the end of January Ben came to stay for the weekend. On the Saturday afternoon he suggested to Alice that they should go for a walk in Gunnersbury Park. It seemed to him she was not in the best of spirits. Where people of his own age were concerned, Ben was too busy fighting for dominance to be observant, but his judgement of people younger than himself was both kind and perceptive.

'So, what ails you?' he said to Alice as they walked towards the shrubbery.

Alice scuffed her feet among the dead leaves. 'You know Dolly Bligh at our chapel?'

'No. Tell me about her.'

'She stayed with her husband in spite of his interfering with the children. They took the children away from her.'

Ben kicked a stone. 'Yes, I suppose they would.'

'A lot of people at the chapel think she shouldn't come any more. But our Minister says if Dolly isn't fit to come to chapel, he isn't fit to be minister.'

Ben was silent. Answers came to Alice readily enough from most other sources, and this experience of talking to someone who did not answer you immediately, and yet was friendly towards you, was unique. When she was upset or had hurt herself, her mother or father would hold her in their arms. Ben gave her the feeling of being held because he took her words and held them.

'At Crusaders,' she went on, 'we pray for people who have done . . . well, wicked things . . . like Dolly Bligh.' She clenched her hands. 'I hate Crusaders.'

'Do you worry about Dolly Bligh, Alice?' Ben asked, a bit out of his depth.

'Well, in a way.' She could not bring herself to tell him about the Drummonds.

They had come to the ornamental bridge over the lily pond. They stood together looking down at the still water. The pond had not been raked, and there was a mass of dead leaves at the bottom. Alice said, 'I mean, it's wicked, isn't it?' Ben was inclined to agree, but he did not think this would help Alice.

'I shouldn't worry about it if I were you.'

'Not worry?' Alice was taken aback. Her father unintentionally generated worry; the Winifred Clough Day School for Girls generated it on a considerable scale.

'Worry doesn't help people. It only puts another burden on them.' Ben had burdened his mother and made her dying harder. Now, when it was too late, he regretted his selfishness. 'Think of it as a bad habit, Alice. Then you'll find it easier to give up.'

Alice felt that everything had been let go. All the worries and fears, the puzzles and muddles and stumbling blocks were running away from her, jumping and somersaulting and bumping into each other while she remained on the bridge, unscathed amid the confusion. 'Not worry!' she repeated in awe. This advice from someone of her own generation had a particular sound, an authenticity of tone which was sometimes lacking in her parents' pronouncements.

'If your mother tells you she's worried about you, does it make you feel happy?'

'It makes me feel I've done something wrong.'

'There you are, then. If all you can do for a person is worry, you'd be as well putting them out of your mind.'

They walked on slowly and came out onto the lawn where the great cedar spread its branches. Chapel *and* Crusaders! Ben thought angrily. His mother's illness might have forced him to learn a lesson or two about worry, but it had left a lot of anger in him with which he had yet to come to terms. He said, 'Perhaps we should put God out of our minds if He worries us.'

Alice gazed at him as though the Emmäus Road ran through Gunnersbury Park.

Claire, at this time, was also having problems with God. She had found a new friend.

Heather Mason, like Maisie, came from a working-class home, but there the resemblance ended. Heather's father was honest and hardworking, as firm in his beliefs and as caring of his children as was Stanley Fairley. Her mother was a capable, generous woman who made Claire and all visitors welcome. The family had been very proud when Heather won a scholarship to the Winifred Clough Day School for Girls. Heather's joy had been in no way diminished after a month at school. Then had come a bitter blow. She was told that, in order to help her fit in better, she must have elocution lessons. Although she had submitted to this indignity, some demon of unacceptability had been roused in her, and from the time of her first elocution lesson her behaviour in class became more unabashedly exuberant, and she was rowdier than ever in the playground.

Her lack of restraint swept aside all the difficulties which Claire usually experienced with her friendships. With Heather, she was always sure of a warm response and never found herself inexplicably rebuffed. If she made unreasonable demands, Heather lost no time in acquainting her of the fact instead of avoiding her company. Heather's anger was as immediate as her affection, and expressed as openly.

But Heather was not a Christian. It took Claire some little time to appreciate this, and it was not until Heather declared herself roundly that Claire fully understood her position. 'Look, it's not that I don't bother about going to chapel, or that I'm not interested, or haven't thought about it. I *have* thought about it and I think it's a load of old rubbish. And so does my Dad and you couldn't have a better man than my Dad.'

Until now Claire had not encountered anyone who did not believe, albeit vaguely, in God. She knew that such people did exist and that the Devil was in them; but the thought that unbelief could go hand-in-hand with apparent goodness and undoubted loving kindness had never entered her head.

'We don't know what goes on in other people's lives,' her mother said when Claire made a guarded enquiry.

But Claire knew what went on in Heather's home: goodness and love and laughter and all without the aid of God! She was shaken. To her, unbelief and goodness were irreconcilable, a contradiction in terms. She worried away at the problem day and night. Once, she tried to talk to her father about it, but he was absorbed in another question of right and wrong, namely the return of the Saar to Germany.

The one place where she might have been able to talk about her problem was at Crusaders. Yet, for the first time, she found herself unwilling to be totally frank. Loyalty prevented her from mentioning Heather by name: she referred to her as 'my friend' and she said to Alice, 'You won't let anyone know who it is I'm praying about, will you?'

'I don't know myself,' Alice said. 'And I don't care.'

While Claire prayed obliquely for Heather, Alice thought of Daphne and wickedness, and wondered if she should give up her friendship and knew that she could not. The most sensible thing seemed to be to do what Ben had suggested and give up God for the time being.

She went to her father. He was reading a detective story, which was one of his few relaxations, and had just come to the first dead body on page 70 – which, in his view, was too long to wait. He put a marker in the book before he put it to one side. 'What is it you don't like about Crusaders?' he asked.

Alice sat silent for a few moments, sifting her objections. Her father, watching her fondly, thought how much she had grown up in the last few months. Eventually, she said, 'The things we pray about.' She put wickedness and the Drummonds resolutely to the back of her mind. 'We pray for people who haven't come as though they had been tempted. I know some of them may have stayed away for the wrong reason – to play tennis and that sort of thing; but we don't *know*, we just assume it.

'We pray for Betty Harris's mother and father and Betty tells us how she has to bear witness alone in a worldly home. I wouldn't ever talk about you and Mummy like that, I mean, praying for you behind your backs with other people listening.'

'I hope you pray for us on your own, Alice?'

'Yes, every day.'

'Does Claire feel like this?'

'I don't think so. She talks a lot about bearing her witness. And she loves the choruses. "Though your sins be scarlet, He will wash them whiter than snow" is one of her favourites.'

'Is it indeed, my little Claire! I wonder which of her sins is scarlet.'

Alice was nonplussed by this response. Her father said, 'Shall we sit for a moment and commit ourselves quietly to Him?'

They sat for what seemed many moments to Alice. The ticking of the clock sounded very loud and down in the kitchen she could hear the puppy crying; she wondered if it had made a pool.

Eventually Mr Fairley moved in his chair and Alice knew she could look up. He said, 'You should never be ruled entirely by your intellect, Alice. Intellectual pride is the sin of our age. And, if I am honest with you, it is the one to which I am myself most prone. But having said all that, I would say to you that you should never force yourself to go against what your intellect tells you. When you have intellectual problems, be still and wait for God to enlighten you in His own time. Don't ever imagine you have outgrown Him. It is your mind that is not big enough to encompass His truth. Always remember that.' There was another silence, during which Alice thought

171

about her erring body and wondered if her father ever erred in his body; Louise had said he might not be lustful but he was certainly lusty, because she could hear the bedsprings squeak.

Mr Fairley looked covertly at his book. After a few minutes, he said, 'I'm glad to have had a talk with you, Alice. We don't talk often enough.' His fingers strayed towards the book.

'What shall I tell Mummy?' Alice asked, perplexed at the inconclusive nature of their discussion.

'That you don't have to go to Crusaders, of course,' he said irritably. 'Haven't you been listening?'

'I love you!' She flung her arms round his neck and hugged him. She loved and adored him, the more so because she had suddenly realized how innocent he was in comparison with herself who had become a part of the wickedness of Daphne and Mr Drummond.

He patted her shoulder, 'My dearest, why didn't you say before if Crusaders upsets you so much?'

14

The forthcoming Silver Jubilee was beginning to colour people's thoughts; the nation was in a mood to be jubilant after so many hard years. Unemployment was now falling steadily and the international scene, if not actually hopeful, was no more discouraging than usual: Mussolini was making placatory noises about Abyssinia, and Germany was celebrating the return of the Saar to the Fatherland. It was time for the Motherland to celebrate: patriotism was in the air. Mr Fairley took the family to see *The Lives of a Bengal Lancer*, having satisfied himself that there was no love interest and, after the initial irritation of Gary Cooper's American accent had worn off, was completely won over by such stalwarts as C. Aubrey Smith and Sir Guy Standing. When the National Anthem was played at the end, the entire audience stood still; even the people who had hoped to sneak out accepted defeat and remained like statues precariously balanced on the steps. A few people sang.

The old lady who called periodically for cast-off clothes was not so optimistic. 'They say things are getting better,' she said to Judith, 'but I can't see it meself. My man tries, no one could try harder. Walked to Camden and back the other day because a mate told him there was work in one of the stores there.'

Although they called her 'the old lady', she was not yet fifty. Suffering from some ailment – probably glandular – she was a lumpish mound of flesh. The bright, intelligent eyes were ludicrously small in the unwholesome, moonlike face. The nose was too flat so that the mouth, having to do the work of breathing, hung permanently open displaying ulcerated lips and splayed, broken teeth. But this was the only display of misfortune she permitted. Over the years she had been coming, Judith had heard stories of her husband and eight children, of the birth and death of grandchildren, but never a complaint, never a demand for pity. In exchange for the clothes there was always a flower in a pot. She would not accept something for nothing. She had a barrow in which she stacked the plants and the clothes. How far she had to push it, Judith did not know.

The old lady was a reminder that times were still hard for some. But who wanted that sort of reminder? The old lady and her family were awkward, unassimilable, the death's head at the feast. People hardened their hearts. 'There is always work for those that want it.' The poor were feckless. It was not only the well-to-do who made this sort of comment. Mrs Moxham, who came twice a week to help in the house now that Judith went out more, said, 'And when some of them do get a job it will all go on drink. I've seen it all before.'

Judith watched the old lady go down the street, wheeling her barrow. What could it be like to live so rejected by your fellow human beings? She did not pursue the thought, nor did she try to follow the old lady in her mind's eye to whatever mean street afforded shelter of a kind to her and her family. But she returned a sharp answer to the woman who came collecting for Jubilee celebration contributions. 'I've other things to do with my money.' The woman marked her down as a Communist.

Judith put a collection box on the hall table and said to the family, 'For everything we spend in connection with the Jubilee, what about putting the same sum in here for the Relief of Distressed Families Fund? Isn't that fair?'

Only Louise thought it fair. She had often seen the old lady pushing her barrow: Louise responded to what was before her eyes — her missionary box remained empty.

Alice, who was practising putting God and His commandments out of her mind, was not prepared to contribute.

When the box was presented to her, Claire's eyes blazed with the new fervour which had her in its grip. 'It's *charity*! Heather's father thinks it's an insult to give to charity.'

'What does he give the unemployed, then?'

Claire, nonplussed, said, 'He doesn't give them charity, anyway. And I shan't either.'

Stanley Fairley would normally have given generously. Unfortunately however, Judith's launching of the scheme coincided with the moment when he was trying to interest her in the plight of the seven hundred Prussian pastors who had been placed under house arrest in Germany. While he was explaining that the Prussian Confessional Synod had issued a manifesto against 'the pagan religion popularized in Germany' she intervened to say, in a manner which he thought flippant, 'While they are making their stand, what about the deserving poor on your own doorstep?'

'Do you realize,' he said angrily, 'that in Germany there are men who are risking their lives to oppose Hitler?' Now, whenever he saw the box in the hall, he thought angrily how easy it was to be a Christian in England, and for some reason this thought prevented him from putting any money in the box.

Heather was providing Claire with food for thought on matters other than charity. She was irreverent about the school and the Royal Family. The Royal Family Claire did not grieve for, because although her parents were loyal subjects, theirs was not an adherence which permitted no criticism. But the Winifred Clough Day School for Girls was for Claire the place in which resided those truths not made available to man by Divine revelation, and its influence on her social perceptions had been greater even than that of her father.

This new friendship, however, offered so many undreamt-of delights that she was resolved that, whatever she relinquished, it would not be Heather. She tried to confide in Alice.

'Daphne's parents go to church and he's got Another Woman; and Heather's family are so good and they don't go anywhere.'

Alice responded with guilty sharpness; 'If you tell Mummy and Daddy about the Drummonds, I shall tell them that Heather is an atheist.'

This struck deep. Mr and Mrs Fairley liked Heather and she was always a welcome visitor – never more so than when Mr Fairley heard about the elocution lessons. For Claire's sake, Heather became inarticulate when religion was discussed, and suffered herself to be thought ill-instructed in this respect.

In Heather's company Claire soon began to gain a reputation for being naughty. She participated in a mysterious pursuit which necessitated locking the bathroom door whenever she had friends to play and getting a lot of water on the floor. 'We just wash things,' she insisted when questioned. In fact, the game consisted of filling the wash-basin and seeing which girl could keep her face under water for the longest time; Heather currently held the record.

At school, Claire was one of several girls who hid alarm clocks in their desks and let them off in the French lesson, which already tended to overrun into the break period. Once she rode all the way home on the back of Heather's bicycle.

On the next occasion when Miss Blaize leant on the rostrum and told the school to sit down, Claire was worried in case she had been seen climbing over the school wall to retrieve a netball from the garden of the adjoining house. It was, however, a small matter of hygiene to which Miss Blaize wished to draw their attention; some girls had been seen to stuff their handkerchiefs into their knicker-elastic; this was not the right place for a handkerchief.

This was the day of Heather's elocution lesson, and one act of madness was mandatory on such days. Heather stood up. 'Please, Miss Blaize, where *should* we put our handkerchief? There aren't any pockets in our blouse and skirt.' There was only a faint Cockney intonation and not a trace of insolence; she gazed optimistically at Miss Blaize, a true seeker after knowledge.

No one present could remember a time when Miss Blaize had been challenged from the floor (except by a girl who had a fit). Miss Blaize looked at Heather as though there was no other girl present. 'That is a very sensible question, my dear.' She turned her head in the direction of the young needlework mistress and smiled her most mirthless smile. 'I think perhaps we should devise something, don't you, Miss Porter?' Miss Porter, scarlet-faced and unsure whether speech was demanded of her, made a small barking in her throat and nodded her head vigorously. The school was dismissed. What had promised to be a considerable drama would dwindle into a needle-and-thread exercise. 'Thanks to you, we shall all be sewing little pouches into our skirts!' Heather was told. No one thought the experiment of engaging in a dialogue with Miss Blaize worth repeating.

In February, Miss Blaize had one of her occasional informal sessions with the sixth form. The informality consisted mainly in their being invited to her room, where a few were lucky enough to find chairs and the rest sat on the carpet. It was Miss Blaize's habit on these occasions to talk about matters not usually touched upon lower down the school. Now, staring in front of her like a sorrowing fury, she spoke of the opportunities which can slip by in life, and of a time when 'we look back on days when we were happier than we knew'. For a moment, Louise thought Miss Blaize was going to speak of love; and perhaps Miss Blaize had permitted herself to stray further than she had intended in forbidden territory, for she came out of her abstraction and began to give advice which, if followed, would necessitate the letting slip of quite a lot of opportunity.

There was a barrel organ playing in the street. The effrontery of it, Louise thought, making that cheerful jangle while Miss Blaize was extolling chastity! Miss Blaize, making one of those intellectual leaps for which she was renowned, now left the subject of chastity and began to talk about marriage. She spoke of the responsibilities of home-making and bringing up children; the husband merited only a brief reference, the existence of young men being barely acknowledged at the Winifred Clough Day School for Girls. Louise, a seeker after pleasures which Miss Blaize did not see it as her business to acknowledge, let alone encourage, listened to the barrel organ.

Louise's friend, Kathleen Church, had never been out with a boy and she was not unrepresentative of this group. As they left Miss Blaize's room, she said wryly to Louise, '*How* are we going to get married and have children? From all we learn at school, we'll have to do it by correspondence course.'

It was the break period. They went into the dining-room where Kathleen bought a quarter-pint of milk with a straw stuck through a hole in the bottle-top. Louise bought a long, iced bun. She had an enormous appetite, but lately nothing seemed to put on weight. In the playground younger girls were chasing one another on the grass, and the middle school had captured the netball courts for practice. By the shrubbery, a group of girls of whom Alice was one, were eagerly discussing *The Lives of a Bengal Lancer*, and the relative attractions of Gary Cooper and Franchot Tone.

'I must get a boy soon,' Kathleen said. 'Do you know, I've never been kissed! If it goes on much longer, no one will want me.' She brooded about this as she sucked her milk. 'How far have you gone with Guy? I mean . . . Have you . . . ?'

'As far as I can without . . . you know . . .'

They walked into the small garden where the kindergarten sometimes had their lessons in the summer. 'Do you remember playing "Fire on the Hill" here?' Kathleen asked. 'I never understood what it was we were supposed to be doing, and I got so upset about it Mummy nearly took me away from the school.' They considered this, looking back at an inconceivably distant part of their lives. Kathleen thought that having survived her ignorance of 'Fire on the Hill' she would probably survive not knowing what to do about sex as well. Faintly, from the school came the sound of arpeggios repeated again and again on a piano.

The little garden was forlorn now, the rose bushes so many dead, bare twigs, the earth hard and dry, scattered with a few dead leaves which had escaped the rake of Chapman, the gardener. Kathleen said, 'Some of the bulbs are coming up under the tree,' and pointed. Louise looked dully at the green shoots, biting her lip, suddenly full of pain. The pain was always there now; sometimes when she was busy she was unaware of it, but as soon as her mind relaxed its guard, it quickened. There was this soundless crying deep inside her, a helpless yearning springing from a well that would never run dry. She could do nothing but fold herself around it and hope to contain it. It was particularly bad on weekday evenings when she seldom saw Guy, and yet hoped that he might find a pretext for calling; while she studied in her bedroom, she listened to the footsteps of people in the street, the creaking of a gate.

It was very cold, and a sleety rain was beginning to fall when the girls went back into the building. Sometimes Louise saw the building as a towering monstrosity, and at others as a paper screen on which sky, roofs, walls and scurrying figures were implausibly sketched.

By lunchtime it was raining heavily, and the girls spent the time after lunch in the hall. An accomplished pianist thumped out a lively quickstep and several couples were dancing, including Claire and Heather. Heather was the leader, manouevring with more energy than grace, while Claire hung light as a feather in her arms. There was a dank smell of wet clothes coming from the cloakroom, and the windows were steamed over. Sweat made dark circles under the arms of the dancers. From the walls the prints of old London looked down and, above the prints, members of staff looked down from the balcony, talking as they watched the girls. 'Just like prison,' Louise thought, 'with all the little cells going off the catwalk.'

A pimpled junior came and sat beside her, gazing adoringly, hoping Louise might dance with her. The child began to prattle about a film she had seen with Myrna Loy and William Powell. Myrna Loy, it seemed, was the very image of Louise.

Louise could not bring herself to dance with the child. 'Look, cherub, I've got the curse, so I'm going to take a rest,' she excused herself; then, seeing the crestfallen face, added, 'I think I've got some pictures of Myrna Loy hidden away at home. I'll bring them for you tomorrow.'

'You wouldn't have a photograph of you?'

'I don't take a good photograph; you're much better off with Myrna Loy.'

The child gazed after her, and Louise was moved by this dim reflection of her own longing.

In the corridor she could hear the choral society singing 'The Wanderer's Night Song' with mournful pleasure. She walked past the chemistry laboratory whence came a smell of sulphuretted hydrogen and went into the sixth form cloakroom. She put on her coat and went out to walk in the streets for the remaining twenty minutes.

As she walked, the rain stopped and the sun came out. Her mother had noticed her unhappiness and, thinking Louise and Guy had quarrelled, had said, 'It will pass, my love. It's all a part of growing up.' But Louise did not want the pain to pass into numb insensitivity, which was the condition in which she imagined most adults spent their lives. She had within her reach the one great happiness beside which everything else was insignificant. How *could* she turn from that immediate bliss in order to qualify for rewards of which older people spoke so vaguely and so joylessly? The deaconess at the chapel had once said to her in a moment of great daring, 'There are sweets you can have off that tree, but if you taste today, you are denied those growing higher up.' Louise did not believe that God would order things in this way, like a game in which you only understand the rules after the last whistle has been blown.

As far as she was concerned, the most stupid thing of all was to imagine that God, having created man and woman and given them this wonderful gift of physical love, would wish it to be treated as a forbidden fruit. It should surely be apparent to any person who had not totally rejected God's abundance that something which aroused such a tender awareness of another person, such delight in the giving of body and spirit, could not possibly be anything but good.

The badness was the sense of sin from which even she was not free. It was strong and dark within her and she had to fight against it as she would have fought against any other evil force, such as Hitler. Love *must* conquer sin. If every lover felt this, why hadn't love changed the sour face of the world? She could only assume that other lovers hadn't been as strong as she, had not been prepared to risk as much.

She turned reluctantly in the direction of the school and at this moment she saw Jacov. He was on the other side of the road, and when she waved he crossed to her.

'Why aren't you at work?' she asked.

'I've got another job.' It was evident he was pleased with himself. 'I don't start until tomorrow.'

'What's this job, then?' He would tell her about the job and she would ask him if Guy knew about it. The need to mention Guy's name drove everything else from her mind.

'It's at the film studios here in Shepherd's Bush.'

'How marvellous!' She was suddenly happy as though she and

Guy must have a share in his good fortune. They began to walk along the street away from the school.

Louise had no wish to play truant, but she believed, against all the evidence, that there was always time to do the thing which was of supreme importance. Time would suspend itself while she dealt with her first priority, whether it was picking pussy willows on the banks of the Thames when she had gone to watch the Boat Race, or feeding the milkman's horse with sugar lumps on her way to catch a train. So now when she said to Jacov, 'Did you get this job through that friend who came to see our plays?' she did not see it as an impossibility for her to talk to Jacov about Guy and still be back at school in five minutes.

'Yes,' Jacov said. 'He said you ought to take a screen test.'

'And Guy?'

'He thought Guy's style of acting was more suited to the stage.'

'Guy would soon learn. It's time British films had another good-looking actor besides John Loder. Oh, Jacov! If only you could get Guy a part in a film now!'

'You'll have to give me a little time. I don't think they're going to put me in charge of casting right away.'

'It's got to be now!' she cried urgently. 'Guy's going to America.'

He stopped and studied her face. There was something about the crinkled eyes which suggested he might be making a calculation. He said, 'Poor little one!' There was mockery in his smile, though whether it was directed at her or himself was hard to tell. He bent forward and rested his cheek lightly against hers; then he strolled on, holding her hand. If the calculation had come out in his favour, it seemed he had not yet decided how to take advantage of it.

They walked without talking until they came to a car showroom. 'When you are a film producer you will be able to drive a car like that,' she said, pointing to a Daimler 15, priced at £450 and described as having 'any amount of snap, deceptive speed and a remarkable suavity'.

'Do you like suave cars, Louise?'

'Look at that clock! I should have been at school half an hour ago.'

'Too late now. Let's go to the pictures.'

She hesitated, looking resentfully at the clock, unprepared to accept its message while she still had things to say. 'This trip of Guy's to America was fixed up months ago. His uncle is paying for it. He can't really get out of going, can he?'

'For you, I would cancel a hundred trips to America! I would even give up this wonderful job which is going to make me famous. I would do anything for you!' He flapped his arms wide, like a scarecrow, and rapped his knuckles on the showroom window. It was always in his gestures that he was most eloquent. If an upraised arm was all it took, he could have conquered the world; if an outstretched hand was all that was needed, no woman could have refused him. He spun round excitedly and pointed to the Daimler. 'I will break the glass and we will take the car and drive away.'

It was typical of him that having half-convinced her that he would do such a thing he should then ask, 'Where shall we go?' Guy might not steal cars, but he would always have plenty of ideas about where to go. Jacov made a face at a man in the showroom who had come to investigate the rap on the window; then he turned away, hunching his shoulders. 'Shall we have a farewell party for Guy before he goes to America?'

She looked away from him at the bare branches of plane trees against the windy, rain-threatened sky. 'At St Bartholomew's Hall, you mean? With all the Dramatic Society there?' Momentarily, her face looked dull, the eyelids heavy, the mouth drooping listlessly.

Jacov wrinkled his nose in dismay. 'We could have a party at my house, I expect – something more private.'

'*Could* we?' She looked at him thoughtfully, making her own calculations now.

'Well, provided my mother . . .' He began to cast about for objections.

'She didn't mind us rehearsing, did she?'

They walked on and eventually came to a cinema near Notting Hill Gate. Jacov said, 'Paula Wessely!'

'Isn't this the one where he paints her in the nude?'

'It's all very innocent, though.'

She hesitated, and he began to tell her that Paula Wessely was really a Continental-style Janet Gaynor. Louise, who was concerned with how long her sanitary towel would hold out, decided that it would be all right, and in any case she would probably be able to get another in the cloakroom.

She had never seen a foreign film before, and was impressed. It proceeded with an ease and authority which American films lacked; it charmed you and had little sly jokes with you instead of shouting for your attention. Jacov put his arm around her, and as his fingers moved slightly beneath her breast her breathing quickened. Sensing her excitement, he bent and kissed her, lightly at first, then harder so that she could feel his teeth against her lips. If this ever happened when they were alone she wondered how long she would be able to hold him. He put his hand against her stomach, moving it slowly, and suddenly all the bits and pieces of her body which had lately been in such friction, irritating and nagging, as though nothing inside her had been properly made, ran together into this one burning centre. She thrust her head back sharply, gasping.

Jacov said urgently, 'Come! We'll go. I know where to go.' He got up, urging her to join him. A man in front turned round and told him where he could go. Louise, cold and trembling now that he had withdrawn from her, whispered, 'I want to see the film.'

Jacov sat beside her, watching her face instead of the screen, sometimes leaning in front of her so that she could not see; when she pushed him away, he would be still for a few minutes and then he would lean close again, lips against her ear, whispering his own racy, if inaccurate, translation of what was taking place on the screen until people told him to be quiet.

When they came out of the cinema, the manager asked them whether they had enjoyed the film, and told Louise she was like Paula Wessely. She was pleased, as she had thought Paula Wessely enchanting. Jacov was not so flattering. 'You are very English. Like the girl in the Ben Travers farces, Winifred Shotter, who keeps promising exciting things that never happen.'

'There's a time and place for the exciting things.'

'No.' He shook his head. 'There is only now.'

In the cinema he had behaved like a wilful child trying to gain attention, but now, face pinched white with cold as they waited for the bus, he looked neither child nor man. So thin, he was more bone than flesh, and with the dark, curly hair blowing around his head, he seemed out of place in the queue of homegoing shoppers. He jigged about, trying to warm himself, looking for all the world like one of the figures on a stick sometimes carried at carnivals. On the bus he was silent. Louise thought about the film. Although it had had a fairy-story ending, implicit in it had been a perception of life that was different from her own. Now, as the bus trundled through the darkening streets, she felt unsettled sitting with Jacov at her side. He, like the film, was different; he cast shadows where previously all had been bright and clear.

'Will you get into trouble at school?' he asked coldly when they parted, some distance from their homes because they did not want to be seen together.

'They won't know. I had private study periods this afternoon.'

This proved unduly optimistic. The adoring junior had reported that Louise had been unwell. When Louise could not be found Kathleen had been sent to her home and, not finding her there, the police had been summoned.

There was a considerable fuss. Louise was kept at home the following day while Judith went to see Miss Blaize. She was not feeling any worse than usual at her monthly time, but she could see the situation was only going to be acceptable to them if they could decide that she was fairly grievously afflicted. She obliged them. Eventually, Miss Blaize accepted the explanation that Louise had 'just sat in the park until the stomach ache got better and then had a cup of tea in the ABC at Notting Hill.' Louise, after all, had a blameless record as far as behaviour was concerned, even if academically her performance was disappointing. Miss Blaize acknowledged to Judith that 'Girls do tend to be unpredictable at this age,' and wisely decided that it was not a matter to be put to the Chairman of the Governors.

At home, Louise lay in bed reading the love scenes in *The Rosary*, and visualizing Guy in the role of Garth, blinded and unable to leave for America.

Later, she heard the puppy crying and went downstairs to console him. The house seemed very quiet. She could not recall a time when she had been alone in it. She picked up the puppy and went into the dining-room, examining the tatting chairback cover on which Grandmother Fairley had worked a swan; noticing how brightly the silver gleamed on the mahogany sideboard, and how the green curtains had faded in the folds to a silvery grey; fingering the crack between the windowsill and the window-frame where the putty, inexpertly inserted by her father, had come away. In the garden the grey cat was sitting on the bird-table eating the scraps of bacon fat, the intricate wire contraption which Alice had rigged up to prevent him swinging lightly as a mark of his passage. There was frost on the grass. Shivering, she turned away, meaning to go back to the kitchen where the boiler was alight, but pausing by the fireplace to show the puppy its reflection in the mirror. It was not interested but, sensing something expected of it, licked her nose. Behind the heavy serpentine lighthouse on the mantelshelf there was a pile of old cards and snaps, and looking through she found one of herself, woolly hat pulled down to eyebrow level, holding Badger in her arms. It must have been taken in the garden of their other house in Sussex; Daddy had written on the back, 'Louise, aged 8, with Badger.' The puppy wriggled and anxiously licked her hand.

The milk book was on the table in the hall together with a note to her father, which must have been put there during half-term week, saying that if the coalman called he must remember to count the sacks.

The drawing-room door was half open, the fire laid in the grate but not yet lit. Her mother must have been sewing last night – the sewing machine was open, a length of dull gold material, probably for curtains, folded and laid by it. On the round table by the window was a small vase of flowers, late Christmas roses, white and pale pink, held in a green sheath of leaves. Louise stood in the doorway gazing at the flowers, which were arranged with such perfect simplicity that they seemed to draw the whole room together, giving it composure and grace.

The puppy wriggled more energetically. She went into the kitchen and began to prepare tea for her mother, something she had seldom thought to do.

15

Spring came early. March was full of promise which April would not keep.

Ben and Angus Drummond were walking through Hyde Park. They had struck up a rather unlikely friendship, and when Angus was on vacation they met in town occasionally. It was early evening now and Hyde Park, in late sunlight, had that air of all things being new which March can give when not tearing itself to shreds. Both young men had been studying hard and Ben, in particular, coveted the pleasures he had had to forgo. He looked keenly at girls with gleaming hair half-hidden under little veiled hats, their exquisitely painted faces so cool, so insouciant, that to involve them even in dreams seemed audacity. 'Now, that I'd like!' he said, passing one such vision. 'Just for the night, to find out what goes on underneath all the gloss.'

'You wouldn't get near her in one night,' Angus said.

Youth gave Ben an utter assurance in the future, combined with an urgent sense that opportunity was being lost to him which would not come again. He said, 'Why don't we head back to town? I know a place in Denman Street . . .'

'My mother is expecting me,' Angus said. 'I can't let her down. She has a rotten time.'

They came out of the park opposite the Bayswater Road and turned towards Notting Hill. Soon they came to a cinema where there were long queues for *Forsaking All Others*. Angus saw the younger Vaseyelins towards the front of the ninepenny queue. 'They won't let you in,' he said. 'It's an "A" certificate.'

'I'll get by,' Katia replied scornfully. 'I do it all the time.' She was heavily made up. In make-up, as in other matters, she was not a neat person and had made a few heavy-handed daubs at her face, creating a patchy, garish effect. Angus thought she looked very Jewish. He could imagine her several years hence running a dress shop in Oxford Street, standing in the doorway, daring people to walk past. She had the dark, magnetic eyes which it is difficult to avoid. While they were chatting, he could not keep his eyes from her face.

A current of energy flowed from her. Perhaps she would not run a dress shop after all – she would do something remarkable. He watched her jogging up and down, every so often glancing at the head of the queue, impatient, demanding. A breeze, light but keen, frisked from the direction of the park. The people passing them seemed incredibly brisk and purposeful, moving towards assignations, whether good or evil, of the greatest significance. Angus had a sudden picture of himself with Katia in years to come, going to exhibitions, knowing the artist, going to theatre parties after the show, living in a world of remarkable people all full of driving energy.

She was saying, 'If you don't think I'm old enough, what about taking us in? I bet you're not doing much this evening.'

'Joan Crawford!' Angus made a fastidious face.

'Who do you like, then?'

'Someone with a bit more natural verve.' He had very little idea what he wanted; he needed someone to be decisive for him.

'Claudette Colbert?' She lowered her eyelids and looked arch. 'A bit of ooh-la-la?'

'I'm afraid I'm just not interested in films,' he said hastily, afraid of appearing ridiculous.

At this moment people began to come out of the cinema, at first in ones and twos, and then in large numbers. Katia said, 'The big film's over.'

Angus and Ben turned away and continued their walk. Light, delicate and tremulous, filtered through the trees. Angus was plagued by a sense of opportunity almost within reach and an awareness of the impermanence of all things.

'How old would Katia be?' he asked.

'Fifteen, sixteen?' Ben was hazy. Katia kept Alice company; if it hadn't been for that, he would have accepted her as eighteen.

'Ripe,' Angus said. 'Wouldn't you say?'

It would not have been at all Ben's way of saying it. He wondered how much experience Angus really had of women. 'Katia is just a kid,' he said. Emotionally, he did not think she was any more developed than Alice. 'Now, what about Alice? She'd make you a splendid wife when she grows up.'

'Alice? The plump one? You can't be serious.'

As they drew nearer to Shepherd's Bush, Angus began to talk

about politics. He said he was thinking of joining the Communist Party, and mentioned a Cambridge don who had greatly influenced him. Ben, bored, did not listen, and as Angus was really rehearsing for his encounter with his father, he did not notice Ben's lack of attention. They parted company outside the Drummonds' house, Ben refusing an invitation to come in. He was going to a party at the Vaseyelins. Jacov had urged him to come early, because he was uneasy about the propriety of having a farewell party for Guy which consisted of himself, Guy and Louise.

'I would not wish to do anything of which Mr Fairley would not approve,' Jacov had said.

'That's going to narrow your life quite a bit,' Ben had told him.

Ben turned into Pratts Farm Road. The gardeners were out, planting, staking, hoeing. Ben did not understand this urge to play some part in the cycle of the seasons, but he felt within himself the movement of a force over which he had no control. He decided to call on the Fairleys before going to the party. Jacov had asked him to bring a girl with him. There were several he might have asked, all pretty enough but none as lively as Louise. So he had come alone. He looked towards the Vaseyelins' house. 'In a few years, when she's thickened a bit, she'll have a jaw like her mother's,' he muttered. There were yellow and white crocuses in the Fairleys' flower borders. and the path was spattered with pink blossoms blown from a prunus in an adjacent garden. As he walked towards the house a breeze stirred, idly floating a scent of hidden bloom more sweet for being untraceable.

Claire opened the front door. 'There's just me,' she said, and he was to understand from her voice the tragedy of this. 'Mummy's upstairs washing her hair and Alice has gone with Daddy to the vet.' Her face came apart as she spoke; tears rolled down her cheeks and she sat on the stairs, hugging her grief. 'Rumpus has been run over.'

Ben sat beside her. 'But he wasn't killed?' He could not imagine it would have taken both Alice and Mr Fairley to present the vet with the remains. In any case, a burial in the garden would surely have been more the way the Fairleys would handle this sort of event.

'He hurt his paw. And the motor cycle went into a tree and the man had blood all over his head.' She brightened as she recollected the latter.

The accident to the dog scarcely explained the passionate tears. 'And how's yourself?' Ben asked. 'No hurt paw, head unbloodied?'

The face crumpled again, her whole body knotted up as if she had cramp. 'I went in next door to tell them about Rumpus. They're having a party . . . for Guy . . . because he's going away.'

'Oh yes?'

Slowly, it all came out. As she left the house she had met Mrs Vaseyelin on her way to catch the Number 12 bus at The Askew Arms. Mrs Vaseyelin had told her that the back door was open, so she had gone round the side of the house and let herself in. There had been no one in the hall, but the cellar door was ajar and she could hear voices. Ben could imagine how intrigued she must have been by this party, how she must have longed for a sight of it. She had stood at the top of the stairs, probably aware that she was not wanted, plucking up courage just to go down a few steps. There was candlelight and laughter. She had the temerity to cast a shadow. Guy had come to see who was there. He had been angry. He had told her she was spying and Louise had shouted, 'Send her packing, she's an awful little tell-tale!' A bad case of guilty conscience, Ben thought.

'I wasn't spying, I wasn't,' she sobbed.

He put his arm round her. Her little dignity had been badly bruised, but it was worse than that. He could see the episode had those recurrent elements of a bad dream: the moment when it is too late to turn back, the unbelievable about to happen, the being caught in forbidden territory. He was sorry for Claire, but not displeased to be given good cause for anger. 'Forget about them. What would you most like to do? Tell me.'

She stared at him. It was a March evening, getting dusk; her mother was washing her hair; her dog was injured; and the older folk she so admired had turned on her. What *was* there to do? Then, suddenly, comfort came to her, warm and crisp, dripping with good sweet syrup. 'You said you could make waffles!'

A minute later when Judith came downstairs with a towel round her head, Ben was alone in the hall. 'Oh dear, I do hope that dog will be all right,' she said softly. 'I don't think the paw is bad, but it's the shock with a puppy.'

'Mongrels are pretty tough.'

'Mummy, Mummy!' Claire called urgently from the kitchen. 'Ben is going to make waffles!'

He looked uncertainly at Judith, but she was grateful for the diversion. They went into the kitchen.

Half an hour later the stretcher party arrived. The dog was wrapped in a shawl and dressed in a doll's nightdress; a bonnet was tied round its head and only its long, brown nose could be seen.

'The vet said we couldn't have done better than to keep him warm like this,' Stanley Fairley explained fiercely as though Ben had challenged his care of the dog. 'He says he has a good chance of surviving.' He went to the wicker basket and laid the dog gently in it.

'Old Mr Ainsworth sent Mrs Peachey in with a little brandy "for the shock",' Judith said. 'Should we, do you think?'

'I don't see why not. Rumpus hasn't signed the pledge, has he?'

Rumpus drank the brandy and hot milk from a spoon, flicked his tongue appreciatively around his jaws, curled up and went to sleep.

The Fairleys settled down to eat waffles in the kitchen. Alice had had her hair cut and she had water-waved it.

'It makes you look different,' Ben told her.

'She brought it back with her,' Claire said. 'You should have seen how much there was of it.'

Later Ben and Mr Fairley went into the sitting-room for a talk while Judith and the girls washed up and kept an eye on Rumpus.

'What do you think about the stand of the Confessional Church?' Mr Fairley demanded. Ten more pastors had been arrested. Ben said he could not understand why more people did not stand up to Hitler.

Outside, it was dark and there were lights in the houses across the road. Ben wondered whether Jacov had been in the cellar when Claire ventured down the stairs. If so, why did it have to be Guy who sent her packing?

Mr Fairley said that the pastors had been sent to a concentration camp at Sachsenburg.

'That makes me savage,' Ben said.

'Some of these stories may be exaggerated, of course.'

'I doubt that.' There was no charity in Ben's soul.

Louise came in soon after nine. Her mother said, 'You're early.'

'I *told* you I wouldn't be late.' She turned away as she spoke and saw Ben standing in the doorway. Her eyes met his with a look of triumph.

16

It was fine and the temperatures were in the seventies for the Jubilee on 6 May. On the wireless it was reported that thousands had spent the night sleeping along the route of the Royal Procession.

Mr Fairley said they would take a tube train from Shepherd's Bush and go up to the City which, historically, would be the most interesting place to be. 'You will be able to see the King's carriage held up at Temple Bar. The sovereign cannot cross the City boundaries except by permission of the Lord Mayor. A great thing, a very great thing! You should be proud to live in a country with such a tradition.'

Alice said she could not travel by tube.

'What *do* you mean?'

'I can't travel in a tube train. That's all. I just can't.'

She was adamant. When it became apparent that her objection, however unreasonable, was genuine, they decided to take a Number 12 bus to Trafalgar Square and hope to catch another bus to the City. Claire objected that she wanted to be in the Park and Mr Fairley said testily, 'Nothing of any historical significance will be enacted in the Park, there will just be a lot of shouting and singing and pageantry' – which was exactly what Claire wanted.

When all was finally settled, Louise said she was not coming. 'I couldn't stand about all that long.'

'There may never be another day like this in your lifetime.'

'That will be all right with me,' she said crossly.

As they were getting ready in their bedroom, Mr Fairley said to Judith, 'Why is it that nowadays we can never go out together as a family? It wasn't like this when they were young.'

'*Because* they were young.'

'Is she really unwell, or is she going to stay at home and moon about Guy all day?'

'Both, I expect.'

When they reached Trafalgar Square the crowds were so dense there seemed little hope of catching another bus. They made their way towards St James's Park to join the crowds lining The Mall. The air was still fresh in the park and a breeze stirred the flags and pennants. People were singing 'Mademoiselle from Armentières' and Stanley Fairley, reconciled to the loss of historical significance, joined in.

There were policemen on horseback controlling the crowds near the Duke of York steps. One grey horse nuzzled a woman's neck and she squeaked in alarm. The policeman turned the horse's head away. 'The lady doesn't want you eating her hat!'

'The Drummonds are going to a party in a restaurant,' Alice said. 'I'd much rather be here.'

'Heather's going to a street party.'

Stanley Fairley said, 'I thought Heather and her family were all republicans.'

'They're having a street party, anyway, and a banner saying, "Lousy but loyal".'

'They're good sorts.' Stanley Fairley looked around at the crowd. He had criticized the money spent on the celebrations, but now that he saw the sincere affection displayed by so many ordinary people he was moved, and thought that the King too was a good sort – not overburdened with intelligence perhaps, but a good, bluff old man.

They descended the steps with difficulty and eased themselves in the direction of The Mall. The crowd was good-natured and at first slow progress was possible, though Claire kept wailing that they would never see anything. When at last they had established a reasonably good position, a woman behind began to push. There was little to be gained by pushing forward, and Stanley and Judith stood their ground, refusing in their turn to push the people in front. She was a big, dark woman with protruding black eyes, dressed in a black woollen frock and wearing a close black hat. Even had it not been for all this blackness, her bad manners would have betrayed her as a foreigner. Stanley Fairley identified her as a typical French madame, a formidable manager with a sense of business as sharp as her elbows. There was in such types a marriage of greed and anarchy, qualities which must not be allowed to triumph over the gentler Anglo-Saxon virtues of tolerance and discipline, especially on this of all occasions. Judith, who did not like being pushed about by other women, was equally determined. Alice and Claire, in whom the school had instilled the principles of good citizenship, closed ranks with their parents. An unspoken war was declared between the

English and the foreign woman. So intense did the combat become that the Fairleys did not notice the great crescendo of cheering. The monarch made his way down The Mall, the Fairleys being rewarded with a belated glimpse of his plumed helmet and a rather better view of Mr Ramsay MacDonald and Miss Ishbel MacDonald.

Now, the foreign woman was forgotten. Long after the royal procession had passed beneath the Admiralty Arch people were shouting and waving. In a sense, the King's celebration was their celebration, a celebration of having come through difficult years together. Strangers linked arms and sang 'Keep the Home Fires Burning' and 'Tipperary'. For these few hours they were members of an enormous family, and their spirits soared with their voices. Mr Fairley told the girls that in other countries when the police lined the streets they did not face the processional route but turned outward to watch the crowd. 'You will never see that in this country.' Alice felt tears of pride in her eyes. In fact, in the park it was the Navy which was lining the route. The sailors looked very young. 'They will remember this as long as they live,' Stanley Fairley said; at which one of the sailors removed his cap and was neatly sick in it.

'What will happen to him?' Claire asked anxiously as a petty officer set in motion the ritual departure of the offender.

'Court martialled, I should hope! They're not made of the stuff they used to be.'

They sat in St James's Park and ate sandwiches and fed the ducks. Then they walked through to Parliament Square and saw the House of Commons, festooned with flags and flowers. Alice and Claire wanted to stay to see the floodlighting but their parents said this would make too long a day of it, and anyway, they must be home in time to hear the King speak on the wireless at eight o'clock.

They walked for an hour by the river, which was crowded with boats noisily hooting sirens; even the old tugs and barges were gaily decorated. In front of *President*, a man was playing a banjo and singing 'Shenandoah', and the rather sad melody followed them as they turned and made their way back to the park. The crowd was larger than ever now as people headed towards Buckingham Palace. Alice and Claire, tired, did not insist on seeing the Royal Family come out on the balcony, although Claire said half-heartedly that she would have liked to see the beacons lit on the hills around London.

They were all tired when they got home. It was twenty to eight. The girls wanted supper and Stanley Fairley wanted to listen to the

King. Rumpus was pounding hysterically on the kitchen door. Judith went into the kitchen to prepare the meal, and Claire was dispatched to take Rumpus for a walk 'at least as far as the double oak'.

Alice went up the stairs. It was cool and shadowy in the house, but outside the sun was still shining and through the landing window she could see the lilac, its blooms pale now, because the tree was old. In his study, her father was singing, 'Oh Shenandoah, I love your daughter, away you rolling river . . .' He had left the door ajar, perhaps in the expectation that his family would decide to join him. Alice tiptoed past quickly and went along the corridor towards her sister's bedroom. She wondered why Louise had not come down to greet them, but allowed her curiosity to be diverted by the linen cupboard whence came a familiar smell. Her mother had been making saffron cake and the big bowl was on the floor. The mixture had risen and Alice, seized by an irresistible childish urge, guiltily scooped a little from the edge and licked her finger. Immediately she had a strange sensation of having opened not the linen cupboard but an Aladdin's cavern in which were miraculously stored all the smells and tastes of her childhood; cinnamon and candied peel being stirred into the Christmas pudding, peardrops acid on the tongue, aniseed balls – bringing a picture of Claire with one stuck up her nostril – the earthy smell of the outside lavatory in her Sussex grandparents' house mingled with the evening scent of stocks in their garden and, very faint and far away, the slightly peppery smell of sprigs of broom which she and Claire had once put under their pillows in the belief that their wishes would come true as they slept. What was it they had wished for? As she tried to recall, so the scents faded. She lingered for a moment or two, reluctant to move, and then walked down the corridor, sucking her finger.

When she went into her sister's bedroom, Louise was sitting on the ottoman by the window, looking out into the street, and she did not turn her head or say, 'Did you have a good day?' Alice told her they had had a good day. Louise looked at her as though she had forgotten where they had been, or what day it was. Alice had never seen her look like that before: Louise had always been the one who knew exactly where she was and what could be expected of the day, whether pocket money, skating at Richmond, or scripture with Miss Blaize.

Alice said, 'Is the pain bad, Lou?'

'I haven't got the curse, Alice.'

Alice stood still and sturdy, rather, Louise thought, as if she was defending goal at lacrosse. She said, 'Perhaps you've got the date wrong.'

Louise shook her head. 'I haven't had it since the beginning of March and I'm very regular.'

Alice just stood there. Louise wondered if she would have to help each one of her family over this difficult threshold. 'You know what that means, don't you?'

Alice was the first person she had told and she watched with interest while Alice made herself accept it. How intent and serious she looked, pondering it as she pondered homework which stretched beyond her accustomed horizon. Next, Louise thought, I shall watch my mother; then my father. There was no doubt in her mind as to the order in which it must happen: the weight of their father's shock would be borne by all of them.

When Alice did not know what to make of something, she stored it away inside herself, unlike Claire who spat it out immediately. Now, when she spoke, she sounded gravely in possession of the situation. 'Lou! How awful these last weeks must have been for you. Why didn't you tell me?' Then, perhaps feeling she had come too quickly to this, she tried to turn aside. 'But it *can't* be, surely? Monica Pilgrim only has a period every six months.'

'I'm not Monica Pilgrim!' Louise's eyes flashed with scorn and it seemed for a moment that the mention of Monica Pilgrim would make her turn from Alice in disgust. Her emotions fluctuated so turbulently she could barely keep a hold on them, and disgust was replaced by a mixture of passion and pride. 'I knew at once. I felt it in my breasts, you see. Some women do. And now . . .' She touched her belly and suddenly her face crumpled, 'I'm sick, oh, so sick! I can't keep it from Mother now this has started.'

Her tears, more than anything else, stirred Alice. She knelt beside her, pawing her shoulder. 'Lou! I'm so sorry, dearest Lou!'

They clung to each other. 'You shouldn't have to be sorry, it shouldn't be like this,' Louise sobbed. 'It's all wrong, the way we've been brought up.' Family, chapel, school, the teaching, belief, aspiration, had sat so lightly on her all these years, how was she ever to have known this would be so difficult?

Her mother called from the foot of the stairs. 'Alice! Louise! I want one of you down here in the kitchen to help with supper.'

Louise said, 'I'll go and tell her now.' It was her moment. She recognized it and was glad and had no thought that, whether she wished it or not, it was also her mother's moment.

'Now?' It was all happening too quickly for Alice.

'I'll feel better when I've done it.' She hugged Alice and then, reverting to their old custom, rubbed noses. 'Will you be here until I come back? It will be a help knowing you're waiting here.'

Alice clenched her hands and nodded. She listened to Louise going down the stairs. Something was about to happen that could not possibly happen, and she wanted to run out of the house and run and run and run. But she must wait for Louise as she had promised. She stood in front of the door, staring at the blue woollen dressing-gown to which, in order to cheer it up, Louise had attached a lace jabot given her for Christmas two years ago. Alice tried to remember the details of that Christmas so that she would not think of her mother at the stove in the kitchen, still unaware; of her father waiting for them to join him for the King's broadcast; of Claire shrilly exhorting Rumpus not to tug on his lead. She could not believe it. Her body seemed about to crack apart the disbelief was so huge.

'Oh, it's you.' Judith glanced over her shoulder as Louise came into the kitchen. Louise did not answer and Judith turned to look at her. Something in Louise's face other than the trace of recent tears made Judith's voice sharp and hostile as she said, 'What is it?'

'I've got something to tell you.'

Judith took a saucepan of Heinz baked beans off the gas-ring and wiped the palms of her hands on her apron. This accomplished, she faced her daughter. 'Well?'

'I haven't . . .' Louise stopped, wondering why she was doing it their way, as though it was unspeakably shameful.

'You haven't what?' Judith had no idea what it was that Louise was about to tell her, but she felt that dread of betrayal from which no relationship, however loving, is ever completely free. 'For goodness' sake, Louise, what are you trying to tell me?'

'I wanted it to be different from this, I wanted . . .'

'Just tell me, will you? Have you broken something?' She knew it wasn't that, but she said it as if to warn her daughter against making worse admissions.

'I haven't got my period, if that's the way you want it. I haven't had it since March.'

There was a pause, then Judith said quietly, 'What are you saying?'

'What you think I'm saying. Only I wanted to tell you differently. I wanted you to understand that it's all right, that I'm very happy and you don't have to . . .'

'Are you sure of this?'

'Do you think I would have told you if I wasn't sure? *You* knew, didn't you?'

She had never hitherto accepted that her experience of life might have been shared by her mother, imagining all things to have been new-minted for her.

Her mother was looking at her as though one of them was drowning. In this moment, Louise saw how much her mother loved her. She saw that her mother had had such hopes for her and that now they had all gone. She watched hope go, leaving the eyes, usually so bright and challenging, without a single spark. She was astonished by this darkness and she wanted to cry out, 'Why didn't you *tell* me!' Though what it was she needed to know, or whether it would have made any difference, she could not have said. 'When did it happen? At that party?'

Louise nodded.

'This will kill your father, you know that, I suppose.' She turned away, one hand pressed to her side. 'Oh, Louise, how could you? How could you!'

Louise thought impatiently, 'It won't kill him. People don't die of life.' She was intensely sad at the inability of those whom she loved to see things her way. She felt much older than her mother, and she wanted to comfort and protect her, to guide her through the confusion into the light of joy and common sense.

'You had better stay here while I tell Daddy.'

Louise's eyes filled with tears at the word Daddy. 'It shouldn't be like this. It's all wrong,' she sobbed.

Her mother, welcoming the tears and not heeding the words, said with bitter satisfaction, 'You should have thought of that before now.'

When her mother had gone, Louise began to feel afraid for the first time. The silence was filled with voices, all disapproving, and she could not pull herself together to answer because there were too many. 'Oh Guy, Guy!' she tried to extract him from this unseen company but failed to find him. He had been so near her during these last days, she could not bear the thought that they might drive him out.

Judith was on her way, bearing the load of grief to its ultimate destination. Much as she pitied him, she needed Stanley's grief to give appropriate expression to this terrible event and already as she climbed the stairs she was preparing herself for her own role as the one who must steer their vessel through the storm.

In his study, Stanley was listening to the King and he put up a hand to stop Judith talking when she entered the room. 'The Queen and I thank you from the depths of our hearts for the loyalty and – may I say? – the love with which this day and always you have surrounded us . . .' Judith stood just inside the door, ignoring Stanley's gesture that she should sit down. 'To the children I would like to send a special message . . . I ask you to remember that in days to come you will be the citizens of a great Empire . . .' The front door opened and shut and Claire and Rumpus clattered across to the kitchen. '. . . and when the time comes, be ready and proud to give to your country the service of your work, your mind and your heart . . .'

Stanley switched off the wireless and said, 'It would have been nice if our children could have been here to hear that.'

'Stanley.' Judith came to him and took his hand.

'What is it?' He looked down at his hand held in hers as though wondering if something had happened to it without his noticing.

'I've got bad news for you.'

He started, eyes staring fearfully. 'Claire! She's been run over!' He struck out boldly, though in fact he was putting in train the process of whittling disaster down to acceptable proportions.

She had wanted to break it gently to him, but had neither strength nor patience and, in any case, what gentle way was there? She said, 'It's Louise. She's going to have a baby.'

He looked at her so blankly she thought he could not have taken in what she had said. As the seconds ticked away the house seemed to lose patience and began to register fretful uneasiness: wood cracked, wind stirred in the chimney sending grit spattering in the hearth, a door banged to and fro. It was as if some vital ritual was being neglected, the chief mourner not fulfilling his function.

'I mean it, Stanley,' Judith prompted.

He sat down, gripping the arms of his chair and staring in front of him, jaw slack. Judith, who had been ready to calm him, felt acutely the lack of wailing and beating of the breast.

'Do you want to see her?' she asked, unable to tolerate inactivity.

'Yes.' The idea seemed not to have occurred to him, but now he hauled himself towards it. 'Of course I must see her.' He stood up, positioning himself facing the door, woodenly, as if on sentry duty.

'You mustn't be harsh with her, Stanley.'

He looked at her in amazement.

Judith opened the door. Louise was waiting on the stairs. She had composed herself and was determined to do justice to what was probably the most testing moment of her life. Some last residue of nervous triviality had, however, to be expelled: she said, 'I've got Claire to mind the baked beans.'

'It's been a great shock to your father.'

This was what Louise needed to strengthen her purpose: however shocked he might be, this time he was going to take note of her. As she came into the room she actually caught him in the act of hollowing his cheeks and pursing his lips in a melodramatic semblance of anguish. She stood still and said nothing, hoping he would not leave her thus too long because she was shaking inwardly and soon it would show.

He said, with a note of appeal she had not prepared herself for, 'Tell me it's not true, my child.'

She lifted her chin to the exact angle which she calculated would express pride but not defiance – for she had, after all, done nothing about which to be defiant. 'It is true, Father.' She had never called him Father before.

'Come to me.'

She very nearly panicked and then stepped forward two paces, unsure whether she had done the right thing.

She is still acting, her mother thought – but then, so is he.

He laid his hands on his daughter's shoulders and looked into her face. He is going to forgive me, Louise thought, keeping her composure with difficulty; then I am supposed to fall on him weeping with gratitude. His eyes traced the lines of her face wonderingly as though it was some precious object which had only recently come into his possession. He said, 'My darling child!' It was his great gift to her and she rejected it promptly.

'I'm not a fallen woman, Daddy.'

He stepped back. Her mother said, 'Louise!'

Father and daughter faced each other, the one concerned with plumbing the depths of the situation in which they now found themselves, the other with illuminating the heights. Mr Fairley's face was suddenly suffused with blood. He said, 'What is it you think has happened? Perhaps you will tell me that.' In spite of his anger he was at some disadvantage, since he needed help from his daughter – whereas she appeared to require none from him.

'Guy and I love each other.' She spoke the not very exceptional words as though they had been coined especially for her and Guy; and, looking at her face, one could only assume that this was indeed how she saw it. 'Everything will be all right,' she said. 'If only you will leave it to Guy and me and not complicate things, I promise you it will be all right.'

The colour drained from her father's face except for two veined patches on his cheeks which burned as though hot wires had been pressed against them. ' "It will be all right",' he repeated. 'Is this all you have to say for yourself? Under what possible circumstances can you imagine that this will be "all right"? Don't you realize how others will regard you, how it will affect you for the rest of your life and those who love you? Can you really imagine that this is a situation devoid of complications? "It will be all right"! If you can be so heedless of this, what will become of you? You will go from bad to worse, like some poor creature who has not had the advantage of . . .'

'All right, Stanley,' Judith warned.

'IT IS NOT ALL RIGHT!'

'It's *right*, then,' Louise shouted, 'You know what *right* means, don't you? Why do you have to make it all so complicated? I'm no good when things get tangled up, I just have to hold on hard to what I know is right and then I can see my way plain and straightforward.'

'Right, plain, straightforward . . . Is it possible that you have lived among us without understanding anything? All that mother and I have tried to give to you over the years, has that meant nothing to you?'

'I know you both love me and I love you. What else is it supposed to mean?'

'You can't argue with her while she's in this state, Stanley.'

'Louise.' He modulated his voice but was unable to keep it steady. His eyes protruded with the effort to reach her and a vein stood out on his temple. 'Louise, every day at breakfast we read the Bible together and we pray. Have you absorbed nothing from this?'

'Jesus didn't throw stones at the woman taken in adultery and *I* haven't committed adultery!'

He spoke in the hushed whisper which could yet reach the back row in chapel. 'You dare to use His name at such a time!'

'I follow His commandments just as you do.' The more quietly he spoke the more Louise shouted. 'I love the Lord my God and my neighbour as myself and those are the two that count because HE SAID SO!'

'The whole street must be hearing every word of this,' Judith said.

Stanley Fairley turned and went to the window, not with the purpose of checking how much could be heard but in order to collect himself, to work out what had gone so terribly wrong. Unfortunately, as he looked into the street the first thing which caught his eye was a FOR SALE notice by the gate of the house opposite. This brought vividly to his mind the day when they had moved in here. He had paid off the mortgage on the house in Sussex and this was the first house he had owned. As he looked up at it he had felt so proud that he could provide his family with this splendid home, and he had thought of the other things he would be able to do for them now that he had a headship. Tears came to his eyes when he recalled how they had worked on the house and garden. There wasn't a shrub he had planted without thinking of the pleasure it would give them all. Only recently he had secretly decided to have a telephone installed. Such little things – they seemed pathetically inadequate now – and yet what joy had gone into the planning of them! What was his life if it was not this house and the physical and emotional capital he had invested in it? And now it had come to this! He had intended to tell Louise that he loved her, that whatever happened he would stand by her instead of which . . . If only she had shown some appreciation of the enormity of her offence (and, coincidentally, the generosity of his response) he would have taken her in his arms. What he would have done after that he had no idea, just as he had no idea of what he should do now.

Judith said, 'Have you written to Guy?'

Stanley Fairley groaned at this example of how relentlessly women reject the essential in favour of the peripheral.

'I *can't* write now,' Louise answered. 'Things have got in the way. I have to wait until I can see it all quite simply again.'

'But you must write to him! Otherwise he will hear it from his mother.'

'I have to wait.'

Judith said, 'Louise, you must *listen* . . .' and then stopped. Her voice was muffled when she went on, 'I think we had all better have something to eat and then we can talk about this.'

She went out of the room. In the kitchen, Claire was sitting on a chair and Rumpus on the mat; both looked very subdued. Claire said, 'The baked beans burnt, Mummy.'

'That's all right; I'll take over now.'

'Mummy, why had Lou been crying?'

Then she saw that her mother was crying violently so that her breath whooped in her throat as if she was choking. Rumpus slunk under the table. Claire raced out of the kitchen and up the stairs in time to see Louise going into her bedroom. Through the half-open door she saw Alice. She ran down the corridor to join her sisters.

'Mummy's crying,' she said.

Louise flung herself down on her bed. 'Oh, Alice, I never thought it would be as bad as this! I thought there might be a terrible row and they wouldn't want me any more, or that they would love me so much they would be able to understand. I couldn't be sure which it would be because Daddy is so passionate and Mummy can be so awfully unsympathetic. But I never thought they wouldn't understand *anything* and *still* go on loving me!'

'What don't they understand?' Claire asked.

'Take her away and tell her, Alice. And don't worry. It will be all right. I *know* that it will be all right so long as people don't interfere. You believe that, don't you?'

Alice nodded. She marvelled at Louise's bravery.

'What is going to be all right?' Claire asked when they were in their own bedroom. She looked as if she was not sure that she wanted to know, but when Alice told her she seemed to take it well. At supper she sat quietly, not eating much, looking from her mother to her father, avoiding Louise. Suddenly, while Judith was pouring tea, she cried, 'Are we going away? Shall I pack?'

Judith said, 'Of course we are not going away, Claire.'

'But we can't stay here!' Her voice was shrill. 'We can't!' The freckles stood out on her pale face like a powdering of nutmeg on milk.

'As far as you are concerned everything will be the same,' Judith said wearily. 'You'll go to school tomorrow and . . .'

'I'm not going to *school*! I couldn't ever go to school again! I'll never go out again. I shall stay in the house for ever and ever and ever!'

Alice was dismayed to find that even at such a time she was resentful of Claire's ability to focus attention on herself.

Judith said, 'I think you had better go to bed. I'll come up with you.'

As they left the room, Claire was saying, 'I won't go to school, Mummy, I won't!'

Alice did the washing up. When she went up to bed she could hear her mother and father talking to Louise in the sitting-room.

Claire was in her pyjamas, brushing her hair in front of the dressing table. Her protests about not going to school, though still vociferous, had the monotony of defeat.

'I shall be going, too,' Alice said.

'People will know, won't they?'

'The Imminghams will have to know. I think that's what they are talking about downstairs.'

People would look in a certain way and things would be said, slyly, or even shouted, as Claire could imagine Maisie doing. How were they ever to bear the disgrace, they who had been so much better than other people? Claire watched in the mirror as her grief spilled over. What would happen to their father? How could he still preach in the chapel and be the best headmaster in Acton and run the sea cadets . . . Her face, pulled this way and that like a rubber mask, was now stretched to the limit. 'And Crusaders,' she sobbed. 'I couldn't ever go again. They'd all pray for *us*.'

She had reached her climax and climbed into bed. Her mother had given her a hot water bottle to comfort her, and she held it against her stomach, snuffling. Her nose was blocked and the muscles of her throat ached. She looked at the window. The curtains were drawn back, and every now and again fireworks exploded in showers of red, white and blue. She resolved to look at them, keeping her eyes open wide, because once the lids began to close she would sleep and then in no time it would be morning. 'I'm going to stay awake all night,' she told Alice. But in spite of all her efforts she was asleep in a quarter of an hour.

Alice could not stay in the bedroom, wondering what was happening in the sitting-room. So she sat on the stairs leading down to the first-floor landing where, although she could not hear anything, she did not feel so shut away. Moonlight slanted through the landing window beneath her: she could see it gleaming on the lino and falling more dully on the floorboards. The stairs and landing had been painted recently and the skirting boards still had a shine about them, but there were dark marks here and there where Mrs Moxham had got floor polish on the paintwork. Alice had not understood why her mother carried on so about it, but now, looking at the dark smears, she whispered, 'Oh Mummy!' and felt the need of tears she was unable to release. In lieu of tears she went into the bathroom and wetted the cleaning cloth. Then she knelt on the floorboards and worked at the smears until her elbows and wrists ached. The smears remained obstinately immovable. It upset her that she could not get the skirting boards clean for her mother. 'Oh Mummy!' she said again, rocking back on her heels. All the scrubbing and ironing and mending, cooking, stoking fires, and then to have this happen! It wasn't a sensible equation that so much elbow-grease should equal so many children growing up good and straight; but Alice felt in her stomach it should have been so. And yet she felt that Louise was right because she was so brave. It was very unpleasant to be thus torn.

Later, she saw Louise come upstairs and go to her bedroom. She wondered whether to follow her but did not. Then, half an hour later, her mother came up and Alice wondered whether to speak to her but did not. Finally, her father came up and went into his study and she knew she must not disturb him. It was dark on the stairs and none of them noticed Alice. At this moment, she thought, we are all in different parts of the house. She supposed it must have happened before, but now, late at night, it troubled her and she hurried back to the sleeping Claire.

She slept restlessly, and somewhere between waking and sleeping the thought came to her that the Leaning Tower of Pisa *had* fallen.

It was a long time before Stanley Fairley went to bed. He was in a state of the utmost confusion. A man of formidable energy, he could usually be relied upon to react with the whole force of body, mind and spirit – whether irritated by the delivery of the wrong newspaper or in denunciation of the most heinous crimes of a dictator. If tears were called for, he shed them, embarrassing his wife during the curtain speech in *Cavalcade*, and startling a colleague by his response to the playing of a barrel organ on a cold, foggy evening, fumbling for silver to make up for all those who passed by. In the Ben Travers farces he laughed louder at the asininity of Ralph Lynn than anyone else in the cinema. Yet now, at what was undoubtedly the worst moment of his life, he actually found himself asking how he should respond; a calculation which, in another person, he would have had no hesitation in denouncing as emotional bankruptcy.

It was, however, as a bankrupt that he faced himself this evening. He would have preferred to have said that he faced his God, that he stood condemned, a man who had failed. But even here confusion set in because he was unable to recount the matters in which he had failed. The lack of words in someone so articulate was almost as daunting as the lack of appropriate response. It meant, for one thing, that he could not pray since, for him, prayer was a dialogue between himself and his Maker, in which he tended to have rather the more to say. Had he been a Quaker he might, in that community of silence, have been held by others stronger than himself. The Anglican church might have provided him with a structure in which he could offer his desolation to God. But his own brand of vehement, aggressive Methodism had not prepared him for the time when the spark went out.

As the hours went by, he sat and stared at the empty grate. He cracked his knuckles and occasionally he groaned; and once he jumped to his feet, baring his teeth savagely. All of which accomplished very little.

In their bedroom Judith longed for the physical comfort of his presence. She thought about the time when she was carrying Louise. How lovingly they had planned for the baby! This poor creature would come into the world as a result of youthful heedlessness, the chance effect of the snatched moment. Louise, at nineteen, could have little idea of how this unconsidered child would cramp her life, tying her to domestic responsibility and a man she might not have chosen had she given herself more space in which to grow. It might not matter so much for Guy to make a mistake. But women must get the answers right from the beginning: it is rare for them to get a second chance.

17

Judith and Stanley Fairley walked down Old Oak Common Road. Several days had elapsed during which Louise had been taken to the doctor, an elderly man who had querulously given it as his opinion that Louise was pregnant. They were late because the groceries had been delivered just before they left and Judith had had to check them. Stanley could not imagine why this should have been necessary at such a time.

Judith said, 'What did you say to him?'

Stanley had telephoned Mr Immingham from the school. 'I just said there was something we wanted to talk to them about. What else could I have said?' he demanded irritably as if she had rebuked him. 'He had a client with him and old Norris was hanging around waiting to speak to me. He's been at the school for over thirty years; you'd think he would have accepted the fact that boys write on lavatory walls, wouldn't you? But every time it happens he behaves as if he was Mother Superior at a convent school.' Judith could tell he intended to occupy his mind with Norris's prudery until he was confronted with the inescapable presence of the Imminghams.

After the first impact of Louise's revelation, when they had seemed to grope their way together, their different attitudes had become more apparent. Stanley saw Louise as betrayed; any other view was totally unacceptable to him. Judith was able to accept the reality and begin to reconcile herself to it. But for him this was not possible. A scapegoat must be found.

As they walked, Judith was already thinking about the next day when she would be seeing Miss Blaize. This would be an undertaking more formidable than the present one, since Miss Blaize could afford to indulge in moral outrage, a luxury scarcely open to the Imminghams.

They were passing semi-detached houses where men were working in the gardens. Stanley Fairley groaned at the smell of new-mown grass and wondered if he would ever again have the heart to work in his garden. It flickered across his mind how many troubles have started in a garden. He looked at a youngish man clipping a hedge, and thought how small his concerns must be; probably there was nothing on his mind except the need to get the hedge finished before his supper was ready. From the open window came the sound of scales repeated again and again on a piano. Tears blurred Stanley Fairley's eyes. They turned down a side road with smaller houses and neater gardens. Judith opened a gate. 'I shall be glad when this is over,' she said.

They heard a door open in answer to their knock. When he saw Mr Immingham standing in the hall, wearing his neat grey office suit, his feet in the soft slippers his wife insisted he should wear indoors, Stanley Fairley felt his stomach lurch.

Mr Immingham took Judith's coat and hat, and Stanley's hat, and put them in a wardrobe to the right of the front door. Then he led them into a room at the back of the house. Mrs Immingham was sitting in a wing-chair by the mottled-oyster tiled fireplace; although she rose to greet her guests there was no welcome in her eyes. Either she had a presentiment of unpleasantness, or she regarded all visitors as intruders. She was wearing a draped dress of soft material and smelt of Devon Violets; her hair was prettily puffed about her face. Judith felt an unexpected pity for her. Mr Immingham invited Judith and Stanley to sit down, offered cigarettes which they declined, lit one himself, and made an attempt at conversation. His wife allowed her eyes to travel to the clock.

'I can't think why you did not *telephone* me,' she said to Judith.

Judith, ignoring the important fact that the Imminghams were on the telephone, said, 'We wouldn't have called on you at this time if it hadn't been serious.'

Mrs Immingham, still under the impression that nothing was so serious as establishing her advantage, said, 'Had you *telephoned* me I would have asked you to tea.'

Judith looked at Stanley who made a grimace, perhaps intended to convey that this was woman's work. Judith was as brief as possible.

The Imminghams lived for Guy. To say that the sun rose with his every homecoming and set with his departure was scarcely an exaggeration. His wellbeing was their chief motivation in life. To learn that Guy was involved in social disaster was only a degree less terrible than the announcement of his death. Looking at them, Judith and Stanley saw the situation in all its stark misery. Here was no fumbling for meaning, no anxious trying for the right response. Mrs Immingham crumpled like a cream bun on which someone has accidentally trodden, a victim of random destruction. Mr Immingham was stricken. In front of their eyes this quiet, kind man withered. Oh children, children! Stanley Fairley thought, you try to give them the future and they throw it down like babes given an expensive toy for Christmas. Mrs Immingham wept and her husband held her hand, his fingers lifeless on hers, seemingly unaware of her as a person. They would have no comfort to offer each other; whereas Stanley and Judith, however much their motives might differ, would see this through together.

'They are both very young.' Mr Immingham spoke without bitterness. 'We should have realized it was expecting too much of them, sending Guy to America.'

Judith looked at him sharply, surprised by his understanding.

'We sent him to get him away from *her*,' Mrs Immingham sobbed. 'Because she meant to have him.' She looked at Judith with loathing as though she saw in her the architect of their misfortune. 'Oh yes! Your daughter meant to have our Guy.'

Judith, who felt that this was probably true, controlled herself and remained silent.

Mrs Immingham, maddened that at such a time Judith should adopt what seemed to her an attitude of superiority, cried, 'And how do we know that our boy is the father? She was loose, I always said she was loose.'

'Our daughter is no more loose than your son is a rake,' Judith retorted. 'And please don't imagine that we ever approved of their friendship. We never thought him good enough for Louise.'

'My wife is very upset,' Mr Immingham said apologetically.

'My wife is very upset, too,' Stanley Fairley countered.

'He will marry her, of course.'

'No.' Stanley Fairley spoke quietly. 'My daughter will not have to marry your son. We have talked this over, my wife and I, and there is no question that they will have to marry.' Although he profoundly hoped they would marry, he said firmly, 'There will be no pressure from us. We have decided that if, when they see each other again, Louise is at all unsure, we shall advise her not to marry him.'

'Not to marry him!' Mrs Immingham echoed. She was unable to understand what manner of people these could be, yet she perceived that out of their perversity might come deliverance. She pressed a handkerchief to her lips, not trusting herself to speak.

'Three lives would then be ruined,' Judith said. 'We shall bring the child up in our home if Louise decides not to marry Guy.' Some feeling of oppression, always there but unrecognized until now, had lifted since she made this decision. She felt as though a very tall building which overshadowed her house had been demolished and she could see for miles and miles.

'I think that's very wise, don't you, dear?' Mrs Immingham said to her husband.

'They will marry.' He looked from one to the other, sad for them because they could not see how inevitable it was. 'You may think they have a choice, but *they* will not think so.'

Yes, he's right! Stanley Fairley thought in relief. Then he thought how superficial Mr Immingham made him feel: this has destroyed him, poor fellow. He was ashamed of his own indestructibility, fearing it came not from strength of character but a craven refusal to drink the cup to its bitter dregs.

Aloud, he said, 'Of course, I blame Jacov.' As he said it, he experienced a feeling of release. The need to blame was very strong within him, but how could he blame the son of this stricken man? He must on no account allow himself to hate Guy if he was to marry Louise. And there was the child to consider: he must be at peace with the father of his grandchild. Yes, he saw very clearly that it was Jacov's fault. It had, after all, happened in the Vaseyelins' house. Years ago, had he not been persuaded, much against his will, to entrust his daughters into Jacov's care at that first party they had attended at the Vaseyelins? Some kind of bargain had been struck, had it not, with honour involved? And where had the first fateful encounter taken place but over the garden wall!

He said, 'I blame myself for allowing this intimacy with the Vaseyelins to develop.'

'Foreigners live so differently from us,' Mr Immingham said, sad and still without bitterness.

Judith said nothing. She thought that the blame probably lay with Louise who was strong-willed and impetuous, but she realized how important it was that they should reach common ground with the Imminghams, and was content to sacrifice the Vaseyelins to this end.

As soon as Judith and Stanley had departed, Mrs Immingham sat down to write to Guy.

The next morning Alice sat by the bedroom window waiting for Claire to get ready for school. How could everything be so different in so short a time? When she was eight, Alice had sprained her wrist.

For weeks afterwards her mind had been pinned down, concentrating on the mechanics of movement she had hitherto taken for granted. So now, life seemed out of joint and each small exchange demanded thought and effort.

'Have you told Daphne?' Claire asked.

'I haven't told anyone. You haven't, have you?'

'No.' Claire's face wore such a look of misery that Alice was satisfied she was telling the truth. 'But I must tell Heather. We tell each other everything.'

'Is Heather more important than Louise?'

'Yes, she is. I hate Louise.'

Claire spoke with conviction. Last night she had dreamt she was standing on the stairs leading down to the cellar; there had been a disgusting smell and the wall beside her was wet with something that wasn't water. She had been terrified.

Alice thought that Claire was being selfish, but she did not say anything because she realized it would only make matters worse for her parents if she and Claire were at odds with each other. Since things had changed so drastically she was more aware of her parents' love, which seemed stronger and of a different quality now that it was being given when it could no longer be taken for granted.

As they left the house Katia came running out of her house to join them. 'I've been waiting for you,' she said. 'We're still friends, aren't we?'

'Of course we are,' Alice said uneasily.

'Only your father doesn't speak to us now.'

'Daddy doesn't speak to *us* sometimes when we meet him in the street.' Alice was voluble. 'Mummy often says, "Here comes your father, let's see if he will notice us." '

Fortunately, Katia's curiosity was allayed by the sight of the postman coming out of Number 23. She ran up to ask him if he had any post for her, and returned with a letter from her boyfriend in Germany.

'Are you going to Germany in the summer?' Alice asked.

'Yes, of course.'

'What about Hitler?'

'Ernst's father is in the Nazi party, so I shall be all right,' Katia said, and added, 'He's a friend of Hermann Goering.'

Alice did not know much about Hermann Goering, but she gathered from Katia's tone that he was important. Although she thought Katia was showing off, she encouraged her to talk about

Ernst and his family so that she would not ask why Louise was away from school.

At ten o'clock, when she was on her way to her English lesson, Alice saw her mother sitting waiting outside Miss Blaize's room. She had her handbag on her knees and both hands gripped the handle. If Alice spoke she would turn, taken unawares before she had had time to summon up her usual confidence. Alice hurried away. When she reached the classroom she was ashamed and wanted to go back, but it was too late.

Miss Lindsay said to the class, 'I think we'll have a discussion today. I know how much you enjoy discussions.' A few girls groaned obligingly.

Miss Lindsay regarded it as part of her mission to suck from her pupils the poison which was fed to them daily in nauseous hymns and romantic literature. She fully intended before she left the school to introduce her pupils to the work of the Marquis de Sade. In the meantime, she contented herself with introducing into the discussion on *Jane Eyre*, Blake's 'The Sick Rose' – a poem she interpreted in the light of her own beliefs rather than Blake's.

'This is one of the few poems which dares to examine the origins of love.' They were unimpressed. 'I want you to copy it out. I will read it slowly.' This, she knew, was one way of ensuring that some of the words lodged in their minds. She watched with sardonic amusement as these dough-faced girls wrote:

> 'The invisible worm
> That flies in the night
> In the howling storm
>
> Hath found out thy bed
> Of crimson joy . . .'

'Now,' she said when they had finished, 'let us turn to *Jane Eyre*. What picture do we find here of love? Why, for example, do you think it was necessary for Mr Rochester to be blinded?'

'Because of the fire?' They were wary; aware that the simple answer was seldom acceptable to Miss Lindsay.

'But why was it necessary to have a fire, do you think?'

Katia Vaseyelin said, 'It killed off Mrs Rochester.'

Irene Kimberley said, 'Because he had to be seen to pay for his past wickedness or the Victorians wouldn't have liked it.'

Miss Lindsay regarded Irene with favour. 'But afterwards, what would happen as a result of his blindness?'

'Jane would look after him,' Ena Pratt said virtuously.

'Ah, now we are coming to something rather interesting, aren't we? This dominating man would become dependent on Jane, that good, meek woman. Some of you have probably read *The Rosary* – not, of course, a book in the class of *Jane Eyre*, though possibly more to your taste. Here, too, we have the blinded hero, and the heroine another Jane. I don't suppose either Florence Barclay or Charlotte Brontë was completely aware of what she was writing.' Miss Lindsay looked contemptuously at the portrait of the author in the front of *Jane Eyre*. 'But the great artists have always known. Never mind the machinations of the plot, Romeo and Juliet end up in the tomb, as do Aida and Radames, Othello strangles his Desdemona. And so it goes in life, too: Cleopatra presses the asp to her bosom and Abelard is emasculated.'

She wondered whether it might shock them into attention if she worked Christ into her thesis, but at that moment she noticed that she had made an impact on one of them. Alice Fairley was crying. She resumed the reading of *Jane Eyre*. When the lesson was over she asked Alice to stay behind.

'Is something worrying you, Alice?'

Alice had been thinking of her mother waiting to see Miss Blaize, but she had no intention of telling Miss Lindsay this. She said the poem 'and all that' had upset her.

'Really, I don't think we can tolerate that kind of prudery in a girl of your age!' Miss Lindsay was far from dissatisfied. Pleasure of a kind with which Alice was not familiar glinted in her eyes. 'These matters are a proper subject for discussion.'

Her gaze was so keen that Alice had the feeling Miss Lindsay wanted to get right inside her skin. Alice shifted her weight from one foot to the other, uneasily aware that something was threatened here of which she had no previous experience.

Miss Lindsay said, 'Tell me what it is in particular that upsets you, Alice.' She spoke softly; there was an eagerness in her eyes that made Alice feel as uncomfortable as if Miss Lindsay had peered lewdly at the private parts of her body. She clenched her hands and shouted:

'I think it was vile! All that about worms and crimson joy!' She ran out of the room without waiting to be dismissed.

*   *   *

Miss Blaize was totally unprepared for what Judith had to tell her. Quite apart from the element of surprise, Miss Blaize, unlike Miss Lindsay, was constitutionally ill-equipped to deal with crimson joy. She sat gazing heavily at Judith, wondering how it could have happened that she had been so deceived in the Fairleys. They had seemed to her to be responsible, co-operative parents, attending all the school functions and appearing to appreciate what was being done for their children; never behind with the fees; only claiming her attention over matters which justified investigation – the children's religious education, a poor school report, a decision as to which foreign language Claire should take and whether Louise should continue with Art in the Upper Fifth.

'But how could it be that you had no idea that this was happening?' she asked, her tone implying that the most unthinkable licence must have been allowed Louise.

'I ask myself that,' Judith said, feeling worse than at almost any time during the last unhappy days.

'Indeed, you must!'

'We shall withdraw her from the school, of course.'

'And the other children? In the circumstances, you would not wish them to remain.'

She is going to make this as difficult as she possibly can, Judith thought, clenching her hands. 'We think it will be better if they have as few changes as possible in their lives.'

'My dear,' Miss Blaize contrived to be at once quietly sorrowful and totally without sympathy, 'their lives cannot but be changed.'

'If we take them away from the school, it will be as though *they* have something of which to be ashamed.'

Miss Blaize thought that if the Fairley children left the school the matter might well be talked about until the end of term; but by the beginning of the autumn term it would be forgotten. If they remained, they would be a source of constant undesirable interest to their fellows. She said, 'You must realize that I have to think about the other children for whom I have a responsibility.' It was apparent that this was a matter which allowed of no compromise.

Judith had hitherto only seen Miss Blaize in mellow mood. Now, massed darkly behind her desk, she seemed a creature whose origin lay in the days of the pagan gods, who might one moment be benign and the next destroy with a carelessly tossed thunderbolt. Here, surely, was power without mercy, a force outside human control.

Miss Blaize began to make suggestions as to alternative arrangments for the education of Alice and Claire.

Judith had seldom felt so helpless. Then, looking up for inspiration, she saw on the wall above the mantelpiece a photograph of Miss Blaize with the Chairman of the Governors. Mrs Brinley Harris was a large woman without Miss Blaize's grandeur. Her lumpish face might have been carved out of a root vegetable for some Hallowe'en frolic, but it had a certain peasant shrewdness which Judith found comforting.

Judith said, 'We don't intend to withdraw Alice and Claire from this school, Miss Blaize.'

'But I have already told you, Mrs Fairley, that it would be best if they did not remain.'

Judith composed herself. For the sake of the children she must not alienate this woman completely. 'My husband has often said that you have given the children so much . . .' What was it Stanley had said? Something about 'abiding truths, the enrichment of the mind . . . and values which they will carry through life with them'. Judith wished that Stanley was here, he said this sort of thing so well. She did her best to sound convincing, and refused to allow herself to be intimidated by Miss Blaize, who was looking as though she was witnessing a whole shoal of pearls being cast before swine.

'I don't think there is anything more we can say about this,' Miss Blaize said heavily when Judith had finished.

Judith got to her feet. 'In that case, I am sure you won't mind if we write to the Chairman of the Governors? We would like her to know how much we value the school.'

Miss Blaize did not rise to speed her departing guest. There was quite a distance from the desk to the door, and Judith felt it was the longest walk she had ever had.

Miss Blaize meditated on what had passed.

If Louise Fairley was to stand condemned, what was it that she had done? She had committed a sin against the church and she had undermined the foundations of civilized society. Miss Blaize examined this statement. Some would consider it an uncompromising judgement: Miss Blaize did not consider the matter allowed of any compromise. If Louise had *not* committed a sin against the church and undermined the foundations of civilized society, then she had done nothing of any great moment, and her offence was no more harmful than riding a bicycle on the wrong side of the road.

Admittedly, Louise Fairley's face, as Miss Blaize recalled it, was not the kind to shake the topless towers of Ilium and bring a civilization crashing down. There were, however, disturbing features. When at morning assembly Miss Blaize looked down from the platform at the young faces upturned to her, the one thing which flowed from them to her was an immense feeling of hope. They would not have said that they were hopeful – many would have claimed to be unhappy, bored, depressed, even – yet every morning, dark though they might consider their private despairs, they gazed at her with faces as yet unshadowed by defeat. Louise Fairley's face was as hopeful as any, but there had been another quality which had set her apart from her fellows. That quality was delight. Miss Blaize had often thought that Louise would make the best of things in whatever circumstances she found herself, simply because Louise welcomed life. How totally she had been deceived! That very delight which she had found so attractive should have warned her that here was a girl who in the secret places of her heart worshipped at an alien altar.

Among the many subjects on which she thought it her duty to instruct her pupils, Miss Blaize had never included sex, marital or pre-marital. As she thought about Louise she did not blame herself for this omission or ask why she should have avoided the subject. But the smell of burning from that alien altar was in the room.

The sins of the one sister must be visited on the others: all the Fairley children must leave the school. Their removal would have to be approved by the Chairman of the Governors. Miss Blaize made arrangements to see Mrs Brinley Harris the following afternoon. The Chairman, a country woman at heart, was gardening when Miss Blaize arrived and put aside her trowel with reluctance. She sat with legs apart, displaying her bloomers, while Miss Blaize told her what was required of her. She was quite prepared to take Miss Blaize's instructions on all matters affecting the education of the pupils. On matters of morality, however, she preferred to trust her own instincts. She noted that Miss Blaize was not proposing to trouble her with the parents' views on the matter. A letter from the parents had been put through her letterbox last night, but she did not think it necessary to trouble Miss Blaize with this. When Miss Blaize had finished, she said, 'Oh, these things happen, you know. No need to take it out on the other two lassies.' Miss Blaize argued. Her aspect was terrible. Mrs Brinley Harris thought the woman might have been grieving at the fall of an empire rather than the fall from grace of one young woman. She looked impatiently towards the garden. The trees were coming into leaf and the room was green in their shadow. She decided to put Miss Blaize down with a bit of scripture: not a bad thing to let her know her Chairman wasn't completely without scholarship. 'When I get something on my mind,' she said, 'I say to myself: ". . . a thousand years in Thy sight are but as yesterday when it is past, and as a watch in the night." '

Miss Blaize left shortly after this and Mrs Brinley Harris returned to the garden.

While the fate of her sisters was being discussed, Louise was having tea at Lyons. She had been shopping for her mother in Shepherd's Bush when she met Jacov. There had been times over the last few days when not only had Guy seemed far away, but it was difficult to imagine he had ever been close. Now, as she talked to Jacov, Louise felt Guy might come strolling towards her and, for one all-too-brief moment, he was there, standing before her, tall and upright, the soft brown hair falling across his forehead. She could see his shy smile and the way he had of watching other young men with interest and admiration, unaware of his own good looks. Oh, that lovely unawareness! She bowed her head.

Jacov said, 'So I told him that if that was all he had for me to do, he could find another assistant. Very sad, but I don't think it is what is upsetting you. Come, tell me about it. I know something has happened. Your father nearly got run over walking past me with his head in the air this morning.'

She told him.

His face took on a bleak look, the mournful eyes seemed to gaze at Louise across an icy waste instead of a cluttered tea table. Louise, not always alert to the complexity of mood, was nevertheless quick to note a change of climate.

'How can *you* be shocked!' she exclaimed.

'I was thinking of your father. I know now what he must be feeling.'

Mr Fairley had made an apt choice, for there was that in Jacov's nature which made him ready to play the scapegoat.

'My father is being unreasonable,' Louise said, finding she must comfort Jacov and not her. 'You mustn't take any notice.'

'No, he is right. I gave him my word and I betrayed him. It is a matter of honour.' He lit a cigarette and she watched him, annoyed that he did not offer her one although she did not smoke. 'Your father was very kind to me. He was my first English friend.' There was no doubting the strength of his feeling for Mr Fairley.

'Thanks for the sympathy,' Louise said. 'It's been a great help talking to you.'

He pulled on the cigarette once or twice and then enquired, 'And Guy? Is he coming home?'

'I haven't told him yet.'

'If he doesn't come, *I* will marry you.' He said this with no great show of energy.

Louise laughed. 'You'd be the last person I'd marry, Jacov.'

'Why do you say that?'

Although he looked mildly crestfallen he was not really surprised; he had not expected that she would want to marry him. Yet it was not confidence he lacked so much as will. If he had the will, what then? She could imagine them both in a darkened room. There would be music playing. They would lie side by side, looking at the streaks of light between the curtains, saying, 'Shall we go out today?' and then turning inwards towards the music, day after day after luxurious day. This fantasy and the immediate response of her body to it, frightened her. She said, 'I don't think you'd make a good husband, that's why.'

Word got around. Had the Fairleys known that Louise had talked to Jacov they would have blamed him; failing that, they blamed their doctor's wife who was known to be indiscreet. Alice and Claire, released from their bond, lost no time in making their own disclosures.

Heather was in the playground doing her jazz band act to a group of enthusiasts. Fingers pinching her nostrils, the other hand flapping across her mouth, she emitted nasal bleats and moans, at the same time jerking hunched shoulders and stamping her feet to the rhythm. Claire waited on the edge of the group until the Broadway Baby had finally said goodnight, then she signalled and Heather broke away from the group.

Heather flung her arms round Claire and swore to stand by her. Further consolation was not called for, but Heather, generous in all things, must attempt to provide it. 'Anyway,' she said, 'The same thing happened to my cousin.'

Claire was taken aback that Heather should think there might be a comparison between what happened to her cousin and the same thing happening to a member of the Fairley family. She wondered whether their friendship could continue in the face of such lack of discrimination. Fortunately, the bell had gone while Heather was offering her disastrous comfort, and they were swept up in the press of girls making their way back to the building. By lunchtime Claire had decided to overlook Heather's aberration, though she felt a reprimand would be necessary were the cousin to be mentioned again.

Daphne assured Alice of her support in less flamboyant terms, but her loyalty was none the less sincere. Daphne would always be ready to stand by her friends whatever happened, so long as it wasn't dull.

Only Irene was shocked. 'I'm surprised at how shocked I am,' she said to Alice. 'I hadn't thought of this happening to anyone I know.'

Alice could see that Irene was troubled by her own attitude and she was grateful for this. She needed someone as confused as herself to talk to; they would be able to puzzle things out together. Hitherto, Alice's friendships had tended to be with girls whom she admired for qualities different from her own – Daphne for her daring, Katia for her intensity and foreignness. In Irene she had a friend with whom she could share, discuss, explore; whose understanding deepened and whose enjoyment enriched her own.

On one subject, however, they seemed unable to help each other. They talked a lot about Louise and Guy and about how their own inexperience might best be remedied. Neither felt very interested in boys, and it was this lack of interest which most concerned them.

'Katia gets worked up about the way men look at her on the bus,' Alice said. 'She even gets so excited reading *Jane Eyre* she can hardly sit still in class.'

Irene thought perhaps they should do something practical. There was a youth club attached to her church which she was sure they could both join.

'After Louise and St Bartholomew's, my parents wouldn't let me join a youth club.'

'We've got to meet boys sooner or later.'

'Now isn't a very good time, though.'

It seemed that in the cinema lay Alice's only hope of illicit excitement. She spent some time at night thinking about her ideal man and did indeed get rather excited. She saw him as someone who might bawl at her one moment, but let anyone else say a word out of place and he would risk his life to ram the words down the offender's throat, for at heart he was chivalrous – as were they all, the screen heroes, chivalrous to a man. She was growing up with a clear idea of what the chivalrous man was like, and would never be put off by a rugged exterior. Rugged exteriors, in fact, were essential. Humphrey

Bogart might have been said to cast a long shadow over Alice's youth.

During the following week, the cinema and life briefly came together.

It was just before supper that there was a knock on the front door. Judith, who was beating eggs, said to Alice, 'That's probably the groceries. Can you take them in?'

Alice opened the front door and there was Guy, a suitcase beside him.

'I've come back,' he said. His eyes went beyond Alice to where Louise was standing on the stairs. 'My mother wrote,' he said. 'I came at once. I haven't been home.'

It was the most perfect moment. Alice could not understand why Louise waited so long before she came down the stairs. He had come to her when she most needed him, just like the hero of a film. Alice wished Louise could have crumpled a little more in his arms, instead of saying, 'You *are* glad, aren't you?' leaning back and looking into his face as though she really wanted an answer, when his arms around her should surely have told her all she needed to know.

Alice turned and ran into the kitchen to tell her parents. 'Guy is here!' she cried triumphantly. 'He hasn't been home. He came here first!'

That night, Alice looked from the bedroom window towards Kashmir and prayed that one day her dreams would come true as Louise's had done. She sighed into the warm night air. If only she had a clear idea of what her dreams were!

Louise and Guy went to St Just-in-Roseland for their honeymoon. One day they visited Falmouth and went down to the harbour to look at the *Herzogin Cecilie* which was taking on a load of grain. 'She is square rigged and jigger rigged fore and aft,' Guy told Louise. It was a hot day and Louise had wanted to go swimming. Tomorrow it might rain.

Guy was very moved as he looked at the ship. He had always had a fear that he would never break away from his mother. Now, he felt as exhilarated as if he had left home and taken to the wild sea. He held Louise tightly to him as he talked about the great days of the windjammers.

Louise, listening, felt a pang in her stomach. Would it always be like this, Guy loitering behind, caught up in some never-never land while she waited for him to enjoy the present moment with her? The dazzle of sunlight on the water must have hurt her eyes, and momentarily she had the illusion that the bright world was tilting like the deck of a ship. She shook her head briskly to get herself back in balance.

They lunched with Louise's grandparents. Guy and Joseph talked about the *Herzogin Cecilie* until Louise said crossly, 'That old ship won't go on for ever.'

Guy bowed his face over his plate, his mouth turned down. After lunch, he strolled down to the harbour with Joseph while Louise helped Ellen in the kitchen. He stood with the light breeze ruffling his hair, and told himself that this was the happiest moment of his life. He was free, yet he was not cast off, dangerously adrift. 'A hard life, but you must learn a lot from it,' he said, squaring his shoulders.

Joseph said, 'Ay,' thinking of the frailty of that lively vessel out in the void, subject always to a force beyond men's comprehension which could overturn it, or smash it on the rocks and the next day be blessedly calm. The main lesson he had learnt was that life is precarious.

Guy said, 'I suppose she'd take a lot of pounding?' The ship was now part of his happiness and therefore to be preserved at all costs.

'Yes, she'll have weathered quite a few bad passages,' Joseph said. 'I'll be sorry to see her go.'

'Don't you get tired of it?' Louise asked her grandmother. 'Always staring out to sea?'

'There's nothing I can do about it, so there's no point in fretting,' Ellen answered. 'You have to learn to accept what can't be changed, otherwise you do yourself and other people a lot of harm.'

Louise laughed and kissed her cheek. 'Whatever else we are, we Hocken women aren't miseries, are we?'

'You're happy, are you?' Her grandmother looked at her, smiling, but with that reserve in her manner which sometimes seemed to distance her from people with whom she had hitherto been talking intimately. 'I was afraid perhaps you felt you had to.'

'I only had to because I love him. Don't you think he's wonderful?'

'*You* won't always think he's wonderful. That'll be the time to talk about loving him.'

18

In December, Louise gave birth to a boy. Guy suggested he should be called George in honour of the old King, but Louise was having none of this romantic nonsense and he was christened James. A few weeks later the nation mourned the death of King George V. Romanticism suffered a more bitter blow in April, when the *Herzogin Cecilie* was driven ashore and holed near Bolt Head in Devon. Guy thought this a terrible thing to happen in the first year of his marriage.

Louise had the baby in her parents' home, but soon afterwards she and Guy moved to Grandmother Fairley's house in Holland Park. As Ben walked along Pratts Farm Road in early summer, he wondered how the house would seem now that Louise had gone. It was some time since he had seen the Fairleys. At Easter he had been to America to see his father's family, and before that he had been studying hard. The American visit had not been successful, and the Fairleys had acquired a greater importance for him.

As he walked up the path he was greeted by a peculiar nasal wailing which sounded one moment like a demented train siren, the next a low animal snarl. The front door was unlatched; he pushed it gently and looked in. Claire, thin as a stalk, dressed in pink jumper, black knickers and stockings, was tap-dancing, red hair flaming round her shoulders, while a big, gawky girl was stamping up and down, making this incredible noise.

Claire stopped as soon as she saw him. She hugged him excitely and then demanded, 'Do I look like Ginger Rogers?'

Ben would have preferred that she look like herself. The other girl said, 'I'm Heather. I've heard ever such a lot about you.' Ben resented her friendliness: anyone would have thought that of the two of them, she was the one who was at home here.

'Are your parents out?' he asked Claire.

'Daddy's on the river with the sea cadets and Mummy is at the YWCA. We're supposed to be mowing the lawn.'

'It's Alice's birthday next week, isn't it?' He handed a small parcel to Claire. 'Do you think you could hide this away until then?'

'Alice isn't having a party because she can't have the Vaselines,' she said regretfully. 'So she is having Irene and Daphne to tea and then they are going to the theatre.'

'The theatre?' Mr Fairley himself could scarcely have sounded more disapproving.

'Oh, it's all the theatre and French films with Alice now.'

'I'll leave you to get on with mowing the lawn,' Ben said. 'I'm going to dinner with Louise and Guy.'

'You'll probably meet Alice on the way back,' Claire told him. 'She's been there this afternoon helping, but she hasn't been asked to dinner.'

'I can't see my sister helping me when I'm married,' Heather said.

'I'm never going to get married!' Claire sounded fierce.

'Well, I am!' Heather was equally vehement. 'And I'm going to have six children.'

They began to argue, Heather laughing but Claire shrill. Ben was forgotten. Eventually, Heather said, 'Marriage can wait. The lawn won't.' Claire put on a skirt and they clattered off to the garden.

Ben stood for a moment in the doorway of the drawing-room. The house had changed. It did not fold around him as it had once seemed to, its warm embrace shutting out the world. Perhaps this was just because it was summer, windows open, a soft breeze stirring curtains, rustling the old Christmas wrapping paper and fir-cones in the empty grate. He was afraid, though, that it was more than that. The family were growing apart. Society should be divided into two categories, he thought: the wanderers and those who remain constant. And by constant he meant as fixed as the star by which the helmsman sets his course. But it began to look as though, willy-nilly, people were wanderers.

He looked at his watch. He had to meet a girlfriend at Holland Park tube station. Not that he was in a hurry: he was not looking forward to the evening.

He met Alice in the Uxbridge Road. She had slimmed down, and looked attractive in a sleeveless dress and a blue beret pertly tilted to one side of her head. As became one who would shortly be sixteen, she had taken a grip on herself in other ways as well, and was more composed. There was no doubting her pleasure in seeing him, however, and she greeted him with the old, faintly conspiratorial grin, as though they shared some innocent naughtiness.

'Aren't you coming to supper?' he asked. 'That's spoilt my evening.'

She looked towards the house outside which they were standing. 'I'm going out with Daphne.'

Daphne appeared at that moment, a cool little customer who greeted Ben with a raising of the eyebrows.

'What are you two getting up to?' he asked, his eyes on Daphne.

'We're going to listen to Mosley,' she said.

'What!'

'Alice is very ashamed about it. But I come to listen to Donald Soper with her, so she feels she can't get out of it.'

'You *like* Mosley?'

'Very much.' She returned his gaze in a manner to which he was unaccustomed in young girls, not provocative so much as appraising. It made him angry: he would have liked to teach her a thing or two.

'He's a Fascist.'

'What then?' Still that level gaze.

'In Italy, if they didn't like Mosely's opinions they would put him away. In Germany, they'd do it if they didn't like the shape of his nose.'

'Why not come and listen, then, since you're all for free speech?'

She had hazel eyes, not hard or bold as brown eyes can be, but quite fearless. If it hadn't been for his girlfriend waiting at Holland Park tube station, he might well have taken up the challenge. A girl worth saving from folly.

The Drummonds went on a cruise in the middle of July. Angus, who was now working at the Foreign Office, had the house to himself. He had grown into a rather severe but handsome man. His face had the look of a person who is withholding something about himself, and this fascinated women. He was already beginning to experience difficulty in living up to the promise of his looks.

Sometimes he saw Katia passing the house. One Saturday morning when he was driving his father's car, he offered to give her a lift.

'I'm only going to the market,' she said.

'Never mind. Jump in.'

She hauled herself in beside him, getting her skirt caught up inelegantly around her thighs. He drove a little way towards the market and then turned into a sidestreet. He stopped outside some lock-up garages; there was a nonconformist chapel on the other side of the road, closed at this hour. It seemed as secluded a spot as he was likely to find between here and the market.

'And what have you been doing with yourself?' he asked in the amused voice which he affected when talking to young women – a tone which suggested there was something faintly ludicrous about their affairs.

Katia told him she had been taking music lessons. She had decided to be a great violinist, and her eyes shone as she talked about her father who, she said, played at concert halls all over the world. Her dark gold hair was knotted on top of her head, a style which she had not mastered but which, drawing the hair away from the face, served to highlight the curve of the high cheekbones and the winged eyes, which she had further emphasized with lavish application of mascara. Angus, whose taste normally ran to the soignée and chic, was startled to find himself exposed to so garish a display. He was both attracted and repelled, an unsatisfactory state in which to find oneself. Katia talked in a disjointed, breathless fashion, her hands moving constantly, adjusting her hair, touching her cheeks, the lobes of her ears, as though to assure herself that she was still all of a piece. While he talked, her fingers hovered around her mouth, tapping her teeth, patting her lips, caressing her chin. She was so conscious of her body that the sun falling on her through the windscreen made every nerve shrill, and she was incapable of paying attention to what he was saying.

'You're the nearest thing to perpetual motion I've come across,' he teased. 'Are you always so restless?'

She laughed and turned her head away, while her fingers moved rapidly over neck, breasts and left ribcage.

'What is it, then?' he asked.

She turned to him, mouth half open, a pulse beating in her throat. He was by now quite agitated himself, and placed a hand on her thigh.

'That's what old men do in the cinema,' she said.

'And what do you do?'

'I get up and move.'

He put his other arm around her shoulders, pressing her against the seat. She was becoming very excited. He had not expected this and was not sure what he should do; his lovemaking was usually carefully planned to avoid this kind of confusion. The feeling of unpreparedness was disturbing. They could go to his home, only the maids might talk, certainly *would* talk. His hand, moving up her thigh, came to the gap between stockings and knickers. 'I'll drive you back to my house,' he said. She was shaking convulsively. Angus, alarmed and rapidly losing his hold on the situation, said, 'Try holding your breath.'

'That's for hiccups, stupid!'

He tried to start the car, but his hands were sweating and slipped on the gear lever; he swore angrily and stalled the engine. She opened the door and, getting out, began pacing up and down on the pavement, cradling her breasts and muttering 'Stop it, stop it, stop it!' to herself.

He got the engine started and called to her, 'Come on, we'll go to my house.'

She shook her head and went on walking up and down, taking gulps of air. Rage boiled in him. 'You're not going to back down now, my lovely.' He was mortified to hear himself saying this in a hoarse voice as though he was playing melodrama.

She began one of her rapid examinations of her flesh. 'GET IN!' he shouted.

She turned and ran. He called after her, 'You're a dirty little Jewess! A dirty little Jewess!'

Immediately it was said his passion evaporated. He was horrified. She had excited him, made him ridiculous, and then rejected him. In his humiliation he had behaved in a manner worthy of his father. He had only said it to hurt, he had not meant it; but it was unpleasant to realize how readily the words had come to him. He must make amends for his own sake as much as hers. She was running down the road. He jumped out of the car, stumbled, and fell on one knee, ripping a hole in his trousers. Grimly, he picked himself up and limped after her. He could feel blood trickling down his leg. He saw her cross the main road, heading for the market. He lurched after her, dodging in front of a bus. The driver shouted angrily, 'Tired of life, mate? What's wrong with the railway arch?'

Katia had reached the market. He was not far behind, but it was crowded and there was a maze of stalls. A girl got in his way, he sidestepped and she sidestepped; she giggled and said, 'Shall we dance?' Angus, extricating himself, fell against a greengrocer's stall and upset a mound of oranges. The stallholder came at him angrily, and Angus thrust money at him – not apparently enough, because the man snarled, 'Think I'm giving them away, do you?' Angus dodged behind a booth and found himself by a stall with an array of patent medicines. The stallholder greeted him warmly, 'Now, 'ere's a gent knows where to come!' He picked up a bottle containing a bright purple fluid. 'There you are, sir, stops bleeding, prevents nasty consequences.' People laughed. Angus saw Katia in the distance and called to her. The stallholder said, 'I wouldn't like to think what might not 'appen with a leg like that, guv.'

He had dreamt of situations like this when he was a child, himself the clown, people surrounding him, mocking and hostile. If only he could catch Katia now and make amends, all the beastliness would be drawn from him and he would be clean and whole like other people. He really believed this, just as once, counting paving-stones, he had believed that if he did not walk on the odd ones his father would not torment his mother that day, and when he came home from school he would not find her crying. He called, 'Katia! Katia!'

She dodged behind a rack of secondhand clothes. Following her, he became involved with a woman who was grabbing a coat; she elbowed him aside. 'I saw it first!' He tried to push past her and she kicked him viciously on the shin. In a rage, he picked up another coat and threw it over her head. 'Have as many as you want,' he shouted.

By the time he had fought free of the secondhand clothes he had lost sight of Katia. He made his way out of the market and stood on the pavement, cold and shaking. How old was she – seventeen? What would happen if she told people he had assaulted her? He saw himself in court. But it would only be her word against his, and who would believe her – what, after all, was she? The words were waiting to be spoken again. He gave a little sob. A policeman came up to him.

'You all right, sir?'

The man's immediate assumption that, whatever had happened, he was the victim and not the wrongdoer, was comforting.

'I had a bit of trouble in there,' he answered unsteadily.

'Better make sure you've got your wallet, sir.'

Angus felt in his jacket pocket; his wallet had gone. The loss of the wallet seemed to set the seal of doom on the morning.

Katia was walking towards Holland Park. She had not liked what Angus had said to her, but now that she had outstripped him she was no longer afraid: she felt exhilarated, and even wished she had let him catch up with her. What would have happened if she had? Her precocious physical behaviour had often landed her in situations for which emotionally she was not ready; but she sensed that this was changing now. She stopped at a greengrocer's shop and bought cherries. Then she walked slowly to Holland Park where she sat under the trees, eating the cherries and seeing how far she could spit the stones. Lovemaking was a bit of a farce. *That* was a discovery:

she would be able to handle it now she knew that. In future she wouldn't be gauche, she would be soignée like Claudette Colbert. Life was opening out for her, she could feel it in the air and in her body. She was in command, and the agitation within her quietened. She would take her time and not let people rush her. In one of the houses which backed onto the park, someone was playing a violin. She listened, and gradually the music transformed her excitement into something deeper and richer. A sudden sound – a car backfiring, perhaps – agitated the birds and for a few moments the sky was dark with wings, but Katia did not notice this activity. The birds flew higher and higher until they lost form and semblance and became ashes blown in the sky. Katia sat thinking of all that lay ahead and was happy.

Grandmother Fairley was no longer able to live alone and remained with Aunt May. Although very frail, she had seemed brighter in spirit since Louise's marriage, a subject of absorbing interest which occupied her thoughts and helped to explain and justify her mournful attitude to life. Aunt May contrived to agree with everything her mother said without seeming to take any of it in.

'I find it difficult to know what goes on inside May; in fact, I sometimes think she has no inner life at all,' Grandmother Fairley complained to Stanley. 'I have realized since I lived here that she doesn't have a Quiet Hour.' As she never allowed her daughter a quiet ten minutes, let alone an hour, this was hardly surprising. 'I have never seen her reading the Good Book. It's no wonder the young ones go astray.' She nodded her head in sombre satisfaction at having thus involved Aunt May in Louise's downfall; she was a firm believer in the sins of one generation being visited upon the next.

Yet, co-existing with her severe moral beliefs was an expectancy of human frailty which enabled her to accept Louise's downfall without any of the pain felt by Judith and Stanley; and it was without heartsearching that she had made her house available to Louise and Guy. The thought of their indebtedness pleased her, and she never failed to say to Louise when she saw her, 'It will be yours when I'm gone.'

Louise spent long hours with the baby. His eyes followed her round the room; when she looked at him and made a sign he chortled. They had such laughs together! She sang and talked to him as she worked, and he gurgled with pleasure; he was the best audience she had ever had. He had great talents, too, waving his arms as though conducting an orchestra positioned above the cot; when she took him for walks in the park he conducted the trees. 'He's very strenuous,' Judith said. 'I can't imagine what he'll be like as a toddler.' Every new object delighted him and he would stretch out his hands to touch. Whatever Louise gave him he accepted and trusted because he trusted her. She marvelled at the miracle of his body; the pearly, dimpled flesh, the tiny fingernails, the limbs that were already surprisingly strong, the indomitable will contained in such a fragile package. Most of all, she rejoiced at his infinite capacity for wonder.

She and Guy had the two top floors of the house and her view was a roofscape: slates gleaming in the rain, smoke from a chimney, a tree thrusting up from a hidden garden, birds, street-lamps and clouds formed her world. She seemed always to be gazing upwards.

It was not all joy, though, and she was conscious, after she had tucked him away in his cot, of how strangely apart she seemed from the bustle of life now that she spent so much of her time watching from the window. Visitors became very important.

On a lovely evening at the end of July, Alice came to supper. Guy was out visiting his parents and Louise looked forward to talking to her sister. She and Alice were very companionable now.

Louise had lost most of the weight she had gained when she was carrying the baby, and to prove it to Alice she put on a navy-blue linen dress she had worn on her honeymoon. It still fitted well, and only pulled a little across the small of her back. Some changes there had been, however: the bridge of her nose had thickened, she was fuller around the jaw and the line of neck and shoulders had a new solidity. The face was as lively as ever and glowed with good health, but life had briskly firmed the delicate lines of youth, and it would be fanciful now to imagine her a beauty.

While she was waiting for Alice she did some of the ironing, and when her sister arrived the linen dress was crumpled.

'Shall I take over?' Alice, who hated housework at home, enjoyed helping Louise.

When Louise had finished at the gas stove she watched Alice methodically smoothing a shirtsleeve to eliminate all creases before bringing the iron down on it. 'Here, let me,' she said. 'I can't bear to watch you fiddling like that.'

It was hot in the room although the windows were open. Louise smelt of sweat, and Alice wondered if she was unaware of it, or didn't care. She was herself fastidious about sweat, and had dress preservers

stitched into her frock; they scratched and were not entirely odour-
less, having a rubbery smell, but they prevented the damp patches
which she considered so disfiguring.

'What have you been doing today?' Louise asked. Although she
was married and was, therefore, the one to whom the really exciting
thing – the making of a new life – was happening, there was no
getting away from the fact that as far as the trivial day-to-day
business of life was concerned, Alice now had the more to report.

Alice said, 'I did shopping and homework in the morning and I
went to the pictures in the afternoon.'

'Surely you could give Gary Cooper a miss on a lovely day like
this!' Louise felt a stab of envy at such spendthrift use of sunshine
hours.

'Jean Gabin, please!'

Alice had moved from the cinema as entertainment to the cinema
as art, though it had to be admitted that the translation had been
eased by the discovery of the young Frenchman.

'Does Daddy know?'

'Yes. I can't keep hiding things. I'm allowed to go once a month
now, provided I tell him what I am seeing.'

'French films are a bit daring, surely? All those naughty made-
moiselles!'

'Daddy doesn't think about them. He just thinks about the war
and the villages on the Somme.'

Alice could smell batter cooking, and wondered what they would
have for supper. Louise said, 'So, it's still film stars with you is
it?'

'There's no one very interesting around Shepherd's Bush,' Alice
said disparagingly. 'Only silly boys with boils on their necks.'

'No one like Jean Gabin? There never will be, you know. There
aren't any heroes. But I suppose you will have to find that out in your
own way. Only, take your time, Alice.' She paused, looking out of the
window, and said, as though it still surprised her, 'Marriage is
forever. It's the whole of the rest of your life decided. That's an
awfully big thing.' She began ironing again, but less briskly than
before. 'It's all right for me, of course, because I was very sure what I
wanted. But even so, it . . . well, it comes over me in odd moments
that I'm not free to do as I please. Even in small things, like going for a
walk, there is someone else to consider. And as for the future, that's
all laid out. I can't say "Perhaps this will happen, or maybe I shall go
another way altogether." Taking a husband is as irrevocable as

taking the veil! So, *you* take your time, poppet. You're growing up much more slowly than I did. Don't let anyone rush you.'

Alice thought it rather soon for Louise to be talking in this old-married-woman way, but she answered peaceably, 'No, I won't,' though in fact she was appalled at the slow rate of her growth in this respect.

They had toad-in-the-hole for supper, cooked as Alice liked it, with nicely-browned batter and crisp sausages.

'Why do you say your future's all laid out, Lou?' she asked. 'When Guy becomes an actor you'll probably move all over the country; Audrey Punter's brother is in rep and he doesn't know where he is going to be from one week to another.'

'Guy has given up any thought of that. He says he'd never earn enough to keep me and the baby.'

'You mean he's going to stay in accountancy?' Alice could not keep the dismay out of her voice. 'Doesn't he mind?' It was the nearest she could bring herself to asking Louise if she minded.

'Perhaps.' Louise looked as though she was considering an unknown man – not Guy, about whom she had in the past always been so sure. 'I think he's disappointed and relieved and ashamed of being relieved. You would understand that better than I, Alice; you're more of a dreamer. What happens when people don't put their dreams to the test? Do they become embittered, or are they glad they kept the dreams intact?'

'I hadn't thought of Guy's being an actor as a dream. I thought it was something he wanted to do – like me wanting to be a writer.' She blushed as she said this, because she did not often speak of her ambition. Louise however was still thinking of Guy.

'He wouldn't be able to cope in the theatre. And anyway he's not a very good actor.' She delivered this judgement with an impartiality which surprised Alice, and reminded her of the way their mother sometimes spoke about their father's sermons.

'But he was so good in *Dear Brutus*.'

'By St Bartholomew's standards he was good. He tried to get into the Questors and they wouldn't have him. When I saw what that did to him I was thankful he decided to stay in accountancy.'

'Isn't it a bit dull, though?'

'You think too much about films.' Louise took Alice up sharply. 'It's time you came down to earth. I didn't marry Guy because he was going to be an actor; I married him because I loved him and it doesn't make any difference whether he works in an accountant's office or sweeps the road.' She scraped the last of the toad from the tin and slapped it down on Alice's plate. 'And what's all this talk about writing? How often have you sent anything to the school magazine, let alone for publication?'

Alice was too taken aback by the unfairness of this attack to see it as a defence of Guy. They ate in silence for a few uncomfortable minutes; then Alice said, seeking to make amends for any criticism she might seem to have made of her sister's new way of life, 'I do envy you living here, Lou. I've always wanted to live in Holland Park.'

'It's nice enough, I suppose.' Louise missed the more congenial company of neighbours in Shepherd's Bush. 'The people aren't very friendly.'

Alice looked out of the window. She could see into the sitting-room of the house opposite; the piano with photographs on it was still there, and had the appearance of not having been disturbed by music since she last regarded it. She looked further along the road towards Number 33. 'Once, when I was here with Grandma, I saw Daphne's father going into one of the houses opposite with a woman. I found out afterwards that they were having an affair. Did I tell you?'

'Yes, you did. You were very shocked.'

Alice felt a need to tell Louise about the other thing which she still found so disquieting. She prepared her way for it. 'Do you remember Dolly Bligh at the chapel? Her children had to be sent away because Mr Bligh . . . misbehaved . . '

'I find *that* shocking! I think any man who gets up to that sort of thing ought to be castrated.'

Alice did not like to say any more.

'Can I take a peep at James?' she asked when they had finished supper.

'As long as you don't wake him.'

Louise was still disgruntled. Bad moods never lasted long with her however, and when they were washing up she put her arm round Alice, and said, 'Perhaps you'll write a story about Holland Park one day, pet, and put us in it!'

When Alice left it was still light, and she walked into the grander part of Holland Park. The houses were magnificent, tall and spacious; looking down the long line of the road and seeing the storeys rise one above the other, the decorated balconies giving way to the rim with the dormers above, the buildings were like a beautifully-layered wedding cake.

The evening with Louise had left Alice feeling not exactly disappointed but a little flat: perhaps she had hoped for too much. Whatever was wrong, Holland Park had no answer to this, and she turned away regretfully from the beautiful marzipan-and-icing world and made her way into the main road.

She walked towards Shepherd's Bush, and then turned into Norland Square. Irene lived here, but Alice did not know Irene's parents well enough to feel that she could call univited. There were lights on in the house and the curtains were still drawn back. Alice could see Irene's father sitting in a chair by the window, reading a book by the light of a standard lamp. How her life had changed! Once it would have seemed impossible that she should be friendly with anyone who lived in Norland Square. Her spirits rose. She was sure she would become a writer, and that she would live in this area and know a great many artistic people, and she would marry a man who would sit in just such a window reading with the light of the lamp falling over his shoulder. She could see his hands holding the book, but not the face. Oh poor, poor Louise! to feel that there was no 'perhaps', no 'maybe'!

Katia usually wrote to Alice during the summer holidays; letters full of hints and allusions, plentifully punctuated with exclamation marks, words underscored, drawings of faces and all so smudged and disorganized that Alice had little idea of what Katia was trying to convey, other than that her exploits were such as to shame the doings of *Jonah and Company*, her favourite reading.

Alice had excitements of her own this year and failed to notice the absence of letters from Katia.

One of the girls in her form lived in Ealing. Alice and Irene had become friendly with this girl, and they now met her for coffee at Zeeta's in Ealing Broadway. On a Saturday morning Zeeta's opened its basement and this room was taken over by the young, of whom there seemed to be considerably more in Ealing than Shepherd's Bush.

In years to come when morning coffee was a time for relaxing tired limbs and aching feet, it would be hard to recapture the intense excitement of walking down the stairs at Zeeta's, hearing the clamour of voices and waiting for one's first glimpse of the occupants of the smoke-hazed cavern.

Within two weeks of meeting there, Alice and Irene had come to know several people by sight, and as they descended the stairs they glanced round in pleasurable anticipation. At first, they merely noted whether the redhaired girl was still the companion of the young man in the dark-blue sports blazer who looked so attractive with his lopsided face and flattened nose. 'He's a rugger player,' Peggy told them. 'All rugger players have broken noses.' Such knowledge, her tone implied, could only be come by in Ealing. After three weeks, Alice and Irene began to look for particular young men. Alice's hero was tall and dark with what Alice took to be aristocratic features and an air of lazy indifference to his surroundings; he was her idea of Chief Inspector Alleyn. Usually he was with a group of young people and Irene assured Alice that, having observed them closely, she was satisfied he was unattached. When he was in the coffee room, Alice was as nervously excited as if they had been the only two people present. She made inconsequential remarks, laughed too much, and was clumsy with her roll and butter. Occasionally, boys whom Peggy knew joined them, but these – being young and callow – were never as interesting as the company at other tables.

Alice thought she had never seen so many handsome, self-assured young men in her life. Unfortunately, for every handsome young man there was an attractive young woman.

'Our families moved to the Greystoke estate at the same time,' Peggy said. 'We all grew up together.'

It did not occur to Alice and Irene that they might lure any of the handsome Ealing men away from their girlfriends. When Alice saw, the next time she came down the stairs at Zeeta's, that her dark young man was sitting alone with a girl, she noted immediately that the girl had striking physical attributes which she, Alice, would never possess. It was a moment of intense pain.

'She just throws it all around!' Irene said scornfully when she and Alice were alone together in the cloakroom. 'And that was Californian Poppy she was drenched in.'

Reassurance of a kind came next week. Irene's hero, a blond young man with a narrow face and lantern jaw, who usually acknowledged Peggy, much as he might a younger sister, came to their table and asked if he might join them. It was apparent that it was Irene who interested him. Alice looked with pride at her friend. Irene, neat as a character from Jane Austen and every bit as sharp, had drawn this young Viking away from girls whose charms were more obviously displayed. To Alice's surprise, however, Irene, having landed her catch seemed inclined to throw it back whence it came. In the company of her own sex she was notably articulate and amusing, but faced with this engaging young man she behaved in a standoffish manner and talked about matters which did not concern him. Alice took pity on him and asked him questions about his life. She soon found herself talking to him quite easily, and even teasing him about wearing a bowler hat when he became a trifle pompous about his job in the City. At the end of the morning he asked her if she would meet him for coffee the following week.

'It wasn't *me* he wanted,' Alice said on the way home. 'But you didn't encourage him. Didn't you like him? You said you did the other week.'

'I didn't like him in close-up: his eyes were too close together.' Irene turned her head and looked out of the window.

'Should I meet him next week?'

'Why not? It's nothing to do with me.'

Alice supposed that ordinary young men held no attraction for Irene; there was probably one man for her and Irene would wait until he crossed her path and then they would strike sparks off each other like Beatrice and Benedict. She sighed, knowing she would never be like that.

The following week she had coffee with the young Viking. They got on well and he asked her to go to the pictures with him. On the appointed day, he held her hand in the cinema, but when he wanted to kiss her she explained that she thought she was a bit young for that, and he accepted it good-naturedly, saying she was 'great fun'.

It was at this time that Alice thought how much she would enjoy telling Katia that she now had a boyfriend. Then she thought it was odd that Katia had not written. When she met one of the twins in the street, she said, 'What is the news of Katia?'

'We haven't heard.' He looked wretched.

'I expect she's having too good a time to write.'

He shook his head. 'She always writes.' He turned away and went on up the street. Alice had never before seen either of the twins when they seemed concerned about anything outside their private world.

She related the conversation to her parents. One morning later in the week, as Mr Fairley was walking Rumpus, he saw Jacov come out of a telephone booth. He decided to ask about Katia, but as he approached, Jacov turned away as though he had not seen him. Mr Fairley was a little disquieted. When he returned home he said to Alice, 'You had better enquire if the Vaseyelins have had any news of Katia.'

It was a long time since he had agreed to any visits being made to the Vaseyelins' house. Alice, feeling this was an opportunity not to be missed, since it might pave the way for further relaxations, lost no time. She half expected Mrs Vaseyelin to answer her knock, since Jacov must by now have gone to work and Anita always went out early to do the shopping in the market. It was Jacov, however, who opened the door. He led her into the big room where, years ago, they had had that strange Christmas party. There had been magic in the air then, but the atmosphere was different now. For one thing, the room seemed to be dominated by Mr Vaseyelin, although he was not doing very much – just standing by the mantelpiece gazing at the clown and the dancing girl. Alice was aware of his pain. She had never known anyone project suffering as Mr Vaseyelin projected it now. The twins were at the far end of the room, frowning at the floor in a moody fashion, more sullen than suffering. Mrs Vaseyelin sat on the sofa, a still figure examining the hands clasped in her lap indifferently, as though she didn't see much future for them. Anita stood behind her, eyes closed, muttering to herself. No one seemed to be looking directly at anyone else. Alice was surprised that they weren't doing anything. She could not imagine her parents being inactive should Claire not return from camp with the Children's Special Service Mission.

'I was wondering if there was any news of Katia,' she said nervously. 'I thought she was supposed to be back by now.'

'They have taken my grandparents and Katia away,' Jacov said. 'Someone wrote to tell us. The letter was not signed.'

They all looked at her now, with the exception of Mr Vaseyelin, and there was no doubting their resentment. Anyone would think I had come to take *them* away, Alice thought. Aloud, she said, 'I'll tell Daddy. He will know what to do.'

She was not sure what her father's reaction would be, but when she told him what Jacov had said, he came with her at once. He seemed at first unaware of the family's hostility. 'I am sure you will find that this is something which can be sorted out,' he said briskly, by no means displeased to take charge. 'But I think you should notify the Foreign Office without delay.'

The man by the mantelpiece, whom Mr Fairley took to be a distant relative, gave a short, bitter laugh. During the whole conversation he did not once turn to face Mr Fairley, but he contrived nevertheless to invest the proceedings with a profound pessimism which brought to nothing all Mr Fairley's energy and positive thinking.

At the mention of the Foreign Office Anita, who had been regarding Mr Fairley with suspicion, crossed herself. Mrs Vaseyelin said, 'First Sonya and now Katia,' as though the intervening period between the death of the one and the disappearance of the other was only an agonized moment of waiting for the completion of a dreadful act.

'It is much too soon to despair,' Stanley Fairley said sharply.

She turned her head away from the possibility of hope. There was neither anger nor surprise, pain nor reproach, in her face.

Stanley Fairley, confirmed in his opinion that foreigners have no idea how to behave in a crisis, turned to Jacov. 'You must go to the Foreign Office and show them this letter which you have received. Katia is a British subject, I take it?'

'No.'

'No!'

'We always meant to do something about it,' Jacov said wretchedly.

Stanley Fairley swallowed his impatience. 'Nevertheless, I think you should go to the Foreign Office. If it will be of any help, I will come with you.'

'If you please.'

Jacov turned to explain to his mother, speaking in Russian as though she no longer had a command of English. Anita interrupted, her little black peasant's eyes glancing slyly at Mr Fairley from time to time. It was plain that she was advising Jacov against accompanying Mr Fairley. Mrs Vaseyelin raised a hand to quiet her. Good manners must be preserved even now; she gave Mr Fairley a bow which indicated that he was to be humoured. The twins now came to him, arguing fiercely in Russian. Mr Fairley looked at the room. The Vaseyelins had lived here for at least ten years but there was little to mark their occupation; this room might have been a place where people had set camp, expecting to move on at any moment. What have they been doing all these years? he thought; what has been going on in their minds?

Jacov detached himself from his family. 'I am ready now.'

At this point, to Mr Fairley's astonishment, the man by the mantelpiece cried out hoarsely, 'My daughter, oh my beautiful daughter!'

Jacov's brothers and Anita watched as they walked down the path, for all the world as though there was some danger involved in going out into the open.

On the bus they were silent, Mr Fairley thinking how typical of the

Vaseyelins that, having conjured up a father, he should prove so singularly incapable of addressing himself to the problems of his family; Jacov impenetrable in his own thoughts.

The man whom they saw at the Foreign Office was polite, but had little information to give and few suggestions to make, beyond a vague promise to do whatever was possible.

'The grandparents owned a chain of stores, you say?'

'Shoe shops,' Jacov said.

'We do know, of course, that a number of Jewish-owned stores have been closed.'

'We all know that,' Stanley Fairley pointed out. 'What we don't know is what happened to the owners.'

The man said, 'Precisely.'

Stanley Fairley paused to give Jacov the chance to speak. The young man had sat for most of the interview staring at a shelf on which there was an untidy clutter of books. He appeared to be imposing an eye-test on himself. Whenever a question was asked by Mr Fairley he screwed up his eyes, focussing on a particular title.

Mr Fairley said, 'What about these . . . concentration camps we hear about now? A meaningless phrase if ever there was one, probably a cover for something rather nasty.'

The man made a steeple of his fingers and looked down his nose at it. Jacov put his head to one side to study the spine of a volume. The man said, 'I have to be honest with you,' – not choosing to answer this question – either because he knew too much or too little. 'We have had a number of enquiries similar to yours.'

'You mean, cases of English schoolgirls who have gone to Germany for their summer holiday and not returned?'

'English schoolgirls, no.'

'To all intents and purposes, she is English.'

'Not for diplomatic purposes, I fear. Please believe me, we will do everything in our power.' He looked at Stanley Fairley. 'You are a relative?'

'I am Mr Vaseyelin's next-door neighbour.' Stanley Fairley was dismayed to realize he had had an impulse to disown the Vaseyelins, and he added resolutely. 'A friend of the family.'

The man suggested that Jacov might like to give detailed information about Katia, and for this purpose he took him to another room. The man returned on his own, and Stanley Fairley took the opportunity to say to him, 'How serious is this, do you think?'

The man shrugged his shoulders. 'I couldn't tell.' Then, for a moment, his impassive calm was broken and he said waspishly, 'These people, why can't they use a little sense! If they can't bring themselves to apply for British citizenship, at least you would think they would stay in this country where they are safe.'

'Then you *do* think it is serious?' Mr Fairley was dismayed.

'If that letter is genuine it can hardly be anything but serious, can it?' The man's mouth twitched in a thin, caustic smile. 'However, I have to tell you that the general view here is that there is a lot of exaggeration. Once Hitler feels more secure, the situation in Germany will improve.' His cold blue eyes looked at Mr Fairley. 'Hitler believes he is encircled. We may have to revert to the flat earth theory, but all things are possible in the best of all possible worlds.'

A few minutes later Mr Fairley and Jacov left the Foreign Office. It was a cloudy day with rain in the wind. 'Would you like to have something to eat?' Mr Fairley asked. Jacov, however, preferred to stay in the open, so they walked into St James's Park and sat on a bench by the lake, watching people feeding the ducks.

Mr Fairley, who had not found this encounter with officialdom reassuring, said, 'Rather a coldblooded type, I'm afraid; but efficient, no doubt.' A child bounced a coloured ball which rolled beneath the bench and Mr Fairley, glad of diversion, bounced the ball back to the child, who immediately recognized a playmate. Jacov dug clenched fists into his jacket pockets and stared at the lake, its grey waters ruffled by the wind. The child's mother came and led the child away. Stanley Fairley stared after it regretfully. 'Katia will come back,' he said. He felt empty and hungry and was aware that his voice lacked its usual conviction. 'I'm not sure about your grandparents, but there won't be any trouble over Katia. She is only a child – even the Germans will realize they have made a mistake.'

Jacov said, 'Yes,' holding himself together because he must not upset Mr Fairley who had been kind.

Soon, a light drizzle began to fall and they got up and walked towards Victoria where Mr Fairley, who was almost faint with hunger and depression, insisted that Jacov must have something to eat. As they consumed baked beans on toast they watched the people in the street: giggling girls in cotton frocks holding handbags over their heads to shield themselves from the rain, a pavement artist laying sacking over his half-completed work, the commissionaire of an hotel summoning a taxi for an elderly woman in furs. Mr Fairley told Jacov that he must visit the German Embassy and contact his Member of Parliament and Jacov, nodding his head, sat back in his corner and wished that Mr Fairley's voice lent itself to a more confidential tone.

After they left the café they caught a bus outside Victoria Station and Mr Fairley read the *Evening Standard*, which occupied him for most of the journey. Jacov looked from the window as they came to streets which had been familiar to him for many years now. Roads ran off on either side of the High Street; he had no idea where they went, had never investigated any of them with the exception of the one that led to St Bartholomew's hall. He did not understand the topography of the neighbourhood and would have had to study his rate demand to find out in which borough he lived. As for central government, this was an area of English life of which he intended to remain ignorant; nothing would induce him to consult his Member of Parliament, thereby inviting the intervention of the State in his affairs and putting the remainder of his family in jeopardy.

'I shall write to the newspapers, of course,' Stanley Fairley said, folding the *Evening Standard*.

'I should be most grateful,' Jacov said politely.

They were travelling together on this bus because Katia had failed to return to England and an unknown letterwriter had said she had been 'taken away'. But even the bare facts of the situation presented them with no common ground. Mr Fairley applied his intellect and imagination to the concept of being 'taken away', and thought he had arrived at a fair understanding of the enormity of it. Mr Fairley had been born in Sussex; he had fought a war on foreign soil and then returned home to marry a Cornishwoman, and the extent of his travels since then had been a move from Sussex to London. He saw Katia's predicament as the result of a particularly unpleasant up-surge of German nationalism. Jacov and his brothers and sister had been born in Russia, had left in the night and slept in cellars in strange houses in unknown countries, they had travelled across a continent and eventually they had come to England, where their aristocratic father now played the violin outside Earls Court station. And yet, Katia had been taken in the night. The footsteps in the moonless street, the knock on the door were, to Jacov, the announcement of the time and place of an appointment from which there was no exemption.

They got off the bus and walked up Pratts Farm Road. Jacov, hunching into his coat, said, 'My father has lost two beloved daughters now.'

Something in his tone disturbed Mr Fairley who was, in any case, unsatisfied with what had passed. He said sharply, 'Look here, you must keep up your hope, you know.'

Jacov said, 'Yes, of course,' and tried to arrange his features into an expression which would be acceptable; but it was the eyes which Mr Fairley was watching at that moment. The lad who, years ago, had snared him in the trap of pity had grown into a man and, looking at him, Mr Fairley was surprised to realize how mistaken he had been to equate Jacov's condition with the deprivation of the children from the slums of Acton. The slums were within the compass of Mr Fairley's life – a terrible indictment of his society, but part of it. Jacov Vaseyelin had engaged his pity under false pretences. Mr Fairley, standing at his garden gate – within a few paces of home and the comfort of tea and saffron cake – looked into Jacov's eyes and saw that the things which for him had stood secure for a thousand years were to Jacov so much ephemera to be blown away in the wind; all the law, the learning, the hard-won human values, all blown in the wind.

He went into his house feeling uneasy in his world, and was immediately set upon by Judith. 'Alice has been telling me that Katia had a boyfriend. Tell Daddy what you told me.'

'His name is Ernst. She didn't tell me his surname, but she said his father is in the Nazi party and he knows Hermann Goering. So if his family is important, they won't let anything happen to Katia, will they?'

Stanley Fairley felt one of his more severe depressions coming on. 'I'll take my tea upstairs with me. I must get down to writing to the newspapers.' As he sat at his desk, he found himself wondering whether Katia would come back. Absurd, of course . . . He took a sheet of paper and laid it in front of him. No words came.

It was not the newspapers with which he was concerned; no editor would have the answer to the questions which he now asked himself. He had faced another crisis during the year, but in the matter of Louise he had been able to take the blame to himself. There was no way in which he could place himself in the centre of this tragedy, if tragedy it was. The only person to blame in this case was God. How could God let this thing happen to a young girl like Katia, who had never done any harm to anyone? He heard himself crying out to God like a protesting child. Yet he read his Bible every day and it was all there. How little he had considered what it meant: the suffering servant, the birth in the stable, the journey into Jerusalem riding on an ass. He had not examined the implications of this for modern

Christianity, had still thought in terms of Lord, King, Almighty, of a Power to be called into action whenever the situation warranted intervention. Had he really believed God was like Jove, up there in the sky ready with a thunderbolt to toss down on miscreants? The truth was that, in the matter of obtaining Katia's release, God was no more effective than the man at the Foreign Office – had, in fact, less earthly power. God, as the Bible frequently reminded one, was to be found not among the captains and the kings, but among the rejected and defeated, among those already in captivity. God was not strong as man judges strength.

'Have I never really believed?' he asked himself. 'Have I only been in love with ultimate authority?'

He could not write the letters while his mind was in such turmoil. He hurried down the stairs to Judith who was taking washing from the line.

'That can wait,' he said.

'You won't say that if you don't have a clean shirt tomorrow.' It looked as if more rain might come; the most urgent need as far as she was concerned was to get the washing in quickly. Even when she finally consented to come into the drawing-room, she was impatient and cut short his exposition of his dilemma.

'Stanley, you are *always* examining and re-examining what you believe!'

'This is different, surely you can see that?'

'It's not different, only more serious. This self-examination is part of your make-up. If only you would realize that and try to avoid it when you feel it coming on, you wouldn't get yourself in such a state.'

' "Avoid it when you feel it coming on"! You reduce everything to the terms of the schoolroom.'

He went out of the room, slamming the door behind him, and barely spoke to her for the rest of the evening. But that night he came to her, wanting to assert himself and yet at the same time like a child asking to be comforted. This mixture of male arrogance and abject need had once roused her anger but now, understanding better, she could give in to him without feeling diminished. She loved him and comforted him and they were at peace.

But it was their very loving which disturbed him when he settled down in his study the next day. In the last year he had lost weight, and with it had gone some of his thrustfulness. Sometimes, when caught unawares, his eyes seemed to start out of his head, not with anger but an emotion more akin to fear. He had that look about him now as he meditated on the nature of love. Love was so vulnerable. In his own life he came nearest to his Christian calling in his love for his wife and his daughters; yet it was in this area of his life that he was most vulnerable. Was vulnerability then an inseparable part of loving, something woven into the seamless robe? Of Christ this was acceptable, at least in his earthly passion. But what of God, who was perfect love? Did the very perfection cast out vulnerability along with other weaknesses? One must suppose so, since the alternative was to regard God as totally vulnerable – a thought so disquieting that neither Mr Fairley's intellect nor his emotions were prepared to have truck with it.

He looked down at his desk. He would write the letters to the newspapers. But suppose nothing came of his efforts, what then? The Vaseyelins would not go away, they would continue to live next door and for a time every morning he would enquire if they had heard from Katia, and then there would come a time when it would be kinder not to ask. After that, would he go about his own affairs, shape the privet hedge, mend the fences, forget?

He picked up his pen and wrote, 'Dear Editor . . .'

When Claire came back from the Children's Special Service Mission camp, her family greeted her safe arrival with a combination of joy and guilt. Claire was not joyful. As the train bore her towards Liverpool Street she had looked with dismay at the soot-blackened buildings and the forest of chimneys belching smoke, and thought how awful it was that life had to be lived in such surroundings. The squalor of Shepherd's Bush had depressed her utterly.

'Why can't Daddy get a job in Suffolk?' she demanded the moment the older couple who brought her home had departed. 'The air is so strong! Not like the West Country air that just sends you to sleep. You *know* the way it always makes me drowsy.' It was apparent to her family that she had had a splendid time and would talk of nothing but Suffolk for the next few days.

It was not only the Suffolk air which had been splendid.

'I have decided I must give up Heather,' she said when she was showing Alice her snaps. 'I talked it over with Derek. This is Derek, the tall one with the shrimping net. He was so understanding; he said he knew I had been trying to win Heather for God, but he thought perhaps I wasn't quite strong enough yet, and that I might be putting a strain on my own faith. I *am* weak.' Her wide green eyes were both enraptured and submissive. 'It was wonderful to have someone realize how much help *I* need.'

Alice was not sympathetic. 'I think you would be daft to give up Heather. Why can't you accept her as she is? She doesn't try to change you.'

'I can't be two people like you can!' Claire stamped her foot. 'It's got to be one thing or the other with me.'

The next day Heather called, and she and Claire went for a walk. They returned two hours later. 'We tap-danced all the way down Old Oak Common Road!' Claire said to Alice. 'What would Miss Blaize have thought!' Alice wondered what Derek would have thought.

Alice had neglected her studies during the previous week, and this evening she sat up late trying to make amends. The girls had been warned that sixth-form studies would be much more demanding than previous work, and Alice always heeded such warnings. Daphne was unconcerned, because it was not in her nature to be intimidated, and Irene had no cause for concern, being one of the most able girls in her year. Many of the girls with whom they had gone through school had now left. Alice found herself balanced between awe at the prospect of her exalted future, and regret for the past when study formed a less important part of her life. She would miss Marjorie Potter, who had one brown eye and one blue eye and was adept at writing rude verse; and Elizabeth Pitman, who fainted in the lessons she did not like and passed pleasant hours in the sick-room with Matron, whom she did like; and Valerie Pewsey, of whom it had been said that if she was still a virgin it was more by accident than design.

These hopes and regrets, the anticipation and the anxiety, worked upon Alice and she found it difficult to relax. When she slept she had a dreadful dream. She woke so terrified that she did something she had not done for many years; she went down to her parents' room. 'I had a bad dream.'

Judith came upstairs with her daughter and sat on the edge of her bed. 'You shouldn't have had that pickle at supper. What was it all about?'

'I dreamt of Katia. She was in a railway train and she couldn't get out. It happened once, at Shepherd's Bush tube station; she got stuck just as the doors were closing, but I managed to pull her free. I couldn't this time. I tried to take her hand, but I couldn't reach her.'

For a moment, it was as though some dark thing of the night had flown in at the window and hovered above them. Judith put her arms round her daughter and held her close. She thought angrily, 'Why don't they *do* something! That useless woman sitting in that airless house; Jacov going off to work looking so sad and helpless; Stanley writing letters no one will act upon! Why don't they go to Germany and get her back? That's what I would do if it were my child.'

Alice said, 'It was so real, Mummy. She *called* me.'

Judith comforted her and then made her a cup of weak tea. 'You mustn't let this prey on your mind, my love.'

For several days after the dream, Alice could think of little else. At the weekend, the young Viking, whose name was Ted Peterson, came to tea, and for a time Alice seemed better. Judith and Stanley liked him, the more so because they realized that little was involved other than Alice's pride in having a boyfriend.

There were three weeks to go before the beginning of term, and one of those weeks Alice was to spend on holiday with Irene and her parents. 'Now you are to enjoy yourself and put Katia out of your mind,' Judith said when she kissed her goodbye. Then, uncharacteristically – for she was not a woman to fill her daughters' heads with fear – she added, 'Be careful of strange men if you and Irene go wandering off on your own. You're growing up now and something could happen that you aren't prepared for. So be sensible.'

Alice had committed Katia to God's care. If He was supposed to have saved Faith Marriott's bunny-rabbit, it was blasphemous to imagine that He could not save Katia. She resolved not to think about it while she was away; thinking about it after she had put it in His hands would be like Lot's wife looking back – a failure in trust which could only have dreadful consequences.

On the whole, the holiday was a success. At first Alice felt a little awkward. Irene's parents were more reserved than her own mother and father, and it took her some time to realize that in their undemonstrative way the Kimberleys were a close-knit family. Mr Kimberley was a civil servant and was reputed to earn over a thousand a year. For a person of such eminence, he was a quiet man. Alice had hitherto tended to equate silence with the gentle submissiveness she found in that other quiet man of her acquaintance, Mr Immingham. A short time in Mr Kimberley's company, however, made her realize that he was neither gentle nor submissive. His comments as he read the daily paper were not as explosive as her father's, but were remarkable for the amount of meaning contained in a minimum of words. This economy of speech interested Alice, because it was so effective. Mrs Kimberley in contrast tended to cast about for words and to leave sentences unfinished; but she did this not in the anxious manner of poor Mrs Drummond, but with an air of rueful disdain at the inadequacy of language to convey the intricacies of thought, the finer shades of feeling. Mr Kimberley appeared to find her unfinished sentences of great interest. They were the first couple whom Alice had met who found real enjoyment in each other's conversation.

Alice, while feeling very gauche, was pleased to be with the Kimberleys, and they were kind to her, although she sensed at times a certain surprise at finding a fourth person in their company.

'You and your parents are very close,' she said to Irene.

'Yes.' There was regret as well as affection in the way Irene spoke of her parents. Alice could understand this. The trouble with loving one's parents was that it made the task of breaking away from them all the more difficult, and she could see that Irene might have the greater problem here. But that was still in the future, and both had much for which to be thankful. In spite of many small dramas and daily challenges, she and Irene had had the blessings of a long, slow childhood. Their parents had not constantly nagged them into activity of one kind or another, or demanded that each moment should be accounted for. There had always been time to watch the wind shaking the leaves of a tree, sooty city smoke transformed by the rainbow colours of sunset, the flight of starlings in the winter dusk, the pattern of frost on a windowpane; all seemingly incidental, but in retrospect very dear, for in these unhurried moments the mind had been eased and fed, imagination nourished, and in future each would retain the ability to detach such moments from the knotted cares of the day.

Alice wrote cards to her parents, to Claire and Louise, and she said she was enjoying herself. There were moments, however, during the holiday when she was subject to unreasonable panic. She did not like the door to the room which she shared with Irene to be closed; yet when she was in a very open place, walking on sand dunes, the sense of so much vacancy affected her balance, and it was all she could do to stop herself from grabbing at Irene's arm.

On their return, the Kimberleys took a taxi from the station. When it stopped outside her home, Alice was almost rude in her insistence that she could carry her case up the garden path. It was important that events should unfold as she had rehearsed them; the intervention of a stranger would require a re-fashioning of the moment of arrival which it was beyond her imagination to contrive or her strength to bear. The front door was flung open, Rumpus tore into the garden and ran round and round in circles, and Claire went dashing after him. Alice was gathered in by her mother and father.

Her father told her that Rumpus had missed her, he had gone round the house looking for her; her mother said, 'I had to give him one of your old jumpers to lie on in his box, he wouldn't settle at night otherwise.' How could they keep on about Rumpus's undoubtedly touching devotion, when it was the return of Katia which was the most important thing? Yet there was something in their greeting – not only warmth but a clinging as though they were holding her safe – which had a daunting effect on her. She pulled away ungraciously, and the distance between her and her parents was greater than it had ever been. In that moment – for it was surely no longer than a missed heartbeat – she saw the sitting-room as if it belonged to the past, like walking into one of the junior school classrooms by mistake.

'Katia's back, I expect?' she said.

Her mother and father looked at each other, not at her. Alice began to talk about her holiday, and they accepted the change of subject gladly. Later her mother said, spoiling her, 'Let's have your washing. I've got the copper out anyway, so I might as well do it.' Her father went out to post a letter.

Alice ran upstairs to the room which had once been Louise's and was now hers. She shut the door carefully before she released her burden. At first she stood like a soldier, hands clenched at her sides, while she addressed God. 'I hate you, I hate you!' She left Jesus out of it, because she could not bring His name to her lips. It was God with whom she was angry. Her whole body clenched itself and she screamed, 'I hate you!' She had never, even as a small child, given way to such uncontrolled rage. It was not only for Katia she cried out, it was at the littleness of life, the constant spoilsporting, the damming of her natural propensity for all the things labelled forbidden. She hated the God of Crusaders who forgave you your sins though they be scarlet, the God of Sunday School who wouldn't even know what a scarlet sin was, the God of the Winifred Clough Day School for Girls who wanted you to lay down a good harvest to be garnered by ages yet unknown but wouldn't have you walk on the grass and would strike you dead if he found you lying on the grass when the sower was about his work, even the God of her mother and father and their mothers and fathers before them Who was faithful to the end of time and went about quietly closing all the doors to the secret places of enchantment, Him she hated, too. She hated each and every aspect of Him; He had been the most negative influence in her life, and although she could not express this in words it was all there in her cry of hate. 'I hate you! I shall never speak to you again!' And – which was more – she told Him He didn't exist. And behold, He didn't! He was gone, just as if she had opened a cupboard and given everything a good shake and a moth had flown out. She was free of Him!

The freedom was tremendous, she felt it travel along her spine, her head was spinning with it; she went to the window and seemed to be walking on air. There was nothing inside her, she had breathed Him out of her, emptied herself of Him. She felt cleansed. The world beyond the window seemed to have been cleansed, too. For a few moments, which were the strangest, most rapturous of her life, she simply saw images without attributing anything to them, saw moving greenness shot with dazzling points of light and did not think of tree, saw swoop and fall and flutter and did not think it bird, saw black and white madly circling red laughter in a dance of crazy ecstasy with no idea of dog and girl, saw it all new as she herself had been new before her parents called her Alice.

It didn't last; how could it? Beside her, wings gently brushed to and fro, alternately lightening and darkening the room, moved by the same breath that stirred the greenness. She put up a hand and touched curtains. She was standing at the window of her room looking down at Shepherd's Bush, and everything was much as it had always been. The God of her childhood had been cast off: but He was still there.

She had thrown down a challenge which had been taken up. Or was it she who had been challenged? Was this what others meant when they talked about being saved, called? She didn't think it could be. They made it sound so comforting, as though something had been settled once and for all. She wanted *that* for herself, had prayed for it, had tried to do the things which seemed to work for other people, but nothing had happened. She had been passed by. So why now, when she didn't expect it, had certainly done nothing to deserve it? Why *this*?

She had spoken in anger to God; the words might have lacked originality, but the feeling of hate had been pure, and it had been waiting a long time to burst from her. And the result had been a momentary glimpse of that other world beyond the walls of Kashmir; she had seen a place where 'thou shalt' and 'thou shalt not' were unknown, where terror and pleasure were inextricably joined, a place beyond understanding and the naming of things. And He was there, in that place on the far side of the wall, which she so desired to enter. If it hadn't been her, she'd have said she'd had a vision.

It wasn't of the order of visions which strip away the old self and send a person out to minister to the outcasts or bring down a tyrant; lepers wouldn't benefit from it, and Hitler could sleep soundly at night. It was an image glimpsed in the blink of an eyelid, and the traces would fade as quickly as those of a dream on waking. But something had been done which would not be undone. From now on she would speak to God; hesitantly, intermittently, reluctantly, fervently she would speak her anger, despair, her joy and adoration, grief and longing: the dialogue, the wrestling, the coming and going of love and hope, the ebb and flow of belief, the finding and the losing of the threads in the pattern, the exhilaration of success and the bitterness of failed expectations; these would not cease. And there would always be God, the God of now and the God beyond the God of now; unattainable, inescapable, unpredictable, suffering from a fundamental inability to obey man's rules, who might demand of one person crucifixion, and of another that she accept the gift of life.

Her face as she stared through the window was the face of a girl still, unfirmed and distractable, more ready for laughter than tears, but with a bewilderment in the eyes foreshadowing the questioning years to come. Although she was so shaken by Katia's disappearance, there was a sense in which it seemed to have been foretold. Her puritan upbringing had laid much emphasis on the need for endurance in the face of injustice, fortitude in suffering and, by their very nature, the virtues commended to her implied a certain grimness in the grain of life. What she had not been prepared for, because she did not merit it, was the laying of a jewelled robe across her shoulders. There was something shocking about grace, an inexplicable quirk in God's behaviour; the struggle to come to terms with it would be her life. But she did not see that now, was only dimly aware of a beginning.

Her mother called that tea was ready and there were crumpets.

The dreams about Katia recurred. Always, there was the train; but in each dream its condition deteriorated. Windows became broken and were boarded up with planks, until eventually the carriage looked more like a cattletruck than a compartment, and it was only the eyes between the cracks which revealed the presence of people inside.

There came a time when the eyes seemed to watch Alice day and night. Then, there was one dream which was particularly bad, the details of which Alice was never able to call to mind, and after that the dreams ceased. This, Alice told herself, must be a good sign.

On the last day of the holidays she went to see her grandmother, who gave her a ten-shilling note because she was going into the sixth form where she would have to work so hard. On her return Alice walked slowly along Pratts Farm Road, thinking about the more responsible life of a sixth-former.

It was late September and the light failed a little earlier each evening, but lawnmowers had not yet been put away and there were roses in bloom in the gardens. The signs of autumn were fewer in town than in the country. Someone had lit a bonfire however, and the smoke was drifting in the direction of her home. It had the putrid smell of a bonfire on a dump where rubbish of all kinds best not investigated had been consigned to the flames. Her father would be annoyed. He was always careful to light a bonfire only when there was a southerly wind which would blow the smoke towards Shanks Alley. Alice could imagine him standing in the garden trying to work out the location of the fire preparatory to calling on the offending householder. There was someone standing on the pavement now; she recognized Jacov waiting for her at the gate of his house. The smell from the bonfire brought a memory of winter fog and the foul breath of the underground. The pitch of the street seemed suddenly precarious, and Alice edged to the shelter of the garden fences. As she came closer to Jacov, she said, 'Any news of Katia?'

'Only this.' He held up a large envelope addressed to Katia; printed in the top righthand corner were the words: Claudette Colbert, Paramount Studios.

'She might have run off with Ernst. Had you thought of that?'

'Perhaps.'

The darkness was encroaching now, but the breeze blowing ashes in the sky had something of summer in it still, and the shadows fell light as a feather.

'She will come back, Jacov.' Alice put out a hand, holding to the garden gate. If she could steady herself, everything would be all right; she would come through this bad patch and find that life had settled down, orderly as it had ever been. She said, 'After all, term begins tomorrow. She *must* come back.'

Elizabeth Berridge's crisp and distinctly English style of writing
established her as one of the most significant novelists of the post-
war years. Now that her best work is at last available in Abacus
Paperback, a new generation of readers will be able to discover the
quiet brilliance of her writing . . .

Elizabeth Berridge

ROSE UNDER GLASS

'*An eye for the beauty of humble and familiar things, and a gift for expressing it in
a language sharp yet delicate. She has a quiet, wicked sense of humour.*'
New Statesman.

ABACUS FICTION 0 349 10303 8 £2.95

Elizabeth Berridge

ACROSS THE COMMON

'*Entirely good and most beautifully written. I love her subtlety and observation and
impeccable characterisation.*' *Noel Coward.*

ABACUS FICTION 0 349 10304 6 £2.75

Elizabeth Berridge

SING ME WHO YOU ARE

'*One of the best English novelists presents something of a tour-de-force.*'
Martin Seymour Smith.

ABACUS FICTION 0 349 10305 4 £2.95

Also available in ABACUS paperback:

FICTION

ENDERBY'S DARK LADY	Anthony Burgess	£1.95 ☐
QUEEN OF SWORDS	William Kotzwinkle	£2.50 ☐
ROSE UNDER GLASS	Elizabeth Berridge	£2.95 ☐
ACROSS THE COMMON	Elizabeth Berridge	£2.75 ☐
SING ME WHO YOU ARE	Elizabeth Berridge	£2.95 ☐
THE HOUSE ON THE EMBANKMENT	Yuri Trifonov	£2.50 ☐
FOREIGN EXCHANGE	Ed. Julian Evans	£3.50 ☐
BABIES IN RHINESTONES	Sheila Mackay	£2.75 ☐

NON-FICTION

STRANGER ON THE SQUARE	Arthur and Cynthia Koestler	£2.95 ☐
NAM	Mark Baker	£2.95 ☐
PETER THE GREAT	Robert K. Massie	£5.95 ☐
IRISH JOURNAL	Heinrich Böll	£1.95 ☐
KAFKA – A BIOGRAPHY	Ronald Hayman	£3.25 ☐
TERRORISM	Walter Laqueur	£2.75 ☐
THE GREAT EVOLUTION MYSTERY	Gordon Rattray Taylor	£3.95 ☐

All Abacus books are available at your local bookshop or newsagent, or can be ordered direct from the publisher. Just tick the titles you want and fill in the form below.

_____

Name _____

Address _____

_____

Write to Abacus Books, Cash Sales Department, P.O. Box 11, Falmouth, Cornwall TR10 9EN

Please enclose cheque or postal order to the value of the cover price plus:

UK: 55p for the first book plus 22p for the second book and 14p for each additional book ordered to a maximum charge of £1.75.

OVERSEAS: £1.00 for the first book plus 25p per copy for each additional book.

BFPO & EIRE: 55p for the first book, 22p for the second book plus 14p per copy for the next 7 books, thereafter 8p per book.

Abacus Books reserve the right to show new retail prices on covers which may differ from those previously advertised in the text or elsewhere, and to increase postal rates in accordance with the PO.